I0691949

THE NOTORIOUS L.E.X.
Dartanya A. Williams Sr.

ISBN 978-1-7326122-5-9

Dartanya A. Williams Sr| Ni Jambo La Publishing

www.dartanyaawilliamssr.com

Instagram:@dartanyasr

Twitter:@dartanyasr

Facebook:dartanyasr

DEDICATIONS

I like to thank a higher power for giving me the strength and blessing every day and allowing me to do what I love, writing and storytelling is my true purpose in life.

I like to dedicate this book to the millions of self-publishing writers of color that have a vast amount of talent that is not being recognized in this crazy ass game of publishing. All of you know who you are, just don't give up on your dreams. Keep writing and drop your Magnum opus on the world.

To my wife Margaret, one of my biggest fans and supporters of my work. You're my best friend and partner in crime words can never describe how much I love you baby. Thank you for all your help on each one of my masterpieces.

To Tamyara Brown thank you for helping me put out crazy wild twisted street tales from the gutter. I really apparel your friendship and tireless hard work on all my novels. And I'm a big fan of your writing that's filled with blazing page turning drama, deep heart filled emotions and off the hook passion and skill. Thank you for everything.

To my brother Chilly Ock who always believed in me and became a big fan of my writing. I love you for all your love and support on each one of my novels. You just don't know what that means to me. Not only you're my brother but you're a great father to your children and a hell of a man. You're a positive role model in the Black community working with the youth with your baseball league you're a great husband to your beautiful wife Chrissy the Bombshell. I'm very blessed to have you two in my life. Thank you.

To Rasheeda now that you're a professor at a university teaching writing it was only destiny that you're doing this now congratulations. Thank you for being the first person that believed in me when I was writing my street tales into five subject spiral books when I could not afford a computer. But you've seen my potential before I saw it taking the time to read them and encouraging me to put my books out. Now I'm five books deep and I wrote over 12 novels. Now I'll never forget you thank you.

I want to thank all the people from around the country on Facebook and Instagram that show me love with my novels. Thank you so very much.

I GET SET UP AGAIN.

It is a hot ass July day. My government name is Alexis Jordan everybody on the streets calls me Lex. I used to be down with one of the most infamous black organized crime drug gangs in the country, the 24th street cartel in Philly. Now, it's time I told my side of the story. I was set up again by someone or somebody to be the fucking patsy for two of my close friends of mine in the gang who were murdered. I jumped ship for other opportunities after being accused of some kind of bullshit in the gang. I was tired of that shit, and I rolled out with Bony Irons and his crew in New York. I assure you I had nothing to do with the death of Binky and Angel. They were my family, and I loved them both. I know I did a lot of wicked shit while I was down with the gang, but I would have never done no shit like that. Now the whole gang wants me dead thinking I had something to do with it. *That motherfucker Mark Pain set me up fucking good after he had it done; he had his people tell Lieutenant Cob AK's CIA hook it up in a way that I did that shit.* I can't lie I jacked some of their shipment of coke before I split. I looked at it as severance paid after all my time of service with the **Banda** *(Gang).* AK ran a tight fucking ship, but we were family. For real though up until all the bull shit started going down. So, I got the fuck out of that outfit. Now I run my thing with the Iron brother's cartel without all the fucking politics restrictions and favoritism. It has been five years of me getting down with the *Iron brother's Bony Tony Iron and Lance Lucci Iron running the whole show.* To me a lot of these New York niggas is really fucking shady, so I must keep my eyes open on their ass for real.

So, one late night it's super-hot outside. I am up in the spot in Sugar Hill, Harlem on 145th street where they drop the product off 149th street in the Bronx with their crew Lola Tippy and

Scooby. Now they always come like clockwork when I work the spot for the drop offs. Then Salem and his partner Big Sammy come and take it up to East Harlem to 3rd avenue to bag it all up. Then it hits all over the streets like a supersonic live organism. I don't care what they say while they're talking shit. I always check it and make sure it's right if it is supposed to be 50 bricks or 500 bricks. It doesn't matter to me I count each one of them motherfuckers. Now we're all in the kitchen area. They come inside of the back door where I let them in all the time when I'm working the spot. So, they drop the shit off in cardboard boxes with beans in plastic bags on top and the coke on the bottom. I'm counting them Lola and Tippy are cool standing there, but Scooby I notice he is all nervous and shit like a cat in a room full of rocking chairs.

I looked up at this nigga I holler at him right quick,

"Are you alright, Dawg?"

"Yeah, everything is everything, why do you say that?"

"Now, I'm almost done counting. I'm supposed to have 300 bricks, that's what Big Sammy told me on the phone."

Then out of nowhere four mask dudes came crashing in the spot from the front door. **Boom!** Rushing in guns blazing from behind me I quickly turned pulling out my pistol they all started shooting at me **Pat! Pat! Pat! Pat!** I quickly ran inside of the big dining room area ducking behind the couch bullets flying everywhere. I'm still blasting back, but I notice those niggas never pulled out their guns to shoot at these mask gun men trying to fucking kill me. Then I hear a loud explosion **Boom!** It rocks the whole place. Smoke is everywhere. I can't see but I'm still shooting. I'm choking from the smoke thinking fast I pull my shirt off and I wrap my T-shirt around my mouth. I looked up and I can barely see the window on the left-hand side. so, I jump up still staying low and I dive out the fucking window **Tisssssssshhhhh!** I land on my hands, and I cut my left hand.

I'm still holding on to my pistol in my right hand tightly. My left hand is bleeding. I put my pistol in the front of my jeans. I take the shirt I had wrapped around my mouth to wipe the blood off my hand. I then took the glass out of it. I get up slow I am a little dizzy but I'm getting myself together I when and looked inside of the house and the coke is gone and so is the crew who dropped it the fuck off. They set me the fuck up not only they took the 300 bricks of coke they also got the 200 bricks of heroin Tony Rome dropped off on me earlier that day and he told me to give it to Sleam and Big Sammy when they make their pickup.

I quickly pulled out my phone out of my jean's back pocket to call Big Sammy to tell him what happened. He's not picking up the fucking phone. So, I called up Bony the phone rings about four times and he picks up.

I said to him, "yo, somebody just jacked all of the product out of the spot!"

He gets really quiet on the other end of the phone then he shouts, "hold on."

He clicks over on the other end. I'm standing there like a fucking fool. I thought to myself I can't believe I really gave this nigga some pussy too. *I said to myself this no-good ass nigga supposed to be my man or something. Just like that this nigga turns on me in a blink of a fucking eye. Wow, once a nigga bust that nut up in you, he's done with your ass for real.*

Now, I can tell he's acting really strange on the phone, and he clicks back over verbalizing *in that slick ass tone of his,*

"Are you all right?"

I can tell by his voice it was sounding funny. This nigga doesn't know *I know this motherfucker good. He's up to something.*

Quickly I reply sharp and cunning.

"Well, my hand is all fucked up, but I'll live."

Now he's trying to smooth talk, me as you know I don't believe not one fucking word that come out this niggas mouth.

"Look, don't worry about it, baby. I'm sending someone there to clean that all up. I holla at you at the spot when they're done." One thing I learn being down with the 24th street cartel always be fucking prepared for anything and write out your obituary when you ready to go to war. I walked back in the spot, and I closed the door and most of the smoke cleared out. I went into the bedroom getting me another t- shirt from out the dresser drawer in the back bedroom. I slipped it on thinking to myself it is time to get busy no time to lick my wounds. Then I grabbed my backpack and quickly walked in the front room. I sat down on the couch. I started pulling out my tools and clips what niggas don't know I have a large ass arsenal of weapons. I built up. I had hidden all over the place just for moments like this about to go down. I'm thinking to myself they had double crossed the wrong bitch for real. I started loading up my pistol's machine gun and four hand grenades in the side of my black backpack. After I finished that I went into the kitchen and found some duct tape in the drawer.

I wrapped my hand up tight to stop the bleeding. I get a cold beer out of the refrigerator, gulping it down fast, saying to myself if this is my last one, I will make sure it is going to be the last one for whoever he's sending here to kill me! I go back in the living room area, and I wait I know what comes next a room full of death and a lot of hot slugs in a nigga's ass for sure. I heard the front door opening fast and I yelled out,

"Is that you, honey?" Pointing my MP-5 machine gun leaning back **Bbbbaaarrrrrrtttttttt!** Hitting the first motherfuckers coming in the door wood and fucking debris flying everywhere and the loud sounds of niggas falling to their death fill the air as well. And all at once all you hear is gunshots and machine gun fire filling the whole house sounding like thunder from out of the sky.

Then I see two mask ass holes popping up on me spitting bullets. I hit the floor flat down as they ran up on me. I gave them the fucking business without the suit. Ripping their shit to shreds they were screaming like a bitch when they hit the floor **Doom! Doom! Aaaahhhhhhhhh!** I kept my head on a swivel, so I was ready for the next person jumping out at me. Don't you know its jackass came jumping into the broken window. I sprayed his ass before he could take one step inside of the house **Kapackatattta! Blang!**

He falls sideways, his blood squared all over the window frame and his bloody body is smoking like a broken stove in the wintertime. His foot still stuck in the fucking window. Then shit got really quiet now it's time for me to get the fuck out of here with the quickness.

So, I pack up my bag, stuffing all the guns I had in different places then I can see red and blue flashing lights shining in the front window. Shit, it's the cops. I duck down low and quickly head for the back of the house I looked out the side window. I know just what to do when they think they have me surrounded. I duck down thinking of another way out this motherfucker. I run upstairs and at the same time I'm reaching into the side of my bag getting one of my hand grenades. As soon as I reach the top of the steps, I hear hard running footsteps and a loud voice yelling, "freeze!"

I yelled back, "freeze this! I pulled the pen and tossed my first one. The four cops who ran in the door started hauling ass back out the door. **Kaboom!** I got another one out and I pulled the pin and I rolled it down towards the stairwell. I'm out the bedroom window and I hang down off the side and let myself go falling to the ground. **Kaboom!** The second one goes off blowing the fucking steps off leading upstairs inside of the house that will give them ass hole's something to think about. *That one will make any of the cops that are in the back of the house run up front to see what happened or help any of the cops that got hurt in the blast.*

I fell all the way on the ground, on my hands and feet, but I popped back up and got ghost. The darkness is a good friend right about now I fled into the shadows of the night. With all of them scrambling from the two blasts from the grenades they were shooked. I ran off into the dark of the night with the cops thinking I have the whole place rigged. I was gone. I got about ten blocks away and I came up on a dark blue not too old Ford truck parked on this quiet block. I pulled out my Jimmy from my bag and popped the lock. I jumped in and reached up under the steering wheel pulling the wires out from under it. I started working on the wires and I started it up in five minutes flat. I took off down the street while those Dick Head cops were running around looking for me. Luckily, I had enough gas in this bitch to drive to Jersey. I went and checked in at motel 6.

I have about 20 different fake IDs that are of really good quality. So, it's no way they will know who the fuck there looking for. Soon as I get to my room, I open the door and I sit on the hard ass bed thinking who in the hell called the fucking cops at the spot. Well, I'm going to rest up and go to each one of them niggas homes and get to the bottom of this shit from the door. They probably think I'm dead, this is where I have the upper hand on their ass for sure.

I'M BACK JACKING MOTHERFUCKERS AGAIN.

I laid low for a month in Jersey at the motel 6 long as I paid them, they did not care how long you stayed. I don't have any more drugs (Cocaine) I just snorted up my last two dime bags this morning and I have a little bit of cash on me. I know I will run out of that soon, too. I had to pay them and get something to eat as well. *I had not been in this kind of situation since I was running around with my crazy ass junkie boyfriend Billy Hawkins back in the days robbing every fucking body we ran across. I just had to get out of my junkie mothers house and get out there in the streets. I was young, wild and fucking crazy. I lied and told everybody my life story that those two niggas ran up in my bedroom. That they rape me at my crack head mothers house. I told anybody who would listen to me that's what made me run away from home when I was only 15 years old. But she did send those two lousy ass niggas into my bedroom to fuck me for her drug debt after she done smoked up all their shit. What my mother and those two niggas didn't know about me.*

That I became a stone-cold killer in the last three months after my birthday. I done killed four niggas in just one week and the crazy part about it I started liking it too. I get a rush from it like snorting coke. But the truth is that those two-ass holes who came at me never seceded at getting some of my pussy. I fucked both of them up with the gun Billy gave me after we robbed three corner store bodegas. All in the same night and the gun was my reward from Billy for a successful heist. I broke the first niggas nose with the butt of the gun, the other one I kicked him in the balls and slugged him in his jaw with the gat. I felt really good kicking their ass. I should have shot both of them for trying to get some underage pussy. Plus, I only had two bullets left in that motherfucker testing the gun earlier that day. I knew I would need them for some real dangerous niggas I run across just in case. I was not worried about those two light weight niggas was not worth the bullets. I knew I could just fuck them up and roll out of there without working up too much of a sweat. Then I came out of my bedroom and cracked my mother in her face with the gun for sending them into my bedroom in the first place. I just pistol whip her ass just a little. She was so high it did not matter that bitch would live. She was bleeding out her mouth. That's all she will go smoke some more crack and the bitch will be fine.

Only thing that was good when I hooked up with Billy was, he taught me about guns, and killing people without having any kind of remorse about it.

So, I had to get rid of the truck I stole to get there so I went out later on that night. I went to the gas station to get some gas with the little bit of cash I had on me and scope out a fucking potential mark. I go into the gas station booth and tell them to give me twenty dollars on five. The fat black woman behind the booth said Tommy will come pump your gas for you. I forgot in New Jersey they don't let you pump your own gas. They have to do it. When I saw him come out, I knew damn well this greasy stain ugly ass white dude was broke so I could not Jack him right quick. So, I'm looking around while the tall ugly gas station attendant is pumping my gas in the truck. I see these white boys pull up in a brand new dark green Range Rover pull up beside me on the left. There are three of them and one of them is looking at me hard at me. I see him right away but I'm playing it the fuck off. I blurted out to him,

"If you took a picture, it would last longer than if I just smiled at him."

He answered with a smirk on his face,

"I will if you let me see a little something, baby," I pulled up my sweater along with my lace bra and let him see my titties and he started smiling and giggling. I pulled my sweater and bra back down smiling my ass off seeing that look on his dumb ass pail face.

He went inside to pay for his gas with that silly ass smile on his grill. The tall ugly gas station attendant turned to me and said, "I'm all done, Ms." Rubbing his hands together. I didn't want to give him anything because I was low on loot, but I was playing it off. So, I had to make it look good.

So,I went in my pocket quickly handing him five dollars, he said, "thanks Miss walking over to pump the gas for the white boys with the new green Range Rover."

He came back out after paying for his gas and started talking loud and bold, "damn baby, if it's like that we can go somewhere and party, I got some really good shit."

I uttered, "oh yeah, let me taste a little.I'll let you know if it's some good shit or not."He flash a bright friendly smile on his ass they love to see a nigga smiling at them. He laughed and he walked over towards me pulling out a big bag of coke. He scoops out some light-yellow powder in a clear plastic baggy with a rolled up hundred- dollar bill holding it up to my nose. *I peeped his pocket with the money in it, but he wanted me to see he had money and he had a fat ass roll of cash too he doesn't know I'm going to get all of it before the night is all over with.*

I snorted up the coke fast and hard and I put on my little act. I looked up at him pronouncing with a grin yeah this is some good shit he's smiling. *I'm lying my ass off to make him feel good.* "So, where do you want to hook up, baby?"

And I gave him my bedroom eyes that way they trick ass motherfuckers every time without fail. We were all down the road at the Loft with a Bachelor party. We all went down to Roger Willco to get some more liquor and to cop some more coke from this black dude at the bar across the street from the liquor store.

"Okay, you want me to meet you over there or what?" "Yeah, I would really like that baby looking me right in my eyes."

I knew I got this mark ass motherfucker for sure.

"What is your name babe?"

"My name is Brad." *He showed all his perfect white teeth.*

"My name is Belinda, sweetheart."

I lied to him right away.

"So, Brad, do you think you can handle this here?" putting my hand on my hips looking him up and down. *I see the lust glowing in his eyes looking at my body. He's craving for some this black pussy like an exotic fantasy rolling around in this white boy's mind.*

"I know I can baby, are you really going to meet me they're for real?"

"Just tell me what room you're in and I'll come over there and fuck your brains out. You will never forget it as long as you live."

I'll tell you that shit for sure with a smile on my face. *I got this ass hole on the hook. All I have to do now is pull his white ass in nice and easy like a fish out the water without a fight real smooth like.* He laughs with his face turning bright red, answering fast. I'm in room 606, but I'll come down and get you to give me your phone. I'll give you my number so we can hook up. I give him my phone and he put in his number quickly, never taking his eyes off of me. I take the phone from him *I slowly touched his hand, and he got a real fucking thrill from that shit I see it in his eyes.*

I looked at the number standing in front of him so he can get more of an eye full of my sexiness, uttering slowly. "What about a half hour or so?"

"Yeah, that would be fine. I see you then sweet thing." He tips the gas station attendant with ten dollars flashing that big bank roll of his. I just smiled watching him jump behind the wheel of the green Range Rover with his two knucklehead friends. He waves at me smiling and they take off into the darkness up the road. I drove off and went over to Wendy's up the street.

I parked and went inside to get something to eat waiting. I knew this trick ass white boy was going to call me. After I ate I went into the bathroom with my backpack getting all my guns together loading up my clips in my tools to go to work. As soon as I was done, I got the call from trick ass Brad what a lot of people don't know is that married men are the biggest trick ass motherfuckers in the world.

I peeped that gold band on his left hand soon as I came up on his stupid ass from the door. I drove over there, and I parked in the back of the hotel. I called Brad back and he came down to get me all smiles. So, I get my black backpack and toss it up on my shoulder getting out the truck smiling back at him. I knew this motherfucker had a dark meat fantasy. I went with him. We both went up to the back door he had stuffed with a rag to get back in and we both went up on the freight elevator. He is feeling up on me. I just push him off a little giggling putting on my little act again announcing with a sexy smile.

"We're going to get it on baby just as long as you got some paper, Mister Brad. we can have the time of your life if you're really good, baby."

My eyes got wide looking him in the face to let him know that I was not playing with him if he wanted some ass he had to come up with the cash. He barked all cocky,

"Oh yeah, I got money, baby. I'll show you when we get to the room. We reach the six floor he's looking both ways all fucking nervous *I know he don't want to be seen with my black ass but yet he wants to fuck me doe.* Now we go off to his room really swiftly he used his electronic key quickly he sticks it in the light turns green.

He pushed the door open quickly, still looking both ways up and down the hallway. That's when I peeped the cameras up top, I put my head down and turned sideways so it doesn't get a really good look at me. I voice to him,

"Where are your friends at?"

"Don't worry about them there right next door in 607 and 608 there getting busy too."

I sat on the bed and I set my backpack at the foot of the bed. I take my tight sweater off and he looks at me in my lace red bra. I stuck my hand out at him with a big smirk on my face uttering out loud, "let's see the money before you get the honey."

He reaches in his pocket with a knot of bills. He shows me the money by verbalizing, "so what is it you want sweet thing."

"Okay, playa I want 300 for everything, lover boy." "300, wow!"

He's looking at me like I'm not worth that much money So, what you think this is. I stood up letting him see the rest of my banging hot figure putting my hands on my hips. I take off my jeans so he gets a real good look at my sexy red panties with my fat ass.

I got it from Victoria's Secret. He sits down on the bed looking up at me while I'm wiggling and gyrating my hips and I turn around and let him see my very nice round brown ass jiggling my ass like loose jelly. Then I started twerking my ass in my red lace panties. He's rubbing and smacking me on my ass. He is having a good time doing that too. I know I got his ass going now. White boys love to see a black bitch do that all of them motherfuckers fantasize about hitting it from the back when we do that shit.

He said, "oh yeah, 300 it is baby now I see what you're working with sugar." He came over handing me the money with his eyes wide. He gives me Three new hundred-dollar bills. I look at them really well holding them up in the air towards the light to see if they're real. Then I stick them in my bra.

I tell him, "All right take your shit off, so we get this shit cracking, Mister Brad."

I quickly grabbed the bulge in his pants. I did it real aggressively looking him right into his eyes. I'm thinking he was going to cum on himself-right then. There with my sex kitten voice he's loving it. He gets all excited taking off all his clothes fast. I took control right from the door, and I laid him down on the bed smiling. Then I sat next to him on the bed getting closer to him looking down at him feeling him up good. Then I leaned down kissing him long hot and passionately still feeling him up. I started kissing and licking him on his neck rubbing his Hard- On until he's really worked up with him getting harder. Then I started taking his boxer shorts off and he lifted up his behind helping me get them off. I tossed them on the side of the bed and I'm grabbing his rock-hard penis jerking it nice and soft. Not too slow neither keeping him aroused.

I didn't want to suck his Dick, but I had to hook his ass good. I've done this shit over a million times or more to men when I'm about to rob their ass for money. I'm doing a hit to kill their ass and he'll never know what him. So now I started licking him from his chest on to his nipples, real freaky like seeing the look in his eyes light up while I was doing it. Then I started licking down to his stomach really working my tongue on his ass he was feeling it too all into it. I slowly went down to his Dick and made it really super wet and slippery with a lot of spit on my tongue licking him slow. I can feel his anticipation until I reached his main vein popping up in the air bouncing up and down on my thick lips sucking it. I grabbed it nice and gently licked around the head of his soldier standing at attention making the big gobs of spit from my mouth dripping down spewing out from all sides of his pink rod. Then I just quickly put my whole mouth around his thick pink meat. I started sucking and licking on his erection like a super head type of bitch. I am bopping my head up and down pecking my neck even faster hearing him moaning loudly, *"Oh shit, you're good, baby!"*

This how I turn these niggas out the switch goes off in my mind that I turn into that real super nasty bitch that most guys just see in porn movie. Jerking off too all day long dreaming about them. Now I'm making loud raunchy sucking sounds, turning him on more and more. While making a lot of spit flowing down his boner. Then all of the spit bubbles are rolling down to his balls making him jump like a frog on a hot rock.

This motherfucker was losing his mind moaning and groaning loud. I'm thinking he's going hit the fucking ceiling. Jumping up and down like he had the holy ghost in his ass mumbling talking in tongues. *He's breathing hard like he's hyperventilating.* I was going up and down bopping my head making all these sucking sounds, jerking it with both my hands at the same time. I'm making it feel better than getting some hot pussy like a got a sizzling tight snapper on his Dick. *I can tell he's ready to blow at any minute now.* I see him sitting up a little more while he was laying down to watch me go to work on his Dick. I make it a real sloppy blow job running down his leg. I know I got his ass good. Then I started slurping on the end of his erection letting him see the spit strings slide down off his one-eyed snake. I suck it back up in my mouth showing him my nasty ass slut tricks blowing his fucking mind. While he's right on the edge of the cliff of ecstasy with a volcanic explosion about to jump off.

Then I just stop cold, holding his super hard erection in my hand looking up at him saying,

"Oh sorry baby, but I have to pee really bad."

" I'll be right back to finish you off sweetheart, okay while I rubbed on his wet Dick smiling."

He sat up out of breath shouting, "okay." While trying to get himself together with a big smile on his face. He laid back down blowing out air holding his head wiggling around.

I got up slowly wiping my mouth off with one of the pillowcases from off the bed. I take it with me. I pick up my backpack at the foot of the bed and run in the bathroom. He never saw me picking up my jeans and also back up off the floor super smooth. I close the door and I wash my mouth out in the sink really good with the mouthwash. He had in there on the sink. I looked at myself in the mirror mumbling this better be a big fucking score.

I take the pillowcase and stick it in my bag. I slip on my jeans real swiftly. I go in my bag getting my rubber gloves putting them on,then I get my Glock pistols putting the silencer on the tip of both of them. I make sure they are both on real tight. I waited a few minutes. Then I came out holding my Glock pistols running over towards the bed he sits up in. I yelled, "Yeah, you know what this motherfucker is, give me all your money!"

He gives me that dumb ass look yelling, "I gave you what I have." I cracked him right on top of his head with the gun **Koolop!**

"I 'm not playing with you, white boy give me your phone ,your car keys, your watch and all that money I saw you with. I'll kill your ass, do it now!"

He is holding his head bleeding with the blood running in his eye as he walks over toward where he took off his pants on the floor. He gets his wallet and phone and walks back over to me handing me that knot of bills, his watch phone, car keys and his wallet.

I take one of my guns and I stick it in the front of my jeans and the other one in the back. I snatch everything out of his hands he's looking like he's about to fucking cry like a little girl in the nude. I pulled the money out of it, took his phone and I dropped it inside of a tall glass of beer on the coffee table. I put the wallet and watch in my bag and the car keys in my pocket. I said open up the safe over there I know you got more money motherfucker! He got his hand up in the air shaking scared to death.

"That's all I got, there is nothing in the safe. I'm telling you the truth."

I smiled at him answering , "oh yeah"!

I walked closer to him and I pointed the gun at him yelling, "last time I'm going to ask you to open up the fucking safe before I shoot your white ass!"

He just looked at me replying with a blank look on his grill, "it's no money in there."

Pooouuufff! I shot him in his right knee and he fell to the floor bleeding. I step up closer as he is yelling in deep pain. I point my pistol at him again and I screamed, "open the fucking safe or I'll shoot your ass again,Brad!"

He's rolling on the floor crying like a little bitch moaning, "okay! Okay! Don't kill me!"

With his hands up in the air dripping with blood from him holding his knee. He stands up hopping over towards the safe bleeding. I got a real good aim on his ass shouting hurry the fuck up!

"I would have not shot you if you would have done what I told you to do in the first place!"

With blood all over his hands from him holding his knee with both hands he hits the combination quickly and the safe door pops open. I get the pillowcase I wipe my mouth off with out of my bag I step up to him yelling move to the side and don't make any funny moves or I put the next one in your fucking head all right! I stick my gun in the front of my jeans and walk over to the safe pulling the money out. It looks like it's about twenty-two grand. *Wow they had a lot of tricking money on hand, not bad.* I walk over and get my backpack, setting it on the bed, unzipping. It poured the loot I got from the safe inside. I took the pillowcase and I tossed it inside the bag. I quickly reach in my bag putting my black mask on. Then I get my backpack. I put it on my shoulder and pulled out my gun. I walk over to Brad, and I stick my gun to his head disclosing, "come on we're going to go see your goofy ass buddy's next door let's go!"

He stands up bitching, "you got all my money why don't you just go now."

I uttered loud, "shut the fuck up motherfucker! You got your Dick sucked, right." He just looks at me without saying a word.

I barked, "well, this is the price you have to pay for you fucking around on your wife out here tricking!" I'm pushing him hard towards the door with him hopping bitching, "aren't you going to let me put something on at least?"

I took my gun and I pointed it at his Dick articulating. "If you say one more word you're going to be known as Brad the Dickless wonder, okay. Now, shut the fuck up let's go mother-fucker!"

I asked, "What's your friend's name?"

"Frank!"

"Okay, move your ass, come on!"

As I smacked him on his white ass turning red! We walked next door with me right behind him I whisper to him real low don't tip his ass off or your fucking dead! I knock on the door hard, and I duck right in back of him. A few minutes later the door opened up quickly with his friend pronouncing,

"Yo, what happened with that black bitch you were trying to hook up with?

I pushed him in the door right into his friend Frank and I popped up on his ass. I hollered, "the black bitch is right here you pale face motherfucker!"

I close the door behind me. I say to him, "shut the fuck up and give me your phone first, Frank!" He gave me his phone and rolled his eyes like a little girl. I take it and drop it inside of the sink. I stuffed a rag inside of it and I turned the water on making sure it filled up and the phone was no more good. I squawk,

"Go, open up that safe before I kill you and your friend over here Frank!" Brad with his voice all broke up in pain crying, "do what she says she already shot me. Frank just opens up the fucking safe and let her get the fuck out of here!"

I yelled at Brad, " you go sit on the bed!" As I walked Frank over to the safe, he pop's it open real fast. As soon as I put my bag down to put the loot inside of it Frank jumped at me and I shot him. **Puuuooofff!** I shot him in the leg, and he fell to the floor. He yelled in pain loudly. I started taking the money out of the safe. I looked down at him chatting with a wicked smirk on my face.

"I told your ass I would shoot you! I don't know what's wrong with you white people when a bitch has a gun in her hand and she says she's going to shoot you. Nine times out of ten that shit really going to happen. See, you white motherfuckers watch too many movies. You think you're going to jump up and save the day. See, but in this movie here your white ass gets robbed and shot! And if you two keep fucking around with me it's going to be an alternative ending to this movie. With me giving each one of y'all two slugs in the dome each fucking dead!"

Soon as I got all the money out putting it in my backpack it's about ten grand. Then I heard this banging on the door. I quickly zip up my backpack and I walked to the door looking out at the peak hole. And I see this white boy yelling, "are you all right, Frank?"

I open the door pulling him inside sticking my gun to his head with that gangster ass muttering, "shut the fuck up!" I pulled his ass inside the door quickly by his arm sticking my gun under his chin. I close the door with my leg. Then I drag his ass inside yelling,

"Oh, you want to know if Frank is alright. Well, there he is shot in his fucking leg!"

I pushed him hard on the floor.

I quickly got my knife from my black bag. I walked over to the window cutting pulling the ropes from the curtains sticking the knife in my back pocket of my jeans. I walked over to Frank and Brad on the floor I tied both of them together I hog tied their ass making fucking navy knots in that bitch it no way they can get out of that shit. After I was done tying their ass up, I told them to get up and I pushed both of them into the bathroom. I reached inside Frank's pocket, getting his hotel key card and the money he had. In the other pocket it's about four hundred dollars. I stuck it all into my pocket. I closed the door to the bathroom, and took a chair putting it up under the doorknob. I quickly grabbed the last white boy off the floor talking loudly what's your name?"

"My name is Chuck."

"Okay, you look like a fucking Chucky too. Now give me your phone."

First, he hands me his phone with no problems. I told him, "now were going over to your room and you're going to open up your safe and give me your money. I'm going to get the fuck out of here okay now. If you fuck with me, I'll shoot your ass just like I did your friends. Do you follow me?

He nodded his head yes. I walked him over to his room with my gun at his back. He opened the door and popped open the safe. I can see in his eyes that this motherfucker was really scared. He was not going to be like Brad and Frank trying to be a fucking hero. I took the money out and he only had a couple grand.

I uttered, "okay give me what you have out of your pockets."

He hands me the two hundred dollars he had on him. I should have known he would break these ass holes. I put all the money in my backpack, zipped it up, swung it back on my shoulder. I marched his ass back to the room next door. I opened the door with the hotel key card. I took him to the bathroom moving the chair from the doorknob pushing him inside with the others crying and bleeding. I closed the door back I put the chair under the doorknob and I'm off to the fucking races I got about 34,000 dollars not counting the change I took off of these ass holes. I rolled out there using the back-exit steps. I'm walking fast until I reach the ground floor exit door that leads outside. I took off my black mask, sticking it inside of the side of my bag. I took my time walking over to the brand-new green Range Rover. I pulled out the keys pointing to the remote. Boo- Beep. I hop in and I'm gone. I head straight back to New York for some more unfinish business. I'm the last bitch in the world a nigga would want to cross because I'll will get you back very quickly.

YOU THOUGHT I WAS DEAD.

I drive right to the Bronx to kill them niggas then get out of town. I know right where that bitch Lola laid her head at. And that bitch made nigga Scooby too. He lives right around the corner from her. I only stopped to sleep in the Range Rover pulling over on the side somewhere and got something to eat. In a drive thru on my way there the only thing I have on mine is revenge. I laid low most of the day. I waited until nightfall and on the real late-night tip. I camped out a few blocks away from Lola house on 80th street. I waited until it was 3 in the morning before I made my move. I drive and park on her block only a door away from her house right across the street. I slip on my black mask and just like AK used to say. All the time it's time to punch in and go to fucking work. I creep up to the front door. I quickly picked the door and I slid in. It only took me a few minutes to get inside of the crib. Good thing I'm not losing my touch when it comes to breaking into somebody's house. If Billy was still alive, he would be proud of me. I close the door softly behind myself. I quickly creeped inside of this dark house. I have been inside of this spot more times than I can really remember. I check the first floor to make sure nobody is there on that floor. I make it up the stairs to the bedroom on the right-hand side. I know that's where she sleeps with her old man Fat Poncho. He is in the game too, but he works with another crew. He's another pussy hound nigga who can't keep his Dick in his pants like all the rest of them niggas that down with them. He tried to holla at me a few times, but one thing about me I might be a freaky bitch, but I don't do fat men. Plus, he knew I was fucking with Bony he just wanted to see if he can pull me or not. Every nigga, I know away want some easy pussy. I creeped up slowly until the door was closed. I turned the doorknob carefully until I got the door open. as soon as I came into the room. She is laying on the left and he's lying on the right side of the bed. I walked over to her side and I put the gun right up to the side of her head. She jumped up feeling the cold steel of my silencer mashed up to her fucking dome she screamed out.

"Poncho!"

He jumps up and I just backed up a little getting in position in a real good gun stance pointing my pistol at him with that smoke a, motherfucker where they stand base in my voice.

"If you move, I'm going to kill both of y'all in two fucking seconds flat. So shut the fuck up and listen!

Fat Poncho sit up a little more with his eyes on fire yelling, "what the fuck is going on in here?"

I walked over and turned on the lights at the switch on the wall on the left. Now they see me with this black mask on and I quickly take it off my head to let them know who it is. I want her to see my face before I blow her fucking brains out all over the fucking bedroom walls. I stick my mask in the back pocket of my jeans down deep. Lola looked up at me in shock as soon as she saw my face. Shewas about to open up her mouth. I shouted at her, "You Thought I was dead right bitch!"

Fat Poncho yelling putting his hand up in the air, "why are you doing this shit Lex? Youwere down with us what the fuck happen?"

I was thinking he was bull shitting me at first but with that look in his eyes he did not know what happened at all.

"Oh, your wifey over there, didn't tell you that she along with Scooby and Tippy set me up. She took 500 bricks of coke and 200 bricks of heroin out of the spot and set me up to get killed by Bony Irons and his killer goons"! Fat Poncho looked over at Lola; she just lower, her head not saying anything. Fat Poncho yelled, "answer me Gawd damn it did you do this shit?"

"Yes, I did but Big Sammy told us to do it. And when did you start taking orders from Big Sammy? I thought Bony was the fucking boss?"

I knew this would hit one of his nerves because he can't stand Big Sammy. They have a beef, going back over position and power within their drug gang called the Iron Boys.

"Look Lex, you know I'm not a bitch made nigga. If I did something to you for me to die by your hand, I would not bitch about it. As you can see, I had nothing to do with this shit!" *He's rolling his eyes looking over at Lola.*

"I see no other way she has to die, Poncho!" I took aim to shoot her in the head and Fat Poncho yelled out,

"Wait, I can fix this!" *Putting his hand up in the air like that's going to stop some bullets or something.*

"Check it out Lex. I'll take you to one of the money drops of Big Sammy that way you get even with him". No, you're going to try something and then I still have to come back here and kill her and you too. Look like I told you I'll take you to his money drop with no tricks and as you already know I don't like that motherfucker and you know that shit from the door. You're right about that okay get dressed and if you cross me your whole family will die. Don't worry I'm going to love to see the look on his face when he finds out that you took all his money from the drop. Suppose Sammy finds out that you help me do this shit? He won't because I have an alibi and he look his wife deep into her eyes. She is nodding her head yes but Fat Poncho while he's putting his jeans and Polo top on yelling over to Lola talking loudly.

"I want to hear it out of your lips say it now bitch!"

You were with me all night. There was no way he could have done it. That's right and stick to your story or I'll kill you my motherfuckin self you hear don't cross me, Lola!

I won't be a baby by this time Fat Poncho is dressed and ready to go. He looks at me saying, "I have to get my gun if I'm going to help you do this shit."

"Lex, you're gonna have to trust me. I'm going to tell you something Poncho and I never want you to forget this shit. I don't trust a living soul on this planet earth but I'm going to let you relieve this debt your wife Lola did to me."

"Okay, he went over to his dresser getting his gun and he slaps in the clip. He sticks it in the front of his jeans muttering, "let's go."

He looked at Lola and said, "I'll be back later and don't talk to anybody about this shit or I will do what I said."

He kissed her and went out the bedroom door with me right behind him. Soon as we got outside, I pointed towards the dark green Range Rover I jacked from the white boys. He laughed, uttering, "that motherfucker bullet proof."

"No! Well, we're taking my truck." Mine is pointing his remote towards his black truck parked right in front of his house. Boo-Beep! I spit at him fast.

"Just let me get my backpack. We're going to need a few things I have in there."

"Oh yeah, like what?"

"How about four hand grenades you got that motherfucker?"

"I guess you're right Lex go get them. Do you have a machine gun too?"

"You know I do a MP-5 and four clips with it."

I quickly go in the whip grabbing my backpack and I jump in the truck with Fat Poncho. I still don't trust his ass but I'm going to see how this shit plays out. If I see one sign of him crossing me. I will kill his ass, go back and slaughter his whole family to send all of them motherfuckers the message. We take off and we ride about 15 blocks and park at this three-story apartment building.

I said to him, "what about the bodyguards?"

It's only four of them about this time that's what makes this so good. I reach in my back pocket and get my black mask out. Fat Poncho reaches into the glove box pulling out another gun and his mask he puts it on fast and he looks at his watch. It's 4 in the morning and I put on my rubber gloves from my bag. Fat Poncho looks over at me talking low.

"Why are you putting on the gloves, Lex?"

"Check it if we kill someone in here, they won't have my fingerprints to pen the shit on me that's why." "Okay you have any more gloves?"

"Yeah, here you go." As I handed him a pair of gloves. He's smiling whispering, "how many people have you killed before Lex?"

"Shit, I don't know how that fat motherfucker from the show the wire said I done killed more niggas than a Chinese cemetery."

"That is a good one. I done killed more niggas to fill up Madison square garden."

" I like that I'm stealing that one but I'm a Sixer fan, so I'll say killed more niggas I could fill up the Liacouras center."

We both laughed as he pronounced with a smirk on his fat grill let's go do this.

We both jump out of the truck and quickly head towards the front door of the place. It's locked so we both got low and I picked the lock rapidly. I opened the door slowly. Soon as we both came inside not too far down this hallway a guy leaning back in his chair sound asleep. Near a large door on the right-hand side. I just creeped up on him taking aim. Puuu Ooofff! Fat Poncho right behind me but when he looked at me before we opened the door, he was impressed. I walked inside and it's four people, one guy with a counting machine and the other one was wrapping the piles of cash putting rubber bands on the stacks. I toss it in a big trash bag on the floor. And the other two men get the bags and take them to the next room until someone comes to pick it up. None of them is armed.

They throw their hands up in the air when me and Fat Poncho are pointing our guns towards them. Then out of nowhere this large man came out from the right with a machine gun pointing he was about to spray some bullets. Puuu Ooofff! **Doom!** *I shot him in the head before he could squeeze the trigger.* He hits the floor super- fast and hard. another fat dude from the left with a saw off shotgun gun **Puuuooofff! Doom!** *I shot him in his neck with the blood gushing out fast when he hit the floor.* Two more men popped out on the left and right behind me. I quickly drop down flat on the floor aiming upward from my back **Puuuooofff! Puuuooofff!** I shot the one on the left in the mouth and the one on the right in the middle of his large ass fucking head. They both crashed to the floor bleeding out with that fucked up look on their grills.

Fat Poncho just looked at me while I was standing back up winking my eyes at him. He Blurted out, "I have to get me one of them shit."

I stepped up pointing my pistol at the money counting people barking okay line up "over there along the wall hurry, up!"

"Don't let me have to kill your dumb ass for some money that is not yours okay move your ass!"

They all lined up near the wall on the right like I told them I yelled, "where is the rest of the money?"

One of the men pointed towards the left where it's another door. I opened the door and looked and the whole room was filled up with trash bags.

"Shit, it's going to take us hours to get all this money out of here."

One of the men looked us in the face muttering well you already said, " None of our money is our money. So, I'll help you get it out of here just as long as we can keep some of it."

Me and Fat Poncho looked at each other then I asked him, "what's your name?"

"My name is Mark."

"Well Mark, if you help us get all of this money out of here. I'll let you have some for sure but how are you going to do that shit?"

"That's easy, did you see that school bus outside there? "Yeah, - Well that's my bus that what I do and to make some real money I come here and do this for Big Sammy.

"You're not scared of Big Sammy knowing you helped take his money?"

"Yo" he has to find me first. *Me and Fat Poncho started laughing and I was thinking to myself everybody is down to make an extra buck when they can.*

"Okay you got a deal Mark, what about the others?"

I looked at them, verbalizing, " will you help us?"

They all looked at each other. One of the tall thin light skin guys mumbled out his mouth, "I will not help you leave me out of this shit!"

I quickly snapped at him, "what's your name man?"

My name is Rick then I asked the dude next to him what about you what's your name?

"My name is Devin and I'm with Rick. Do what you have to do. He puts his hands up in the air."

"Okay you're the last man in this shit. What do you have to say?"

31

"My name is Darrell. Hell yeah, I'll give you a hand fuck it."

"Okay, Mark, go get the bus and park it over here on the side so we can quickly put the money in there."

Mark replied loudly, "Sounds good."

I look at Poncho telling him, "You go with him and check shit out for us, okay."

I looked on the side and saw a little bathroom. They both go out the door. I walked up to Rick and Devin with my gun on them shouting right this way I'm putting you two in the bathroom over here. Rick cried why we had to go in there. Because I said so nigga now don't let me tell you again!

Devin spoke,"come on Rick man just do what she said man."

With Devin pulling him by his arm inside of the small bathroom I just looked at both of them just when Mark was putting the bus where I told him. I was about to close the door when Rick blurted out fast, "you'll never get away with this shit.

"Big Sammy is going to hunt you niggas down and kill you both!" **Puuuooofff!** I shot him right in the middle of his fucking head for talking shit. Devin just looked up at me with blood on his face from the blow back of the shot. I hollered in his face what about you, nigga you got something to say? He spoken swiftly, "I change mind. I'll help you if you let me live, please.

"Sure, Devin is welcome to the money team."

Now Mark and Fat Poncho came back inside, and we made a chain tossing the bags to one another putting them inside the back of the school bus. It doesn't take us long to get most of the bags in the school bus working together as a team. We could have taken them all, but the clock was against us because Fat Poncho kept jabbering that the next shift will come in at 7:00. So, we had to work fast and get ghost like a motherfucker. To me we had more than enough reason to get greedy.

I yelled, "let's get the fuck out of here."

Fat Poncho hollering back at me, "yeah, you're right let's roll. I spit to him right quick give me your phone number right quick he gave it to me."

Fat Poncho went to his truck Devin jumped on the back along with me getting in closing the back door of the school bus. The dude Mark jumped behind the wheel of the bus, and we took off down the street like a blur. I go sit up front with him on the side telling him to drive towards the docks. I called Fat Poncho. He picked up on the first ring. I told him to go to the docks. We should get there in no time just keep following us up there okay.

"Yeah, good idea, baby girl."

He made sure not to call out my name and I still have on my mask ducking down for no one to see me as well. It took us about 20 minutes to get there. I tell Mark to pull over. I called Fat Poncho uttering, "yo, put your mask back on while we unload these bags."

He just giggled and hung up the phone then I saw him turning his truck around and parking it backwards in the back of the school bus.

Devin and Mark got off the bus with me helping me take the trash bags filled with money stuffing them in the back of Fat Poncho's truck. After we were all done, I walked over to Mark, verbalizing, "thank you for all of that money."

As I stood closer to him smiling, making him feel more relaxed. **Pooouuufff!** I shot him in the middle of his head, and he fell to the ground. Devin tried to run **Pooouuufff! Pooouuufff! Pooouuufff!**

I shot him three times in the back of his head. I just saw blood mist flying in the air before his body hit the ground face first. I just looked over at Fat Poncho shrugging my shoulders.

Fat Poncho muttered, "damn, Lex your one cold bitch! I barked you better know it, and don't you forget that shit neither, fat man!"

"Wow, I thought you were going to let them live?"

"You know fucking well soon as Big Sammy would catch up to them, they were going to Rat us the fuck out for sure."

"Yeah, I guess you're right so what about all the rest of the money on the bus?"

"Just call one of your thug ass boys that you trust and tell them to come get the bus that's all."

"We just toss these two niggas in the fucking river and call it a day!"

"Okay, help me pick this nigga up." He walks over to Devin body picking him up by his shoulders. I quickly grabbed his feet walking to the end of the dock. It's still a little dark out with the sun about to come up on the horizon. We both started swinging him back and forth and let him go with the flow, in the air and Splash! Now we go get Mark's body and walk over towards the edge of the dock. This guy was a little heavier than the other dude. We were both huffing and puffing, swigging him and letting him go Splash! Fat Poncho quickly called up his boy Moon and told him to come ASAP! Telling him it's a life and death type of thing so he had to haul ass to get there.

Moon on the other end of the phone uttered "he was on his way."

We both got on the school bus as Fat Poncho pulled out a fat pink color bag of coke. We both snorted it up quickly talking shit about Big Sammy we both felt good about taking his loot this nigga was elated. *That made me change my mind about killing his fat ass.* Surprisingly his boy Moon came fast driving the bus off we jump in his truck, and we got the fuck out of dodge skirrrrrtttt!

While were driving back I told Fat Poncho, "I'm going to get the fuck out of town and keep getting up like a motherfucker." *I just told him that shit. I'm going back to kill Scooby, Tippy, Bony*

Irons, his brother Lance Lucci and his sidekick. Mikey, before I get out of town that way, I feel better about myself.

"Check it out,baby girl, we're going to my little hold up garage. So, I can give you your cut and get your Range Rover. Shit that's not mine. I jack that motherfucker from some white boys. I shot two of them and only got 34,000 dollars out of them pussy ass motherfuckers."

"So, you need a whip, then right?"

"Yeah, you got another one for me."

"Sure, I do for you Le?

"I have a 2012 explorer I can give you but it's not bullet proof like this doe."

"That's cool just as long as it runs good Poncho man. What year is this right here?"

"Oh, this shit here is a 2019 look. I was thinking that when it really smooths me, and you can hook up and do some more things together."

"Yeah, I would like that."

"So, what else you have in mind because you came up with this one nigga? so I don't smoke your wife for crossing me."

"I know but shit worked out really good, right?"

"Yeah, it did but like I said what do you have in fucking mine because I have other shit, I want to do okay."

"Yo, Lex, just think about it."

Then we pulled up at his large garage and rolled down his window pointing his garage remote towards the big white steel doors. Then it's a loud hydraulic sound from the garage doors coming up as he drives in the parking lot. When I looked around inside, he had about six cars and four trucks. I get out and we both get to work pulling the bags out inside of the truck setting them up on his tool table. After we got the bags on the table and on the floor near the table, Fat Poncho set up two money counting machines on top of the tool table. And we got busy but I'm getting fucking hungry.

"Yo, when are we going to get something to eat up in this bitch?"

"I'll run to the drive thru and get us a couple egg and cheese muffins. Is that good with you?"

"Yeah, anything will happen right now for real."

"Okay I'll be right back just keep counting Lex."

He jumps in his truck pointing his remote to open the doors and drive out quickly. As the door started coming down while I'm still counting all this dope boy cash with rubber bands around it. It is a pain in the fucking ass. 15 minutes later the doors came back up and he drives back in parking on the right and side He gets out with the bags he went to Mickey Dee's.

TWO DOWN AND TWO TO GO.

He set the bags up on the tool table winking his eyes at me. I grabbed the bag open, and he got me a sausage egg and cheese sandwich. I pointed to Fat Poncho.

"All right it's your turn to keep counting nigga I need to eat something before I fall the fuck out! "He's laughed, while he's eating and counting the money with the money machine flapping and clicking. I ate and got back. It took us about three hours to count all that shit. *I can't front. I'm glad I pulled this job with him so I can have some money to make moves. The nigga was all right I was thinking he was going to try some slick shit and I would have to kill his ass. but like he said it all worked out. Now if I could put a crew together, I can do bigger jobs and really make some money. That one thing about getting big money once you get it you get used to it. Because you want it all the time too fuck that shit.*

After it is all said and done, after we count both big piles of loot, a grand total 20,000,000 split two ways. Not bad. We could have got more but why be greedy. Now Fat Poncho pulls out a zip lock sack of coke from out his tool table. Why did he do that Shit? have not had no good high-grade cocaine in a fucking while. *I can tell just by looking at it that it's some real raw Dawg shit.* I used to snort shit like that every day hanging with the 24[th street] cartel gang. So, we snorted a little blow and drank some beer. Now I'm ready to roll after I get buzzed off the blow. I ask him where can buy some really good shit from. He looked at me, utter loudly, ``What, you didn't like that?"

"Yeah, that's what I want some more of what we just had."

"Well, we're all Gucci than baby girl!"

I'll hook you up with my plug, but he doesn't fuck with every street person around. I can call him but he's expensive.

"Yeah, hit him up and tell him I want an "O" (Ounce)."

"Okay, but it's going to take him some time to deliver that for you."

"Well, call me I'm not waiting around. I'm going to go get some rest. We were working on the late-night tip. We both started giggling, "give me those keys to that Explorer so I can go."

"Here you go." He hands me the keys. I looked over at it and it was white. I was not crazy about the color but what the fuck. It's a gift from one crook to another. Four wheels beat the shit out of two heels any day of the fucking week. "So, I put all of my money in his black and gray old tool bags he gave me. We put them in the back of the white Explorer. Along with my back-pack I put a couple grand in my pocket. I bump fist with Fat Poncho.

He told me with a smile on his fat grill, "it's good working with you Lex. I'll call you when the coke comes, okay. I'll talk to you later. I jumped behind the wheel, and he hit the button to let me out there. I took off like a jet fighter pilot with my gun in my lap. *A bitch like me don't trust a living soul on this planet earth for real.* Zrooom!

I pull out of there and I drive to downtown Manhattan. I park in one of the real crowded parking lots. The tall thin African dude with fucked up yellow teeth was not going to take it. Until I gave him a hundred-dollar bill for himself and paid for the parking too. I walked up to the Levi's store then I went to

15th & Broadway. I roll over to AEO & Aerie and I tell you. I really got my shop on for real in that motherfucker. That white girl in the store was kissing my ass all the way out the fucking door. I wear one of all black outfits out the store. I liked walk-ing out the store like a real fucking square bitch out here in the fucking world. I brought some nice leather bags to put the money in. I go get my whip. I take the money out of the old fucked up tool bags and put them in the nice brown and black leather bags. And as you know I'm watching my back looking around to make sure nobody is peeping my ass doing this shit.

Now I drive to the Baccarat hotel & Residences on West 53rd street and check in with my power suit on. I look like a fucking power broker doing things and I get one of the best suites on the 10th floor. Soon as I go up to my room and I tip the bellhop this tall white boy who keeps checking me out looking at my ass. Only thing he made me think about getting some from a real thug nigga who knows how to put it down on a bitch for real. I just wink my eye at his ass and close the door real fast in his face. Then Fat Poncho calls me telling me that his man is there with the coke. I replied, "Does he have two O's instead of one?"

He asked him and he answered he had it. I told him to bring it up to the Baccarat hotel.

"What's his name?"

"His name is Chi- Chi."

He says it's 20 large and he knows where it's at. I barked. It must be some real good shit for 20 large. He started jawing loud, "it's the fucking best!"

I tell him to come on with it. I'm trying to get high and don't take all fucking day with that!

Fat Poncho spit back to me all snappy, "he'll be there, don't worry about it and he hangs up."

I order some room service right after I ate, I had steak and eggs and it was off the fucking hook too. I sit back and light up a cigarette then I get the call I pick it up really quick, "who is this?"

"Yo, this is Chi- Chi. I'm in the lobby. I'll be right down." I quickly head down to go get this coke from this dude. I get down to the lobby looking for this dude.

I hear this guy walk up to me. "Are you Lex?"

"Yes, that's me babe." *This fucking guy is gorgeous he's looks half* black and Puerto Rican or something. *This guy is smoking hot doe.* "So, you're Chi-Chi."

"Yeah, that's me, you got something for me?"

I see he has this little gift bag. It looked like a little shopping bag to me. I know the coke is in there. "Yes, I do!"

I looked in my pocketbook real fast. I had all the money, but I wanted to get this hunk of a man up to my room, maybe make something jump off. So, I fumbled just a little and I said, "you want to know why I was rushing to get down here you want to come up and get the rest of the money for you? I'm so sorry. "

I knew he'll fall for the bullshit act. I'm putting on as I hand him the 20,000 swiftly. He takes it real smooth, sticking it in his pocket. He replied with his eyes getting wide, "that's alright. I'll come and get it from you sweetheart."

I smiled, giving him a hot sexy stare. We both walked back towards the elevator and *now I'm really checking this mother-fucker out damn. He keeps looking better, big strong arms, and a lot of tattoos. It looks like he is packing some meat down there too.* The elevator came and we both got on and I holler at this fine ass motherfucker, "where are you from Chi- Chi?I was born in Philly but now I live here in New York in the Bronx. It's all right but it's not like Philly for real."

" Wow,you know what, I'm from Philly, born and raised". "Oh yeah, what part?"I'm from South Philly."

"What about you?"

"North Philly before my mom died and I came here to New York to live with my father."

"Okay."

The elevator rings **Bing**" it my floor and he voices me super smooth. "I'm not trying to be too forward but you're a really nice-looking woman. I must say Ma"

I giggled, "you really think so with your hot looking ass."

He laughs as we walk to my room now, I know he's checking me out as well. I open the door with my card key. Then he asks me, "So how long are you here in New York for?"

"I'll be here for another two weeks before I go back to Boston. That's where I live now."

I had to tell him a real quick lie. He closed the door behind himself as we both walked into my suite. He's looking around.

"Wow, this is a really nice room you got here."

"Shit, it cost me enough loot. Okay let's see the goodies Mister black and gorgeous."

He started giggling, pulling the coke out of the little gift bag with all the colorful gift paper red and yellow. He set it on top of the table in my room and I rolled up a hundred-dollar bill. I pulled up a chair and sit down in front of the table and I scoop some of it up. I blow it in my mouth first to see what it's hittin for. Damn Soon as it hit my throat, I knew this was some good shit Fat Poncho had. Then I snort it in each one of my nostrils and I put my head back and bang.

The cocaine started working rapidly on my brain. I look up at him articulating wow this is some good coke that has to be some Peruvian flake. Chi-Chi just smiled and nodded his head. *He knows I'm right, but he won't say anything.* I walked to the nightstand and went in one of my bags and got the loot. I pulled it out and counted it swiftly. I walked up handing it to him looking him up and down with my sexy bedroom eyes niggas fall for that shit every time. I gazed at him in his deep brown eyes, "you going to keep me company for a while, right. Fall back and have some champagne."

He just pulls up a chair sitting next me disclosing, "I'm not in a big rush over here."

"Good why don't you get some champagne glasses while I scoop up some of this coke and put it on a tray and we can continue this conversation on the bed."

"Sounds like a winner to me, Ma."

I quickly grab the silver tray from off the pushcart. I dump a big pile of the coke on top of it. I quickly sat the tray on top of the bed and took off my black power suit top kicking off my shoes. Chi- Chi came up with a bottle of Louis Roederer Cristal and two glasses. He handed me one. He pops the bottle of champagne pouring me some in my glass fizzing and bubbling up. Chi- Chi sit next to me, we tapped glasses , and both started sipping on the champagne. I got up fast, turning on some music on the CD player on the nightstand still holding my glass of champagne. I set it down quickly taking off my blouse picking up my glass of champagne sipping on it. Sitting on the bed next to him holding my glass in one hand and rubbing on his leg with the other.

I turned on some music saying, "do you like Cristal?"

He said, "I had it a few times but it's really expensive. Shit with the money you're making off that coke nigga you can afford it. I just got a cut. Almost all of that money goes to my boss Angel. "Well, it sounds like you need to be your own boss with your fine self."

As I lay out some lines of cocaine on top of the table and said, "come on motherfucker don't tell me you don't snort coke."

"Yeah, I do Ma." With his big Hollywood smile, that's when there was a knock at my door. I go to get it and it's room service with some more Cristal champagne at the door. I tip the nice young lady who brought it up to me on a cart. I told her, "I'll take it from here just close the door for me honey.

I pushed it inside as she closed the door like I asked her, and I pushed the cart close to the bed smiling.

IT'S BEEN A LONG WHILE SINCE I GOT SOME.

He has been over the pile of coke. I made lines out of it and he snorted up two lines. while I pop the champagne getting us some glasses. I pour us each a glass. I hand him his glass of champagne. We both sat on the bed and we tapped glasses with me and said, "to new fast friends."

He chimed in, "to a real hot Ma-Ma." He looked me deep in my face. He drank his glass down and he leaned over and kissed me. We kissed long and super wet then I drank down my glass of champagne. Now I leaned on him and started kissing him again, pushing him down on the bed. He placed both his large hands on my ass. Now we're grinding on one another like two hot in the ass teenagers. I said to myself fuck this. I started taking off my blouse but soon as I did that, he started helping me take my bra off. I'm pulling at his jeans.

Taking them off as well. I opened up his jeans, but he jumped up standing on the side of the bed taking them all the way off. At the same time, I'm taking mine off too, looking at his hot body. I can't wait for him to come hit my hot wet kitty. It's been a long while since I got some for real. He got his clothes off first down to his blue boxer shorts and looked up at me and started climbing up on the bed slow and sexy like. I'm lying on the bed with my black panties on and I cocked my legs open to let him know. He came up on this bed and he better tear this pussy up too. Or I just be wasting my fucking time.

Well as soon as he came up, I grabbed both my ankles putting my legs up in the air higher. He pulled me towards him. Then he quickly reached down, taking my panties off. I lift my ass up a little more to help him out. He got my panties off and he tossed them on the side of the bed taking his boxers off super-fast. Then he grabbed my left leg pushing it back with one hand and taking his other hand grabbing his thick brown man hood. Then pointing it towards my dripping wet coochie ramming it right inside with force. He didn't do it too hard. **Oooooohhhh!** As soon as he got his large one eye snake all the way up in me. He quickly grabbed both my legs and he started stroking putting his back into it with a hump in it. *That let me know he really wanted it and he's not playing any fucking games neither. Gawd Damn! He's fine and he can fuck good too. Most the time those pretty niggas don't know what to do with the pussy when they get it.* He is putting both my legs on his big strong shoulders. This man is like a bull on the rampage, and I'm so turned on with him pounding my pussy. To The soft R&B beat playing on the radio. I feel like I'm going to cum and he just got started. He got right to it.

With me looking up at him grunting. He knows what he's doing too. With each stroke my cunt got wetter and its running down my fucking leg too. Then he leans down to kiss me, and I reach up grabbing him around his thick brown sexy tattoo neck. I took my other hand putting it right on his tight bronze buns pulling him closer inside of me as he was pumping harder. I use both my hands on his ass pulling it more up in me. **Oooouuu!**Right at this time he's really hitting it now and I'm soaring up to the clouds gyrating my hips back on him hard. sweating up a storm with our sizzling hot flow. I just let it go climaxing. "**Oooohhh** shit!"

I started squirting my head and Chi-Chi kept going even stronger like a runaway train on a track. I looked up at him and he's focused on rocking my world for real. He's doing it well too! We both yelled in deep lovely pleasure. I can't lie I'm getting out of breath trying to keep up after I cum again. It was like I blasted off to the fucking milky way now floating among millions of stars. I can tell he's holding on to me tighter mumbling, "he is about to cum stroking harder and harder and **Boom!**"

He lets it go. He is shaking up and down like a tree in a fucking tornado. It likes to get pulled up by its roots. His face all twisted up. I thought his head was going to pop off his shoulders right then and there. I can see the vein in his neck popping up. I can feel all his hot baby gravy shooting up in me. I feel like I'm about to cum again. It felt so good. Then he just collapses on top of me breathing hard and so am I. His sweat from his head is dripping down on top of me in my face. He kissed me and we started French kissing long and hot. Then he said, "I'm about to get up off of you, but I don't want to come up out of you for real."

Take your time, don't do it real fast Chi- Chi."

"Okay Lex,I won't baby." We both started giggling loud and he did take his time. I open my legs a little wider and he gets up off of me real slow. As soon as he did, he laid next to me, putting his big arms around me, kissing me on my cheek and my lips again.

He asked, "you want some more coke?"

"Yeah, line some up for me and light up a smoke for me, baby."

I pointed to where my cigarettes were on top of the nightstand. I sat up. As he takes out two cigarettes at the same time handing me one. Then he started shuffling the white powder making four fat lines on top of the smooth surface. I quickly sit on the side of the bed getting closer to the nightstand as Chi- Chi hands me the rolled up hundred-dollar bill. I snorted up the two lines of the blow. As Chi- Chi poured me some more champagne and himself a glass. He hands me my glass and all I can think about is fucking round two smiling.

"So, did you think about what I told you about working for yourself?"

"I would love to, but I don't have the loot to start up anything."

"Don't worry about that I have to do a few things but on the weekend.I can set you up with something really nice to get you started. "

"I'm down if you're really for real. I'll do it."

"Okay look I'm telling you now if I hook you up and you burn me, I'll kill your ass. I don't care how good your ass loot. I don't play when it comes to my loot Chi- Chi I'm telling you."

"Look if you put me on, I'll take care of fucking business for real Lex."

"I'm just saying Mister Sexy."

MORE PAY BACK ON THAT ASS

Me and Chi- Chi kicked it just a little more. I took him in the shower and let him hit it from the back. I leaned up on the large white tile shower wall cracking my ass open wide real sexy like bracing for the impact. He took his time sliding his rock-hard manhood inside of me, nice slow and hot shit. I wanted to cum right then and there with his huge butter pecan color Dick of his Ooooh Poppy. He didn't waste any time putting his hands on my hips with the water coming down on both of us rocking my pussy like it was the last one on earth. It did not take me long before I started squirting out a hot orgasm with the warm water coming down all over my body. I felt light-headed and out of breath with a tingling sensation rushing throughout my whole body. *Wow, it's been a long-time since I came like that home boy. Really knew how to put his thing down, but I would never let him know about it.*

Then I when laid down and when to sleep after that good fucking. He put it on me. Getting high and he stayed with me until nightfall. When he woke up, he announced he had to roll. He gave me his number and I walked him to the door. We kissed. I told him I'll call him and let him know when we can hook up and sell some products.

He said, "Cool, Ma." He paused and I could see that pussy whipped look in his brown eyes.I went and laid back down on the big king size bed. I laid around watching TV. I waited until it was late at night before I made my move. I took a little nap and got up. I got washed and dressed and put on an all black shirt, jeans and sneakers. I went out the back exit of the hotel to get my car in the parking lot. I hop in and I drive back up

to the Bronx. This time I drove up to 82nd street where Scooby lived. I parked about three cars from his front door so that I wouldn't miss seeing his ass. I know he is about to go to his night shift working in the dope house. I see his home boy Tippy with two other niggas I don't know I seen them before, but I don't know their fucking names just some thugs want, be motherfuckers from around the way niggas. But they're going to find out what it is tonight for sure. I quickly go in my backpack, get my black mask and put on my rubber gloves. I got my silencer screwed on fast. I put on my mask.I quickly came up on the same side of the street they were on. I know their waiting for that nigga. All of them are talking shit to one another loudly. As I creep up on them, I have my pistol already pointing at it. The first dude turned around and it was too late. **Pooouuufff! Pooouuufff!**

I plugged Tippy first. He hit the ground hard and fast with blood shooting out. One of the other niggas ran like a little bitch. The other dude pulled out his gun on me, but I had the drop on his ass. **Pooouuuff!** I hit him right in the middle of his fucking head keeping my head on a fast swivel.I quickly turned towards the top of the steps **Pooouuufff! Pooouuufff!** I shot Scooby coming down the steps holding a gun. I hit this motherfucker right in his neck. He was holding his neck dropping his gun with blood gushing out like a fucking geyser in the woods. His fucking flunky's that was by his side I shot him in the mouth, and he die with Scooby sliding down the steps landing on top of him bleeding like a stuck pig. Soon as I went to roll out three more henchmen came out the house shooting their machine guns. Coming after me **Ratta tat tat tat! Barrrrttttttaaaaa!** I duck behind this big truck on the left as soon as they ran up on me. I crawled all the way under that motherfucker with the hot lead following me just missing me. shit.

When they ran up to see where I was at one of them was stupid enough to duck his head up under the truck **Pooouuufff!** I shot him right in the face. The other two started shooting their machine guns **Baarrraaatttt! Baaarrrraaaatttt!** Glass and debris flying everywhere with thousands of holes inside of the truck smoking. I climbed out on the other side seeing all these sparks and smoke flying while I'm moving from under the truck. Soon as I got under the truck. I swiftly grabbed the dead man's machine gun and I slowly stood up. Taking aim when they both looked up, the shock on their face was worth more than a million dollars for real. **Baaarrrraaaatttt!** I shot both of these ass holes. They both hit the ground hard making a loud death scream. I quickly walked to my whip up the street soon as I got to my truck, I heard a woman screaming I hopped in my truck, and I took off my mask and I fucking floored it. I drove up to the corner and made a hard-right turn and I was gone.

I drove to New Jersey to one of Big Sammy dope spots. It took me about two hours to get there. I hung around until the sun came up and he never showed up. I wanted to kill his ass and Jack's ass too. But I'm watching them bring in packages. I saw that there were about ten men so I'm gonna have to work fast. I only have three hand grenades, so I have to make it work for me. I jump out of my truck with my backpack. I go around the block, so I scope out a car to jack right quick. I rolled up on this old model Ford. I take out my Jimmy from my backpack. I stick it in the car door and pop it in two second flat. Before I get the car, I find a long stick branch from off the ground. I jump in closing the door. I reach up under the dashboard pulling the wires down. I take out my knife from my pocket and I cut the wires.

I found the right wires, so I made them touch seeing them starting to spark and I tied them together making the car start up I put it in gear, and I pulled off nice and smooth. I drive the car not too far from the front door. I stop. I take out about four rubber bands and one of the hand grenades and wrap it around the steering wheel. I take the stick and I jam it in between the driver seat and the gas pedal. I get out and I put the car into gear. The car takes off driving towards the front door on the left. I take out my black mask putting it on, and I pull off my shirt and my bra. I put my gun in the back of my jeans. Then I put my MP5 machine gun on my shoulder making the strap tight, so it doesn't fall off while I'm moving around fast. I take out one of my hand grenades in my jeans pocket. I put my bra in the bag and my shirt deep down in my back pocket.of my black jeans and I started running towards my truck and jumped in driving towards right near the back door in the driveway on the right-hand side. Soon as the car crashes into the front door **Kaboom!**

Its Rock's the whole house. I jumped out the truck and began walking swiftly towards the back door. two men came running out from the backdoor, yelling to see what happened. Soon as they see me with a black mask on and my titties out the two of them are looking up at me. One of the men said, "what the fuck".?

The second man asked, "who is this freak over here!" I quickly draw my pistol with the silencer on the tip **Pooouuufff! Pooouuufff!** I shot both of them in the middle of their head. They both hit the ground fast and hard. *Shit Annie Oakley don't get shit on me. I'm one bad bitch with a gun.* I ran toward the back door holding my gun by my side three more guys came running up looking at me like I was crazy before shooting at me missing.

I shot back with more accuracy then those three fucking amateurs with a gun **Pooouuufff! Pooouuufff! Pooouuuff!** I shot one in his neck the one behind him in his eye and the last man I shot him in the mouth blood shooting out every fucking were. *I looked at the bloody bodies on the floor whizzing in blood gushing out thick like a fucking horror movie on acid.* I'm talking loud to the dead men on the ground now saying I got to bounce y'all psycho bitch reporting for duty. Then popping up from the left are four men with machine guns shooting at me. I got flat down on the floor as they all came at me hard and fast. Soon as they got close, I got my hand grenade in my hand pulling the pen *and gave God some more friends to hold close to his bosom*

Kadoom! Dumb ass motherfuckers I got all four of them in one shot all I see now is body parts and blood scattered all over the floor like a war zone.

The smoke is getting really thick from the car on fire at the front door, so I have to work fast. I ran out to the driveway. I jumped in my truck, turned it around and I crash right in the back door. I jump out because I know just where the dope room is. I ran inside of the dope room with all this smoke. They had a shopping cart right beside one of the tables. *Today is my fucking day y'all. I'm ripping a hole in the world's ass just like it did me from birth.* I started tossing the keys of dope inside of the shopping cart and I pushed it up to my truck like *I was in fucking Walgreens or something.* Open The hatch back door, throwing them inside.

After I was done, I went back and got another cart full of keys of dope throwing them inside at breakneck speed. I close the hatch back. I quickly put my shirt back on giggling on how my titties out worked with their ass holes and taking off my black mask. I jump back inside my truck and backup out there hauling ass. Soon as I'm driving up the road towards the expressway while I'm blasting the radio. I see fire engines with the sirens blaring, blowing past me going towards the house. I'm driving nice and smooth back to New York. I pull out my pocket some of that coke I cop from Chi-Chi fine ass. DMX tracks blasting on repeat. It didn't take me long to get back to the hotel because of traffic but once I get a little rest.I'll be back on the move to see who I can dump this shit off on for a nice price of course.

I HOOKED UP WITH THE JUNGLE CREW.

I parked in the hotel parking lot. I leave the bags of drugs inside the truck. I just covered it up with a couple dark color blankets Fat Poncho had in the back of the truck. As soon as I get to my luxurious room the whole room smells like white linen fragrance, I love that smell. I toss my backpack on the red crush velvet chair I pull out my phone setting it on the nightstand with my smokes then I take off my jeans and I flopped right in the king size bed Gawd dam I was burned the fuck out. *The best thing in the world is after doing your dirt you come and chill in luxury. It lets you know what you put your ass on the line for from the door.* I slept until it got dark outside. My phone is ringing, waking me up in a sleepy daze. I don't want to come out for real.I picked up my phone on the nightstand near the bed. I reach over, putting it to my head and asked,

"Yeah, who is this?"

"Yo, it's me Poncho baby girl!"

"Hey what's up with you?"

"Shit, if I had your hand, I'll throw mine in. Please tell me who knocked off the dope house in Jersey?"

"I don't know what you're talking about man."

"I been chillin all fucking day and night my nigga."

"Yeah, whatever Lex that nigga Big Sammy is going crazy first his money drop spot now his dope spot. I'm loving it. He said, "it was some crazy bitch with a black mask and her titties out."

"How do they know that shit?"

"Because they have the outside surveillance camera footage,

they know if it was your Lex mask or not"

"Well, how Biggie spit that shit I'm like the motherfuckin gingerbread man catch me if you can."

He's laughing his ass off on the other end of the phone saying, "I knew your crazy ass did it look; I have a buyer for some of the Fentanyl if you're interested?"

"That's what that shit is?"

"Yeah, and you took most of it, they use that shit to mix with the heroin to make it more powerful for the junkies to come back faster than a motherfucker."

"Then after two or three of them overdose off that shit they sell more of that dope mix what a way to market your fucking product. *We both laughed* Damn I'm thinking that's shit was heroin."

"How many did you get Lex?"

"I don't fucking know I didn't count that shit. I just tossed it in the fucking truck and got the fuck out of there."

"Check this out, give me a key for a finder's fee and I'll help you get rid of the shit?"

"Okay what can I get for a key of that shit you think"

"Shit you can get 37000 to 35000 a key here in New York it's your shit but if I was you."

"I would start out high and take no less than 35000 or 30000."

"Yeah, that sounds just about right okay set it up Poncho and if you set me up nigga you know you're dead."

"You still don't trust me Lex?"

"Hell, no I don't trust a fucking living soul on this planet motherfucker."

Poncho laughed and said, "I'll call you in about an hour or so and I'll tell you where to meet us at. "Okay one." He hangs up so I go to get myself together for this bull shit if I smell anything funny, I'll kill everything that's moving. So, it didn't take me long to get ready. I got washed and dressed. I put my hair in a ponytail right quick, loaded up my guns and got something to eat while I was waiting on the call. Soon as I got done eating a steak and eggs a rich motherfucker's breakfast and I'm full as a tick now puffing on a Newport kicking back.

Poncho called me,"yo, what's up. Lex baby you ready?" "Yeah, I'm ready where you want me to meet you? Right here at my garage you know where it's at, so you feel safe". "It doesn't matter to me big man if shit is not right you already know what's going to happen, right?"

"Look everything is going to be cool okay and I need to holla at you about that shit we did too"

"Okay, I'll be there soon. We can talk then one!"

I already have my Glock pistol in the back of my black jeans. I make sure I have my other pistol with the silencer on it and I have my MP-5 with two clips in my backpack ready to go. I light up a Newport and I make sure I still have some of that good ass coke I brought. I took out enough to snort out of one the O's (Ounces) I brought. I put it in a little plastic sack scooping it up swiftly. I fly out the door going to the parking lot of the hotel. I know I'm parked on the sixth floor. I looked around to make sure nobody had their eyes on me. I opened the back hatchback. I started counting the keys I jacked when I was done its 47 keys not to fucking bad. I put the blankets back on top of them, I jumped in my front seat, turned on some music on the radio and took off. It took me about a half hour to get to Fat Poncho place. I beep the horn to let him know I was outside of the gate. The gate started coming up real slow. I saw two other people I don't know near Fat Poncho talking shit and smoking cigarettes. I pull in really fast *I'm sizing these niggas up the short one looks like fucking Bushwick Bill from the Rap group the Ghetto Boys. And the tall one he's cute looks like Jamie Foxx.*

I can tell there both some real deal killers but if they get out of hand, I'll kill both of them before they can blink their fucking eyes. I put my backpack on my shoulder and I took out my keys and jumped out as the gate came all the way down. It got darker inside of the join when the gate went down with one light shining where they were standing. I walked towards them real smooth as they were all standing by. Fat Poncho's tool table I walked up to Fat Poncho said, "yo what up baby girl?"

"Everything if we're going to do some business?"

I bump fist with him smiling, "Sure thing, Lex this is my man Moon and his partner Stump."

I bump fist with both of them and the dude Moon said,

"I heard you got some Fentanyl for sale. What do you want for it?"

"Yeah, I have what you want if you're ready to buy."

"I want 20,000. A key and we can rock and roll right now brother."

Moon said, "that's not bad but if you come down just a little to 20,000 a key. I can take four of them off your hand right here and now."

"I have 80,000 cash money honey. "

I look over at Fat Poncho. He is nodding his head yes with a smirk on his fat brown skin grill.

"Okay cutey show me the money and make my sky's all blue and sunny."

Everyone started giggling. He reach over on top of the tool table grabbing his bag then I see that little ass hole fucking make a move. I whipped out my pistol and pointed right at his oversize black water head.

"I'll blow that big ass head of yours off of that little ass body motherfucker!"

He put his hands up in the air with his eyes getting wide.

"I was getting my smokes sweetheart." He showed me all his fucking yellow teeth. He is getting his pack of cigarettes really slowly from off the top of the tool table. With his fat ass black fingers. He laughed looking up at me. I like her Poncho man! They all started laughing. Moon, still giggling, pulls his money out of the large gray gym bag. He showed *me the money with a smirk on his dark grill.*

"I got you right here Ma- Ma." See now show me your shit looking me right in my eyes *This nigga is serious as cancer.* I pointed my remote in my left hand towards the truck. I quickly walked over, never taking my eyes off of any of them still holding my pistol.

I'm playing it off real cool **y'all,** *but if a nigga twitch,* **I'll wet up shit right quick from my thick black hip. Niggas will get lit!** I put my keys in my jeans pocket and my gun in the front of my jeans and I picked up five bags of Fentanyl. I close back my hatchback. I walked back still keeping my eyes on them niggas. I'm switching my ass off and it looks like all their Dicks are hard. I call it being hard core bitch radar. Every real gangster I know want to live fast and fuck all the time. They never know if that their last day to breathe breath on this fucking earth! I set it on top of the tool table and said, "check it out, playa."

He quickly grabbed one of the keys of Fentanyl he reaches in his pocket pulling out this white tube. He takes his hand and pulls out this white test strips out of this fucking white tube showing it to me first. I nodded my head. I don't know what the fuck he was doing I just act like I knew. He sticks it in the white powder just taps it real fast. He stands there shaking it the strip comes up with a little red line more towards the right. He shows it to me, "it's positive."

He looked up at me, "wow, this is some really good shit."

He nodded his head at me putting the white tube back in his pocket. He hands me the bag, "here you go, Ma."

I take the bag of money and put the strap on my shoulder. I

reach over to grab one of the bags of Fentanyl. I tossed it at Fat Poncho leaning on the tool table. He smiles, catching it in midair and he quickly puts it in his tool drawer. He winked his eye at the two of them, both giggling. I just walked back to my truck with the bag of loot he just gave me. I hit my remote, always keeping my eyes on them. I know all of them are looking at my ass as I'm putting it on the passenger side seat, close it back and hit my remote. **Boo-Beep**. I walked back over to where they were standing. Stump asked me, "can I buy you a drink, sexy?"

With a cigarette hanging from his thick dark lips. "Sure, what you got brother?" He quickly walks over to their black GMC on the left-hand side of the garage, opening the door pulling out a bottle of gin and its cold. I looked and smirked, "man, I love gin and it's cold too."

"Yeah, I keep it in my cooler in the truck."

"Hey Poncho, get us some cups."

Poncho clapped his and jump up, "Oh, you didn't say nothing but a word, nigga."

He quickly reaches up in another one of his tool cabinets pulling out a sleeve of red cups handing each one of us one. Stump opened it up and started pouring everybody some. Then Poncho pulls out a big bag of coke, dumping it out on top of the tool table. He is chopping it up with one of his business cards and it reads **Fat low life crook his whole life is off the books**.

I'm just fucking with y'all heads y'all know what I mean. doe!

Then he rolls up a 50-dollar bill and hands it to me uttering lady's first with a wide slick grin on his dark grill. I took it out of his hand and started snorting the first two lines and boom it was some raw Dawg shit here.

I asked, "where you get this shit from while I'm holding my nose." They're all laughing at me.

"From your boy Chi- Chi why?" My shit doesn't taste like this. I pull my bag of coke out of my pocket and let him taste it.

He looked at me, "it's the same shit, girl you're tripping." While he's holding his head back letting the drug drip back into his nose. So, I let Stump and Moon taste it and they both agreed the same shit putting his hand up in the air and a big smile on his dark brown face.

Stump asked, "where are you from, Lex?"

I replied, "South Philly born and raise you better know it nigga."

"Man, I'm thinking you're from the Bronx all this time you act like you're from here."

"If you ask me all of them bitches is no fucking joke like you baby."

Moon told me too after Poncho told me you took down that joint all by yourself. That was a real nice piece of fucking work. I said, "shit when I was in Philly, we done took down about 35 banks, so a fucking dope house is a piece of fucking cake."

"Well, me and Stump got a job lined up. My man Vita scouted out this drug dealer in Philly and Poncho told us you were from Philly. So, this shit is like perfect timing for these Puerto Rican Cats. The dude's name is Raymundo from F and Allegheny. You know the area right"

"Oh yeah like the back of my hand. I know that dude he's down with the FEC Front & Erie Clique." A guy that was in the gang with me was down with that drug gang at one time."

"So, what do you think? Can we take them?"

"Depends on who you got with you."

"Well, I wanted to know if you could help us out on this shit because you know Philly really well".

"I don't know about this shit I just met you, niggas. That's like asking for a blow job and you never even brought me fucking dinner."

All of them started laughing.

I was thinking after we knock his ass off, we take the drugs up to Boston, mix some of the heroin with the Fentanyl and double the money. We would give you a nice fat cut of the loot."

"Now that sounds like a plan but I'm good right now." While I'm sipping on my drink, *I'm still eye balling these niggas and I'm fucked up off of that coke.*

Fat Poncho continued, "Look, that score we did together was good but it's not going to last forever, Lex. Come in with us we can stack this shit up until we can chill out for about a year or two years or so".

"Let me think about it, okay. Is that what you wanted to talk to me about?"

" Yeah, and to tell you that Big Sammy got a green light (Hit) out on you. I know you can take care of yourself, you are going to need some people around you that you can trust. All of us here hate Big Sammy so we're not going to sell you out. Plus, it's good to get out of town for a little while. Anyway you know what I'm saying".

"I told you before that I don't trust anybody. How do I know anyone of you don't sell me out for that fucking loot?"

"I can tell you right now Big Sammy is not going to pay any-body else. He kills niggas after you done did the job for him killing somebody. He is going to smoke you, so he doesn't have to pay your ass. The three of us right here know that already. Other stupid ass greedy motherfuckers don't know what we know about that nigga. If he finds out I told you where that drop spot was at, I'll be in the same boat you're in."

"Well, you're right about the money. I know that's not going to last, but it's your wifey. I'm worried about her. She's going to rat us out, I'm telling you."

What he doesn't know I can tell by the look in her eyes that's she's fucking Sammy, but Poncho don't know it yet. Stump and Moon looking at Fat Poncho and I can see in their eyes they both are agreeing with me, but they don't say anything.

Moon changes the subject, "so when you were in Philly did you have your own crew?"

"No, I was part of a crew."

Stump asked, "So who were you down with? I can't wait to hear this shit?"

"I was down with the 24th street Cartel." All three of them stare at each other like they were blown out the fucking water. Their mouths dropped open. *I saw the look on all their faces. It was like I told them that I was riding shotgun with the devil and I was sticking a hot pitchfork up a million motherfucker's asses burning out their ass hole.*

Moon looked over at Fat Poncho, "get the fuck out of here for real?"

I rolled up my sleeve while I was sipping on my drink and said there is nobody on the planet brave enough to wear this tattoo on their arm if it was not real. *All of them looking closer to my ink the skull with two Glock pistols Chris crossing one another and in thick block letters the 24th street cartel under it.* Moon yelled out, "oh my fucking Gawd. No wonder you could have taken down that dope spot by yourself, Ma." I heard so many stories about them on the streets and when I was in prison. They ran the jail.

Stump looked up at means began speaking, "I heard a story about them taking out the whole MMC (The Mass Murder clique) in Coney Island. That the cops were too fucking scared to go up there to pick up the fucking bodies."

Stump cuts in, "I got one better Boss Coo- Coo was the baddest motherfucker in New York. I heard he done killed 85 niggas personally himself and that's after he took over after Jay Loot stepped off. And when he did take over Boss Coo- Coo ordered more than 400 people dead and the 24th Street cartel took him out. So, I knew right then and there nobody was badder than the 24th street Cartel. They still to this day run all of boss Coo-Coo's territory here in New York."

"Yeah, that's true, Shakim and Jump are holding that shit down right now."

"You're right he's the big man so are you going to get down with us or what?" *He looked me right into my eyes to see what I'm going to say.*

Moon with both his arms up in the air yelled, "yo, we really could use you with this job. If we're going to pull this shit off right."

"Alright, I'll do it only if y'all go and get the right tools (Guns) for us to work. we all have to split everything equally with no bull shit or squabbles. The first sign of that shit and I'm gone."

All of them nodding their heads in agreement as I bump fist with each one of them. We continue to get fucked up talking shit. We all agreed to meet back up the next day to put the game plan together to do the gig. I jumped in my truck and Fat Poncho hit the remote letting me out lifting up the gate. I waved at Stump and Moon. I drove out swiftly. I went back to my hotel room. It didn't take me long to get there. Hell, I don't know how I did it because I was twisted. I made it back all in one piece to my room. I toss my backpack on the chair then flopped on my king size bed with all my shit on. I was knocked the fuck out.

The next day I got up around 11 and I was still high as a motherfucker. I'm used to it just as long as I can still function. I quickly take off all my clothes and jump in the shower and get my shit together. So, I can check out of this joint and get back to work. After I get washed, I do my hair. I just brush it back putting it in a gangster bitch ponytail. I get dressed and pack up all my shit. I double check to make sure I don't leave anything. I scoop out some of that coke I brought. I refill a smaller sack so I can snort. I stick it in my jeans pocket then I repack the two O's (Ounce) in my suitcase. I made sure I got all my loot as soon as I was going out the door to go meet everybody. My phone rings, I answer it while I'm still on the move. It's that fine ass nigga Chi- Chi asked,

"Yo, what's up baby? What are you doing?"

"Look, I have to make a run. I'll holla at you later on tonight. Is that alright with you babe?"

"Sure, I will call you later on so we can hook up"

"Sure, I'll see you then." *I just lied to him. I don't want him to know what I'm doing.* I go to the front desk, I pay them, and I roll out with my new suitcase that has wheels on it and I head towards the elevator. So, I can go to the garage to find my truck. I don't know where the fuck I parked at because I was so fuck-ing high last night.

While I was looking around for my truck, I noticed that some-body was following me. I know they're not cops, it's a man and woman both are white in their mid-30's rich well to do motherfuckers. They look like spooks (CIA). They don't know that I'm on to them. So,I played it off but if they get too close to me you know. I'm going to blow one of their fucking heads off from the door. They keep their distance I know once I jump in my truck, I can lose their ass when I drive the fuck out of here. They both get in their dark blue Volvo the same time I get in my truck once I find it. But I sit back looking at them to see if they're going to pull out now, they know I'm on to them. I reach in my jeans pocket pulling out a hundred-dollar bill. Then I pull out my gun with the silencer on the tip nice and calm cracking my window just a little. They're not too far from me, they pull out slowly, but I started up my truck. I ride past them fast and I shoot **Pooouuufff! Pooouuufff!** I hit their front two tires and I took off heading towards the front entrance. I ride up to the booth with a hundred-dollar bill in my hand.

I smiled and greeted the attendant, "hi, are you doing today handsome? Look, I'm in a big hurry young man, just let me out and you can keep the change."

The young clean-cut white dude smiles just got wider, "Sure thing, Miss. Have a nice day and thank you!"

I took off driving. I can see in my rear-view mirror the same white well to do man running up to see where I'm at. He's huffing and puffing. I made a Sharp right turn, and I was gone, giggling.

It doesn't take me long to get to Fat Poncho Garage. As soon as I'm outside of the gate I beep the horn three times our new code. The gate started coming up. I make sure nobody is still on me. I see that I'm cool before I ride in there. I drive in and I park on the left-hand side but when I jump out my truck. I notice it's a little more cleared out as I'm walking up closer, I see two new people. *As you know I'm sizing their ass up, both covered in tattoos but the real dark one on the right has a tattoo that says,* **Faya au ufe** (Do or Die) *in Swahili.*

I walk up and Fat Poncho bumps fist with me and asks, "What's up, Lex?"

I bump fist with Moon and Stump Fat Poncho greets me, "hey, I want you to meet Juicy."

I bump fist with him, "what up?"

He replied, "It's all good, Ma. Justchillin. And this is my man, Vita."

I bump fist with him, "**Kuna nini kaka!**" *(What's up brother) His mouth dropped open and replied,"***Mini ni mzuri Da Da** *(I'm good sister)* **Nzuri** *(Good).*"

Fat Poncho cuts off and asked, "what the fuck did the two of y'all say?"

Everyone started to laugh. I just said to him, "

"What's up brother."

He responded to me, "that's he's good, sister. "

Fat Poncho asked, "what language is that anyway, Lex?"

"That's Swahili,brother."

"Well, how the hell did you know he spoke Swahili?" "Because his name is Vita that means war in Swahili and his tattoo on his arm says Do or Die."

"Okay, I didn't know that shit." He smiled and nodded his head.

"What other languages do you speak Lex?"

"Nine fluently so far."

Vita said, "See now I know it's true that you were down with the 24th street Cartel because all of them had to speak Swahili fluently or you could not get in the gang."

I looked at him and asked, "how do you know that shit?"

"I put in some work with some of Kim's people and they told me."

Fat Poncho cut us off, "okay, let me show you our new toys we got. Lex check it out. As he waved his hand for me to see what he had. He pulled the cover off and on top of the table with all these guns lined up on the long steel table. It looks like a fucking gun show display. I'm looking at machine guns handguns with all the clips and bullets plus my favorite hand grenades.

"Wow, you were not fucking around when I told you tools Poncho."

"Yeah, I hit my man up right here Vita." *He's holding his Dick putting his fist in the air Winking at Me real nasty. I'll fuck him, but I might have to put a bullet in his black ass for acting up after I give him the pussy.*

He smirked, "Well, my name is not war for nothing."

I started laughing shit you got that right while I'm picking up the machine guns checking them out.

"Now this something you can put a hole in a nigga's ass for real!"

Moon came up beside me and started talking, "I feel you Ma. Are you rollin wit us? you going to see why they call us the motherfuckin Jungle crew hot chocolate!"

"Oh, I'm glad you know my shit is hot, but I'm here to make the bodies drop!"

"And niggas getting knocked!"

He started laughing and had a dreamy look in his eyes. *Then I just winked at him and put one hip out. This nigga looked like he was turned out looking at some real gangster pussy.nAbthugs fucking wet dream with a blow job. I'll have all these niggas eating out my fucking hand in a month. I'll train their ass to bow down to the real gangster queen!* So, me and Vita is both checking out the guns *and oh yes were checking each other out on the fucking low as well. Man, I'll have this nigga pussy whipped overnight if he come fucking with me.* Fat Poncho walks over to us, "Yo, I have to go back to the spot Lola said something happened at the house. I got to roll, I'll be right back."

I looked him right in his eyes, "if you go back home right now you will not be back, my nigga. For real. When does she ever call you and say something is up at the crib? Never, right?"

He nodded his head knowing that I'm right. His face is filled with pain and now some fucking payback, plus some flip the strip on a bitch ass in a minute expression on his grill.

Moon, step up with both his hands up in the air, "she's right if you go back to your spot, it's a fucking set up Dawg, don't go!"

He looked at both of us and Stump walked up standing in front of him and said, "if you go out that door without taking any of us with you, you're going to be dead in the next hour. I'll pick out a really fly ass suit to lay you out my nigga."

"Oh, you too man?"

"Yes, Lola has been waiting on this for a long time now!"

Vita chimed in, "if you don't listen to us, you're a motherfuckin newborn fool let us roll nigga. You're wasting time, let's roll baby come on!"

Fat Poncho looked at all of us with his eyes glowing and he knows that bitch is trying to play him and take his ass out. He puffed on his Newport blowing out a big cloud of smoke, "okay, let's ride."

I picked up the AR-15 and some extra clips and two smoke bombs. I put six hand grenades in my backpack. I say to him, "now you are thinking with your scroodle, playa"!

I quickly walk with him to his black Benz wagon. *I can tell this nigga is smoking hot mad knowing this bitch betrayed him just like I told him she would. Stump and Moon jump in their whip. Juicy and Vita slid in their truck as were all rolling out of the garage with a three-truck murder convoy to the spot. The bat cave doors went down and were off to the fucking races.*

 We are in front of his crib in no time. Fat Poncho is ready to jump out all hot headed to get busy.

I pull his arm, "Fat Poncho, wait you're gonna have to cool down before you roll up in the spot, Dawg. Just sit tight."

Soon as I said that we see four goons walking out his front door. I know three of them its Sleam and his goon squad Zoro, Fat Bernard and some nigga I never seen before. He's really big, black and fucking ugly.

Sleam goes back inside with Zoro and the two of them on post looking around. Fat Poncho asked me,"So what's the play here?"

I replied, "we only need three down ass killers to take them out. you're going to be our ride out this motherfucker after we smoke their ass okay. Call Stump and Moon. I don't have their numbers."

Stump picks up on the first ring, "yo, what's up when y'all going to make your move?"

"Give me the phone."

Fat Poncho hands me the phone, "yo, Stump you come up here with us get out your truck in about five minutes. Let me holla at Juicy and Vita, okay." I hang up, handing Fat Poncho the phone. He calls up Vita he picks up after it rings twice in his heavy ass killer voice of his,

"Yo, what y'all waiting on. Let's do this."

I tell Fat Poncho to put it on speaker right quick.

"No, not yet you go check the back then call us as soon as you get their text with the skull emoji and help mop shit up."

"Alright." He hangs up and he gets out of the truck walking towards the back. I get out saying to Fat Poncho you stay here keep that motor running. I jumped out with Stump this little ass nigga with a big old gun. I wanted to laugh then it hit me. I told him, "Go ahead of me." I lift my machine gun and get in my gun stance. I'm right behind him. It's dark outside and creeping up fast on the right-hand side of the street.

I yelled to Stump, "bum rush their ass!"

Stump stepped up and took aim. **Kadoom!** Shooting that big black ugly motherfucker. Right under his chin he fell sideways with blood shooting up on the door. I opened up on Fat Bernard ass with him trying to draw on me at the same time but I beat him to it.**Kapackatacka!**

Hitting him in his chest and stomach that motherfucker started squirting out like a fucking water plug on the corner with his eyes getting wide with shock knowing that he's going to die. I quickly rolled on the ground towards the right, came up and took aim **Kackapcatka! Kapacktacktawo! Sizzzzzsssss-ssss!**

Glass flying everywhere coming down on me like hard spitting rain in the wintertime. I shot the two niggas in the window on the far right. One fell out of view and the other is hanging out the window of broken glass like a fucking bloody ass rag doll. That was Zoro sorry ass. Stump is already up the steps blasting that little fucking hand cannon he had. **Kadoom! Kadoom!** *I'm thinking to myself that little black motherfucker moves really good and fast. I like that shit.* I run up the steps behind him fast as lighting. This man shot two more men, but they could not see him. The house is dark downstairs. I hugged the wall, staying low. The only light we can see is shining in the stairwell on the right.

A shadowy figure darts in the doorway. I turned to shoot and its Vita looking at both of us. He quickly stood next to me on the wall in the dark front room and whispered, "**Hautapata Rah azote** *You're not going to have all the fun.*" *I just smiled and tapped the stump.* I pointed out to him that I was going up the steps. Then out of nowhere I see flashing red and blue lights from the window outside.

What one, the bitch made motherfuckers call the cops? What is the world coming to when a drug dealer has to call the fucking cops?

Vita and Stump looked up at me in pani. I just smiled at both of them. I reached in my backpack getting a smoke bomb.

I barked, "follow me. Let's go!"

I went first running up the steps. I tossed the smoke bomb staying along the wall. As soon as I got to the top of the steps the smoke was getting thick, but I can still see two men coming rushing out one room on the right and another one on the left shooting **Pat! Pat! Pat!** - **Pat! Pat! Pat!** I was already low. I just got lower with the bullets just missing me and returned fire as soon as they were shooting **Kapacktaka! Kapackatkata! Kapackatkatack!** *I tell people all the time most shooters will not be accurate when you are shooting back at their ass at the same time. these niggas here will never be real gun slingers. When you* *run across a real gun slinger like me. Now it's too late for their ass because I smoked their monkey ass. I looked down at their two bloody dead bodies saying never fuck with a real crazy bitch like me.*

Vita didn't come all the way up the steps he just got in position at the opening of the stairwell helping me kill the man on the right-hand side popping out the room like he was jack in the box now his funky ass will be in a fucking box. Plant your stupid dead ass in potter's field when you have no family to claim your bullet riddled fucking corpse trying to be a gangster. Shooting the man on the right **Kadoom!**

Stump took care of the man on the left shooting him right in his Dick. The man screamed falling backwards to the floor bleeding out. **Kadoom!** Stump shot him in the head for the Coup De Grace finishing him off blowing haft his fucking head off his shoulders. Vita ran all the up the steps stepping over the body. Stump just dropped on the floor hugging the wall winking his eye at me. By that time the cops are running in the fucking door all gun ho like they were going to take us down or something. These ass hole crackers motherfuckers never ran across a bitch like me before. I slide down to the floor on the wall near the bedroom. On the left we can hear the cops yelling up the step.

"Come out with your hands up and toss out your guns and you will not be hurt!" Loud and authoritative *Like who is going to believe that shit with these fucking crackers.*

I stood up and I had the hand grenades. I tip over to the stairway slowly and smoothly. I heard them coming up slowly. I pulled the pen and I looked down and dropped it down. The first cop saw it fall to the step. It was too late for his ass as the cop behind his partner dove **Kaboom!** The explosion rocks the house shaking. I ran towards the bedroom on the left kicking the door in **Doom!** Vita is right behind me, and Stump is bringing up the rear where all guns are blazing. As Sleam is holding a gun up to Lola's head yelling, "you come any closer and I'll shoot the bitch!"

I laughed and opened fire on both of them, Kapacktacka! Stump and Vita just open fire as well along with me. **Kaplow! Kapacka!** *They both fell to the floor backwards, all bloody their death screams fill the room like a bad funky ass smell from hell.*

This is why I wanted Fat Poncho to wait in the car because no matter what I was going to kill that bitch and I didn't want him to see that shit. I looked at both of them in a large pool of blood I yelled, "we have to get the fuck out of here and fast before more cops get here come on!"

The downstairs of the house is on fire that will hold them off while we make our escape the fuck out of there. I started running towards the back room on the right at the same time. I pulled out my phone and I called Fat Poncho. He picked up asking, "what the fuck happen?"

"Don't worry about that, just go around the block and meet us in the back. Call Moon and Juicy tell them to get the hell out of here now!"

The whole house is getting really smoky fast. We get to the back room. I lift the window super quick.I hang down and let myself go from the window ceiling. Vita did it next and we both stood there to break stump fall with him being so short. Soon as Stump let go, I saw more flashing red and blue lights behind us. By then the house is rip roaring with fucking flames in the front of the house.Out of the darkness two cop cars came speeding up. I got low in the yard Vita and Stump did the same with the red and blue lights flashing from the right-hand side of us ducking.

I looked at both of them and they *looked like they wanted to shit on themselves. I see Fat Poncho out of the corner of my eyes in the distance, but they don't see him in his whip chillin.* I'm smiling and whispering, "it's time to play fast ball like a motherfucker fellas."

I quickly reach into my trusty black backpack. I pulled out two hand grenades *and for some crazy reason I can hear in my head an announcer at a baseball game over a loudspeaker yelling play ball!* I stood up slowly, still staying kind of low. I pulled the pen and with all my might I threw the first one. Next, I did the same with the pen on the second one and I threw it quickly. I know I put some mustard on that bitch too! I yelled at both of them. "Let's go!"

We all hauling ass running towards the left in the dark. We can hear one of the cops yelling, "hey, you stop before I –"Kaboom!

That motherfucker landed right on the fucking hood of his police prowler the second one when off **Kaboom!** *Shit was flying everywhere. That* one hit his front left tire. I'm one bad bitch! We all quickly jumped inside of Fat Poncho's Benz wagon with me getting in the front seat

"Are you having fun, yet sweetheart? Let's go!

Stump said, "man this is one crazy bitch but she's good doe!"

Vita yelled, "Go! Go!"

Jumping in the back seats and off we go. I go inside of my pocket barking. "Well boys you wanted me to roll with y'all so what do you think?"

I quickly started scooping the coke out the sack I had in my pocket and all of them were yelling whooping and hollering loud. We drive back to the garage blasting hip hop music of *Cardi B's Bodak Yellow* while I sing every fucking word to the song the whole way their having a good time. I keep hitting repeat. Soon as he gets to Fat Poncho's garage doors, he rolls down the window sticking his hand out the window pointing his remote as the door starts coming up, he quickly pulls in. We all jumped out and Fat Poncho pulled me to the side, and he asked, "did you kill her?"

I looked him in his eyes uttering back, "yeah, I did we all shot that bitch up and she had it coming to her my nigga!"

His eyes are looking sad but he's trying to hold it in looking at the others not too far from us not saying a word his eyes told the whole story. I just patted him on the back.

"She was going to kill you and the rest of us don't worry about it okay."

"I know how you feel that bitch made nigga Bony Irons had a hit squad to come kill me.As you know I came out on top just like we did today it's all part of the fucking life. Fat Poncho looked up at me mumbling you want to know what your right let's get fucking high. We bump fist and walk over with all the others soon as Stump when to his truck parked inside of the garage a bottle of cold gin, I tapped Fat Poncho giggling saying do your job and get the fucking cups nigga. All of us started laughing as he gets the cups out of his tool table cabinet giggling.

Vita said, "look, the coke is on me after that shit tonight Ma!" He pours out a big pile of coke on top of the tool table with a wide smile. An hour later as we're all getting high talking shit with one another, we can hear this knocking on the garage door. We all looked at each other and Fat Poncho yelled out, "relax, that's probably Moon and Juicy." As he quickly went to the door he peeks out and its them as soon as he opens up the door both of them came in quickly,

Moon shouted, "yo, that shit is on the newsman put it on CNN right quick I'm telling you, yo!"

Juicy uttered, "man that bitch is fucking crazy man I done murked all kinds of motherfuckers, but I never smoke no fucking cops.

I can see in his eyes this nigga is scared to the 3rd power or something. I'm trying to see if these motherfuckers are going to get shook with my hand on my pistol behind my back. I should kill

this nigga Juicy right now before this scary ass hole tell anybody about what happen tonight. I just looked at both of them playing it off smiling as Fat Poncho grabbed his TV remote out of his tool table. He quickly pointed towards the wall where the flat screen is at. The TV announcer announced, "four cops dead and ten people killed at a house in the Bronx. The police are calling it the house of horrors. Others are calling it the Bronx massacre. While all of them are looking up at the TV screen. I'm snorting some more blow thinking of killing this nigga who looked shook. Moon he's cool about it, but I can tell with this other dude Juicy what Jay-Z say pressure burst pipes.

ANOTHER HOT ENCOUNTER

Fat Poncho looked up at me and to everybody looking them right in their eyes, "they don't know who did it. So were all good, okay anybody that can finger us is fucking dead so were good."

Well, I'm glad he said that to this bitch made nigga. I'm thinking I have to thin out the fucking heard right quick. I see Juicy calm down after Fat Poncho talk to Moon as well. It's that ass hole Juicy who is scared. Vita came up beside me, yakking,

"I love the way you move out there Ma you had training." I looked at him smiling replying sarcastically, "yeah, bye the fucking best. What about you?"

"Well, my brother Tumar was down with the bloods and my father Jitta was down with the five percenters, so I have a life-time of fucking training you know what I mean Ma."

"Where are they now?"

"My brother is dead, and my father is back in prison, but he will be back out really soon."

"Well, you're lucky my father was a junkie faggot mother-fucker. He's dead and my mother is a crack head who is from Southwest Philly." *Shit I didn't go into my two brothers Steve and Victor two crackhead thieves who stole the little bit of shit I did get when I got it.* Vita came up to me real close and whispered, "I wanted to thank you for getting us out of that shit. I have a way for you to thank me but first I want to get high before we both start fucking."

"Oh, I'm with that hot ass hand grenades throwing bitch."

"Oh, you're trying to get me wet. I was wet after I smoke them ass holes standing in the window like the fucking ducks at the carnival. *I put both my hands on his ass sticking my tongue out at him. We are standing face to face and the shit is fucking sweltering hot vibes between us shit my nipples is fucking hard now.*

"Oh, you're one wild bitch. I like that I'm really feeling your sexy frames and your twisted brain. I knew after we fuck it's going to be off the chain. Soon as I was going to say a really good comeback Fat Poncho announced, "he was going to take off in the morning to Philly and be ready to ride at eight." I looked at him uttering loud, "the Iilly that the way we say it back home Dawg. He smiled then I quickly grabbed him by his arm Is those two niggas cool."

They better be if not I'll let you do what you love to do is kill shit. I bump fist with him smiling, you know it. He looked at Vita and grinned not saying a word walking away.

"Vita, you said after we fuck it's going to be off the chain well my hot ass thug friend. I'm going to show you the fuck game!"

The nigga started giggling, he's to fucking black in his face to blush. *That's when I noticed how sexy his eyes were after looking at him closer.* We both walked over with the others, and we started snorting, drinking and telling war stories of all kinds. Then we started talking shit laughing at death and the fucking police.

I mean we got fucked up then me and Vita slipped in the back to the bathroom. He quickly grabbed me kissing me I pushed him off me yelling,

"No hot in the ass teenage grinding bull shit! You are going have to whip that bitch out and fuck me like when you just got out of fucking lock up after five years nigga!" *I know that set his soul on fire.* He's leaning back with a deep wicked smirk on his dark grill and a sinister twinkle in his dangerous eyes. I quickly took my gun from the back of my jeans and I set it on top of the sink.I took my black jeans off and I pulled down my black panties so we can get this shit on right here and now.

"I bent over the porcelain throne looking back at him with my sex kitten glair shouted, "I know you're not waiting for a fucking golden invitation motherfucker!"

Why I say that shit for that nigga came at me like a fucking bull in the china shop. He took his gun off himself, setting it next to mine on top of the sink, unzipping his jeans, taking them off, whipping out his big black tube steak pointing it at his smooth dripping wet target. I felt the head of his Dick entering my sugar walls. It's really wide like a helmet on a soldier pushing up. He slides inside of my twat nice and easy but I'm dripping wet before shit jumps off. Once he got that hump in his back the shit was on. *Ooowwww.*

We have a nice super-hot groove going on right from the door rocking and *I started getting wetter with each hard-trusting sweaty ass stroke I'm about to cum and we just got started.* This nigga is jack hammering the shit out of my coochie with his big black thug Dick. Then he started smacking me on my ass too and each time he did it more juice started running down my legs like a fucking waterfall. We both groaned loud its music to both ears. After about twenty minutes of doggy style, I want to be Sally Star and ride this big black beast this nigga is slinging to me fuck that. I quickly turned around pushing him off from me really hard, hitting it from the back. I looked at him in his gorgeous black grill grabbing his milky wet hard on to the left, I lifted his erection soft and gentle. So, we can fuck face to face. I love that shit. I lifted my left leg and took its big thug meat and made it fit to my soaking wet hot pussy working my hips sticking it all the way inside me kissing him at the same time. As he started grabbing both cheeks of my around brown ass pumping and jumped right on top of him holding him around his thick black tattooed neck. *Without thinking about it I wrapped both my thick chocolate legs around his hips getting it really good too riding it like a fucking cowgirl.* We both thrusting our hips together with the loud sounds of smacking meat. The both of us making loud sexual noises filling the not so big bathroom echoing are hot fucking turning us both on even more.

I'm sucking and licking on his tattoo neck whispering a whole lot of hot shit in his ear. *"Oh, you got that good thug Dick nigga work it harder up inside of me! Yeah, baby knock a hole in this motherfucker baby!" He's mumbling back to me, stroking even harder and harder.*

"That's just what I'm going to do with your sexy black ass! And I had to tell you that gave him more energy to fuck me like a wild man."

Hitting my Gee spot Whom! I let it go. I could not hold it anymore. I started squirting my hot love juices gushing out dripping down both our legs to the floor.

While he is pumping me like crazy, "ooohhh shit! I can't lie" I'm fucking out of breath, and I know I can hang. He had to be ready to cum soon. I see it written all over his handsome dark face trying to hold it back. Just like I knew it was about to happen Bang! He's coming. I can feel his hot baby gravy fill my sweet spicy honey hole. I'm thinking it's all over with his face all twisted up, but he kept going, grunting with his man hood still hard as a brick.

I said to myself I must take a break pulling apart from leaning on the wall of the bathroom. I was hyperventilating getting my mine right. My head was light breathing hard looking up at him with his hard-on still popping up in the air smiling at me. I asked, "what you take before we started fucking Gawd dam!" I hit his erection not too hard as it's bouncing up and down. I'm giggling looking at it with a fat head and thick veins popping out the sides of it and the cum dripping out of his one-eyed snake.

He said to me out of breath, "I can't front that never happened to me before." *I just laugh knowing he is just talking shit I know he took some Viagra or something but I'm not mad at him because it was really good too.* I looked for a rag so I can wipe myself off. Vita came up behind me reaching under the sink, getting me a nice new yellow wash rag and some pink dove soap bar. *I talk to him real sexy like,* "thank you and I kiss him." I mumbled before that shit wore off. I want to go get in the bed so I can cum about three more times. He started laughing, talking out of breath, " let's get something to eat."

Then we can get back at it with your sweet chocolate ass. He smacked me on my ass hard, "oh I like that shit."

I just giggled and started washing myself off with him standing beside me at the large sink washing himself off too with his gray wash rag with his own pink dove soap bar. I washed up really well and got my black panties off the floor. I can feel his eyes on me while I am slipping them on. I turned around and I was right with him smiling his ass off. He doesn't *know I have eyes in the back of my head for real*. I put my black jeans on, and I reached over and picked up my gun from off the sink sticking it in the back of my jeans. I make sure it's really good there.

I quickly get my fat sack of coke from out my right-side pocket pulling it out. I roll up a 20-dollar bill, scooping some out. I took about two snorts and Vita came up to me talking low. "Let me have some, baby girl."

I hand him the bag with the rolled up 20-dollar bill he snorts some. He walks over to the sink holding the coke and 20-dollar bill in his left hand. And he takes his right hand turning the water on just a little letting the water run on his long finger and he takes his wet finger sticking it in his nose. I walked up taking the sack with the 20-dollar bill sticking in it out of his hand as he went and got his gun. From off the top of the sink walking back over to me hugging me. I snort some more coke. "Alright nigga, let go get something to eat and we can get back to some more hot sex motherfucker. I walked up rubbing his bulge in his blue jeans. *His eyes get wide with a big grin on his good looking dark brown mug of his.* "Okay come on." We walked out the bathroom and the only one there was Fat Poncho sitting on top of his tool table talking on the phone puffing on a blunt. We could smell the pungent odor as we walked up with thick smoke lingering in the air. I said, "where is everybody?"

"They rolled out and said they will link up with us in the morning when it's time to go."

"I bet you five thousand dollars one of them bitch made niggas is not going to show up."

"Well, we will see about that shit." *as he blows out a big cloud of smoke like he doesn't believe me his eyes say it boldly.*

"I'm telling you and I know which one it's going to be too Poncho."

"Oh yeah, which one of them then?"

"That nigga Juicy I seen it in his eyes he was fucking shook you know where that nigga lives at?"

"Yeah, and I know where his rich bitch he's fucking lives at too. That's where he's at all the time, don't worry, I can put my hands on him if I need to be."

"Okay watch I'm right again we're going out to get something to eat you want something."

"Oh, y'all don't have to do that. I got Big Mama Red coming over here with some grub right now all y'all have to do is fall back I got y'all."

Vita barked out with a smile, "yeah, she has been wanting to get with you for a minute now and she can cook her ass off too."

I looked at Vita and asked him, "who is she anyway? She runs a speakeasy around the corner from here. We always buy food from her on the late-night tip. You don't seem like the jealous type, Ma. "

"Oh, no, never that play-boy. I was just asking so I know what kind of people y'all fucking with because were really hot right now with them four cops getting killed."

"You're right about that but I've known my girlfriend for a

while now and she's been wanting to get with me for a long time now before I hooked up with Lola". *He never told me that he was fucking big mama the whole time he was with Lola. Niggas don't tell you that shit just the bullshit.*

Soon as he said that it was aloud knocking at the garage door. He hops up and he quickly walks to the door. He opens the door helping her with her bags and it is this light brown skin heavy set woman with a black and pink flower dress on. She was carrying two big plastic bags, setting them on top of the long steel tool table. Soon as she came closer to us standing at the tool table, I can smell the food hit my nose. "Wow, I love home cooked food."

Fat Poncho set one the bags he helped her with on top of the tool table. He looked over at me introducing us, "Lex this is Mama Red.Mama Red this is Lex."

"Hey girl, how are you doing? Nice to meet you". She bumped fists with me and yelled.

"I hope y'all is hungry because I hooked y'all up for real. Where are the others?"

Fat Poncho answering back quickly, "they all rolled out don't worry we will eat what them niggas missed Mama, trust me."

Me and Vita laughed.I can't wait to eat now smelling that food. She smiles when I get a real good look at her while she's unwrapping the food from the three bags. The aroma fills the whole room with down home delicious food that will fill your soul as well as your stomach. She looks like she's about in her early 30's, very pretty, a full figure woman for sure. She looks like my aunt Mi-Mi from North Philly but a little younger. She has fried chicken, green corn on the cob, beef and pork ribs and baked beans. I came over to help her with the food after she pulled out the paper plates. She's fixing Fat Poncho's plate, stacking it up too as I make Vita plates than mine. Fat Poncho went to his refrigerator on the right-hand side of the large garage walking back with a big plastic pitcher of red cherry Kool aid setting it on top of the tool table. He gets the red cups giving each one of us one grinning wide and pouring us the ice-cold ghetto beverage. We all loved each other from back in the day.

I can't lie, I can't remember the last time I had some for real. We're all standing up. I started to eat my food when Big Mama Red said, "hold up y'all putting her arms up in the air. We have to give thanks."

"Thank you lord for this food we are about to receive. Thank you lord for each day you give us every day in Jesus name we all pray. Amen."

All of us said amen all at the same time while Vita rolled his eyes. He started eating his food. It's still hot and man did I throw down.I really enjoyed it too. *I wish I could cook like this. I can't cook to save my fucking life from the door. I never had nobody to show me how. My mother just stayed fucked up all the time.I ran the streets from the time I was 12 years old.* Soon as I was done, I helped to clean up with Big Mama Red. She asked me, "where are you from Lex?"

"South Philly."

"Oh yeah, I have a family from Phill. My cousin who lives in South Philly, his name is Boba Lou?"

"Yeah, I know Boba Lou. He's an old head he has a speakeasy on Stillman street."

"Yeah, you do know him. He's crazy, girl." We both started giggling. "I didn't know you were from that area. It's a small world."

We both walked back over to where Vita and Fat Poncho are both talking to one another smoking cigarettes. Soon as we walked up, he reached into one of his tool cabinets pulling out a big zip lock bag of cocaine. He pours some out in a big pile and he starts chopping it up with one his business card. Mama Red leaned on him after he chopped it up. He scoops some of it up from his rolled up one hundred dollar bill holding it up for Big Mama Red. She smiles snorting up the white powder with his hand on her fat yellow ass. Then he started snorting some himself. He pointed for us to come join them and we did. Big Mama Red pulls out a bottle of Vodka out of her large black leather coach bag that matches her outfit and her shoes. She poured it inside of her Kool aid and she turned to us and asked, "would y'all like some?"

I stepped up holding my red cup as she poured some in, smiling her ass off. Vita waves it off with a smile and we get high for about an hour or so having a good time. Fat Poncho shouted, "look we have to get some kind of rest before we do our next job.I have a room for y'all upstairs. I'm going to turn in. I'll show y'all where it's at,come on" So, I get my backpack and me and Vita follow behind them walking towards the left to this large stairwell. we get upstairs and he points towards the left telling us, "there you go I holla at y'all in the am."

He's rubbing on Big Mama Red's large derrière in her flower black and pink dress walking inside of the room on the right-hand side. He closed the door and we can hear them giggling from the other side. Me and Vita walked inside of the room and it's really nice too. With a queen size bed everything in the room is dark blue. The bed, covers, the rugs, and the curtains. I can tell that a woman hooked this room up and it smelled good as well. We got in round two. The pill did not wear off yet, so we got it in again and I had two more super-hot orgasms. I fell asleep feeling good after I got my shit off. The loveliest evening, leaving a big wet spot in the middle of the bed. The next morning when I got up it's 7:00. We both only had a few hours of sleep but we still got up so we can roll out and go to Philly. Fat Poncho came and knocked on the door telling us, "Everybody will be here soon so get ready okay." He's talking to us from the other side of the door. He told us the bathroom is on the left-hand side. I'm still high, but I still jumped up and got in the shower. I went downstairs to get my things out of my suitcase in my truck, some fresh underwear, my deodorant, my jeans and top, I got dressed and I was ready to go and so was Vita.

We both go downstairs in the garage. It's 8:00 A.M. We waited for everybody it's 8:30. Stump and Moon show up a little late but no Juicy.

Fat Poncho said, "we're going to wait until 9 and we're all going to roll out. Big Mama Red came downstairs pulling Fat Poncho to the side talking to him while we all started talking with one another. Now it's 9 and still no Juicy. Fat Poncho waves towards everybody to all come together. Fat Poncho announced, "look y'all we can't go anywhere with this nigga out there, so we have to take care of that then roll out to Philly."

Moon said, "You right we don't know if he's going to tell somebody that we were there last night."

Stump chimed in, "I agree, and you were right Lex."

Fat Poncho looked me in the face like a man and agreed, "yeah, I have to Admit you were right, Lex."

"Okay, then everything has to stay in this room right now." As I looked at everybody.

"Just give me the address and I'll take care of it."

Fat Poncho said, "No, we're going with you."

"Well, if you do, I'll still do it myself and then we can go do this job."

Big Mama Red uttered, "I'm going with y'all. where are you going?"

"I'm going to Philly baby and I'll be back to get you okay." "No, you didn't say that shit last night, nigga. I waited all this time on you to get rid of that low life bitch! Now we get together and you're coming back for me. Oh no that just won't do with me, honey."

I just giggled blurting out, "just give me the address and I'll be back, and we can all go together."

"Okay Moon, will take you there and we will be here when you get back okay."

"Sounds good to me brother." I looked him right in his eyes. Telling all of them I got one hell of a plan.

" Check this out. I tapped Moon to follow me over towards Fat Poncho. He walked with me and I said, "could you excuse us for a minute, Big Mama Red, please? She just nodded her head with a wide smirk and walked a few feet from us. *But I can hear her mumbling. I'm the one who told you to go kill that motherfucker before he snitches on y'all.* "Look, do you have an old nighty Lola had around here, big man."

"Yeah, I do but what the fuck is you going to do Lex fuck the nigga or kill him?"

"No, it's just another distraction that all youniggas see. You don't think outside the box when it comes to killing a mother-fucker, that's why I'm so good at it."

Moon said, "yeah, that's good when the guard is checking you out then you smoke his ass on the spot. Now give that man a fat fucking blunt, for being so smart!"

We all chuckled loudly as Fat Poncho looked at me, smiling and yelling, "you're one sick bitch, but I like it, I'll be right back." Moon just looked at me still laughing. It took Poncho a few minutes and he came back with a red see through nightgown handing it to me.

I looked at Moon, "give me the keys." He tosses me the keys saying, "let's do this shit!"

"Sure!" Vita walked up in front of me talking with his eyes getting wide. "I want to go with you." I put my hand on his big chest, "you wait here dark and sexy."

He looked at me and nodded his head, yes. He didn't say a word. I kissed him. Then I quickly went over to the table filled with guns looking for another pistol and found one with another silencer now. I have two and I'm ready to go to work. Moon saw me doing it so he went and got one too for his pistol. He winked his eyes at me smiling. I made sure I had enough bullets in the clip. I jump inside of Moon's black GMC truck getting behind the wheel driving towards the large garage doors. Fat Poncho hits his remote letting us out as I pull out fast to the street. I asked him while driving, "how long you knew that nigga Juicy?"

"For about 10 years now I never knew he was like this for real."

"Well, sometimes you really find out about people when shit goes down you know what I mean."

"So how long have you known Poncho?"

"All my life we grew up together. Him,me, Stump and I never like Lola, no good ass. She's been fucking around on him the whole time they were together. "

"Why didn't you tell him about the shit if he felt that way about her?"

"We did, he would not listen to us. What about you and Vita? Does he know about you and Chi- Chi?"

"I would not care if Poncho told him about that shit man. Like he told y'all, I'll tell him myself. I fuck who I want to, and I just don't fuck anybody neither know why?"

"Yeah, please do I want to hear this shit."

Because of the way I live I never know when I'm going to get my head blown the fuck off because I'm a real gangster bitch. Plus, I love real dangerous men that turn me on. They don't live by the rules of this fucked up society that's rigged for rich motherfuckers to fuck us over every day of our lives. And before I go, I want to cum about ten times and go out in a blaze of fucking glory. I don't care about living and I don't care about dying. It works for me. We both started laughing and he looked over to me still giggling, "well, that does make a lot of sense."

"Look when it's all said and done niggas is going to say I was a no-good whore a killer or whatever. I don't give a fuck about none of that. I'm living for right now!"

"Well, I feel you on that one. CanI ask you something" "Well, you asked me everything else. So, what's stopping you now, nigga?"

He started laughing, "okay my nephew is a writer he would love to meet you would you sit down with him?" "What's his name?"

"Kaleam Savage, that's his pen name. His real last name is Scott. He's really good but he needs to meet somebody real like you. Everybody says they're real, but I have seen you in action, so I know firsthand what a real gangster is". "A real gangster bitch. I'm twice as dangerous don't you forget it motherfucker!"

We both started laughing again. "I'll have him talk to you after the job in Philly okay and this is between you and me alright."

Moon is telling me where to go as I drive, and he told me to get off at the next exit. I made the hard-right turn and Moon pointed, "you need to pull over and get your outfit together because we're almost there"

"Okay." I pulled over towards this park area. I quickly took off my shirt then my bra and I opened the trunk door. I stepped out and I took off my black jeans and my panties and I tossed all of it in the back seat. *I knew that nigga was watching. I did not give a fuck niggas been trying to peek at me since I was 14 years old when my titties got bigger.* I slipped on the red nightgown, and I reached in the back of the truck going in my black backpack getting my black latex gloves putting them on swiftly. Then I grabbed both my guns, one had the silencer on one already. I jumped back in behind the wheel I screwed on the second one.

I got it on tight and ready to go sitting both my guns in my lap. I looked over at Moon and asked, "okay, where too, Mister Moon?"

Moon asked, "Do you have another pair of black gloves?"

I answered, "yeah".

I reached back in my backpack on the side and handed him a pair. He put them on fast, looking me up and down. Moon is looking right at my titties while I'm driving. I shouted, "if you take a picture with your phone, it will last longer."

He took out his phone too and held it up at me uttering, "your right." He took the picture; I blew a kiss at him with both of us laughing.

Moon is laughing, talking loudly, pull up into that gated complex over there with your crazy ass. I drove towards the gate as Moon told me the guard is a fat white dude. Take care of him and I'll show you were. That nigga Juicy live with this rich white bitch. I drove up to the booth where the fat white man was. As soon as I pulled up and rolled the window down, he was looking with his eyes glued on my titties. I barked at him, "my face is up here Mister!"

" Oh, I'm sorry, who are you here to see?"

Pooouuufff! I shot him in the middle of his fat white head. He fell backwards and I jumped out stepping over his fat bloody body. I hit the lever to open up the gate. The arm went up really fast. I jumped back into the truck and took off with Moon telling me to ake another left over here. I pulled up at this nice light brown brick apartment building.

Moon instructed. "park right here. He's on the second floor. Come on." He jumped out with me with his pistol with the silencer on it.I quickly walked towards the front door. So, I stroll in there all nice and sexy with both of the silencer pistols behind my back. The skinny white dude at the front desk is a faggot. He's Rolling his eyes like a little bitch. "How can I help you,Ms. thing?" I announced to his ass, "yes, give me the key to the elevator to the second floor please."

"Why should I do that? You are not part of the management of this building or a resident here."

Moon walks up behind me mumbling, "so much for the shock value baby girl."

We both smile at one another and I took my pistol in my right hand and mashed it up to his forehead yell, " I tried to be nice you faggot ass motherfucker. Give me the key or that big black nigga that's fucking you in your little white ass froggy style won't happen anymore, okay!" He hands me the key yelling, "okay! Okay!" Real snotty I snatched the key real fast Moon took aim **Pooouuufff!** Shooting him in the head. He fell backwards to the really nice white marble floor. I quickly ran behind the desk, and I dragged his ass all the way under it out of sight. Then I hear the elevator doors open Bing! I stayed low under the desk. Moon just walked behind the desk getting a rag out of the top desk draw acting like he was cleaning the desk. When this older white couple started walking off and he just smiled as they just walked by him smiling. He's just smiling back at them speaking politely, "good afternoon." showing all his teeth. *White folks love to see a nigga cleaning with a smile as they both walked out the door not paying him any mind at all.*

I peeked up seeing them go out the door. I stood up as we both quickly walked towards the elevator while I had the key in my hand. Soon as we were about to step on to the elevator on the right-hand side the one on the left-hand side came down Bing! And this security guard steps off walking towards us. I pushed Moon on to the elevator and I put both guns behind my back smiling, and he looked up at me and his whole face turned bright red. Because he can see right through my red nightgown and he likes what he sees. He stops to get a better look at me **Pooouuufff! Pooouuufff!** I shot him in the neck and his eye. He fell backwards to the hard-white marble floor. Me and Moon quickly dragged his ass on to the elevator car. Moon hit the button and I stuck the key in and turned it. Right quick so we can get to the second floor. Bing! I turned the key so the elevator would stay there as we go and kill this motherfucker and we have to ride back down. Moon pointing whispered, "this way Lex."

We quickly walked up to the big light brown pretty door on the right-hand side of this really nice place. I'm on the left and Moon is on the right. He backs up a little and **Boom!** Moon kicks the door in first. I see Juicy on this large bright orange couch fucking this white bitch doggy style huffing and puffing. I take aim as soon as he sees me. He's in shock with his eyes getting bulging out of his head, but he jumps up trying to reach for his pistol on the right. **Pooouuufff! Pooouuufff! Pooouuufff!** I shot him in the middle of his big black head.

Then I hit him with another one in his stomach and the last one right in his fucking heart. The blood splatter all over on the back of the couch and on the lamps. He fell on the floor face first making a loud thumping sound as the white girl jumps up. She is nude, screaming her head off. **Pooouuufff! Pooouuufff!** Moon shoots the white girl in her face twice and she falls backwards to the floor. **Doom!** We just looked at one another quickly stepping towards the front door. Moon steps in front of me stopping doing a curtsy giggling. "Moon, you're fucking just as crazy as me nigga let's go!"

Moon yelled, ain't nobody as crazy as your fucking ass Lex, believe me!"

We both run out the door to the elevator but there's blood all over the elevator floor. nowhere to stand without stepping into the blood all thick on the floor. I yelled out that we have to get to the video room and get that tape before we get out of here.

"Your right, I know where it is at.Moon looked at me spitting fast, "come on!"He runs towards the exit door on the left and we go down to the basement. He quickly opens the gray steel door we started walking down this long bright hallway with all white walls then we reach the room, and he points to the door smiling mumbling this is it! Moon kicks in this door on the left **Boom!** It is two old white men with their rent a cop cop corny ass blue uniform sitting down drinking coffee with all of the surveillance cameras on the wall in front of them. The whole room smelled like burned roast beef, coffee and old cigarettes. Moon spouted out I got a real treat for you two old motherfuckers! As he sticks his gun in both their faces waving his hand to me shouting, "hey baby show them" I stepped in front of him while the two old white men started smiling as I took out both my guns from behind my back. One of the old men cried out, " you don't have to kill us, Miss. just take what you want, we won't say a word about this shit!"

I uttered, ``You're right, you like what you see? We sure do look so lovely!"

The second white man yelled out, "I wish I was twenty years younger. I would show you a thing or two girly." We all started laughing that broke the ice and made me and moon not to kill them both. I giggled, "okay we still have to make it look good over here fellas let's find something to tie you guys up."

I took the wires from the DVD players hooked up to their whole system. While both their eyes were glued on me the whole time while I was tying them up there were both giggling the whole time like schoolgirls. Moon took the video DVDs out then he picked up the machines smashing it on the floor. **Blang**! Then he took both of their wallets out of their pockets, then took out both their licenses very swiftly and he showed it to both of them talking in their faces. "If any of you guys say something I know where you live remember that shit okay!"

They both nodded their heads, still looking over at me. *It's like these two old men are having a real good time.*

I gave them a little show. I tweaked my fat ass making it clap jiggling up and down for them. I'm thinking they were going to cum on themselves right then and there. I blew a kiss at both of them and they both waved back at me with their Dicks harder than times in 1939. We ran out the door. Moon barked at me. "We should have killed both of them if you ask me, Lex."

"Those two old fucks had the time of their life they aren't going to say shit Moon let's get the fuck out of here!" We get to the end of the hallway we go up one flight back up and we head towards the exit door to the large gray steel door. Moon looks both ways walking out putting his arm around me walking slowly towards the truck not too far from the exit door. It was like it a walk in the fucking park or something nice and cool like. Right before I jumped in the truck Moon slapped me on my ass laughing running around opening the door. I did not say anything while he had that big smile on his grill. I took off nice and smooth and jumped on the expressway blasting the radio. *Drake's Hotline Bling is on while we talked about what happened laughing the whole time.* It did not take us long to get back to the garage. I parked behind the row of trucks and cars on the left-hand side. As soon as I jumped out of the truck Vita walked up to me and mumbled, "wow, you look really hot in that red teddy."

I replied in a soft seductive voice, "you like it, baby?"

I got real. I kissed him feeling the heat again with the two of us. He pushed me up on the car grinding on me I told him, "you know how I feel about grinding on me like some fucking teen-agers you know I don't go for that kind of bull shit, nigga."

I quickly pushed his ass down to his knees, opening my legs really wide. I pushed my hot box right into his handsome black mug. *Out of the corner of my eyes I can see Moon peeking from the other side of the truck. I didn't care I'm going make this nigga eat my pussy right here behind this truck.* Fat Poncho walked up and announced, "I hate to break up you are sitting on this nigga face session, but we have to get the fuck out of town right now y'all!"

I pushed Vita back off of my hot smooth shaved cunt getting wet and we both started laughing. As Fat Poncho walked away shaking his head giggling. I looked at Vita, "he's right we do have to get the hell out of town." I went to the back of my truck to get my suitcase to change my clothes. I took it out and I closed it back. I started rolling my suitcase and I put my black backpack on my shoulder to the bathroom in the back. Fat Poncho grabbed Vita by his arm following behind me and said, "let her get dressed so we can get the fuck out of here all right." Big Mama Red chimes in, "he's right we have to get out of here right now."

I went into the bathroom, and I changed my clothes real swiftly. I came out. Fat Poncho pointed at Moon, "you ride with us.Vita you drive with your girlfriend and Stump in the green van."

Vita asked, "why the green van, Poncho?"

Its bullet proof like my Benz that's why, nigga. Is that good enough for your ass?"

"Oh, hell yes that's just what we need out of this motherfucker for real. You can thank me later nigga let's roll!"

We all started laughing. "Stump you packed up all those guns."

"Yeah, I got it all done bro. Let's get out of here!" Vita jumped behind the wheel, and I quickly put my bags in the back of the van. Stump helped me and he jumped in the backseat with his cigarette hanging from his thick dark lips. While I got in the passenger seat I pulled out my little coke bag and snorted some while leaning back in my chair. Fat Poncho Reaches his arm out his window of his black Benz wagon with his remote in his hand opening the doors. He drives out first with Vita right behind him as the garage doors close quickly. Vita follows right behind Fat Poncho driving the van. Then my phone rings. I look at the caller ID, "it's Chi- Chi. I will get it."answering "hey, baby what's up?"

Vita is looking over at me all crazy.

"I'm just chillin 'that's all.

"Well can I come over and see you tonight baby? I have been thinking about you all day." "Yeah, so what you've been thinking about baby."

"I was thinking about how good you whipped that hot Coochie on me that night. I can't get it out of my mind. Don't tell me your fine ass big Dick nigga like you is pussy whip over the two times we fucked that night?"

He starts laughing and *Vita hears him through the phone.*

Vita is tapping me on my legs with his face all twisted up getting upset while he's driving the van. I tapped him back on his leg hard and yelled, "keep your eyes on the road nigga!"

Chi- Chi mumbling back at you talking to me baby. "No just somebody I'm in the car with that's all."

"Look, what time can I come see you tonight baby fuck all this small talk shit...." Then from out of nowhere **Baaaarrrrtttttt! Baaaarrrttttttt!** *I can hear the bullets bouncing off the van sounding like large sized heavy ass rocks hitting the side of the van. While Vita is swaying from side to side.*

I said, "what the fuck is somebody shooting at us?"

Chi- Chi screamed at the top of his lungs, "where the fuck you at, I'll come help you baby!"

"Look, I'll take care of this shit myself, I'll call you back!"

I hung up fast and I quickly climbed in the back seat of the van getting my black backpack. I got two of my hand grenades. I grabbed my favorite machine gun, the MP-5 swiftly slapping in the clip.

I cocked it back **Click- Clack**. I quickly jumped back in the front seat. I called Fat Poncho and he picked on the second ring. I said, "we have a group of cars on our ass take off like the fucking wind me and Stump will take care of them!"

He yelled, "you sure?"

I replied, "you know me like you said I kill shit!"

I hung up and Stump looked over at me with all his yellow teeth showing and I bump fist with him laughing. Then I hit the button on the window, cracking it just a little. **Kapackack-atack! Kapackackata!** Stump slid over on the same side as me cracking his window just enough to start blasting at these niggas with his hand cannon going to work on their ass. **Boom! Boom! Boom!** We're both spitting bullets towards this dark sedan that's shooting at us. All I see is sparks flying from their guns. As we both go back and forth there is a fire fight on the black top under the Dull yellow lights. I started spitting again and we both tore their ass up, shooting out the window. We hit two of the shooters in the car. From the corner of our eyes we see the car sliding towards the side of the road in the darkness disappearing out of view.

We have the upper hand because the van we are in is bullet proof but as soon as we took care of them another car came speeding up shooting at us. As soon as we fucked up the first car of shooters. I can't front Vita was doing some real hellafied driving not letting the cars with the attackers get by. He swayed from side-to-side driving like a demon from hell. I don't know where he learned that shit from, but he was driving his ass off for real while me and Stump went to work on their ass.

The second car with three masked goon gun men even in the darkness I can see death glowing in their eyes like the children of the corn movie. Soon as they came up super swift me and Stump worked together fucking them up. All I saw was glass and blood flying in the air with the twisted metal from the bullet holes. I took care of two of them in the back seat. I sprayed them with so many bullets it was like a wash in blood.

Stump blew the dude face off in the front seat and ripped his chest open as large as the fucking Grand Canyon. The driver in the second car of shooters lost control after Stump shot him in the back of his fucking neck **Boom!** *Gawd dam when I saw what happened it looked like a watermelon exploding with all of his brain fragments landing all over the side of the window.* The car crashed into a large group of cars on the right-hand side, and it blew up at impact. **Kadoom!** Just as were about to go up the ramp to the expressway I yelled to Vita to slow down nigga! He looked over at me yelled back, "are you fucking crazy" "Well, I already know your fucking crazy, but you want me to slow down Lex?"

"Yes, slow down enough so I can toss these fucking hand grenades on these ass hole's on are tail!"

Vita, still driving his ass off, looks at me smiling, spitting out fast. "That's a good idea, but when all this shit is done, we need to talk bitch."

Stump laughed his ass off. It filled the car like loud hip-hop music booming.

Now we're on the expressway and little by little Vita is slowing down. As the last car of shooters is speeding up, I have my hand grenades ready. I set them both in my lap. I have my finger on one of the pens on the hand grenade looking out the window timing their ass as they started coming towards us. I hit the window just a little lower and I threw it hard. **Blam!** It hit the hood of the car and bounced up and hit the windshield **Kadoom!**

Damn that Jawn blew that motherfucker to Smithereen. All you see is fucking glass, twisted metal and flames shooting up in the air as the car crash into the guard rail on the left-hand side of the road **Doom!** Then Vita floored it, driving off faster up the blacktop under the glaring lights of the expressway going by like a crazy blur in an Alfred Hitchcock movie. I quickly rolled the window back up. Stump quickly hits the button on his window to roll back up still holding his gun and a cigarette hanging from his big lips. His sinister giggle that will haunt the soul of most people. I reached over and turned on the radio blasting it loud going in my pocket pulling out my coke sack snorting it right out of the bag. I quickly handed back to Stump some of the coke to give him some uttering, "this is for a job well done nigga!"

He took the bag out of my hand smiling and still giggling l snorting some of the white powder out the bag laughing dam we make a hell of a team girl! Vita looking over at me barking really angry, "like who the fuck was that on the phone before those niggas came up on us, Lex?"

" You really want to know Vita"

"Yeah, I do want to know!"

"He's a guy I bought some coke off of. I found him sexy and I fucked him. This happened before I met you okay mother-fucker!" *A I stuck my finger in his face and I screamed.* "And let me get something straight with your black ass from the door nigga I am not your woman okay! And I hope you get that through your thick ass head. I found you sexy too and you're lucky I gave you some pussy! So, if you want to fuck up a good thing here keep talking shit and you will get no more of it for real!"

"Okay! Okay! You can get your finger out my face while I'm driving this fucking van bitch."Stump giggled his ass off in the back seat blowing out big clouds of smoke. I see Vita looking at him in the rearview mirror with his eyes on fire. I wanted to finish cussing his ass out, but I chilled out. *Just as long as he knows that I am not playing with his monkey ass. This nigga just doesn't know that a woman like me it's never any shortage of Dick.* I reached and turned on the radio blasting the music and snorting some more coke from my little sack sharing it with Stump. I did not give that nigga Vita none of it.

I snorted up the last of it out of the bag then I tore the little plastic bag open and started licking it. This nigga is watching me the whole time. While I'm licking it, not saying a word. I'm not paying this nigga any mind listening to the hard-hip hop beats. I'm feeling the groove for two more hours of ignoring this motherfucker until I see the welcome to Philadelphia sign.

"Vita while I'm tapping him on his leg, I have to call Fat Poncho and find out where they are so we can all link up together."

While I'm making the call, this nigga is rolling his eyes at me like a little bitch. I just smiled and nodded my head to the music holding the phone up to my ear. I reached and I turned the music down, verbalizing loud enough for both of them to hear me. He's waiting under the bridge near the exit when we get off, I hang up. I see both of them nodding their heads letting me know that they heard me.

"Okay when you come off the ramp let me drive so I can take y'all to my people's spot."

Vita nodded his head yes not really wanting to look at me. He is still pissed off with me shit I'm high now after snorting the rest of that blow, so I really don't give a fuck that this nigga is mad at me. Vita drives down the ramp he drives just a little more and he pulls over. I jumped out walking around to the driver seat pulling out my phone at the same time. I got behind the wheel and I called Fat Poncho again. He picked up a quick spit, " where are you at now?"

"I'm coming to you right now as soon as you see me just follow me, okay."

I drove up and Fat Poncho saw me, and he started following me in the green van. I drive towards Fairmont avenue about ten blocks away. It didn't take me long to get to the spot. I parked across the street from the crib. Fat Poncho parked not too far away from where I was at as I walked up to the door. I knock on the door hard and this tall light skin dude came to the door screaming at the top of his lungs,"who the fuck is you knocking on the door like that?"

I asked, "where is Rock?"

"Look, like I said before bitch. Who the fuck are you?"

I whipped out my pistol super-fast mashing it to his fat yellow head yelling, "I don't have time for this bull shit where the fuck is Rock!"

"He's downstairs with his woman Tia."

"Okay take me to him right now or I can air your yellow ass out. I'll still get to holla at him anyway." I step all the way inside the house, and I close the door pushing him back. As soon as I walked in the room Rock, he saw me with the gun to this dude's head. He pulls out his gun. Then he steps full ward pointing his gun. He looked good and yelled, "is that you Lex?"

"It sure is motherfucker!What you not glad to see me nigga?" He lowers his gun laughing and he quickly walks up to me giving me a big hug giggling and laughing.

"What up, baby,girl?" Rock taps the tall light skin dude and tells him, "it is all good Spank. This is Lex, she's the one who put me in the game."

I put my fist out for him to bump it. Work on it!

just bump fist with her she was not going to kill you nigga or you be dead already trust me. He smirks, bumping fist with me quickly, then I see this nice-looking short woman walking up. Rock said, "hey honey, come here, I want you to meet somebody who is a real family over here.Tia this is Lex. Lex, this is Tia."

"It's nice to meet you and I stick my hand out for her to shake it."

She did it all slowly looking over at Rock. I said, "Look Rock used to work for me, and nothing went on alright. I know what you're thinking honey Rock is a good man and he always looked out for me when we worked together alright. Look I need to holla at you right quick, okay?" "Step into my office, baby girl."

Tia is following right behind us Rock turned around talking nice to her look baby I need to talk to her I be right back. Tia snapped back, "look let me talk to you right quick!" He turns to me with his eyes getting wide mumbling low. "I'll be right back Lex and they both walked in the other room."

I pulled out my phone calling Fat Poncho he picks up on the second ring yelling, "Yo, what's up, Lex? "

"Give me a few after I talk to this dude so we can have a hold up spot for us to set up shop okay trust me I got y'all okay call." Vita and Stump and let them know everything is cool.

"I need to talk to this nigga his old lady is in his ear right now you know how that goes right?"

"Yeah, I do. I hope we don't have to come all the way here and have to smoke some more motherfuckers."

"No, it's all good this nigga use, to work for me all right just chill I be with y'all in a few, okay."

"Okay, if you say so Lex."

"Now we came to Philly now you want to kill shit right?"

"Oh, hell yeah, I know how you niggas here roll fucked that."

"Yeah, whatever nigga just chill the fuck out I be out in a few."

I hang up with this nigga and Rock came walking up spitting quick, "she's just tripping that's all."

Come on waving at me with a big smile. I followed him downstairs to the basement. He turned the lights on, and I looked around. "Wow, you really hooked up down here the last time. I was here."

He points towards the chair at the really dark brown table the whole place smell good and really clean with the deep fragrance of Febreze." Soon as I sat down, he said, "yeah, the last time you were down here you killed Maxine dumb ass remember that?"

"Oh, hell yes you have to Admit that bitch had it coming after all the times I let her slide with shit." "That bitch was trying to fucking play you I don't know why she did but she paid with her life."

"Yes, she did and as you know that goes for anybody trying to play Poppy."

We both started giggling loudly. "Who are you working

for now, Rock?"

"Nobody I have my own plug I was fucking with Kim for a minute now she's too busy fighting with AK and them over price and everything else."

"Yeah, so you got a hold up spot for me and my crew"

"Yeah, I got a warehouse on Hope Street. It was nice too. His eyes gleamed at the sight of it.

"Shit, the gang used to have a spot-on Hope Street. I know I bought it from them and another one on Old York Road. That one used to be Kim's joint but when AK went to Miami, he sold me the Hope street joint."

"Good, I'll hook you up after the score, okay. Now look who is talking about playing a motherfucker you didn't come here without taking down shit Lex." He looked me right into my eyes real deep.

"Okay, I can drop five large on you, and you give me the keys. Rock."

"Now that's the Lex I know, and love. I have to tell you my peoples keep that place spic and span clean. So, don't y'all go fuck up the place now."

"Oh no, Rock you know me I love to live in luxury. You know I don't play that shit living like a fucking slob. I'll be right back; I'll go get the loot."

I quickly went out to the van. Vita rolled down his window and asked, "So what's up, baby?"

"We're all good, I just have to give him a little something and I'll get the keys."

"Sounds good, are you still mad at me, Lex?"

"No, we got shit to handle nigga. I don't have time to stay mad at you. We will finish talking later. Okay, let me get this money all right." I go to the back of the van and get my suitcase. I pulled out seven bands.

"Stump, I need something to put this shit in."

"I got you, Lex." He reaches into his bag, getting a black plastic bag handing it to me. He asked with smoke coming out of his mouth.

"Can we trust these motherfuckers, Lex?"

"Yeah, we're good baby!"

I touch his face with his wide teeth smile.

"Good shooting tonight with some more training you're going to be one badass motherfucker."

"So, who is going to train me, you?"

"Yes, me nigga. Let me go up in here and take care of this shit." I quickly walked over to where Fat Poncho is parked, he rolled down his window looking at me whispering.

"What's up, Lex? What did they say?"

"I have to give him a little something for the warehouse. I'll take care of it. All of y'all just can give it back to me out of your cut, cool?"

"Yeah, I'm with that so what do you think, Mama Red?"

"Yeah, I'm down it's not a fucking dump is it?"

"No, you're going to love it."

Fat Poncho asked, "hey Moon, what do you say about this shit?"

Moon said, "Yeah, I'm down with it, but I'm with Mama Red just as long as it's not a fucking flea bag joint,I'm ready to go to work baby."

" Okay, good. I will be right back with the keys." I walked back over to the house and knocked on the door and the dude Spank opened it. He walked with me to the basement and I'm keeping my eye on this nigga while I got this bag of loot. I went down the steps and I sat back down at the table. Rock came from the back with Tia and they both sat down looking serious. I put the bag on the table smiling at both of them talking loudly. That's seven bands right there.

He pointed at Tia and said,"Get that for me baby." Tia took the bag and looked inside of it. Her mouth dropped open and she gasped.

I shouted, "Now with your peoples here know that I'm in town. Oh, don't worry if any of them open their mouth they will not open it again."

"Okay and I'm letting them know too. I will smoke their ass too just to know that shit."

  "Yo Spank, give her the keys now if you need any blow let me know, okay."

"Sure, I'm good for right now Rock and thanks for this, my nigga."

Spank handed me the keys and lowered his head.

"Look, you're the one who put me on and now I'm really doing my thing. Now let me walk you to the door. We walked up the stairs. I whispered to Rock, "you did not tell your wifey about us. Did you?"

"Oh no you know me I know how to keep my mouth shut baby girl." He gives me that old nasty man wink. I just smirked. We both started giggling as he opened the door for me, I hugged Rock, "thank you."

I quickly walked to the van. I jumped behind the wheel. I pulled up where Fat Poncho is parked, and I rolled down the window.

He did the same. I yelled out, "it's on now nigga follow me let's go!"

THE WAREHOUSE PALACE

I pulled off with him right behind me and we drove to the Hope Street warehouse in North Philly. It took us no time to get there. I pulled in the back of the warehouse, and I jumped out yelling "were here y'all."

Fat Poncho pulls up right beside the green van and they all get out. I see that look on their faces. Moon walks up barking all crazy "I told you Lex. I'm not staying in some raggedy ass fucking place I'll go stay in one of the hotel's here in town. Call me when y'all need me fuck that!"

I said to him, "you're about to eat your words motherfucker. Come check this shit out!"

I smiled open the large steel door with the keys and pushed it in really hard. Stump is right behind me along with Fat Poncho and Big Mama Red. I turned on the lights on the left-hand side. I said to everyone that, "each room has its own bathroom and shower so you can do what you have to do in your own room. I am telling you you're going to love it."

All of them started going awww. Soon as they walked in, they looked around with their mouths on the fucking ground. This place looked like a fucking palace. Vita and Moon came in real slow looking around and they could not believe their eyes. Vita said to Moon, "from what I see so far you can go to that hotel, Dawg. I'm laying low right fucking here for real all of us started laughing and it echoed in the large space."

The first thing they all see is the white tile floor super clean with this black leather couch set, gold glass end tables with gold lamps that look really expensive on each end of the couch and loveseat. On the left is a long bar fully stocked with the neon lights glowing on the shelves they pop on as we walk up and track lights along the ceiling that are gold.

I pointed at each of the rooms. "Y'all have not seen shit yet! Come on, follow me."

I'm waved at them and there all looking around like they never seen a place like this in their fucking life. I walked over towards where the long black petition towards the back is at and I pulled it back. It slid back nice and smooth, and they all saw a state-of-the-art new gym with all kinds of new exercise equipment. Then I walked them over to the large bathrooms on the left. I show them that real fast each of them all had their mouths open wide. They couldn't believe how nice and Sharp the bathrooms were too, with white marble with four large showers. I pointed towards the right," the kitchen is over here. We all walked over towards it. Right in front of all of them is a brand-new kitchen, a light brown backsplash and cooking hood, and a large stainless steel eight burner stove with the original red brick all around it. The dark cherry wood cabinets and a light brown wood Subzero refrigerator.

A kitchen island with a dark brown marble top. I turned to Big Mama Red, "this is where you can throw the fuck down right here, baby!"

Big Mama Red yelled, "shit, I can do a whole lot of fucking throwing down in here girl!"

"Whose place is this, Lex? Some fucking millionaires or something girl?"

"No, this used to be the gang's joint. Rock brought it off them when AK went to Miami.

Fat Poncho uttered, "I can see from this place the gang was not fucking around Lex."

"Yeah, this is just one place we had after we're done. I promise we will have a place just like this in less than six months. Watch!" Stump chimed in, "shit, he just might sell it to you Lex. After we make a few scores and shit."

"I have a place in mind but for right now this is home. Y'all let me show y'all the upstairs rooms after that I'll show y'all the third-floor lounge. I used to love coming here it so fucking plush right up my alley."

I looked over at Moon and spread my arms open, "see it doesn't look like nothing from the outside for a reason brother just keep that in mine."

Moon nodded his head, "you were right I did have to eat my words this joint is off the hook."

"Come on y'all so I can show y'all the rest of the place so y'all know where you are going to sleep at". They all started following me up the steps on the right-hand side of this large, beautiful place. I go up the steps with everybody quickly behind me. We all get to the top of the steps in this large well-lit hallway with hardwood floors that are shiny and new like a hospital floor. *And the whole place smells like white linen fragrance. I love that shit it smells rich from the door.* I point at Moon spitting at him quickly, "now you go in there and you tell me what you see brother."

"I know! I know you're going to ride me all day about this shit man I was fucking wrong all right."

Everybody is laughing and I said, "no I am not going to ride you all day about this shit. I just want you to see that I'm not the one to be fucked with, that's all my brother."

We all laughed. I playfully pushed him to the room on the right-hand side of the place. I opened the door to the first bedroom and the shit was large and plush. Black carpet with a big queen size bed,a big 50-inch flat screen TV on the wall, a black bedspread black and white curtains, two black lacquer night tables on each end of the bed and a black hand carved dresser drawers and a big bathroom on the right with a huge shower.

Everybody peeked inside the room with all of their eyes looking in deep admiration and smiles. I say to him this is your room.

"Wow for real?"

" Yeah, this used to be Uzi-Boy's room when we were all staying here."

I shout , "go check it out while I move on with my next surprise delight for the gang." Everybody giggled as Moon went and jumped on top of the bed and I waved my hand for everybody to follow me.

We walked down the hall just a little and the next room had a light brown pretty ass door.

"Okay Poncho and Mama Red are you ready for this here?" They both jumped up and down like little kids in a candy shop, "yeah, We ready come on with it, Lex"!

I quickly opencd the door and their mouth dropped open and they said, "awwwww shit!"

Now this room was done up in all light blue light blue carpet, a king size bed with a white silky bedspread and a giant flat screen TV on the wall. Awhite bar and desk on the right with light blue curtains and the bathroom had light blue tiles with blue and white towels. They both ran inside of the room smiling, jumping up and down like they were on the fucking price is right or some shit.

I announced, "this used to be Rush's room with him and his wife and then I pointed up at the crystal fully stocked bar and the chandelier. I asked happily, "So what do y'all think?"

Fat Poncho said, "this is off the hook Lex thank you bumping fist with me and Big Mama Red giving me a big hug giggling loud this is significantly better than a fucking hotel for real! You got that shit right Mama Red! As they both sit down on the gigantic bed smiling from ear to ear. Stump said, "What about me, baby girl?"

"Hold on. brother. I got you!" I got you just chill your next nigga come on!" We walked not too far up the hall and came to the next room. The door on the left-hand side is a black door. I asked, "are you ready my nigga?"

"I'm surely ready Lex!"

"Okay, here we go!" I open the door. This room is done up in black and white with a queen size bed with a zebra bedspread black carpet black and white curtain, a giant flat screen TV on the wall and a black lacquer bar on the right-hand corner and a very large bathroom and shower. I asked again, "Do you like?" *With my hand up in the air looking at him.*

"Oh, hell yes, I likes." He ran up and hugged me.

"Wow, it is way better than I thought it was going to be Lex thank you."

"Oh, you going to fucking work for this shit nigga, you just know that shit!" I pushed Vita out in the hallway while Stump was checking out his new room all excited. Now I grabbed Vita in his collar, and I got right up to his face looking him deep in his sexy ass eyes of his talking low, "now if you act right, you might get some pussy tonight!"

He started giggling. I replied, "you're not still mad at me, are you?"

"No fuck that I got what you were saying I'm goo. I'm a grown ass man baby you said what you wanted to say and so did I. That's old water under the fucking bridge Ma."

"**Nzuri!** *(Good)* Come on." I pull him down to the end of the hall and we stand in front of the door. I'm shouting to Vita, "you ready for this, Mister black and sexy?"

"Yeah, baby I'm always ready" I opened the door and his mouth dropped open and said, "wow!"

This room is twice as big as all the others, but all the rooms are big. Vita looked at me and asked, `` Now, whose room was this?"

"This was AK and Jackie's room. He looked at the big king size bed. The whole room is done up in white and gold. The king size bed have a gold spread with gold tassels on each end of them. A 60-inch flat screen TV up on the wall with gold end tables on each side of the bed with two large gold dresser drawers and gold curtains with a very large picture window". I showed him the bathroom, smiling, pulling him by his arm. The bath has two sinks, two toilets, a bidet and a huge shower with light gold tiles and gold and white towels. I looked at him and announced, "this is how a motherfucker should be living that's why I do the crazy shit I do. I lived in squalor when I was young and I'm never going back to that shit, or I'll die trying to live the fucking way. I don't want to settle for any bullshit."

"I feel you Ma."

"You're right." He kissed me long, deep and wet.

"Vita, let me take a shower before we get into it because I want you to lick my pussy until I cum three or four fucking times. Fuck that!" He licked his lips and replied, "suppose I told you I don't eat pussy."

I put my hand on my hip and smirked, "well, if you don't, I'll find a nigga somewhere tonight that will, and you can go sleep in the fucking lounge until the nigga is done doing It."

He nudged me and I bumped my hip into his. I went and closed the door and took off my clothes quickly. I ran and jumped in the shower turning the water on closing the large glass doors washing up my body. *I know dam well this nigga eats pussy when I had him in the garage. I pushed his head down there that nigga was going to eat my pussy out behind the fucking truck who he thinks he's talking too with that bullshit.*

Soon as I'm washing up hitting all my hot spots, I hear the door open with all this water coming down on me. I looked over with my body all lathered up with soap. Its Vita holding his large black erection I turned around soaping up my ass good and I opened the crack of my ass bending over putting my hands up on the light gold shower walls. He comes up behind me and I reach back to give this nigga a hand pointing it right at my ass hole for him to stick it in nice and slow. He's pushing with his hot tight tattoo body, and he slipped it into my ass. "Oh shit!"

I bend just a little more, opening my legs wider as he puts his large dark hands on to my thick hips. He's starting to gyrate his hips to work his man of steel into my anus. The soap made it easy to slide inside and he started off slow pumping sliding it in and out of my ass and I'm still holding open my ass cheeks feeling his lovely meat up in my ass hole. I'm pushing back with my thick legs and my ass cheeks bouncing on the back of his dark strong ass hairy legs. Now I'm starting to get that good sensation inside of my ass while he's fucking me with the water coming down on both of our hot brown bodies.

The faster he started stroking me the better it started feeling. It got to the point where I started feeling the G Spot in my ass. I moan out loud, "yeah baby fuck me good."

Vita started pumping and humping on me hard slamming that thick black sausage in my ass hole. It really started feeling good with me groaning loud and the water going all into my mouth with me in deep passionate pleasure. Now I'm rubbing on my pussy at the same time he's stroking my ass hole and the combination together is fucking electrifying. I started squirting when I felt his hot nut shooting up in my ass, we both were yelling, "aaaaawwwww! Ohhhhhh Owoowwwooo!"

We both were screaming so loud I'm thinking it would have shattered the glass on the large shower door for real. I turned around and kissed him with water coming down on both our bodies. I feel so free and sexy right about now getting my shit off. Now he's washing my body with his large strong hands soaping me up all along my back, my ass and my titties. I can just melt like butter right about now. I got a sponge and I started washing him and got him all lathered up with soap feeling his strong arms and his chest listening to him moan every time. I'm rubbing on him, it's turning me on. Then I just rinse myself, off my mind is floating on a fucking cloud feeling so good and I stepped out the shower on to the mat. Before I can reach and dry myself off in a deep daze, he stepped out of the shower quickly grabbing one of the large white towels and he started drying me off, kissing me on my neck nicely and tenderly. He dried me off by rubbing the water drops from my body rubbing on my ass kissing me I reached up putting my hand on his face kissing him more.

I stopped and I grabbed him by his hand, taking him to the bed slowly. I lay on the bed on my back opening my legs wide pushing his head down to my freshly shower pussy. Yeah, and I'm holding the back of his head all the way up in it too pumping and gyrating my thick brown hips too. He started off licking it slow at first, I'm thinking he don't have any coochie eating skills whatsoever but then that nigga really started getting in to the better he got at it. I just started leaning back just a little more and the wetter I got the better it started feeling with my love juices flowing down I started pumping my smooth drenched snatch a little faster and now this nigga done turn into Mister Cunnlingus. Wow my eyes started falling back in my head. He was doing such a good job on my pussy. I'm rubbing his head at the same time I'm steady pumping my super wet cunt in his face. And he was lapping it up like a fucking pro too. I looked up at him while I'm moaning in deep pleasurable bliss.

I can really tell he's really enjoying licking me up and down with all of my cunt juices on both sides of his handsome black mug and dripping off of his chin. Then he really started to really concentrate on my clit sucking on it and I thought I was going to hit the fucking ceiling I started squirting shooting out and he never stop sucking on my fat sticky clit. He just lifted his chin, so it doesn't splash all in his face letting all of my hot love juices flow down my legs onto the bed.

That move let me know this nigga know what the fuck he's doing for real. After that he started making a loud sucking sound and slurping shit that made me have another hot ass orgasm Ohhhhhh shit! Aaaaawwwww! My head is light and I'm seeing fucking star's right about now I started pushing his head back off of my pussy and he quickly held me down on the bed still licking I can't lie I just could not take it any more I had to jump off the bed pushing him away from me.

Getting to my feet and I'm out of fucking breath. He's looking up at me with both sides of his dark grill with pussy juice dripping down off it is smiling and giggling loud. I'm blowing out air and I even started laughing, "I didn't know you suck pussy better than that porn star nigga Mister Cunnlingus. Gawd damn!"

I thought I was a freak. I'm looking at him rather than the bed with a giant wet spot in the middle of the bed. He gets up off the bed and he started taking the gold bedspread off the large bed looking up at me and he's still hard as a rock with his manhood pointing right up at me. I'm shaking I can't even stand the fuck up I'm so lightheaded and dizzy leaning on the wall holding my head. I just went and climbed back on the bed laying at the head of the bed grabbing one of the large pillows.

I laid down at the head of the bed long ways away from the wet spot. I pointed to my cigarettes, "Vita tosses me my cigarettes please, baby."

He throws them underhanded, and I catch them in mid-air with one hand. I just winked my eye at him as he just smiled going into the bathroom washing his face and hands. I'm lying on the bed floating on a fucking cloud laying back puffing up a storm. Vita came over to where I was laying, kissing me, I can taste the mouth wash from his lips and grabbing my cigarette pack from out of my hand taking one out lighting one for himself smiling at me blowing out some smoke with his eyes glowing. After I was done with my cigarette I sat up and put it out in the large ashtray on the nightstand. I laid down and I fell asleep.

PLANNING THE JOB

Three hours later I woke up smelling some really good food floating in the air. The aroma was filled with mouthwatering flavor. I looked up and I saw Vita knocked out sleep with his mouth wide open in the big chair not too far from me on the right-hand side of the bed. I slowly sat up on the king size bed getting my smokes from off the nightstand. I light one up and I get lightheaded all over again. I have the cigarette cocked in my lips while I get up looking for my panties on the floor then my jeans slipping them on quickly. along with my top so I can go find out what everybody is doing now. By the smell alone I know Big Mama Red is throwing the fuck down again plus I have to get my suitcase and backpack from out of the van. I don't wake up Vita. I quickly went out the door and went downstairs to the kitchen and sitting at the island is Moon Stump and Fat Poncho. As soon as everybody saw me, they started smiling with Moon speaking nicely, "so did you have a nice nap?"

"Matter of fact I did, and I came about five times, so I worked up a really big fucking appetite too!"

"All of them started laughing. Big Mama Red shouted, "I'm almost done. You can help me serve everybody honey."

"Where y'all get the food from?"

"I sent Stump and Moon to the store while you and Vita were taking y'all nap after me and Poncho had our little nap."

She giggled, "what did you fix Big Mama?"

"Oh, just Catfish nuggets with some spicy cabbage and some cornbread. "

"Wow, I never had Catfish nuggets before."

"Oh, girl you going to fucking love it once you had some baby girl Lex. Here, hand that over to Moon and Stump for me, please."

She handed me the two plates of food and I had to say after smelling the hot food on the two plates it made me even more hungry. I walked over towards the two of them with the food handing it to them with wide smiles at the same time. Big Mama Red came over, handing her man Poncho his plate. She walked back over making two more plates. She shouted, "your boy so he can eat. I pulled out my phone from my pocket and called Vita. It rang four times before he picked up. When he finally did I shouted, "hay baby come on downstairs and eat with us, alright." "Okay, I'll be right down."

I hung up and put my phone back in my pocket. I walked over to the long marble island with the two hot plates of food. We sat down and Big Mama Red came sitting down next to Pancho, "now it time we give thanks. oh lord thank you for this food we were about to eat and may you bless each and every one of us in Jesus's name." Everyone shouted, "Amen."

Vita walked and asked, "did I miss a room full of crooks and killers asking Jesus for his blessing."

Big Mama Red barked, "look no matter what we all do we need Jesus in are life okay Mister nonbeliever."

"Yeah, whatever but the food sure smells good, what is it?"

I answered, "Catfish nuggets and spicy cabbage."

We all started eating and it's out of this fucking world delicious. After we were all were done eating, I started speaking to everyone I'm glad were all sitting together so we can go over the house rules you fuck up you clean up it just that simple. "So, Poncho and Vita, I would like for you two to go over the plan on how we're going to do this job."

Vita replied, "I have a little map I drew up. Let me get itb out of my bag and I can go over with everybody while we're all here. I will be right back."

"Could you get my bags while you're at it, baby please? "Sure, thing sweetie as he walked towards the door to go out."

A few minutes later he comes back with both of our bags. He goes inside of his bag with his map with his master plan. As me and Big Mama Red cleared the island off with all the plates as soon as we both wiped and cleared everything off. Vita set his map he made up for all of us to look at going over everything we have to do and the supplies we need to pull this shit off. After he was done explaining everything we had to do.

"We're going to hit them Tuesday a week from now, that's when they get their drop of drugs."

Now the money is in one house and the drugs are in the other he points to the house on Hilton Street this is where the money is more guarded. We're going to hit them all at the same time.

"Are you sure we have enough people to do this shit?" "Yeah, if we do this shit right. Yes, we're short now that Juicy bitched up on us and we had to take care of his ass.

So, you're telling me we're short of a wheel man, then, right? Yeah, we are short two men. It was going to be Juicy and his brother Teddy. I said, "don't worry about that, I'll get us some wheel men just be ready to go on Tuesday while we get our supplies."

Fat Poncho said, "Are you sure you got this Lex or if not, we can hold it off for another month or so until we get somebody."

"Yeah, I'm sure I got this. I'll get two people who know what they're doing and if they fuck up.They will be dead after we do this shit."

Everybody started laughing out loud. I say are we done for now y'all Fat Poncho said yeah for right now we are. I quickly walked over to big Mama Red talking low do you have any sandwich bags or something I can put this coke in? Yeah, hold on baby she hands me a couple sandwich zip lock bags. I quickly stuck them in my pocket.

"Thank you Mama."

She just smiled, winking her eye at me. she is cleaning up and putting the rest of the food up. I put it on the floor, opening my suitcase. I put my black backpack next to my suitcase. I found one of the ounces of coke I had inside of scooping out enough coke to fill up the sandwich zip lock bag halfway. I close it up to go upstairs swiftly.

I put my backpack on my shoulder. I'm pulling my bag with one hand and pulling out my phone with the other Vita came up behind me talking. I'll take them up to the room for you baby, taking both my bags, the one off my shoulder and the other one out of my right hand.

"Thanks, baby, I'm going over here to the gym so I can make some calls so we can get the right people to do this job."

He said, "Okay, I'll be upstairs waiting for you." He winked his eye."

I just giggled walking back down the steps over to the gym with the zip lock bag of coke in one hand and my phone in the other. Now I called Rock up. He picks up after the phone rings four times as I sit down at one of the exercise machines saying "Yo, is this Rock."

He replied, "yeah, it's me Lex what's up baby girl."

He recognizes my voice right away. "Hey Rock, baby I need a big favor from you brother. I really hope it's not about some money Lex."

"Oh no, my nigga what I need is some good men for this job I'm about to do."

"Oh Yeah, I got you I know some real niggas that can use the work right about now."

"Yeah, okay I have some keys of fentanyl. Can you move it?"

"Is water wet sweetheart?"

We both started laughing and he said, "how many keys do you have?"

"I have ten for you to sell. I'm give you five for yourself if you hook me up some thorough ass thug niggas to put in this work."

"Oh, hell yeah, I'll call this nigga up right now stay by your phone."

"Lex, I'll call you right back." He hangs up. I light up a Newport leaning back waiting for him to call me back before I can take a few puffs. My phone rings. I get it real quick, "so what's up?"

"They said they will meet you tomorrow here at my crib about around 10 P.M."

"Okay, cool now they won't try to jack me. I hope you told them I will kill their ass if they come with some dumb shit."

"No, I would not do that to you Lex baby. This nigga is a thorough ass fucking crook and fucking revolutionist nigga who is super smart he's not about jacking people he's doing dirt with."

"What's his name?"

"His name is Kenyatta X so you're going to bring the Fentanyl with you when you come right?"

"Yeah and thank you so much Rock for this".

"No problem baby, I'll see you tomorrow. One!"

Now I'm sitting alone. I put my phone in my back pocket and I put the bag of coke in my lap getting a twenty-dollar bill out of my front pocket, rolling it up and I started snorting the coke out of the bag. While I am getting high, I'm thinking to myself all of this shit better work. After I get a nice fucking buzz, I go back upstairs to my room, and I sit on the bed next to Vita on the end of the bed. Vita asked, "are we going to be able to trust any of these new guys coming in on this shit?"

"No, not really but if anybody backs out this shit right now, we came all the way up here for nothing then."

"I know what you're going to say if anybody crosses us, you're going to kill them right?" He laughs. I blurted out, "yeah right on the fucking spot too!"

He puts his hand out for me to hand him the bag of coke I had on the bed next to me. So, we got high some more until we fell asleep cuddled up with one another. The next day we got up at about 10 A.M. We both got washed up and dressed. All of us had a lot to do that day getting all the other supplies we needed. We already have the guns and shit. Fat Poncho gave out all the assignments after we all sat down and ate breakfast and Big Mama Red threw down as always with bacon and eggs and some down-home grits with butter biscuits.

Shit, I can get used to this shit here, but Fat Poncho doesn't know that I'll be running this gang after we pull this job off, he just doesn't know it yet. Now he got Stump and Moon to go out and get the masks and rubber gloves. Vita went to get keys made to the warehouse before everybody else went out so they can get back inside the warehouse. So, me and Vita went to the local hardware store to have keys made and came back to give them to Fat Poncho and Big Mama Red.

Then me and Vita headed back out to get the rope chains and overhaul Poncho and Big Mama Red is going to go get us more food and some weed.

Fat Poncho said he had to have it because he ran out and he needed some more to get his head right. So, we all rolled out one by one me and Vita when out first we hit the hardware store first getting the chains rope and something they did not put on the list. I knew we might need a chainsaw. We had to go to another store to get the overhauls. We both went to this army & navy store. We took our time shopping, making a day of it. Shit and even stopping to get lunch too at a nice restaurant in center city like a regular couple. This about the closest thing me and him will get to a fucking date.

He doesn't know I'm going to demand that he take me out and spend some money on me after I fuck him again just to be fucking with his mine for real and see how he's going to act to test him. We came back to the warehouse. Nobody is there, we have the warehouse palace to ourselves. So, we put the bags of what we brought in the back of the gym.

"Vita, I can use another drink he told me too as we went to the bar in the lounge area in the crib." *I can see in his eyes glowing with lust what he had on his mind and that was getting some more pussy I knew it before he kept rubbing all the fuck on my ass soon as we got in the house.* Vita is wanting more sex from me now that were all fucked up after our lunch together having a more than a few drinks and snorting coke we both were high sitting at the bar talking shit.

I was not in the mood but to get this nigga more under my control. I was going to do something freaky to his ass no man can resist and have him wrapped around my pretty little finger. With him keep grabbing and feeling on me at the bar I just pushed him off me really hard. I stood up and I pushed him over to the black couch playfully not too far from the bar area. He fell backwards onto the couch laughing. I got down on my knees unzipping his jeans and pulled out his trouser snake with his eyes getting wide and a big smile on his black grill. I sucked his Dick on the black couch in the lounge room on the first floor. I'm thinking anybody could have walked in on us at any time. I think that made both of us more excited about this shit but at this point it was on and popping.

He loved it but I did not put my all into it like I mostly do. I think I jacked him off more than sucking and licking but he enjoyed it because he came r fast anyway. So, I really didn't have to turn into that super head bitch all men dream about. I went into the bathroom, washed my mouth, came out and he had a few more drinks at the bar.

I went and laid down on the couch in the lounge area near the bar on the first floor by myself. While he flops down on the love seat with a big smile on his face and I go to sleep.

When I did get up, I looked at my watch and it was 8:30. I looked up at the love seat and Vita was not there I know I have to get myself together for my meeting with these hoodfella niggas.

So, I walked in the gym after hearing somebody moving around its Stump working out.

Stump uttered, "So look who it is sleeping beauty over here?"

He is giggling. I just smiled, giving him the finger. I walked away and went upstairs. I'm walking past Fat Poncho and Big Mama Reds room and she pops her head out the door after I walked past, and she asked, "you didn't eat girl?"

"No, I'm good, Mama. I have to go get ready for this meeting thanks anyway."

"Okay, we didn't want to wake you up when we came in, I told that nigga Stump downstairs in the gym to tell you that your food was in the microwave."

"Well thanks. I'll get it when I come back as I quickly walk to my room. I open the door and Vita is sitting up watching the movie Shottas."

I love that movie, he yelled, "why don't you sit down and watch it with me blowing out a big cloud of smoke from his blunt?"

"No, I have to get ready to meet these niggas to see if it's going to work out with us."

Now you mean to tell me you're going to know after one meeting that you're going to know if these niggas you don't know is going to work out."

"Yes, I can. I started taking off my clothes asking him where's my bag, baby." He points towards the left. I quickly picked it up and set it on the bed, opening it up and getting my black top and black jeans. Vita asked, "why do you wear so much black Lex?"

I joked, "you don't know I'm the fucking undertaker. I come to burry any motherfucker in my way you didn't know nigga?"

He started laughing. As I put on my clothes real fast I get my guns making sure I got one in the back of my jeans and I put the silencer on the tip of my other gun and I set it in my pocketbook.

"I need you to help me put some of this fentanyl keys in the van for me please".

He got up and answered back, "okay."

I can see in his face he really didn't want to do shit, but you can get men to do all kinds of shit for you after you sucked his Dick for real. I grabbed five bags out and I handed it to him, and I got five more of them then I put them in my black coach bag. I got the five bags in my pocketbook, and I carried the other five in my arms down to the van. I followed him outside to the van. I tell him to set them in the tire well under the spare tire space. I watched him set them in there. I did the same and he put the tire on top of the bags of fentanyl and he shut it smiling at me. I close the back-van doors and I kiss Vita on his cheek.

He asked, "Are you sure you don't want me to go with you when we've been together all day? We had a really good time too." I smirked and I kicked it to him, "as you already know I can take care of myself Vita, I see you when I get back okay."

He walks me to the driver's side door and speaks smoothly.

"Be careful, I know you can take care of yourself, I'm just saying doe."

He closes the door looking up at me. I say move away from the van I have to go he steps back smiling and I pull off really fast.

I get to Rock's crib in no time I'm a little early, but I did that to check these niggas out I parked across the street from the front door. It's kind of dark where I parked so no one would see me in the van. I sit and wait, lighting up a cigarette keeping an eye out. After an hour or so I see three niggas coming up to Rock's door its 10 O' clock on the dot. One dude is big, the other two are about six foot something but strong I can tell from their build I jumped out and I walked across the street. I came up and rang the doorbell. The dude Spank that works for Rock came to the door opening it and he announced that, "everybody is downstairs right this way."

I follow him towards the basement door. I walked down behind him and sitting at the head of the table is Rock. He stood up and introduced me, "here she is on time like I told y'all. Lex, this is Kenyatta X. He stands up, bumps fist with me and greets me in Swahili, "**Yin udadewethu** *What's up sister?*"

"**Ngiyaphila kuze kube manje** *I'm good so far.*"

Rock points toward the other two dudes and this Duba, "hey, what's up?" he shakes hands with me, and this is Amir nice to meet you sister and he just nods his head. Rock asked, "I have to ask before we get started what was y'all speaking?"

I looked at Rock, answering him with a smile, "that was Zulu. "I sat down at the end seat as all of them sat down looking up at me and Kenyatta X said, "I heard you are looking for some men to do a job. What kind of job is it? Some of the people I worked with in New York came here to take down this drug dealer named Raymundo at F & Allegheny."

"Yeah, I know him, we were thinking of taking him down too. How many people have you got to do this shit?"

"Five so far."

They all started laughing Duba looking up at me barking.

"You came up here without enough people, you are going to need about eight good men, sister."

"Well, that is why I'm here. Can you help me other than that you're just wasting my time?"

Kenyatta X answered, "if you have some people just as good as you are, we can do this shit."

"How the fuck you know I'm any good or not my Zulu speaking friend?"

"Well Rock told me you were down with the 24th street Cartel. They are some real niggas like my people that's the only reason I'm sitting down with you in the first place."

Duba pointed to my arm, "I want to see your tattoo, so we know what rank you were when you were down" I smirked, and I turned to them lifting up my sleeve. I can see all of their eyes getting wide when I lift up my sleeve.

Amir blurted out, "well, Gawd damn. she was a fucking lieutenant why don't have her roll with us doing that job and fuck the New York niggas."

Kenyatta X, "no she put the crew together so we're going to work with them. Look, you're going to need about four more people on this job and I have a fucking army of niggas, but it just might be to many hands in the pie. I want to make sure all of my people are going to get paid after all this shit is done."

"You can take my word on this shit you will all get paid you can ask Rock that am stand up peoples." *Rock nodded his head at them reassuring Kenyatta X and his crew that they we were telling them the truth".*

"I will take both y'all word for it if not if anything funny is in the air. I will kill everything that moves, Ma believe that."

"You are a man of my own heart, so we have a deal, then, right?"

I stood up and he also got up at the same time shaking my hand. "Yes, we do **Udadewethu** *sister."*

"No, not sister **Ndlovkazi** *queen.* "

"Okay, I'm sorry queen!" All of them started laughing. "Okay, I'll go talk to my people and we set up a time so we can go over everything we have to do so give me a number so we can get this shit done. Okay this is how we're going to do this Amir gave her a phone. Amir stood up and walked over to me handing me a phone saying once you turn it on don't turn it off okay, I'll call you around six so that give you time to talk to your peoples after that we will link up with you. Okay that sounds good I turned the phone on looking up at all of them. Rock asked, "are we done here?"

Kenyatta X replied, "for now we are."

Rock looked over at me okay did you bring that thing with you. Yeah, I did your gonna have to help me take it out of the van. Kenyatta X asked, "So Rock, what is it she got for you?'

"Some keys of Fentanyl."

He looked up at me. "How many do you have, Ma?"

"More than you need, why?"

"Well, why don't you give us some of the keys of that shit and that will cover us for helping you out."

"I was going to ask you that, but it just might be a big ass take for us to split on this job, so you're going to have to make up your mind. What the fuck you want Dawg?"

He looks up at me smiling with his eyes wide.

"We can work something out after the job my gangster queen."

Rock chimed in, "hold up let me get my shit and then y'all can work something out all right, motherfucker!"

We all started laughing. I put my black coach bag on the table "here are the first five I said that's for you the other ten are in the van."

I took out the five keys, setting them on top of the table. Rock stood up pulling this phone out calling his boy Shank he picked up fast on the first ring.

"I need you and Jadon to help Lex take some shit out of her van, let's move!"

We both go up the steps by the time we got to the front door

Spank and his other worker I never seen before name Jadon this nigga is huge too.

I turned them and announced, "y'all going to need something to put it in before we walk over to my van fellas"

Shank chimed in and said, "I'll be right back a few minutes later he came back with two really big gym bags mumbling, "this will do the trick, Ma."

I replied, "yeah it sure will as we walked over to the van parked across the street."

We walked very quickly over to my vehicle. I opened the back-van doors and I pointed to the tire well space.

"There up inside of there up under the tire." One of them lifted the tire up and he set it on the ground then both of them started taking the bags of fentanyl out putting them in their bags. I stepped back reaching down in my coach bag putting my hand on my pistol with the silencer on it and them niggas didn't have a fucking clue. While I stepped back to keep an eye out. Good thing I did because out of nowhere out the corner of my eye two niggas came popping up on my right and then two more of them on my left.

The men on the right came up barking, "you know what this is bitch!"

I turned to look at them while Jadon went for his gun and the men on the left yelled, "you will be dead before you try it big man so drop the gun!"

I looked over at Shank and he was all slow to react to this shit like he knew what was going to happen. I knew right then and there he set this shit up. I quickly turned with my coach bag from my left to my right pivoting from side-to-side **Pooouufff! Pooouuufff! Pooouuufff! Pooouuufff!**

They all hit the ground hard and fucking fast. I shot all four of them motherfuckers and I pulled my pistol all the way out my bag. I put the gun right up to Spanks head. "You set this shit up right, nigga!"

Jadon looked over at me, pulled his gun out and Spank was yelling at him, "yo, Jadon shoot this bitch Dawg!"

"You are going to let her put a gun to my fucking head man!"

I yelled to Jadon, "you see that nigga when they came up, he set that whole shit up!"

Jadon turned the gun on Spank, taking aim and not moving. Spank shouted, "you, big dumb ass motherfucker. you're going let this bitch fuck with your mine Jadon man!"

"You knew me all your fucking life man come on"! I pulled my phone out hitting the speed dial to Rock. He picked right up and asked, "what's up Lex?"

I yelled, "bring your ass outside right now!"

Rock came running outside with Kenyatta X Duba and Amir Rockwhat the fuck happens, Lex?

"Looking at the dead men on the ground bleeding. Your man set me up, so I killed his punk ass boys! "

They were all looking down at the four bloody bodies on the ground. Rock barked out in a panic man we have to clean this shit fast. I'm still holding my gun to Spanks head. Rock shouted, "Kenyatta, Duba, Amir gave me a hand right quick!"

As he's looking down at the bodies on the ground, they quickly drag the bodies stuffing them under my van. Rock pulled out his gun, sticking it in Shanks' back shouting to me, "all right."

"Lex, I got this shit you can lower the gun before somebody comes by here and sees you."

"Good thing you and me, is all right other than that you would make me feel like you were setting me up or something."

I lower the gun looking him deep in his eyes as Rock quickly said, "I'm going to take this nigga in the house and lock him down so we can get the work!"

"Yo Kenyatta, stay here and keep an eye for me please while I deal with this nigga!"

He looked at him uttering fast, "hurry up motherfucker. Jadon go get the truck and bring Zig Zag Tone and Bee-Bee with you hurry the fuck up too." I stood there in the dark at the back of my van along with Kenyatta X Duba and Amir.

Kenyatta X said, "That was some good shooting, **Ndlovukazi** *queen."*

Soon as he said that speeding up the street is a truck and then another truck came riding up on the sidewalk boxing us in. I'm thinking it's another attack as I lift my gun and take aim. A young light skin dude jumped out the truck with his hands up in the air and yelled, "don't shoot girlfriend. I'm here to help get these bodies out of here. I'm Tone. I work for Rock! And this is Yak"! *As he points to him and I lower my gun, smiling.*

Then the other two men came out from the other truck talking low I'm Zig Zag and this is Bee-Bee the four men quickly pulled the dead men from under my van quicker than you can fucking blink shit they must have done this shit before. They toss two of the dead men in one truck and two of them in the other truck. Then the dude named Yak asked me, "where are the drugs?" I pointed at the two gym bags on the ground in front of me. He quickly picked them up and jumped in the truck and took off. Soon as the two trucks took off my phone rings, I get it real fast and its Rock on the other end said, "I need you to step into my office, please."

I said, "I don't know about that shit after what just happened a couple of minutes ago!"

"Look, I did not know that nigga was going to do that shit plus you can watch me take care of his ass."

"Shit you might be doing that shit, so he doesn't talk and tell it all."

"I would never do any foul shit to you Lex."

I looked over at Kenyatta X and his boys whispering "just hear him out if you don't like what he's talking about Ma shoot his ass in the fucking head and roll the fuck out! We won't stop you queen." We all started laughing as we walked towards the house. Duba rings the doorbell and Rock gets the door waving at me to come downstairs.

I let them go down the stairs first pulling out my gun soon as we get down there, as he got the nigga Spank tied up in a chair, he's all beat the fuck up with blood coming out his mouth. Were all standing around him mean mugging his ass he is sitting there crying and shaking like a tree in a bad storm. Rock pointed at him, "he's all yours, Lex."

I asked, "did he tell you anything?"

"No, I just looked at him. I took out my pistol, but I took the silencer off the tip holding it in my left hand. I took aim with my right hand shouting, "good night shit bag!"**Kapacka!** I shot him right in the middle of his fucking ugly ass light skin head. His head is leaning back with the blood dripping out. "This is the second time I had to kill somebody down here and you need to get better people. That nigga tried to set me up once you let him hear about that fucking Fentanyl."

"You're right, Lex but we did take care of it right away Ma so were all good now?" *With his hands up in the air as if that was going to satisfy my mistrust, I should shoot is fucking ass right here and now.*

"Well next month motherfucker make sure you have all of my loot. I don't want you to join your boy Spank in the ghetto here after because you know I don't fucking play when it comes to my loot."

I turned to Kenyatta and his men and announced, "I holla at y'all later after I go talk to my peoples alright".

"Yeah, you do that we'll be ready to go as soon as you call us back on that phone, we gave you Lex okay let me walk you out to the door." He walks behind me along with his two Henchman, but I notice they all have their guns out by their side.

I don't know if this is to protect themselves or they're going to fucking off me or what. So nice and slowly I pulled my gun out too and held it by my side just in fucking case any one of them want to get cute. We get to the front door the dude Amir open the door Duba getting in his gun stands and Kenyatta X going out right behind him and I'm getting ready as well for whatever these niggas are getting ready to do. Kenyatta X waits for me on the steps smiling, pulling the door close he points for me to stay behind him winking his eye. We walked down the steps and we started to walk towards my van, but he stopped with his men right in front of him looking both ways up the street. I whispered, "what's going on?"

He replied quickly, "he just got a text from his peoples that the TTS niggas *the Toe Tag Squad their rivals* were in the area. While I was killing that foul nigga, who told those dudes to rob you for the Fentanyl. It seems he was trying to take care of us as well. What they don't know is that two of them are our men out here on post *Kahseam* and *Jabara*."

He waited still looking up both sides of the dark street than he said were going to make sure you get out of here safe before shit jumped off if not, you're going to be in the mix right along with us. I said to myself shit let's have it then as all three of them walked me to my van I jumped in my whip. Kenyatta X taps on the window so I can roll it down as soon as I do, "don't pull off until I pull up beside you to follow you home, okay."

I just nodded my head yes and he continued, "I have a black GMC truck I'll be pulling right up in a few, Ma."

"Yeah, I got you KX." He quickly walked to his whip parked a little further down the block. I just sat there with my pistol in my lap ready for whatever. Just like he said he came pulling up looking at me pointing for me to take off with a deep smirk on his face. I pull off driving up Fairmont two blocks and I'm ready to make a left turn to 16th street. Just as I'm making the turn by Fairmont being a two-way street, the car that was sitting across the street from me in the left lane came speeding out with another car coming up 16th street **Baaarrraattta! Baaarrrrtta!**

Spitting hot led at me but at the same time Kenyatta X in the GMC black truck speeding up **Kapacktttackat! Kapacktakta!** Shooting at the gray sedan that was shooting at me. I was ready to pull over and jump out and help them shoot these motherfuckers up when out of nowhere two more black trucks came up shooting at the gray sedan. All I see out my driver side mirror Sparks spitting from the muzzle flash going back and forth from all the guns locked into battle. Then popping up out of nowhere I see red and blue lights flashing from out my driver side mirror. I slow down and pull over to see what happens halfway up the block.

I see Duba jump out the black GMC truck with a big ass machine gun shit it looks a like a fucking 50 caliber **Kackac-doon! Kackac-doon Kackac- doon! Tacta tact tact tatcatck Doon! Doon!** Ripping the cop car to fucking shreds as the cop car started speeding up backing up burning rubber, I'm laughing my ass off watching these cops getting the fuck out of there like scared little rabbits. Now I pull off getting the fuck out of dodge I speed off down the street. I get about ten blocks away from where all the shit went down. I look in my rearview and I see this black truck. I'm talking out loud to myself that can't be them. The phone they gave me started ringing. I pick it up fast. "I love the way you guys' work."

"Thanks Ma, and I can hear all of them laughing out loud. Look, we're gonna have to get ghosts, make sure you talk to your peoples **Eyodwa** *One!*"

I just giggled looking back and they were gone. I lit up a Newport saying to myself these niggas are fucking crazy. I'll love to be working with them from the door. I make it back to the crib as soon as I walk in the warehouse. I hear the music banging, and everybody is sitting around on the couch and at the bar drinking, having a good time. Moon jumped up from the bar with a drink in his hand and a cigarette cocked in his thick lips and this older good-looking black man by his side. He yelled, "hey Lex, I want you to meet my father Jitta pops is going to be joining us on this job."

I shake his hand speaking over the music playing well. "Nice to meet you pops!"

"Just call me Jitta, baby girl. I just love this place y'all got here."

I answered, "Well I'm glad you like it Jitta."

I quickly looked at everybody else in the room to see if they wanted Moon to bring his father in on the gig. By the looks on their faces everybody was cool with it. So, I said to myself if they're cool with it why rock the boat. I just hope he's good as Moon says he is we damn sure can use another wheel or trigger man on the set. I wave and speak to everybody in the room while Moon and his father Jitta go sit back down at the bar in the lounge area. I walked up a little closer to everyone.

"I'm glad all of y'all are down here. These guys are solid. I saw them in action."

Fat Poncho pointed to Stump sitting at the end of the bar to turn the music down as soon as he did, he said "oh yeah what happened?"

"These niggas try to jack them not only did they take care of them they smoked the cops too."

Vita said, "that's good, how many guys did they get?"

"As many as we need."

Fat Poncho asked, "are you sure we can trust these motherfuckers?"

"Yeah. Moon cut in fast and said, ``When are we going to meet them?"

"Well, I came to talk to y'all before I set up a time for them to link up with us."

Fat Poncho looks at big Mama Red then back at me mumbling sarcastically, " we have to meet these niggas then we can see if they're going to work with us."

"So, what time do you want me to tell them to meet up with us here?"

"Tell them around six tomorrow is cool."

"All right that's what I'll tell them, then I quickly pull out my phone calling Kenyatta X. The phone rang three times before he picked up.

"Yo what's up this is Kenyatta?"

I said, "yeah this is Lex they all agree so you can come at 6 alright."

"Okay I'll be there one!"

I hung up then I went and walked around at the back of the bar making me a drink of Vodka on the rocks as Moon turned the music back up. I walked over towards the couch with my drink nodding my head to the soulful music pumping sitting next to Vita. He is smoking a blunt blowing thick smoke then he hands it to me. I get my puff on as me and Vita had our little chitter chatter flowing. We sat in the downstairs lounge getting our groove on then one by one each one of us went upstairs. The next day I woke up smelling that delicious aroma of Big Mama Red hooking something up some down home and off the chain for sure. I rolled over and Vita is not in the bed with me. I get out of bed and go take a shower so I can get myself together. I'm still a little high from last night. I dressed as soon as I was done, I snorted some coke, got my gun and I went downstairs. I walked to the kitchen bumping fist with Big Mama Red asked, "what you got jumping off today girl?"

"Oh, just some bacon and eggs and some home fries with some flat jacks."

"I can get used to this shit! Well, you better get used to it for now girl here take your plate while it's hot baby". I quickly grabbed my plate as I see Vita Moon, Fat Poncho, Stump and Jitta sitting at the table not too far from the kitchen island laughing, talking and bullshitting with one another while they were eating.

LINKING UP WITH THE X MEN

Vita saw me and quickly got up and walked over to me. "Hey, good morning baby."

"Good morning, Vita." I wink my eyes at him, and he smiles as I sit down to eat. I waved my hand at him giggling, "go over there with your friends so I can eat nigga" He is laughing his ass off walking back to the table where they are at. Big Mama Red came and sat with me keeping me company . Big Mama Red spoke low, "look at them there just like little kids when they all get together."

"I see." As we both laughed. After I ate, I kicked it with Big Mama Red snorting coke while the boys went on and on talking shit about their glory days. We laid around in the lounge getting high until the evening when Kenyatta X and his men came to the crib 6 on the dot. It's a big knock at the door. I quickly went to the door to get it. I open the door. It's Big Duba, Amir, the guy I did not meet yet in Kahseam and the man himself Kenyatta X. He said to me, "this Kahseam you did not meet last night pointing at this brown skin handsome motherfucker." *I'm saying to myself he can get some for sure.*

I quickly bump fist with Kahseam. He's smiling checking me out from head to toe on the low. Amir looked up and blurted out, "Wow, this is a nice joint you can never tell from the outside."

I smirked and raised my eyebrow, "that's the whole point, brother right."

This way so y'all can meet the boys I'm waving my hand for them to follow me inside."

I know they're all looking at my ass. It's a black man's favorite pastime. Fat Poncho is sitting on the love seat along with Moon and his father Jitta is sitting on the couch. I point to each one of them and introduce them, "this is Poncho, Moon, Jitta and over at the bar is Stump and Vita."

Each one of them walked up and they all bump fist with one another and shaking hands I point towards the extra chairs, nice and polite like Stump brought out from the back of the gym for us sitting around so we all can hear the master plan. I have to admit Moon, Vita, and Fat Poncho worked it out with Kenyatta X and Big Duba.

I was really impressed with the way Kenyatta talk he don't use big words he just speaks really clear with power in his voice this nigga knows what he's doing at all times. Now I see why he has so many soldiers that will follow him into hell and come out the other side of it. He reminded me of AK but a little younger. Now,I'm hyped we all have the game plan. It only took us all but two hours to know what we all have to do with this big job. Fat Poncho and Kenyatta we can go over it two more times at the same time tomorrow and a few more times over the weekend to make sure everybody gets it down. We all agree to it. Kenyatta X was all business he did not want to get high with us he said he will get high after the job is fucking done.

They all rolled out the door as fast as they came. I was fucked up getting high all day, so I went to bed with Vita stumbling behind me. Soon as I get upstairs in the room and shut the door this nigga Vita wanted to get his Dick sucked. I was not in the fucking mood, but I got down on my fucking knees and I did him right quick and I jack off the rest of it out his love muscle getting the sticky Jizz all over my fucking hands. I go wash my hands off in the bathroom. I came out taking all my clothes off and I lay on the end of the bed with my legs cocked open ready to go and I'm feeling good high as a fucking kite. He when to take a piss as he was coming out, he stood in front of me all fucking wobbly. He got down on his knees all slow and taking his time to lick my hot twat. Now that it's his turn to do me I can see that he doesn't want to do it. But I pushed his head down there right in the middle of my wet cunt pumping right in his fucking face. This, nigga is licking me out good at first don't you know this nigga fell the sleep eating my pussy out. I looked down and his head is bopping up and down and not licking me while I'm on the end of the bed. Now he's nodding like a fucking junkie who just shot up two bags of some good dope. I looked down and I slapped the shit out of him! **Packa!**

He jumps up yelled, "what the fuck you do that shit for?"

I said, "never in my whole life did. I had a nigga fell the sleep on my good hot pussy nigga. It's going to be a long while before you even could smell this good pussy over here motherfucker!"

I stood up and looked him up and down and if he thinks about hitting me. I got my black bag at the foot of the bed where I keep it. I'll blow his drunk ass brains out. He took a couple steps towards me, talking loudly but I was calm knowing what I'll do to him if he was going to do it. He jumps bad on me but I'm getting closer to my bag. He's yelling talking shit I pulled the covers back on the bed and I jumped in the bed. He didn't see me reach down getting my pistol. I set it close to my titties and went to sleep.

DON'T GET MIXED UP
IN THE BULL SHIT.

The next morning, I got up a little early. When I was in the bathroom getting washed. I get a little more of the dog that bit me last night by snorting some coke from off the sink. Then I got dressed made me a drink at the bar in my room looking at this nigga laying across the bed still sleep. I get some of my clothes together so I can wash them. I put them all in a small trash bag I had in my suitcase. I tossed the clothes inside. I quickly got my trusty black backpack, tossed it on my shoulder and headed downstairs to the laundry room. Only one strange thing is that as soon as I go downstairs. I don't smell any food cooking. I go down the basement that's huge and super clean. Big Mama Red sent Stump to get washing powders and bleach the other day. Good thing she's here with us because that's something men never would have thought about until they need it.

I toss my clothes in the washing machine then soon after an hour or so I can smell the food with that blazing flavor aroma in the air. Big Mama Red is up now throwing the fuck down. I'm still feeling that little of that groove buzzing high I had last night sitting back in the chair smoking a cigarette while my clothes are drying. When my phone rings I look at the caller ID and its Rock. *I'm saying to myself what the fuck he wants.* I put the phone up to my ear asking,"yo what's up Rock?"

"Hey Lex, I need your help with something."

"Yeah, and what's that Rock?"

"I really don't want to tell you this over the phone, for real I need to see you face to face."

"Look Rock I know you really helped me and my crew out with the spot, but I also gave you some loot for that shit too."

"Look, I should have let y'all stay there without asking you for some loot. That was my girl on my ass about that shit so I had to do it, but this is some life and death shit right now. I need you really badly."

"Okay I'll be there in an hour or so."

"Thank you so much!"

He hangs up I'm thinking to myself what the fuck he needs me for. I take my clothes out the dryer and quickly stick them in my little trash bag. I go upstairs in the kitchen still thinking about this nigga Rock and his life and death bull shit statement. Big Mama Red said, "hey girl you're up early still preparing the food non-stop and talking to me at the same time."

"Yeah, I was washing my clothes. I'm done now look I just got a call from Rock he said he needs me saying it's some life and death kind of shit."

Her eyes widened looking at me in my face.

"Oh yeah, well don't get mixed up in some bull shit to get you hurt girl."

I've heard that shit all my life." He hooked us up, so I have to see what the fuck it is first.

"Yeah, but you still don't owe him shit. He made you give him some money to stay here with Lex."

"Yeah, I know but I still have to check it out."

"Look, I know you have skills up the ass girl, but you need to stop playing the fucking superhero bitch and pick your spots too girl. I'm telling you."

"Your right look, I'm going to roll out of here. I'm pissed at that fucking Vita."

"What did he do, girl? can you tell me?"

"I don't give a fuck about telling you that nigga he fell asleep while he was eating my pussy out! So, I smacked the shit out of him."

We both bust out laughing all loud and shit. She's still laughing Big Mama Red in between chuckles, "that nigga woke the fuck up then right!"

"Shit that nigga wanted to kill me girl but I was ready for his ass if he wanted to make a move. I had my pistol by the foot of the bed."

"You would not have killed him, would you?"

"I would have blown his head and his Dick off right on the fucking spot, girl!"

"Look, I'm going to get the hell out of here don't tell that nigga where I'm at okay Mama."

" Oh, I got you girl, don't worry!"

"You're not going to eat?"

"Yeah, I'll take a plate to go alright so I can eat on the run."

"Sure, let me wrap it up for you, Lex."

She wrapped up the food for me on a paper plate and aluminum foil, some good old home fries, sausage and eggs. I just love this woman's cooking for real.

We bump fist after she hands me my plate winking her eyes at me. I quickly took my clothes upstairs and tossed them on the bed to make sure I had everything I had back downstairs. We left out the door jumping in the van. I'm taking off blasting the radio driving up the street. I'm eating my food and driving at the same time some real nigga shit. When I got to Rock's house, I was done eating my food. I tossed all that shit out the window on the sidewalk when I jumped out of the van. I walked up to his crib, and I knocked on the door. I hear some voice on the other side of the door said, "who the fuck are you"

"I'm the nigga Rock called to come the fuck over here that's who the fuck I am."

After a few minutes the door flew open, and I see this tall ugly ass nigga. I never seen before I'm looking around and he have a house full of niggas and it's really smoky filled with chatter and music.

The ugly nigga who let me in is eyeballing the shit out of me. As soon as he went to pull his gun out but as fast as lighting, I beat his ass to the draw. I whip out my pistol pointing it at his head and that nigga was in shock. *He had that look on his face because he was wondering how I whip out my gun so fucking fast. Holding it right in his fucking black ass ugly mug.* Coming out from behind a few niggas standing around and the thick smoke is Rock all sweaty and jumpy "yo, Tone that's my peoples."

Tone said, "man you better get her she's the one with the gun in my fucking face!" *Still holding my gun on this big ugly ass dude,* I asked, "what the fuck is going on here Rock and who are all these niggas?"

He said, "First off please lower the gun and don't kill my man Tone. He's helping me out with these TTS niggas they came and snatched up my girl Tia and her mother last night."

"What?" I lowered the gun from that big black ugly motherfucker's head as I looked up at Rock.

"Why you didn't call your revolutionary niggas you hooked us up with to do the gig?"

"I did it because they want money and all I have is enough to pay some of my people and the rest is the flip money I have to give to my plug! These kidnappers want five million dollars So, what the fuck you want me to do?"

"I need you to talk to your people to help me get my girl and her mother Miss Glow." *I used the line Big Mama just said to me,*

"What you want me to be some kind of fucking superhero bitch now?"

The dude Tone started laughing, Rock looked up at him to mean mugging him and he stopped laughing.

"That was a good one for Rock!"

He's yelled, "were wasting time while you're making jokes when I have to make this move on them niggas before they kill my girl and her mom's! Please Lex could you ask them for me please if they say no least, I know you did ask them for me."

Then it popped in my head really fast. I had a great idea: I can work without asking my crew or Kenyatta and his people.

I said, "get the papers for the hope street joint we're staying in and I'll get you girl and her mom's back for you."

"I don't know about Lex. I paid over three million for that joint and I can sell it for ten easy."

"Are you really putting a price tag on your main bitch life along with your future mother-in-law who will let you get away with all kinds of shit? Knowing you with all your side pieces of ass! You know damn well your mother-in-law is going to sniff out one of them and tell your girl for sure. Shit after you save your mother-in-law's life her mom might even suck your Dick good without telling your girl about it."

I see he's really thinking about that shit his mother-in-law must be one of them old ass bitches who suck a mean Dick. He pulls out his phone and it rings, then he said , "yo, Jadon go in the back in the safe and bring me my steel box out of the office for me, please."

He hangs up. "I'll have my lawyers change everything over and put your name on the deed."

" Okay sounds good and if you cross me Rock, I'll kill you, your girl and your dick sucking ass mother-in-law too so don't fucking play with me alright."

" Come on Lex you know me I would not do that to you." Jadon came upstairs with the small gray steel box in his hand. Rock quickly took it out of his hand. He pulls his keys out his pocket opening the box he quickly flipped through and he pulls out the papers handing it to me.

"Here it is Lex."

I took it out of his hand reading it and I asked, "who the hell is Viola Green?"

"That's my mother."

"Okay, do you know where they have them? Do you have a tracker? "

"No, I just made sure I got some soldiers so we can make a move on them niggas. "

"Alright let me make a call."

I walk away from them a little *but I'm thinking to myself if this shit is going to work, I'm going to call Pat Black and see if she has any pro trackers on call.* The phone rings about four times before Pat picks up, "what's up Patty?"

She knew my voice from the door.

"Yo,what's up Lex you're the only one who calls me that what's up with you?"

"Look I'm in a real tight spot right now. I need a tracker ASAP."

" Well, I have a guy but he's going to want about ten bands from the door."

"Okay I can do that."

"Are you sure the last I heard about you is that the 24th street cartel wanted your head on a silver platter?"

"And you're back in town?"

"Yeah, I'm back in town. I'm going to get all that shit straightened out."

"Plus, I know you're not a snitch and you like money." "Yeah, you're right about that okay. I want five bands for hooking it up now. I know you got a few dollars, or you would not have called me up and I'll call up Shank."

"He's one of the best in the world. He's an ex-marine and he can find a tick on a hairy dog's ass."

I giggled. "I never heard it said like that before."

"Okay hit him up, have one of your people meet me at Broad & Sedgley avenue."

In one hour and have you man meet there as well. So I can get him started. "Well, what's his name?"

"His name is Malika."

"Malika?"

"Yeah, that's his name, girl! "

"What does he look like?"

"He's a tall dark skin good looking dude with a beard like all the young dudes in Philly have nowadays."

I'm thinking to myself if she's describing him like that, she must be fucking him. She utters, "he's going to be dressed in all black!"

I barked back, "I'll be there. I have a green van. Okay tell him that."

"Okay, sounds good to me Lex. **Moja.** *One!*"

"Moja!"

I walked over towards where Rock and Tone is standing and announced, "where on it. I got a tracker for you. I have to run to the spot and get some loot. To pay these people put you men on standby and be ready to go!"

"Okay, I will thank you for doing this Lex."

"Just make sure those papers are changed on Monday morning or you will be smoking blunts with the devil that same after noon." Tone started to laugh but Rock looked at him hard.

I looked over at Tone while I was walking out the door. "You can laugh nigga that was funny!"

I walked out the door, shutting it behind myself. I quickly get to my van. As soon as I started up the van and took off my phone rings, I pulled my phone out of my pocket and looked at the caller ID and its Vita. I don't want to get it but I hit the button mumbling, "what the fuck do you want?"

"Damn, I'm calling to say I'm sorry and you talk to me like that Lex?"

"Look your right you are sorry! Your one sorry ass mother-fucker for real! I'm busy, I don't have time for any of your bullshit!"

I hung up on him driving back to the spot to get this money out of my suitcase to get this party started right.

RIDING INTO A DEATH TRAP

It didn't take me long to get to the spot as soon as I jumped out of the van. I made sure to put my black backpack on my shoulder so I can put the loot in it. I walked in the door. Fat Poncho and Big Mama Red are sitting on the couch listening to music all cuddled up. Fat Poncho asked, "what's up Lex?"

"Well, I'm working on something so we can own this joint."

"Oh yeah like what?"

"Well, I don't have that much time to explain everything, but Rock's girl Tia and her mother got kidnapped." I just got a tracker to help find them and for me doing that we get to keep this join. *I just love the look on both their faces after I said that. That's good but you better hope he doesn't double cross you after you finish the work.*

Big Mama Red shouted, "I told you not to get mixed up in that bull shit, Lex. He's trying to use you up girl." Everybody knows if you cross me, you'll be dead before sundown. They both start laughing as I dash upstairs to my room. I go inside, and Vita is not in there. I get my bag under the bed. I pull it out and set it on top of the bed thinking of all the bullshit I have to do to get the things I want to have. I opened it up. I take out 15 bands. I counted it to make sure it's right and I see what I have left. I quickly tossed the loot in my trusty black backpack. I pulled out a little more coke out of one ounce and it is low now, but I still have another one on deck. I rolled up a ten-dollar bill and started snorting some while I was putting some of it in the zip lock bag. I wiped some of the coke dust off my nose feeling the drip from the blow. I put a lot of the white powder in a zip lock bag and put it in my pocketbook. I get my other pistol loaded with the clips I put in my pocketbook.

I have the one with the silencer in my pocketbook and the other Glock pistol I stick it in the back of my jeans. And off I go back down out the door with my backpack on my shoulder. I came downstairs and walking out of the gym is Vita staring me down. I don't pay him any mine I walked to the back of the gym where we have all the machine guns in green military trunks. Vita is looking me up and down I just when towards the back of the gym and got me a machine gun an MP-5 and four clips. I put the four clips in my pocketbook, and I carry the machine gun in my hand as I'm walking out towards the front door. I just looked Vita up and down back rolling my eyes not saying a word and I kept walking towards the front door real cool like. I waved at Fat Poncho and Big Mama Red, both snickering. I went out the door and I didn't look back jumping in the van. I toss my machine gun on the seat next to me along with my pocketbook burning rubber out of there.

I looked at my watch I'm making good time, but I want to get their early just in case some other shit jumps off *never trust any nigga in this crazy ass game.* I drive to Broad & Sedgley as soon as I'm three blocks away a truck came speeding up on me superfast from out of nowhere hitting the side of my van on the driver side **Blam!** The van just moved a little I'm laughing my ass off they didn't know this motherfucker is bullet proof and it so fucking heavy.

I looked at this big GMC truck all fucked up and the whole front hood was smashed in. I jumped out whipping my Glock from the back of my jeans getting in my gun stance. I'm taking aim looking up at them. Both these mask niggas in the smashed-up truck are knocked the fuck out from the impact with smoke shooting out the fucking engine. **Kapacka! Kapacka! Kapacka! Kapacka!** I shot both of them ass hole's giving them two slugs each two in the head and two in the chest. It was like shooting fish in a fucking barrel. I went back to my van digging in my bag getting my rubber gloves in the side pouch super-fast, I slipped them on while still looking around. I ran over to the smashed-up truck with the two men I just smoked. I looked around to make sure there was nobody around looking. I open the door of the truck I reach in with their bodies slumped over all bloody. I pulled down their mask looking at them with a quick glance at them. I see they had beards. *Now I know who tried to set me up* I quickly put my gun in the back of my jeans, and I jetted back to my van and drove up to the corner.

I saw this tall dark skin dude with a beard standing there. I pulled over, rolling the window down and asked, "you work for Pat Black?"

He answered, "Yeah baby she didn't tell me you were so fine, doe!"

"Yeah, whatever nigga where you parked at?He points.

"I'm over there you got the money?"

"Yeah, you got something to put this shit in."

"Yeah, I have something in the car."

"Okay, I jumped out with my black backpack on my shoulder while I'm walking with him."

I'm looking around. I asked, "where is the other dude the tracker?"

"He's in the car, come on."

I walked across the street with him where he's parked, he jumped in his whip getting this black plastic bag. I had him five stacks. He put them in the bag while this big muscle dude sitting next to him asked, "where is mine at?"

"What's Your name again?"

"My name is Shank bitch!"

They both started laughing, "well Shank after you get the job done then I give you your fucking money and by the way I'm a psycho bitch not just some random bitch that's out here okay."

He jumped out the car and smirked, "alright Miss psycho bitch let's get started with this job so I can get paid."

"Come on." I waved my hand, but at the same time I pulled my pistol out with my other hand mashing it up to Malika head, "you're lucky you have to give that loot to Patty or I would have blown your fucking brains out, nigga! I know you set me up with them niggas down the street I killed both of them."

His eyes told it all without saying a word. I raised my eyebrow and frowned, "this is not over!"

He smirks rolling up the window and he pulls off. *This nigga really doesn't know me he's like all the rest of these young punk ass motherfuckers who think they can get over on everybody.* As we were walking across the street to my van.

"I would have killed him if he set me up!" Shank growled.

"I should have done it, but I don't burn bridges after this is done, I'm going to kill him don't you worry."

I see the cops speeding past with their lights flashing. They must have found those two assholes I had to take care of. We reached where my van is parked, and I jumped in, "I'm taking you to Rock spot, so you can get to work."

I pull off swiftly with the music blasting, he just nodding his head to the hot hard beat not saying a word. We pull up in front of Rock place now he asked, "before we go in who are the people that got snatched?"

"The dude named Rock, his girl Tia and her mother Miss Glow got them last night."

"Do you know where?"

"No, I don't. I have to ask him."

"Did he say who did it?"

"Yeah, the TTS ass hole niggas.We had a run in with them last week, but Kenyatta X and his peoples took care of them right quick."

"I know them, thanks now I know where to start and I know just where they hang out at."

"While we were coming here some people following you, they look like spooks (Spies) to me."

"Are you sure about that Shank?"

I've been in this game for a very long-time, sister. I know spooks when I see them.I saw them checking us out as soon as I linked up with you. When Pat Black told me about you I didn't believe her when she said you were down with the 24th street cartel and AK's CIA hook up but they got their eyes on you honey for sure."

"What do they look like? "

"The reason I ask is when I was in New York I saw this older white dude and this woman checking me out at the hotel."

"Well, I saw two white men, one young and one older and this white woman."

We both got out of the van heading towards Rocks front door. Now I see he has people posted outside. I know the two guys he has outside Yak and Zig Zag walking up in front of us. As soon as they saw me, they waved, "she's cool! "

Zig Zag blurted out, "but who is this Lex? It's the tracker his name is Shank they just looked him up and down saying go head in pointing at the door."

We walked in the door and Rock came walking up with Midnight, Tone and Bee- Bee.

"This is Stacks. He needs to know something from you so he can get started."

"Alright, need for y'all to step into my office."

We all go downstairs, we all sit down at the table as Stacks, uttering, "where did they grab your girl and her mother?"

"At her mother's apartment in center city on Pine Street."

"I need you to give me a good running car and a bottle of Jack Daniel's."

"Is that it?"

"Just give me the address of the apartment on Pine Street."

"You sure you're not going to need any of my men to help you?"

"Yeah, after I find out where they have her, then I need all of your men with every gun you got."

Rock looks over to Bee-Bee go get him the car he needs. Bee- Bee gets up from the table with a real serious look on his grill going upstairs and out the door. Rock pointed and yelled, "Midnight go over to the bar over there and give him that bottle of Jack. Are you sure that's all you need man?

"Yeah, just give me your number when I find them, I'll call you."

Midnight handed him the bottle of Jack and spoke, "here you go brother."

Rock gives him his phone number, spitting it fast and Stacks puts the number in his phone. While we were waiting for Bee-Bee to come back with the car I pulled out my zip lock bag of coke. I dump some out on the table and roll up a twenty-dollar bill I made about four lines on top of the table. I snort two of the lines and I hand the rolled up twenty to Rock sitting next to me. He snorted the other two lines of the white powder. He hands me back my twenty-dollar bill back smiling giggling, "that some some good shit, Lex."

I barked, "yeah, it is the fucking best my nigga."

Shanks' eyes widened and he touched his nose, "I'm down for some nose candy over here until he comes back."

I looked up at him and nodded my head, "okay I pour a little more of the blow on top of the table in lumps and clumps. I hand him the twenty-dollar bill while he is shuffling it with one of his business cards he whipped out. He's shuffling the white powder all fancy with a lot of speed as well I can tell this was not his first rodeo Shank started snorting the coke off the table like a fucking Hoover vacuum cleaner. Soon as he was done, he put his head back , "wow y'all was not bull shitting about that where you get that from?"

"From a friend of mine in New York." Bee- Bee came back downstairs handing the keys to Stacks."

" It's a dark blue Chevy Truck parked near the corner on the right-hand side of the street."

Okay he stood up speaking loudly I'll call y'all when I find out where there at, he bumps fist with me, and Rock saying don't worry I'll find them brother. *When he looked up at Rock real deep letting him know everything was going to be alright. That was the first time I ever saw Rock looking nervous about something and I don't blame him.*

Then Shank looked over at me, "have that money ready after I find them and you and me, need to sit down and talk about your little hook up." We both started laughing as he gave me his phone number and I gave him mine after that he went up the steps.

Rock shouts to me, "what the fuck is he talking about?"

"Nothing, just some bullshit that's all. Do you think he's going to find,Lex? *"With a deep worry look on his face.*

"Well, the person who told me about him said he is one the best in the world and we're going to find out if it's true."

Rock said, " I just don't like sitting around here, just waiting around makes me feel helpless or something."

"Well, that's what we have to do brother. I have a good feeling about this dude. He's going to get the job done, we just have to be ready after he finds them."

We sat around talking shit about back in the days when I was selling dope for the gang but time seam, like it was going so fucking slow too. When he rolled out the door it was 11:30 A.M. We sat around and each time somebody's phone started ringing we were all jumpy then at 5: 15 P.M. Shanks called Rock with excitement in his voice , "he found them." He started sending pictures of his girl Tia and Miss Glow to prove to him that he really found them. Rock is showing them to me and the others then he calls me while I'm looking at the pictures.

"Lex, they have them in an old warehouse in North Philly on 3rd street. We are going to need about ten men. They have eight men watching them, two men on the left, two men on the right and two men in the back, some more men inside."

I uttered, "all right you stay there just in case they move them we are on the way."

I looked up at Rock and blurted out, "you are going to need about 12 good hard-core men for this shit." "Okay, I'm going to coach this shit and you're going to be my quarterback taking it down the field in the last 10 seconds of the game."

Tone screamed at the top of his lungs, "man, I don't take orders from no bitch!"

Rock said, "you will today, or I'll take care of your ass right here and now!"

He pulls out his gun holding it by his side looking him right in his eyes.

"Lex is the best at what she does motherfucker so listen up really good!"

Midnight looked up at Rock and said, "look, why don't we go upstairs."

"So, we can tell the rest of these niggas all at the same time Lex."

"Sounds good to me so they can break up the little tension between Rock and Tone."

We all go upstairs Rock makes the rest of the guys that have been hanging around talking shit all day, smoking and drinking now it's time to put in some work. We had to work fast before they made another call giving him his instructions on where they wanted to drop the money off. Rock quickly gathers everybody up, making them come into the large living room.

Rock shouted, "Everybody listen up! We have a location where my people are at, we have to move quickly on this shit! Lanie, Big Luke, Brick Head are the guns Devan you drive and keep your eyes open. Yak you drive Tone and Midnight, Jay Flow ya'll the guns. Bee- Bee you drive Zig Zag Kevey and Frank Snow y'all the guns. When we get there me and Lex is going to tell y'all what sides to hit in this warehouse so keep your lines open don't be fucking around on your phone. Doo- Bee you are linking up with me and Lex Jadon you stay here, and hold shit, down for me okay let's move out!"

Everybody is quickly heading towards the front door. I let Doo-Bee drive the van I sat in the passenger side with my MP-5 loading in the clip Rock is in the cargo area with his AR-15.

It doesn't take us long to get to where all near 3rd & Erie hanging back, so we don't get spotted in the area. From 3rd street to 2nd street, it's a large abandoned warehouse and all around it is a dirty ass car scrap yard parked near the scrap yard getting ready to move in.

We all are on the back-street shit hole not too far from the warehouse, sweating bullets ready to rush in not knowing how many people are inside.

I call Shank he picks up on the first ring,

"yo I see y'all here. Where the fuck is you at?"

" I'm in the scrap yard waiting on y'all fuck that. So, you are going to help us do this shit then."

"Oh, hell yes, I want to make sure I get my ten big ones. I can't get it if your fucking dead."

"You're a funny guy just keep your eyes open, and I'll show you how I work nigga."

Stacks hangs up laughing. I barked, "okay, made the conference call, so everybody knows what to do, Rock."

"You better know it."

Rock pulls out his phone hitting a conference call and all his men's phones ring at the same time. Each one of them started picking it up.

Rock shouted, "okay call it, Lex!"

I announced, "okay Lanie, and his crew take left Tone you, your crew take the right now. Zig Zag and his boys take the back. Now we're going straight up the middle."

Rock looked at me like I was crazy or something, he raised his eyebrow and folded his arms. I just winked at him saying, "we're all going on three in five minutes."

I waved my hand smiling for Rock to hang up the phone.

"Are you fucking nuts bitch? What's with this straight up the middle shit!"

"Yo, Rock my van is bullet proof okay they will never know what fucking hit them."

He gave a small smile and mumbled, "I love the way you think you're a crazy bitch!"

"Now you did say you wanted me to quarterback this shit right."

"Yeah, I did say that shit."

"Well, you're Bill Belichick and I'll be Randall Cunningham!"

"Don't you mean Tom Brady nigga."

"Tom Brady is the GOAT but I'm an Eagles fan until the day I die. If I'm dying today, I'll be Randall leaping over mother-fucker's head driving into the end zone!"

"This is my fantasy play book nigga just go with it"! Rock snicker checking his machine gun.

Rock yelled, "all right let's do this like Brutus!"

Rock Pulls out his phone making the call they all started picking up Rock calls it off One two three!

Doo- Bee steps on the gas heading straight towards the large steel gray door of the old warehouse picking up more speed. **Kadoom!** He crashes right through the fucking door like they were made from tin flying up in the fucking air. Soon as I leaped out the van, I'm in my gun stance and all hell is breaking out all around me but I'm spitting bullets like crazy staying focus **Kapckatataka!** I'm staying low I hit the first three niggas they went down fast screaming before they hit the ground dead. Gawd damn it's more people in here then I thought it was. Then I'm on a fucking roll picking motherfucker's off left and right. **Kapackata tat tat tacka!** five more men popped up and I'm mowing their ass down like grass with Rock right by my side getting his shit off but he's looking around for his girl Tia and her mom.

I'm doing the same thing looking up so I can see where Tia and Miss Glow are at and I can see Big Luke, Lanie and Brick Head finish off four more people gunning their ass down. Everything is moving fast and furious all around us. *I know there's no room to make any mistakes or it will be your last one for real.* I can see them yet with all the noise of gunshots and machine gun fire going on all around us with the loud sounds of people dying and yelling. I'm looking from left to right to see if I see any more men popping up out on me and this place is fucking junky and foul. With all kinds of shit everywhere old cars are big pieces of metal. So, you would never know where somebody would jump out on your ass and the smell is bad with all the garbage everywhere in this Dall lit funky ass joint the stench reminds me of death.

I'm not scared to die but this is one place you don't want to die at because it already looks like hell from out of your apocalypse nightmares for real doe. I look on my right and Rock is getting busy with Tone, Midnight, Jay Flow and Zig Zag, Kevey and Frank Snow rushing in from the back helping them out. All I see is muzzle flash and blood flying up in the air as soon as five more motherfuckers pop up on us out of nowhere.

Everything gets quiet and walking up is Lanie, Big Luke, Brick Head and Jay Flow. I waved at them holding my machine gun then Midnight and Tone came walking up holding their machine gun waving back at us. We quickly see that we're all alright Rock yelling out keep looking around for my girl and her mom y'all were all about to spread out and start looking around. All I can see is dead twisted metal and bodies in pools of blood along with garbage all over this fucking place. Zig Zag came running up screaming back here! Me, Rock and Lanie run back there as Frank Snow and Kevey quickly cut the duct tape off their wrists.

Tia and Miss Glow is huffing puffing and crying once they seen us. *Frist thing that pops in my mind is this could be a fucking trap to get us out in the open I just got that feeling.* I shouted out let's get the fuck out of here before some more of them is around in this fucking death trap when they took the duct tape from Tia's mouth, she yelled out up there look out! Soon as she said that **Baaarrrtttta! Baaarrrtttat! Baaarrrtttta! Baaarrrtttta!**

Shots are coming from up top from the metal tear about ten feet away from us. Rock dives on top of his girl Tia and pulling her mother Miss Glow down to the ground. It's raining fucking bullets hitting Kevey, Frank Snow and Jay Flow ripping them the fuck open with blood flying everywhere. I'm ducking behind this big piece of twisted rusty metal getting all the way down flat with Midnight.

He's right beside me and the smell is really getting to me now that I'm on the floor in this shit. I looked up at Midnight and I pointed to where the bullets were coming from. I hear these loud banging sounds crashing into shit coming towards us. I can hear this loud skidding sound from tires getting closer and closer. I looked up and I can see debris in front of us moving and flying in the air.

Me and Midnight quickly get out the way and just missing us we looked up and its Doo- Bee rolling the window down yelling let's get the fuck out of here! I jumped up to my feet helping Midnight up then we both went over and got Rock his girl Tia and Miss Glow. I quickly open the sliding doors on the van pushing everybody in. Midnight, Rock, Tia and Miss Glow as soon as I pushed her in. *My fucking heart is racing fast hoping we can get out this funky ass place alive and if I'm going to die I damn sure don't want it to be the fuck in here!* **Baaaarrrtttta tat tat tat! Baaarrttta takacka!** I just jump behind the van ducking and I'm getting low shooting back at them **Kapackataca!** Then I can see Lanie is hurt but he's still alive on the right penned down along with Big Luke and Brick Head hiding behind some twisted up old car and some scrap metal. I'm giving them the signal where the shooters are at up above them. I started counting in silence one two three!

I jumped a little from behind the van and started shooting **Kapackatakat!** Alone with Doo- Bee shooting upward from out the window of the van. Then I see the dude Stacks running up with a machine gun shooting up at the men on top of the iron tear, then he disappears behind some scrap metal after he killed about four of them. Then I can see him popping out giving it to them, keeping them busy shooting at them ducking and diving out the way shooting back at him. I'm waving for them to run and shooting at the same time helping Stacks out yelling at Lanie Brick Head and Big Luke to come on you can make it hurry the fuck up!

Big Luke is helping Lanie while Brick Head is shooting upward to cover them, and they all make it to the van jumping in **Doom!** I quickly ran towards the passenger side door shooting back at them using the door as a shield I jumped in closing the door super-fast yelling at Doo- Bee take the fuck off nigga now! He backs up swiftly hitting this big piece of metal **Kadoom!** He's laughing shouting man this thing is like a fucking tank just hole on y'all were getting out of here right about now! He pulls off hitting shit in front of him moving it right out his way as you can hear the bullets hitting the van. It sounds like rocks and pebbles hitting the top and sides of the van. *All of our hearts are racing fast hoping we get the fuck out of this shit hole alive!* Doo- Bee knocking shit out his way flooring it.

He crashed right out the side doors **Kablang!** And he picked up more speed as we crashed out that fucking warehouse. He looked over at me smiling, uttering, "if you don't have a name for this motherfucker, I'm calling it the beast!"

I started laughing, replying with a smile, "well, that's her name for here on out now!"

We drove back to the crib as soon as we pulled up and before we could get out.I stepped out of the van as all the others were quickly going into the house. The dude Shanks came walking up to me, "you're just the person I wanted to see."

I bump fist with him and said, "I saw you shooting, you killed a lot of them ass holes and you kept their ass busy too thanks."

LI know it was fucking hairy in that motherfucker. I told you I was going to help y'all out not get killed."

We both started laughing.

"Shanks, let me get my backpack so I can pay you brother. Thank you so much!"

I get my black backpack out of the van. I quickly get my bag, I close the door and I hit the remote *Boo-Beep* locking it up. I looked at the van well for what I could see with it being dark outside now it had a few dens in it, but Doo- Bee was right this motherfucker is a beast. I walked with Stacks to the house. Jadon is standing in the doorway bumping fist with me and Stacks with a big smile on his light brown grill mumbling loud nice work.

We were on our way downstairs so I can pay the man when Tia walked up standing in front of us before we can get down to the basement. She came up hugging me like we were old fucking friends or something talking nicely thank you so much, girl I didn't know what we would have done without you.

I played it off with Rock and her mother standing there replying with my ghetto Swag. A friend of Rock's is a friend of mine. We both started giggling along with the others in the kitchen area right where the basement door is at. She bumps fist with Stacks telling him thank you to brother, your good man to have around. He just nods his head without saying a word with a little smile.

Then her mother Miss Glow lowered her eyes and said, "I would like to thank both of y'all for saving us."

I said I know Rock would have done the same thing Mom. We both waved and quickly went downstairs. We both sat at the table. I set my backpack on top of the table and unzipped my bag. I started pulling out the bands, stacking it up on top of the table as he counted them and putting the money into his dirty brown backpack bag, he had with him. After he was done, he barked out with a smile.

"It's all here, honey thanks if you need me again just give me a call you have my number. I can always use a good tracker in the line of work I'm in. Now tell me Lex what line of work are you into drugs, bank robbing, murder for higher you tell me shit you damn near done them all."

We both started laughing and I shouted out with laughter now you can add kidnapping recovery to my resume. We both started snickering he replied, "let me get another hit of some that good ass coke before I split."

"Sure, thing but you have to do something for me doe. Yeah, and what's that you almost got me killed today as it is already Lex. I pulled the zip lock bag of coke out of my pocketbook saying I need for you to find that young boy who set me up today. He looked at me, uttering man Pat Black is not going to like that shit. *I dump out the coke on top of the table looking up at him. I pull out a card from my bag chopping up the white powder.*

"Look, I don't have to try to talk you into this shit. You know damn well you would kill him too you said it yourself early today, nigga."

I'm shuffling the coke on top of the table. I know he's going to help me but I want him to make up his own mind about it,doe. He nodded his head, "your right I would kill him too okay this is between you and me right. He snorted the coke off the table after he was done.

Stacks cuts in and announces, "I'll call you and let you know right where he's at a little later on, okay. "

He's looked up at me with a smirk on his dark chisel grill. But you have to give me some more of this blow. It's good. "Okay you find him, and I give you some more, a whole zip up bag full."

"Can you give it to me now."

"Oh no nigga you should know how I work by now I didn't give you the loot until you found Rock girl and her mother."

"Yeah, but we can trust one another now."

"Yeah, that's true but let me get something to eat, wash up and get that funky ass warehouse stench off of me. It's all up in my nose now and I can't get that smell out of it."

He chuckled, "yeah, you right about that shit man that place stank something awful. "

"And when you find him, it won't be a hard job and you get all the blow you want to snort, and you can go on to your next job."

"Okay, I'll call you after I find him. We bump fist I stood up getting my bag. He did the same and we both went upstairs.

Rock came down real fast talking to Shanks.

"Thank you, man, after I drop off this loot to my plug. I'll have some more money for you helping us out."

"I appreciate everything you have done for us for real."

Shanks replied, "okay now don't say you're going to hook me up with something and don't do that shit now."

"Oh no, I'm a man of my word man you can ask Lex that shit right."

"Yeah, he's a man of his word Stacks now can we get the fuck out of here so I can get that smell of that fucking place off me, please!"

We all started laughing as Rock quickly went up the steps to his peoples sitting down in the kitchen smoking, drinking and talking loud as hell. Me and Shanks came up behind him and were both about to walk past all of them gathering up talking shit about the long deadly adventure they had today.

Miss Glow asked us to stay for dinner and all that shit I told her nicely that I had to go. I wave at my new bestie Tia as Jadon walks me and Shanks to the door. As we were walking to the door Tone, Big Luke, Brick Head, and Lanie and some woman I don't know fixing him up are in the front room thanking us.

Tone stood up from off the couch and. Rock shouted, "you can keep the truck."

Shanks replied quickly, "tell him I said thank you. I have to go if he needs anything else he got my number."

We both waved as he walked out the door. I walked to the van while he went to his whip. Rock just gave him the 2010 Chevy. I waved goodbye and I took off back to the crib. And I know just who name I'm going to put the warehouse in my uncle Big Hank he's the only family member who have not try to fuck me over the years.

I make it back just in time to take a shower get something to eat and for Kenyatta X and his people to go over the plan again I know what I have to do but it's good to have it drilled in your brain. One of the good things I learned from the gang is knowing your job so good you can do it with your fucking eyes close. This time when they came it was just three of them Kenyatta X, Amir and Big Duba that fine ass Kahseam was not there. I was still focused on the job at hand we all are doing the job on Tuesday. We have two more days, and I can't wait to do this shit. Vita had his eyes on me the whole time at the meeting. I do not even look at his sorry ass. When Kenyatta was done talking to us, I walked them to the door he said to me real low I need to holla at you right quick. Big Duba and Amir kept walking to the truck soon as they got in.

He said to me, "I heard what happened. That was brave of what you did."

"Well, I do what I do, you know what I mean. No that was above and beyond the call of duty Ma I'm glad you on my team."

He bumps fist with me, and he quickly walked to the truck getting behind the wheel and he took off.

I went back in the house, everybody was drinking and getting high. I joined in having a good time talking with Moon, Stump, Jitta, Fat Poncho and Big Mama Red but I still did not have anything to say to Vita. *Even after we went to bed, I slept on the red crushed velvet Chaz lounge in the room Vita is still downstairs with the others still getting high.*

SOME REAL FAST PAY
BACK ON THAT ASS.

It's 1:30 P.M. When the phone rings loud waking me up, I get the phone right quick. I'm all groggy looking at the number and I don't know it and I recognize the voice of Shanks.

"Yo, your boy is at the Clock Bar on Germantown Avenue having a good time. You better come before the bar closes and you can catch his ass really good too."

I yelled, "I'm on my way."

I quickly put my clothes on swiftly and I got both my guns. I put a silencer on my gun I keep in the back of my jeans. I go in my suitcase taking out some more coke out the ounce of coke I got left putting it in a zip lock bag for Stacks I stick that in my pocketbook real fast. I made sure I had extra clips and my black backpack when I went downstairs. That led to the gym. I heard the music and happy voices in the lounge area in the other room not too far.

While I go get reloaded to get busy on somebody's ass tonight. Pat Black just have to be mad at me because this nigga has to die! I pulled out six hand grenades out of the green trunks where we keep machine guns and hand grenades. I packed up what I needed in my backpack and walked in the other room past them.

I see Stump, Jitta, Moon and Vita are still up with some female company of three women at the bar in the lounge area. I hear the soft music and chatter and giggles from all of them. I wave at all of them walking by and some of them wave back at me but not stopping what they were doing having a good time. None of them played me any mind their all into each other smoking weed snorting coke and drinking liquor. Dancing slowly to the hot beat with the lights down low. *Shit I'm not mad at them if Vita was not such an ass hole, I just might be down there with them having a good time as well or up in my room getting my brains fucked out all night. But no, I'm on some get back shit now because I'm a person of fucking principal don't cross me, or I will get you back.* I quickly when out the door jumping in the van putting my backpack on the passenger seat beside me ready to go and fuck something up. It only took me 15 minutes to get there, but I had a hell of a time looking for a parking spot. I got lucky my second time around the block. I quickly got one on the same side of the bar but a little down the street but I'm good. I won't have too far to go if I have to run to it.

I walked up the street and it a lot of young people standing around outside of the bar then looked up and see Stacks waving towards me to follow him. I walked with him, and he pointed, "see, he's over there in the middle of the bar with two women and five dudes is with him too."

I just winked at him, "I got it from here."

I got closer to him while we're in this crowd of people with the loud music and smoky dim red lights inside the bar. I reached in my pocketbook I quickly hand him the zip lock bag of coke uttering low thanks you can roll if you want to. He quickly sticks it down the front of his pants and mumbles, "Oh, I'm not going to miss this for the world." He smirked.

I inch up closer to him and then I make my move I acted like one of them dumb drunk broads who's happy to see a nigga. Ego will fall right into place like most good-looking motherfuckers. I giggled and then shouted over the loud music, "oh Malika, I have not seen you in a long-time baby." I jumped up to hug him. He hugged me back softly with a big smile on his dark grill opening his arms. I got my hand on the trigger of my pistol inside of my pocketbook with the silencer **Pooouuufff! Pooouuufff! Pooouuufff!** I put three slugs in his chest, and he fell to the floor. I quickly walked away as his boys to see what happened to him sliding down to the floor as I quickly side-stepped them. And walked towards the front door working my way through the crowd walking fast but not too fast to be noticed. Soon as I got to the front door ready to walk out, I heard a woman screaming and a few men yelling, "hey, stop that bitch right there!"

Shanks is right behind me. I get outside the door of the Clock Bar, but I don't run. I lean on the car nice and cool like. I lean up on the car directly parked in front of the bar and I pull out my pistol real smooth with the silencer on it out of my pocketbook and I hold it up taking aim. **Pooouuufff! Pooouuufff! Pooouuufff! Pooouuufff! Pooouuufff! Pooouuufff!** I hit the first four niggas out the five of them running out the bar yelling at me like they were going to do something. I'm hitting them in the head and chest. Only one nigga backed up after seeing his boys hitting the ground fast and hard and blood flying in the air. A lot of the people out there started running out of the way. I just started walking fast up the street with Shanks laughing his ass off talking with laughter.

"Damn, them niggas walked right into it. Lex they never saw it coming to them."

"I know I'm good." I looked *up and smiled, still giggling.* I made it to my van hitting my remote and I asked, "you are coming with me.?"

I'm looking him right into his eyes. He knows that look if he doesn't he must have never got any pussy before then.

"No, I'll holla at you later. I have a hot date believe it or not that's why I wanted some of this good ass coke you had thanks baby girl you be careful."

I yelled back with my wicked ass smile, "you don't know what the fuck you're missing over here nigga! Damn, I'm thinking you was going to jump inside of this van and fuck me real good then eat my pussy out because I'm nice andwet now after I smoke these niggas!"

"If I knew that I would not have somebody waiting for me Ma, your one bad bitch doe watch, your ass with these mother-fuckers!"

"I'm not worry about these lightweights want a be gangster niggas! Those punk ass niggas can't fuck with me I'm the real deal."

"You're right about that shit Lex I'll talk to you later. one!"I jumped behind the wheel and I took off down the block. I drove right past the bar looking over and all I saw was nosey people jumping up and down in chaos standing around looking to see what happened. I drove right past the bar down the street, and I called Pat Black up. The phone rings about four times and she picks up, "look, your boy Malika is dead. He tried to set me up when I dropped that money off to you."

Yeah, I know Shanks told me about it, he told him not to do it and he did it anyway. Well, as you know I don't let nobody cross me, so I hope you're not mad at me."

"Just now I talked to him about it, and I told him to watch his ass. He said he was not worried about you, and I told him he doesn't know you like I do and that the way it goes in the game I tried to tell him."

"Well, I smoked him and a few of his homeboys too and I told him before he pulled off when I gave him the money for you. He was lucky that I didn't kill him then because you wanted your money."

"I know he told me that too, but you know how young guys are, they think they know everything. So, you and me, are good for real than Patty?"

"Yeah, it's not your fault you told him, and I told him myself so you and I are good and if you need anything as a way just give me a call okay Lex. **Moja** *One!*"

"Moja!"

I went back to the crib and arrived faster than I rolled out. To kill that nigga on some, get back on that ass. I guess some niggas have to learn the hard way.

Now I'm thinking I'll make up with Vita and me and him can get back to fucking each other like crazy and I can cum three or four times and get high. But as soon as I came in the door even with the lights down low, I saw Vita on the couch with his father Jitta gangbanging one of their hoes they had in the spot. I know his tattoos from anywhere. I walked past them not saying a word. I'm not mad at him he just let me off the hook for fucking with him anymore and he knew I'll see him.

I go up on the third floor and taking all my shit up their as well.I'll just talk to him in the morning about it and I can go and do my fucking thing. Now I'm up in the third-floor lounge having a little party by myself until I fall asleep about 4 in the morning.

The next morning, I laid around and when I came downstairs everybody is thinking it was going to be fireworks jumping off because I see Vita and his father fucking them ho's they had last night. I just got my food Big Mama made Fish and grits. I sat with Vita and he's kind of fucking surprised.

I just talked to him nice and smooth. We had fun and were all still family with the gang. We have this job that is coming up and he can do his thing and I'll do mine. It was smooth like Fat Poncho was holding his breath thinking that was going to break up the gang right before the big job. But he saw we talked it out and it was all good.

After we ate , Big Mama Red went up to the third-floor lounge to talk.

She began to speak, "I knew you were not going to be mad you can get any man you want to get. Niggas,think they have the only Dick in town some time.

I smiled, "girl, I have my eye on that fine ass nigga Kahseam that's down with Kenyatta X crew."

"Yeah, that nigga is fine. Shit, if Poncho fuck up on me, I'll get with that Big Hunk of a man Duba he can handle all this shit right here girl and he'll love it." "Look, I had to kill a few niggas who tried to set me up when I went to help Rock out."

"Girl, I told you not to get into that shit you can't trust nobody nowadays. So,you get them papers from Rock Yet?"

Yeah, I have the papers, but I have to get the papers changed over tomorrow."

"Make sure you right on top of his ass too I don't trust that nigga for real you when and saved his girl and her mother make him give you some money too fuck that."

"No, this place is enough for right now. I'm going to have him selling product for me right after that. So, I'm slow walking his ass again. "

"What do you mean Lex?"

"You didn't know I had that nigga selling drugs for me when I was down with the 24th street cartel girl."

"Wow, I didn't know that shit."

"Lex the more I find out about you the more I find out how much of a boss bitch you are."

"Shit, before I jump ship on the gang, I use to run half this fucking city girl no bull shit. I believe you after I seen this place."

"So, you know what name you're going to put this place in?"

"Yeah, my uncle Hank. I told him to sell my place after I jump ship with the gang, and he gave me every fucking dime back too. But as you know I blew it all partying my ass off. I never do that shit again. This time I'm going to build up and keep shit this time around."

"Well, you are a little wiser this time around you know what else you want to get after you get this joint."

"Yeah, I'm going to show it to you next week after we get this job done but I'm so glad you put your foot down and came here with us. You are like my big sister."

"Aaaawww girl, I dig the shit out you too and your better woman then me. I would have fucked that nigga up if I see him fucking some strange ho and me and him are still fucking!"

We both started laughing. "Me and Big Mama Red have gotten tight over the time we've been together in this place but every time I get close to somebody something fucked up happens.

I'm hoping this time nothing crazy happens between us and I really don't trust Pat Black ass. After I had to smoke her little boy toy for trying to fuck me over. The next morning when I got up and got myself together early to make sure Rock kept his word. About changing the names of this place. I got washed and dressed. I double check my guns and I'm out the door I got to Rock house quick. When I came up to the door, I was thinking he might have got out of town or some shit on me then I have to track him down and kill his ass. I'm knocking really hard on the door and Tia opens the door.

"Hey what's up Lex please come on in. Rock is upstairs getting dressed. Girl, have a seat until he comes down."

Tia sits next to me. "I'm glad you are here so I can thank you face to face. I was wrong about you". "So, what were you wrong about? I was thinking you were a real selfish wild bitch who will kill anybody without a care."

"Well, you got it half wrong Rock is family and anybody that's family nobody is going to fuck with him or anybody he cares about. But about me being a wild bitch. No, I'm a psycho bitch and nobody better not fuck with me or my family, you dig."

We both started laughing. "I'm having a party next week at the club and I'd love it if you would come, Lex."

"Okay let me think about it, girl." I'm not too much into parties with people who are civilian types."

"I don't know what you mean by civilian types." *Whatfucked me up was she had a real puzzled look on her face like she doesn't know what I'm talking about.*

"Look I'm going to say this and not to seem too rude, but I'll let Rock tell you what I mean by a civilian because your man is affiliated like me. That's all I'm going to say right now."

"What you mean affiliated like a gang get the fuck out of here."

"Look, just go talk to Rock before I say too much okay. "

"I know he sells drugs, but he's not down with no type of fucking gang his friends be here to help him out with things that's all. "

Right at that time Rock is coming down the steps hearing what we're talking about. Tia sees Rock, she starts yelling, "will you tell your girl over here that we are not affiliated like she says we are!"

Rock looked at her then he looked at me not wanting to say anything.

Rock uttered, "Lex, I will be with you in a few please let me talk to her right quick."

Tia barked," no, I want you to say that shit right here in front of her. I want her to know that were not a fucking drug gang!"

Tone in the other room along with Big Luke looking at me then looking at Rock. He looked at her, "baby, I wanted to talk to you alone as he came up holding her hands. She pushed his hands down yelling like a little kid or something, "what you want to tell me say it in front of her."

I just looked up talking loudly. "I'll be in my van when you're ready to roll."

Tia is going off yelling, "no, you're not going anywhere I want him to say it right now!"

Rock whispered, "baby, she right we're affiliated my crew is called NPH North Philly Hustlers. I was down with the 24th street cartel before I went on my own when AK and Uzi- Boy gave me my blessing to go on my own with my crew. I'm still affiliated with the 24th street cartel as well."

"That's why me and my mother got kidnapped?"

"Yes, because we're making a lot of money and the TTS is another drug gang who hate us because we're making more money than they do, okay."

The doorbell rings Tone quickly walks to the door with his gun in his hand Tia is looking then she's looking at me not wanting to say she's wrong with that look on her face. I'm saying to myself this bitch acts like she's 12 years old or something that the fuck she thinks is going on around here.

But I did not know this bitch was that naïve I didn't know niggas like this was still running around here because of the way I came up super ruff.

Tone opens the door and it's her mother Miss Glow Tia jumps up running off her mouth, "Mom, I didn't know Rock was in a drug gang I'm thinking he just was selling drugs along with his legitimate shit!"

"Girl what the fuck you think what was going on around here with the fucking five condo, three car dealer ships and the four high rise apartments bitch! You better wake up and smell the coffee because the beans are burned."

Everybody started laughing. Miss Glow hugged her, "it is not your fault, baby. I kept you just a little too sheltered baby girl there, not laughing at you. I'm

just a funny bitch when I want to be."*Miss Glow is looking around at us to stop laughing, making Tia feel bad but we're still giggling. That was funny.*

Rock cuts in talking look mom I have to go take care of a few things with Lex and I'll be back baby meet me at the high rise for lunch okay baby. She just nods her head not saying a word.

He walks up to Tone barking, pointing his finger at him to make sure they're cool. "I'll be back alright he bumps fist with him." He waves his hand at me uttering, "come on Lex the lawyer said he'll see us at 10 O'clock and that downtown traffic is a bitch."

He pulls out his phone calling Midnight, "hey bring the car around my nigga. I'm right up the street here." He looks at me talking to Midnight and is going to take us and he'll drop you off here after we're done while I head up to the high-rise cool.

"Yeah, that's cool."

I hear the beeping horn outside. That's him. He quickly kissed his girl, and he kissed his mother-in-law on the cheek uttering, "talk to her for me please."

We rolled out the door with Big Luke walking us outside to the car and he went back inside.

Soon as we got in the back seat of this black Cadillac Escalade.

"Man, you didn't tell that girl what was going on?"

"I did. She just wanted to see shit her own way."

"Maybe I have been in the streets too long that bitch sees everything is going on and she still doesn't know what time it is. That's fucked up."

"Look, I'm thinking her mother is telling her what's going on and as you know I had to keep her in the dark about some shit so it would not hurt her."

"Yeah, you're right about that. So, you're going to marry her?"

I was thinking about it. She keeps bugging the shit out of me about it."

"How long have y'all been together?"

"For about three years now. I met her when I was fucking around on this other bitch I was fucking around with."

"You're not ready to be with one bitch I know your ass nigga."

We both started laughing. We made it to 15th & Walnut Street Midnight drops us off. We quickly walked in the nice and smooth we went up to the front desk and told the guard we were here to see Mister Gold tell him it's Rodney Wilson. He quickly calls after a few minutes the tall white man said go right on up it's the 10th floor. We went on until everything was nice, smooth and very quickly the name I signed on the papers. Hank Jackson soon as we were done, I called him right in the office to let him know what was going on he said to me.

"I hope you keep this place this time you're not getting any younger now."

I replied, "shit, I'm only 26 years old."

"Yeah, too old to be running around without a roof over your fucking head girl."

"Yeah, you're right."

"Look, I need some money so I can fix up these new spots I just brought and for myself too."

"I'll hit you off Friday. Okay I'll see you then Lex and I hung up."

Mister Gold shakes my hand, verbalizing," everything is in good order and here is my card if you need anything at all okay."

I replied, "yes, nice meeting you, Mister Gold."

"Oh, just call me Mike all my friends call me Mike you take care, Lex."

As we were leaving from out of there waiting for Midnight to come to pick us up on the corner of 13th & Walnut Rock.

"See, it's all done and nice and fucking legal too! I told you that I was not going to fuck you over Lex."

"You knew better nigga!" We laughed about it, Midnight came around and picked me up.

"This is where we part, I have to go take care of something else. Midnight is going to drop you off at the spot he opens the door for me. I talked to you later.

Lex and he kissed me on the cheek. I jumped in the truck, and he took off down the street as soon as I got inside of the Cadillac Escalade.

"Lex, I want to thank you for saving my life in that funky ass warehouse."

I replied quickly, "you're welcome, brother. Look if you need anything at all just let me know."

"Okay ,don't say shit like that and when I call on you to do something you bitch up on me, now."

"Oh no, that's not me, Ma just let me know and I'll be there for you."

"How long have you been down with Rock"

 "A couple of years, why do you ask"

"Because I just might be putting my own thing together and I'll need some really good men like yourself."

"Don't worry I would let Rock know about it before I call you in on my thing okay."

He doesn't say anything. I can see he's smiling in the rearview mirror. He turns on some music while we're stuck in traffic. It took us a whole fucking hour to get back to North Philly. Midnight drops me off right in front of my Van. I looked at my watch. It's 12:30 P.M. I just wanted to stop and get me something to eat and go back to the crib and relax. I pulled off. I drove about four blocks when this dark sedan came up and cut me off parking right in front of me, I looked right quickly in my side mirror and it's another dark sedan right behind me. *Looking like one of them cars, Dick Head government agents drive.* An older white dude looks *just like an old CIA spook with his cheap dark suit on and round mirror glasses on.* He jumps out the sedan in front of me yelling, "I need to talk to you Lex step out the van!"

With his hands up in the air waving at me with base in his voice. When I got a good look at him it was that same white dude from the garage in New York. I stick my head out of the window at the same time I reach for a couple of my hand grenades out of my black backpack, and I quickly put them in my pocketbook.

I yelled out, "what the fuck do you want from me?" I need to talk to you Lex, don't worry if I wanted to kill you, I would have done it this morning when you pulled up at your friend Rock's house.

"I don't know you, asshole. How I'm know if you're not going to kill me you, cracker ass motherfucker!"

He's walking closer to me, and I whip out my pistol yelling don't come any closer say what you have to say right their whitey! He puts both his hands up in the air shouting,

"You don't have to call me names, I just need to talk to you, Lex!"

I put my pocketbook on my shoulder, and I open the door of the van very slowly looking in the side mirror and I see this white woman standing by her sedan boxing me in I see she have a gun by her side. I put one of the hand grenades in the back of my jeans. I am making sure it is down there good. So, it didn't move around and pull my black shirt down on my left side before I got out of the van. I have my hand on my pistol with the silencer inside of my pocketbook.

I barked, "you're a pain in the ass. I don't know what you want the fuck from me!"

I acted like I'm going to walk towards him, and I pulled the trigger. **Pooouuufff! Pooouuufff! Pooouuufff!**

The older white man dives out the way of my line of fire. I quickly spin around grabbing the hand grenade I stuck in the back of my jeans pulling the pen at the same time I threw a fastball the hand and the white woman ran screaming. **Kaboom!** I quickly reached and got another one and I through at the sedan in front of my van it hit the roof of the car I hit the deck **Kaboom!** I quickly got to my feet and staying low I jumped in the van the older secret agent man started shooting at me when I closed the door of the van with the bullets just missing me.

I kept the van running, so I quickly back up on the car behind me while the secret agent man is still shooting at me in the van. But the bullets are just bouncing off it. I hit the car in front of me **Kablang!** Then I stepped down on the gas pedal hard flooring it is speeding up **Bang!**

I smashed the shit out of the sedan in front of me and I sped up the street. I'm looking in my side mirror seeing the car on fire smashed in half like a fucking soda can. I'm giggling saying to myself damn I fucked both of them cars up!

I got about four blocks and I made a Sharp right turn, and a cop car came up on me with their lights flashing. I sped up and the cop car gave chase hot on my ass. I made another left turn and out of nowhere another cop car came speeding up on my driving right beside me.

I see the cop pointing at me from the window yelling for me to pull over. I pulled the wheel of the van right quick towards the cop car hitting **Kabang!** Smashing in the side of the cop car. The cop was so pissed off rolling down his window and he started shooting at me. **Pat! Pat! Pat!** Well, he fucked up because I got a little closer to him quickly rolling down my window shooting back at him then I tossed a hand grenade right inside of his patrol car. As soon as he saw it, he jumped out. **Kaboom!**

I sped up just a little more and the cop car behind me still was giving chase and when I got to the corner of another block, I just hit the brakes **Eeeeeeeee! Kadoom!** The cop car behind me smashed right into the back of the van and it was crushed in. I just pulled off fast flooring.

I'm looking in my side mirror seeing the smoke shooting out of the smash cop car laughing my ass off as I made my getaway. I make it back to the crib and I hear all this huffing and puffing echoing in the large space was I'm coming in the door. I walked towards the gym and all the men were all working out. Vita, Moon, Stump, Jitta and even Fat Poncho I waved, and they all waved back as I'm walking. Fat Poncho Asked, "Are you ready for tomorrow?"

JACKING THESE DRUG DEALERS

"Brother, I was born ready. You Know that!"

He laughs and he winks his eye at me. I go towards the steps, and I go upstairs chuckling at these macho men barking. I go up to the third-floor lounge. I turn on some music from the CD deck near the bar *as Jay-Z's I have 99 problems and a bitch ain't one* flows out the speakers. I sat my black backpack on the bar stool. I make myself a drink of gin on the rocks relaxing my mine for a minute. I took off my sneakers, sat on the bed and put my drink down on the nightstand after taking a sip.I pulled out my zip lock bag of coke. I put it on the nightstand. I lit up a Newport and I started dumping out some of the coke on top of the smooth surface getting one of my credit cards chopping up the white powder making lines like it's my second nature. I roll up a ten-dollar bill. I snort two lines fast, rocking my ass with a blast. And I heard a big knock on the door. I looked up and Big Mama Red asked, ` ` Do you want some company?"

I just smiled, waving her inside quickly gigglin. Big Mama came and sat down in the chair near the bed, "shit all of them niggas is working out. I came upstairs to ask you how things go with the paperwork."

"It worked out well. Let me show you."

I got up and I walked over to my backpack pulling out the large envelope and walked back handing it to her.

She pulled out the paper from the envelope all excited she's read through it and asked, "who the fuck is Hank Jackson?"

That's my uncle, he's a property realtor and the only person I can trust with this kind of thing."

"Okay girl, let me get a drink so we can toast to this shit."

She jumps up going to the bar on the left-hand side of the room. "Lex, I don't know how you can drink that gin girl. It's too rough and Manley for me. I have to have some smooth vodka."

She quickly walked back, sitting back down raising her glass.

"I wish you all the luck in the world with your new place girl!" We tapped glasses together and I said, "thank you I worked hard to get this joint!"

As I say under my breath laughing almost getting fucking killed. We both fell out giggling and got high and we laughed and talked for a little while. Then I told her I was going to take a nap because I got up early. Big Mama Red understood smiling, she rolled out and I laid down and I fell asleep. Later, that evening Big Mama Red woke me up so we can all eat together and I'm glad she did. She made Fried Chicken greens, baked macaroni and cheese that was fantastic.

We all had a good time eating together and we were all in good spirits. We laughed and talked with one another like a crime family supposed to do watching each other's backs in this dirty ass line of work were all in. I went to bed early, so I can get ready for our big day with the robbery. The next morning, I get washed and dressed. I'm all excited and ready to go. I came downstairs to eat breakfast before we all rolled out together.

Only thing was that I felt bad for Big Mama Red because broke me. She wished she could have been a part of what we were doing. At 9PM. Jabare, one of Kenyatta X's men, came and picked us up in his big GMC truck. *Kenyatta did tell me that Jabare's truck was also bullet proof, so we had nothing to worry about. Now I'm with team A.*

It's me, Stump, Vita, and Kenyatta X. It takes us about hour to make it to F & Allegheny but were a block away from where our target is at waiting on team B with Indoe driving one of Kenyatta's men and this nigga is fine too. Fat Poncho, Moon, his father Jitta and Big Duba. It's 10 P.M. We all have earpieces, radios and were all on channel two so were all on the same page. Soon as team B came riding up, we all can hear in our earpieces the voice of Kahseam on the lookout. He announced, "the money people are rolling up now, get ready!"

Kenyatta X to Jabare shouted behind the wheel, "go!" Jabare drove fast to Hilton street making a Sharp left turn to the corner house timing it just right when they opened up the gated-up house he drove right up on the pavement.

At the same time, I am behind the wheel with team B is right behind him driving towards the end house on Keim street the little block on the right-hand side. I have on my black mask and my bullet proof vest on gripping my AR-15 machine gun. I jump out first Stump is right by my side with a Bushmaster machine gun. *Something his little hands can handle.* The big gate in front of the house is open so I rush inside the door swiftly and I can see the deep shock on the three men faces ready to shit on themselves with our weapons all in their fucking grills. *Instant death at the blink of an eye.* We bum rushed the crib inside of the large front room pointing machine guns on the men holding three big black duffle bags filled with loot.

By this time Vita and Kenyatta X are in the house holding their machine guns on them as well. I yelled, "hit the ground now two of the men quickly hit the ground fast."

One of the men had a smirk on his face like he was not going to get on the floor. **Rata tat tat tat katacka!** I shot him in both legs and he fell to the floor yelling in deep pain bleeding.

"I told you to get down on the floor motherfucker. I'm not playing with you, give us the money!"

Vita stayed by the door while Kenyatta X came up grabbing one of the bags of money. I picked up a bag and Stump grabbed one.

As soon as I'm about to run towards the door with the bag.

Somebody came running down the steps yelling and shooting at us **Kapackatatca! Kapacktatacka!** We took cover but at the same time were shooting back with more fire power on their ass.

Me, Vita and Stump lit their ass up smoking three of them fast Vita yelled out, "let's get the fuck out of here now!"

At the same time at the other house on the corner of Keim street Big Duba came up to the door of the porch house and knocked on the door with a metal battering ram like the cops use **Kaplang!** Moon and Fat Poncho ran inside the door then Big Duba and Jitta covered the door. As both men were on a swivel with their machine guns ready for whatever. Moon and Fat Poncho both have large gym bags on their shoulders and run upstairs to the big dope room on the right-hand side of the crib.

Soon as they came up towards the room the men guarding the room with the drugs knew they were coming. We watched them on the surveillance cameras on the wall and they started shooting the minute they saw them. The two men on post guarding the dope room are shooting it out with Moon and Fat Poncho. Back and forth with them in the huge space. At the same time the women that were inside of the room working with no clothes on are running out screaming at the top of their lungs running and falling down the steps.

Some of the women were getting hit with this dash of death running out the door with all the bullets flying everywhere in the fire fight in the hallway. Fat Poncho and Moon backed up outside of the room on the left and right side of the wall near the dope packing room. Moon backs up taking aim towards the wall where they were standing at shooting **Ratkatackatack!** He predicted it just right, hitting both men ripping them apart with hot lead. They both are yelling falling to the floor dead.

Fat Poncho peeked inside of the door right quick seeing both men dead on the floor gushing out blood like a Fossett got turned on. They both ran in the dope room, and they set their large gym bags on top of the large steel tables in the dope room. They pushed all the bags of drugs in the bags. *The smart thing Fat Poncho and Moon did was they had another large, long bag within the bags they had so they can get as much dope inside of the room.* They both got as much dope as they could carry, and they call down the steps to Big Duba and Jitta both toss down two big bags of dope Jitta and Big Duba quickly gripped them up and Moon and Fat Poncho came running down the steps with the rest of the bags of drugs.

We got to our truck first. I have the big duffle bag on my back. I quickly open the door of the truck tossing in the bag in the back looking around at the same time making sure we were cool.

I jumped inside simultaneously. Kenyatta X got in the truck along with Vita and Stump jumping in the front seat with the big bag of money slamming the door. He yelled, "let's go!"

Jabare quickly turned the truck around and took off. Right behind us is team B with Indoe behind the wheel right behind him and we are gone. Once Jabare got about ten blocks away, he slowed down and was driving nice and easy like if it was a fucking Sunday drive on the parkway.

Indoe goes another direction, but we all know we're all going to meet back up at the warehouse. Two hours later we were all in the warehouse palace that I own now. We just took down a big-time drug dealer. I'm on a fucking high now. Big Mama Red and Jabare are counting all the money on top of the table that Stump, and Moon took from out of the back of the gym. I'm sitting on the couch with a big glass of gin on the rocks and snorting coke with Kahseam, Moon and Fat Poncho. We talked a whole lot of shit with the hot hard hip-hop beats flowing. Big Duba is drinking beer and smoking weed in the love seat and sitting right next to him is Indoe and Amir getting their puff on. Vita, Stump, Moon and Jitta are sitting at the bar chopping it up.

Kenyatta X is smoking weed along with them, but he keeps getting up checking on them counting the money. Big Mama Red told him to go sit his ass down and relax we're all having a good time after a big score like this. I sat their getting to know Kahseam big strong black fine ass. I whisper in his ear after they count this loot, "I can give you a private tour of the place."

He started giggling I would like that shit. After another hour or so we took down close to two million dollars, but it was only 300 keys of coke and 2000 dimes of baggies.

We split everything down the middle, and everybody was happy. Kenyatta X said, "He has another job lined up for us next week in Southwest Philly".

We all agree even doe most of us were high as shit. *I was horny for this big hunk of a fucking man, and I took him upstairs to get my brains fucked out so I can cum about ten times and pass out.*

We slip away from everybody partying and I take my cut from the robbery upstairs along with this fine ass man. We quickly headed up to the third-floor lounge. As soon as I closed the door, he had his eyes locked in on me and nothing else. I like that he's not looking around at all this bullshit, his eyes are filled with fire and lust. We started kissing, taking each other's clothes off very quickly.

I took off my bra, but I let Kahseam take off my panties as I leaned back on the large L Shape leather couch area. He quickly pulled my black lace panties down off my legs, never taking his eyes off of me. I like that shit I love when a nigga just concentrates just on me.

When he leaned into me sucking on my titties, but this was different he was sucking on them with deep passion and working his way down to my stomach. *Most of the time when a guy gets down to my stomach, I start to push their head down there real fast, but I let him go down on me slow, wet and super-hot too. Wow, it was so exciting because he took his time but when he got to my pussy. I'm pumping my hips fast and hard. He might be some kind of revolutionary black power motherfucker, but he sure knows how to lick twat. I'm still pumping my hot wet pussy all in his face even after I started Cumming, he lifted his head higher and he let all my love juice flow down.*

Right on the couch and down on the rug without it getting all in his face this nigga knows what he's doing then. After he made me cum, I stood up looking down at him smiling.

"Okay now it is time for me to ride the lightning baby get up on the bed with your fine black ass!"

He started giggling and getting up on the bed. *I know that shit turned him on.* When he was getting on top of the big bed, I just could not take my eyes off his thick black Dick pointing up in the air like the liberty one in center city standing tall with a set of big brown balls. I walked up on him, and I started stroking his thick black meat, jerking him off gently keeping it hard. He's leaning back enjoying it. He's moaning looking up at me before I jump on top of it and give this nigga the monster truck ride of his fucking life.

I started licking and sucking the head of his long, rock-hard dick. I made it really wet making a loud sucking sound. He looked like he was about to cum with me sucking on his Dick to get it really wet to ride this motherfucker good. Then I put my whole mouth on his Dick for me to get on it and ride him like Sally Star. He jumped about 20 feet when I did that shit to him wiggling my tongue all the head of his man of steel he was jumping like crazy. I let myself down slowly on top of his erection guiding his hard-

On with my right hand making it fit inside me Oooohhh! When I got on top of him and I got all of his anaconda inside of me I lean forward, and he put both his large hands on both my wide ass cheeks pushing me down on his huge slippery throbbing manhood. I started pumping along with Kahseam and we started getting a super-hot groove going on this really feels good. I'm digging my nails into his chest he didn't mine with me whipping this good hot juicy cunt on him. *I can hear him moaning under his breath trying to hold it back.*

Were both making loud sexual sounds the harder he started stroking me I started feeling that fantastic sensation inside of my clitoris is on fire then **Boom!** I started Cumming again like crazy but this time it's like a fucking geyser shooting up all over the place.

But Kahseam would not stop stroking my pussy making me feel even better **oooohhh"** the pain and the pleasure I'm riding him like he's a wild black stallion of all my fuck dreams. With every hard stroke I'm floating into the fucking heavens were both breathing hard sweating up a storm. Both of us screaming crazy shit to one another filling the whole room. Kahseam fine black ass is huffing and puffing mumbling dam this pussy is so good baby! *I got this nigga is in a deep pussy trance whipping it on him for real.* I'm moaning jumping up and down on his Dick like a rodeo rider on fucking steroid still digging my nails in his chest. *This kinky ass motherfucker like that shit.* I'm yelling leaning down in his face oh you like it baby! I been wanting to fuck you the minute I seen you, nigga! He's groaning out of breath saying oh me too baby! Me too! Making the couch rock with a loud bumping sound.

Now I can see in his handsome dark mug he's ready to cum himself thrusting his love gun upwards ready to burst like a bubble. Then his face got all twisted up yelling and I can feel all his baby gravy shooting up inside of me. Oh, it's so hot and oozing I'm about to cum again when I collapse on top of him all of my sweat is dripping off my face on to his while were kissing, I didn't want him to take his erection out of me still feeling so good.

When he did after another twenty minutes later, we sat up on the end of the bed and I when inside of my pocketbook pulling out my zip lock bag of coke. I dump out a big pile on top of the nightstand and I quickly sticking it back in my pocketbook. I started chopping up the large rocks into small ones. I say to him how about if I put some this coke on your Dick and lick it off good would you like that shit?

He started smiling, "yeah baby, I would love that kind of thing jumping off. Well, your going have to take a shower first and after I do that to you your going have to do me, I call that a little snow in the valley of love."

He started chuckling, "your one crazy ass bitch."

"No, I'm a psycho bitch who is very nasty and kinky just like you, nigga. Now let's get fucked up really good and do some more nasty ass crazy shit to one another."

He fell out laughing.

I said, "why don't you make us some drinks to flow with this coke. And he did and came back sitting next to me on the bed.

I have to admit the Dick was good too. So, we sat up on the bed nude thrill bumps up to my ass hole getting high having a great conversation with an intelligent thug. and I have to say he really had a good head on his shoulders and on his third leg as well. He's smart funny and not bad on the eyes his body covered in tattoos. It was like making love to a great work of fucking art with his muscular sexy body I just could not keep my hands off him while we were talking.

What I really love about us talking he did not want to talk shop just about each other and what we want to do in the future like running shit like a real fucking boss. After we got high, I jumped in the shower he was trying to fuck again. I told him no were going to do some of that nasty shit I was talking about after we wash off. I took him out of the shower drying him off and myself I sat him to the end of the bed I pulled some more coke out my pocketbook, and I got a big glass of gin with a lot of ice. I got down on my knees then I sprinkle his Big Dick with some coke. And I pour some of that gin from my glass on him and I started sucking it making him jump and shake like a twig in a fucking hurricane.

After I was done blowing his socks off, I thought that nigga was going to have a fucking heart attack. Then it was my turn I cocked my legs open wide, sprinkling coke down on my pussy. But this time I push his head down their pumping my cunt all in his face with my hands-on top of his fucking head making sure he doesn't miss a spot. Then I pulled his head back just a little, pouring my glass of gin on my pussy letting him lap it all up good.

BACK AT IT AGAIN

After he was done, I went to sleep with him laying his head on my chest. He went home early the next morning. I gave him my number and told him to don't forget me. He said after the night we had he would never forget about me. *I said to myself they all say that shit once they get the pussy, but I had fun doe so what the fuck.*

The next morning when I got up and ate breakfast Vita was acting funny. "Yeah, but on the surface, things are cool."

I did not give a fuck after I seen him fucking that ho with his father. Niggas can dish it out, but they can't fucking take it. A week blew by fast, and we had another meeting Monday night with Kenyatta X and his crew. It was for are next job at 51st and Woodland Avenue with these Jamaican niggas moving large amount of weight of coke.

We had another three meetings in a row about the job. The last one was on Wednesday, and we all had it down tight. We're going to hit them dread head motherfuckers next Thursday.

All that week we ran around getting all the tools we need to get busy boxes of bullets, weed, Philly blunts wraps, liquor and yes, more coke. Me, Moon and Stump make sure all the guns and machine guns are loaded and extra clips just in case anybody gets cute, and we have to laid there ass right where the fuck they stand. Kenyatta X, Big Duba and Fat Poncho make sure we have all the jeeps and cars and other trucks ready for the switch. Jabare and Kahseam went out and stole two big bread trucks we needed to do this job.

Thursday night at 11: 30 we were all ready to go. All of us are dressed in all black masks and black rubber gloves and bullet proof vest. Big Mama Red drives me Fat Poncho and Vita in her new Jeep Poncho brought her to shut her up. *She talks to me all the time and she's tired of just cooking, cleaning and washing clothes like a fucking maid. I told her don't worry I got my eye on something she can be a part of. She likes that idea.*

Moon drove Stump and his father Jitta to the location we all agree to under the bridge at 31st street. It took us about half an hour to get their Big Mama Red pulled up beside the two bread trucks sitting up under the bridge in the dark along with Moon's whip. We quickly unpacked the guns from the back of the jeep Moon Stump and Jitta were also unpacking the GMC truck moving like crack commandos on a fucking mission. Big Duba and Amir help us put the guns into each one of the trucks we were riding in.

Truck one Jabare is the wheel man. It's me, Fat Poncho, Stump, Amir and Big Duba. In bread truck two Kahseam is the wheel-man Kenyatta X, Moon, Jitta, Vita and Indoe. I made sure every-body double checked their machine guns and I made sure I have my trusty black backpack.

Kenyatta X did the same with his men before they got inside of the big steel bread truck. I'm ready to kick some ass fuck the names. We load up in the first bread truck. Soon as Big Duba got in last he bangs on the side of the truck three times to let Jabare know were all inside of this steel coffin with a Dall light. I love the discipline of Kenyatta's crew. I hold on to one of the straps with my left hand. I'm holding on to my machine gun in the other as the large truck pulls off.

While we're going over the bridge it feels like we're going up a hill or something when nobody is talking. I'm just looking at everybody having their game face on. I know I will not get that rush until I jump out the truck and start handling shit. After the truck makes a big turn now it feels like it's going downhill now and another big turn and bumps in this with this hard steel under my ass.

Then I hear Jabare yelled, "where almost there get ready!" *When we went over the plan Kenyatta X told us it's an old pillow factory on the left-hand side of Woodland Avenue on 51ˢᵗ street they move all the drugs in big bales of foam marked with big black X's on the bails. They have been peeping them for a month now. He was glad he hooked up with us so we can pull this shit off right with people with these kinds of skills. He said he did not have enough men trained for this kind of job.*

I'm thinking that's a bunch of bull shit their going to set us up at one point and I'm thinking today is that day because shit been going to fucking smooth. I always trust my gut feeling with shit like this.

Now my juices are fucking flowing I put on my black mask then I cocked back my Bravo machine gun.

I quickly put my black backpack on my back. A few minutes later I hear Jabare yell, "okay, let's hit it now!" Amir, sitting right across from me, quickly puts on his black mask and announces, "remember you're with me, let's go!"

Big Duba open the steel doors and we hop out in this big loading dock area soon as we got out it's like world war fucking three jumping off. But when I see Kahseam sitting in the truck while I'm getting busy shooting at these Milli Vanilli looking like motherfuckers. I wink my eye at him, and he blows a kiss back at me.

He goes back to shooting at the niggas on the dock. My training kicks back in fast, staying low but I'm locked in focus. I love my job smoking ass holes for a living.

Fat Poncho and Stump got low in front of us staying behind the truck. **Kacpackatat tat tat tat!** *The two of them are laying down cover fire for us. They smoked about four of the mop hair gunmen.* We started running in front of them at the same time Kenyatta X, Moon and Vita did just like we planned ripping motherfuckers to shreds. Shit I'm wet right about now for real!

I wanted to laugh seeing some of them fucking running instead of fighting back like a fucking man pussy ass motherfuckers! Indoe and Jitta come up shooting covering us **Kapackataka! Katakatkacka!** *They cleaned out about six more of the long hair assesholes' with blood and screams of death falling off the dock area. The shit was crazy, but I love this kind of shit doe.*

When we first road up shooting at them it looked like it was about 100 of them niggas, I ran up with Amir stepping over the bloody bodies lying all over the place. We both lifted up two of the four bay doors on the huge dock area. I'm getting ready for more of them to jump out of the fucking woodwork, but nothing happens once we got inside. All I hear is this loud sound I take aim. It'sJitta and Indoe lifting the other two bay doors Jitta told them niggas ran let's go to work. Moon ran up on top of the dock waving the two bread trucks in closer.

Fat Poncho Big Duba, Vita, Stump, and Kenyatta X carefully walks inside checking things out. Kenyatta X came back with the others, "All right Stump. Jitta y'all know what to do we have to work fast just in case they come back let's go!"

"Yo,Lex, Amir, Moon and Vita get on post like we planned to stick to the strip."

Stump and Jitta went and got the forklifts. Kenyatta X and Fat Poncho pointed out all the bails with the X on it that had the coke inside.

The two of them in about half hour to load about 50 bails 25 inside of truck one and 25 inside of truck two working their ass off.

Kenyatta X yelled, "that's enough let's go!"

Fat Poncho and Kenyatta X made sure of two of his other men. Saboo and Lamar came with cars and jeeps because they knew the inside of the truck was going to be a tight squeeze with

25 bails. We rode back to Kenyatta X's crew warehouse at 2nd

& Greenwood, and we drove up to the big junky ass dock area. Big Duba jumped off the truck along with Indoe from the other truck and quickly ran up unlocking the doors. Some of us got out of the bread truck and others in the jeep with Saboo.

Kenyatta X came up telling us when they were done unloading the bails. He's going to get Saboo and Lamar to take us back to their crib. *I'm thinking to myself if they're going to double cross us why they're not doing it right now.* After they were all done getting the heavy ass bails of foam inside of their warehous.

Fat Poncho walks up to Kenyatta shaking his hand, "it's really nice doing business with you, big guy, good work!"

Fat Poncho nodded his head, "the same here my man. You told me it was going to be a piece of fucking cake!"

They both started laughing loud. Then they both hugged one another still laughing.

Fat Poncho said, "I'm going to need some help getting them bails off that truck when we get back to the spot."

Kenyatta X said, "if you got somewhere to put them, I can send you Indoe and Amir to help you get it off." "Sure, as you unload your thing, and you can send them over were going to get the fuck out of here." "Alright as soon as we were done loading up the bails." They continued talking shit with one another.

Fat Poncho complimented, "great job everybody! They all were bumping fist shaking hands with one another but I'm thinking something is up with them, but they are putting on some great acting jobs.

DOUBLE CROSS ON THE DOUBLE CROSSERS

The minute they make their move I'm going to smoke every last one of them niggas. I have to tell Fat Poncho not to trust their ass now that the job is over with.

I know niggas like this smooth and sneaky. I wave down Fat Poncho before he gets up on the bread truck to drive off.

"Poncho, look I need to holla at you before you pull off."

"Okay, what is it you want sweetheart?"

"Look Poncho man, I don't trust them this time around."

"You don't trust them, why?"

"I just don't know I got that feeling this time. It just too much coke this time to split up niggas is greedy." Kenyatta X came walking up to drive us.

"I will tell you the rest at the spot just think about it okay."

I walked with his driver Saboo this nigga is fucking huge along with Stump and Jitta to his jeep. Fat Poncho jumped behind the wheel of the bread truck Moon Vita got on the truck with him and they took off. It took us no time for Saboo to drop me and Stump off.

Fat Poncho was right behind us parking and we all went inside feeling good about taking down the pillow factory caper. We all were taking out all the guns and machine guns as soon as we were done. I went and talked to Fat Poncho as soon as we got inside the door. He asked, "Are you serious about what you were talking about Lex?"

"Yes, I'm telling you they're not coming back here to help us there coming back here to Jack everything we got I'm telling you man. Well, we will be ready for them if they want to fucking Double cross, us after we been working so good together. Fat Poncho gathered everybody together inside of the front room lounge area telling the rest of the crew. *We are all glancing up at him waiting for him to speak.* Check this out y'all Lex believes that Kenyatta and his crew is going to cross us after this big job here.

Stump spoke up first with a cigarette cocked in his thick lips,

"if she feels that way, I think she just might be right she was all the other times."

Jitta cuts in talking loudly waving his hands around when he talks like he does all the time. "I was not with y'all on the other shit, but if you all think there coming back here to fuck us, we should get ready right about now.'

Moon uttered, "he's right."

Vita jumps in and shouts, "I think it all bull shit, but I'll be ready if it happens."

We all get ready and started snorting smoking and drinking at the bar at are lounge when Big Mama Red came downstairs with us getting high. Fat Poncho is sitting on the couch with Big Mama Red all hugged up when his phone rings he gets it real quick, "yo, what's up?"

"Yeah, this is Indoe man were here to help you get your shit inside the crib."

He sits up fast waving his hand giving all of us the signal to get ready.

Stump Moon and Jitta go out towards the back door with their machine guns. Soon as they step outside, they hear loud voices shouting at them from the darkness drop the hardware boys! Me Fat Poncho and Vita walked out the front door in the front of the crowd of men with are guns and machine guns ready to fuck something up.

Standing up front is Kenyatta X yelled, "before y'all start shooting we have all of your peoples at gun point! And we will kill all of them if you don't drop your fucking pistols, and machine guns! I want all of you, niggas to put your hands up in the air slowly or we will start raining bullets down on you mother-fuckers immediately!"

I looked up at them with my eyes on fire I knew this shit was going to happen I scream, "fuck you!'

We all are standing with are guns and machine guns locked into a fucking Mexican standoff with them. But I have to say they have more niggas heavily armed then us.

Kenyatta X calmly pulls out his phone shouting, "bring them out so they can see them, so they know were not fucking playing around with their ass!"

The whole time I'm looking for Kahseam, but all the men with him have black mask on and I can't tell which one of them is him. After a few we see these big ass goons with black mask and machine guns pushing Stump Jitta and Moon in front of them all tied up for us to see them.

Kenyatta X yelled, "okay, now put down your guns and none of them will get hurt! Now I want all that money and the drugs I don't have all fucking night!"

I step up and holler, "no! You motherfuckers is going to do this shit to us after all the shit we have done together!"

Kenyatta X laughed, "well, I came to take it all back from y'all just put down the machine gun or you're going to die with the rest of them!"

Out of nowhere we hear this loud deep whistling sound **Wisssssssssssss! Boom! Boom! Boom!** *The explosions making the ground shake* it feels like it was going to open up and swallow me up into darkness for good. All hell break loses all around us, **Kapackata! Katatacka! Katacpacka!** Its thick smoke every-where in the chaos and gunfire. I'm shooting like crazy, and I can't see shit in front of me I see hordes of men in black mask with machine guns with flashlights on top of them. I'm shooting blindly moving from left to right trying to kill everything moving.

All the sudden **Woooofff!** I feel this Sharp pain in the side of my neck I pulled it out real fast it's a thick steel dart I started feeling dizzy and I blacked out. When I finally came too, I have a fucking Godzilla size fucking headache like my head is about to pop wide the fuck opens at any second. Everything is all fucking hazy and I'm seeing shit double and the room seem like it was still moving around on my ass. I looked up and I see this fat white dude with a cigar in his mouth blowing out smoke. He is dressed in this army green get up.

I tried to move, and I notice I was all tied up I'm looking around and everybody is tied up in chairs to Big Mama Red is on the right of me and Fat Poncho is on the left wiggling around trying to get lose out of the chair were all sweating up a storm. *These motherfuckers are going to torture the shit out of us why they just didn't just smoke us from the door.*

The fat man in the green gets up started screaming, "okay, Mister Cesar wake her ass all the way up for me, please." **Wassshhhhh!** This super tall ugly ass motherfucker tossed a cold bucket of water right in my face.

"Okay now, that I have your fucking attention right now Miss Jordan, I want you to listen to me really good!"

I'm choking and spitting out all this water out my mouth and I can see all of his men standing around with black mask and machine guns I should be dead. Well, if they didn't kill us all by now, they must want something from us, and I know what it is too. The fat white man looking all of us up and down speaking. I got some good news for everyone of y'all you're going to work for me for here on out.

Then this white man came walking up to me that I recognize this older white dude standing next to the fat man. the last time I seen this motherfucker I threw a hand grenade at him when he stopped me in the green bullet proof van. I should have killed his white ass in New York!

He walks up to me looking down at me rolling his fucking eyes like a little bitch as the fat man started talking, "well, you two know one another as he giggled. Let me introduce you two officially this is Mister Price Mister Price meet Miss Lexus Jordan aka the notorious L.E.X. is what I call her."

Mister Cesar and his men started laughing looking at Mister Price. I'm looking up at all of them and they all look like ruthless fucking killers and it's not a miracle were all not dead. Mister Price started talking *looking me in the face pointing his finger in my grill.*
"Yeah, she tried to kill me two times already Joe. And Miss Pinky quit because of this bitch!"

Then the Fat man said, "let me introduce myself I am Lieutenant Cob. We have mutual friends name AK you were one of his best soldiers in the gang."

"Yeah, and I know you set me up, too with that fucking Mark Pain shit. You know dam well I didn't kill Angel and Binky that was some real foul shit you did!"

"I cannot lie I did do that to you, but I can fix that shit for you **Dada** *(Sister)*."

"I'm not your fucking sister you cracker ass motherfucker okay and I work for myself and nobody else motherfucker."

"Well, I hate to tell you this, but if you thought I fucked you over the first time you will really be all fucked up if you don't do this shit for me now, baby girl."

"Oh, really check this shit out fat man my life is already fucked up plus you set me up with the gang to get killed asshole!"

"Like I told you I can fix all that and you and AK could be good friends again."

"Now how in the fuck you going to do that? When it is a price on my fucking head asshole!"

"Well, I have a video tape with Mark Pain talking about setting you up to take the fall now if you play ball with me, young lady. And I will give it to AK and show it to him along with some other things that will prove you didn't do it without a doubt Lex."

"So, what is it you want me to do to get this so-called video tape? I have a client who is Turkish, and he wants someone to kill his competition who also is Turkish. I want you to do this for him and to kill him also."

"Okay, I'll do it for 40 million I'll do it. I'll give you 20 and no more plus you tried to kill my peoples. Look I was going ask for 60 I was cutting you a fucking break that's 20 for each one of them dead and as you know that's fucking cheap fat man!"

"Okay than, 40 million and I'm going to need you to give me the names of his French hook ups, before you kill the Turk's."

"Now you want to give me a measly 40 million for two hits and you want names of some French ass hole middlemen."

"Now the price just went up to 75 now! It is no fucking way I'm going to give you 75 million dollars to do this shit you are really crazy. Well look at it like this fat man you know I speak Turkish and French so they can't get shit past me so good luck finding someone like me to do it. And your right I am fucking crazy everybody knows that shit fat man!"

All of Lieutenant Cob's men started laughing; they all stopped when he looked back at them giving them the evil eye.

"Well, I can let the police know how busy you've been since you escaped the Bony Irons hit on you. How the fuck did you know about that?"

"I know about a whole lot of shit, but I have to say nice work to you killed about ten of them, not counting the cops you blew up in the Bony Irons dope house. And I know about those three white boys you robbed the four cops you killed or was it five because one of them just died after you blew his ass up with a hand grenade. Also, I know about thirty other murders maybe more not counting last night."

"Oh, Mister CIA black bag operation is going to call the Po-Po on me you have to be fucking kidding me call them! You think I give a fuck you already know I don't by now! You know if I did, you'll do about six life sentences after they done with your ass right."

"Well, I don't give a fuck make the call to the police or just kill me and get it over with Fat Man I'm not afraid to die!"

Now I sit back and watch his fat ass pace the fucking floor chewing on his cigar. Then the tall ugly man calls him over and I can tell by the look in his eyes he about to tell him that he needs me.

He started whispering in his ear and the fat man face is all twisted the fuck up nodding his head. He walks back over to me talking louder puffing on his cigar blowing smoke in my face, "okay 60 million and let's rap this shit up okay Lex."

He looks at me smiling from ear to ear if my hands were not tied behind my back, I would have given him my middle finger.

"See, you still don't fucking learn now its 80 million dollars now and a million dollars for any man I get to help me. Fuck that! It is 250,000 and that is the fucking going rate Miss Jordan!"

Mister tall and Ugly looks at the fat man Mister Cesar said look you're the boss. But we need to get her locked down right away with this shit so we can go give her the million a man and what she wants we have some big shit going on here Joe. *Then the ugly tall man with the scars on his face looks lieutenant Cob in the eyes.*

"*Your* right, okay, Lex you got it 80 million and a million a man you have working with you and no fucking more!"

I have to go *lieutenant Cob points at all of us* Mister Cesar cuts all the duct tape from the back of our hands in the chairs one by one. I can hear Fat Poncho is mumbling with the duct tape on his mouth. Lieutenant Cob is pointing at him shouting see what the fuck is it you want to say Mister Cesar take that shit off his mouth. Soon as he took the duct tape off his mouth, he is yelling out, "who the fuck is y'all the secret squirrel Swat team or some shit! And who the fuck is you!"

Lieutenant Cob walks up on him getting in his face yelling, "I am the big fucking Kahuna. All I have to do is wink my eye and your fat ass is fucking dead! And I don't give a fuck if you're working on this operation or not so shut the fuck up, okay! Lex is running the show from here on out and if I hear one bad thing out your crooked car Jacking cocaine snorting fat ass your dead. Are we clear?

Fat Poncho looking up at him with fire in his eyes pissed off mad dogging him. Lieutenant Cob shouted out Mister Cesar!

He stomped over swiftly mashing a gun to Fat Poncho's forehead Lieutenant Cob yelling in his face, "nod your fucking head if we are clear on what I just said to you or your dead lard ass!"

Fat Poncho is nodding his head yes. Mister Cesar takes, the gun mashed up to his head from Fat Poncho's head smirking at him. *We can see in Mister Cesar eyes he wanted to kill him.* Lieutenant Cob walks over to Big Mama Red standing in front of her uttering, "well sweetheart your free to go if you like you can go back to the Bronx and take care of your father Earl. He is sick with prostate cancer, now your mother Miss Esther could not get in contact with you to tell you since you took off with the fat ass car jacker Poncho over here."

Big Mama Red looked up at him *muttering with a shock glair in her eyes.*

"How you know all this shit?"

"I worked for the CIA, so I know a whole lot of shit about people's life. Just like I know about your brother getting killed by them crooked cops about six months ago."

"Now that you brought it up maybe you could help me with some get back on that ass hole. Why do you think I could help you with that sweetheart?"

"Well, you're giving them niggas a million dollars to put in some work so that what I want, and I want some money too fuck, that! And yeah, I'm staying on the team here."

"Smart girl so what you think you should get?"

"250,000 the going rate like you said. Everybody started laughing."

"Okay you got it!"

"You go girl speak your mind I like that shit."

"Yeah, I'll let Lex know about them cops in a couple months' time. Now what about you?"

He points *at Stump.*

"Mister Samuel Carter aka Stump mother Ann Carter retired Nurse every Sunday she goes see your father Eddie Carter who is doing life right?"

"Yeah, your right I want some my money to go to my mother can you hook that up."

"Yeah, run it past Lex and I'll have Mister Price and my secretary Miss Ward to take care of it. Now as you can see good people if you're going to work for me. I want you to be happy, but what I'm asking all of you to do is very dangerous. Most of y'all is used to danger so it should be a fucking piece of cake. It is in every one of you here fucking DNA from the door. All I ask for is your loyalty if you run away on me you will die with no questions ask along with your family's as well so don't fuck this up."

He paused and took a breath from speaking. He pulled on his

cigar and let out smoke.

"Now we come to you Vince Porter aka Vita that means War in Swahili. Your mother doing life for drug trafficking along with your father doing double life for killing two men who crossed him in a 50 keys heroin drug deal."

Vita sitting up taking the tape off his risk talking loud *pointing up at lieutenant Cob*, "yeah, and I want to put money on my mother and father's books, and I already know what you are going to say run it past Lex."

"Right! Smart man, damn all of you guys caught on fast. Lieutenant Cob pointing at Moon smirking." He took another puff of his cigar.

"Let us move on to Mister Michael Wilson aka Moon your mother Alma works in a nursing home. Your father over here Josh Wilson aka Jitta just got out of jail for bank robbery and your porn star sister name Ronny Knocks. Why I tell you all this is that I know all about your family and low life friends you hang out with so don't think about crossing me! Mister Price will be with you guys to make sure you get some money and everything you need for this operation."

I stood up and spoke, "that you have us working with you when do this whole operation goes down?"

"I will let you know. I have to work on a cover for you so you can get close to them, okay. So, you can get the job done okay. So, I'll let you know after I get that done."

"Alright, so what do we do in the meanwhile then?"

"You train and wait for me to tell you when shit is ready and there will be no jobs just lay low until you hear from me your no good to me dead or in jail okay."

"So, what happen to Kenyatta X and his crew?"

"Oh, there still alive I have plans for them too my peoples took them away to another location."

"Oh, now we have a babysitter to keep an eye on us as well."
"Look, like I said Mister Price is here to help you not to spy on
you if you are going to do the job or not it is all up to you, I am
not begging you to put in this work over here, honey." *He looks
me right into my eyes.*

"So, what about my money you said you're going to give me for
the job?"

"I will give all of y'all some money for right now and next
week I will give you half the money. The other half when the
job is done."

Mister Price came walking up telling us, "Look, Lieutenant Cob
I don't know about working out this building here. Lieutenant
Cob pronouncing well they do have to train before doing the
hit it is your call, Kenny."

Mister Price talking loudly, "I want to take them to my farm."

I started screaming and I jumped up getting in his facem,

"No fucking way this is my joint now if we are going to train it
is going to be here motherfucker!"

Lieutenant Cob gets in between the two of us talking calmly
okay looks like I must make the call it is my operation. He looks
at both of us announcing, "you and your crew will spend one
month on the farm to train and that is its, Miss Lex!"

"I want shit done right, I don't care how much you get high or
whatever the fuck y'all do I got a lot of shit riding on the line
here and for the kind of money. I'm spending here looks like
you will never get another opportunity of a lifetime again over
here Lex."

I was pissed off, but he is right about the loot doe, so I muttered
"okay, and I want some money tonight fuck, that shit!"

"Okay I'll give you some money tonight. And I want the coke
we just Jacked too."

Lieutenant Cob gets right up in my face replying, "you're really pushing me you should be dead or in fucking federal prison, but I need you for right now."

"You can have the fucking coke but don't make me regret this shit Lex!"

I looked him right in his face spitting fast **Hautahurumia** *You will not be sorry."*

" **Nzuri** *(Good)* make sure you got your crew in check or I will have to cancel their fucking contracts on the spot okay."

Fat Poncho jumps up towards Lieutenant Cob Mister Cesar quickly grabbing him by his neck.

The other two large goon mask men in all black with machine guns pointing them at Big Mama Red, Vita, Stump and Moon when to jump to help him. Lieutenant Cob screamed at all of them, "you sit the fuck down or I will fucking cancel all of your contracts, right now! And just use Lex to do the job so sit the fuck down now!"

They all stopped stepping back as Mister Cesar is choking him. I walked up to them and yelled, "do not kill him motherfucker, "I need him alright so let him go!"

Mister Cesar gives me that wicked smile *then he looks over at lieutenant Cob nodding his head yes* as he lets him go and he falls to the floor **Doom!**

Fat Poncho is gasping for air Mister Cesar looks down at him uttering loudly, "your one lucky ass fat ass piece of shit next time you will be dead Lex or no Lex! And that goes for the rest of y'all one fuck up and you are all dead!"

Big Mama Red runs over to check on Fat Poncho on the floor. Lieutenant Cob talking loudly with his hands up in the air,

"Okay now that were done with all the fun and games, Mister. Cesar could you please get my suitcase out of the truck so I can give Lex and her associates some of this money. So, we can get the fuck out of here and do what we have to do tonight. "

Mister Cesar looks at everybody and he quickly walks out the front door I walked to the bar verbalizing, "I need a fucking drink after all of this bullshit.

Stump replied fast, "I'll join you on that one baby girl! Big Mama helps her man up off the floor as all the rest of them followed Stump to the bar.

"Make everybody a drink."

When Mister Cesar and Lieutenant Cob walks over towards us at the bar drinking. He just looks at Mister Cesar as he opens the suitcase, I hold it up for him as he is grabbing the money out of it wrapped up in big stacks inside of plastic wrap like big bricks. Lieutenant Cob set a hundred thousand dollars for each one of us on top of the bar counter slamming them down in front of us. *I can't front all our eyes got wide as the fucking Grand Canyon for real. He is articulating to us all in a daze looking at this stack of loot in front of us.* This is a little taste for each of you to retain your services and to let you know I am really fucking serious too.

Lieutenant Cob looked at me speaking now, "that should give all of you some real motivation to do the job. I have to go!"

As Mister Cesar quickly close the large steel suitcase and they both when out the front door with all his mask henchman. Soon as the door close Mister Price shouts,' "okay all of y'all got your money to get you started now it's time for all of us to roll out to the farm tonight let's go!"

" Come on pack your shit up right now take what you're going to take with you got one hour to get ready I'll be outside waiting with my men for y'all."

So, we all pack up are shit fast getting ready to go to this farm he calls it none of us want to do this shit, but it looks like we have no choice of our own right now. Never in a million years I think I will be working with all this shadowy secret government underhanded black bag shit going on. But it is the best hand for right now, so I am going to fucking play it no matter where it leads down it better than being in fucking jail, or dead I know that shit. I think this is one big trap with all this loot he is throwing at us for all of us to be working with his ass full time or something I just got that feeling. *I gust it nice to have a crew of professional killers and crooks on the payroll to do dirt for your ass and get the fuck away with it that's life in America for you.*

The hour blaze past swiftly we all packed up walking out the warehouse ready to go Mister Price is standing in front of this large black steel tank looking like a military war machine vehicle. With about eight of his men dressed in all black toting their machine guns. I am pulling my bags glancing over at everybody and I walked up to each one of them asking if they were all right. They just nodded their head yes not saying a word. I can see in their eyes that they were not happy about this fucking arrangement, but it is better than going to prison or being shot on the spot.

Mister Price men are lined up on the left and right as we all started getting on the black war machine bus Moon and Stump got on first. Then Jitta Fat Poncho and Big Mama Red I got on last after I locked all the doors up from the warehouse. Soon as I got on Mister Price close the doors talking nice and polite, "okay here, we go good people."

He pulls off quickly on to the dark streets I walked over while the bus was moving where Big Mama Red and Fat Poncho is sitting, I stood up holding on while the bus is moving, I looked at him asking, "are you alright, Poncho?"

"Yeah, I'm cool but what the fuck you got us all into over here Lex?" *Staring me into my eyes.*

"You act like I had all of this bullshit planned or something, nigga!"

Vita sitting behind them *popping his head from the seat cutting in speaking* it is not her fault were in this shit, but she did tell us that Kenyatta X and his peoples was going to fucking double cross us. Stump sitting in the backseat with a cigarette cocked in his mouth he leans forward speaking up with his eyes getting wide every time she tells, us something it fucking happens. Moon stood up out of his seat talking loud, "look were all in this shit together it is not Lex fault were in this we all can be dead if that crazy ass army dude did not know she has skills did you ever think of that shit y'all. Every one of them had a blank look on their grill."

TRAINING AT THE FARM

Jitta uttered, "my son is right plus I never got a million dollars to do a fucking job before, so the shit is all gravy if you ask me."

Fat Poncho yelling out, "your right that is a lot of fucking money, but you must live to fucking spend it!"

I answered fast, "well, your right about that, but let us all agree if any one of us fall on this mission. One of us will make sure somebody in our family gets the money."

Big Mama Red replied, "that sounds like the right thing to do so what about you Lex if you fall who will your money go to?"

"My uncle Hank if my crack head mother gets any of that money, she will smoke herself to death within a fucking month or so for real."

We all started laughing loud. *It took us about an hour and a haft to get to this farm in upstate Pennsylvania. It looks just like any other regular farmland with cows, horses, chickens and pigs. They have eight hard working farm hands all of them are white Frank, Billy, Andy, Kenny, Rick, Sally, and the two cooks and housekeepers Netty is Black, and Miss Janet is Hispanic. All of them are nice people and down to earth you would never know there all ex-CIA operatives.*

When you see it, but underground it is like a super large bunker with a shooting range and all the sleeping quarters is up top six cabins nothing to fancy but no TV or Wi-Fi for are phones. Netty fed all of us breakfast in the morning in the big farmhouse the food was good I have to say Big Mama Red liked that someone else is doing the cooking for her for a change. And Netty cooked her ass off for real down-home style we just loved it just like all the farm hands. Netty and Miss Janet made up all are beds and washed all our clothes when we go underground to train with Mister Price. I cannot lie I learned a lot of shit from him while we were there, and I found out that he was cool not like I think he was he is super fucking smart too.

We did the same thing every day we ate at 7A.M. And we stopped at around 3P.M. Sometime a little early. What was driving us crazy with no TV and phone the whole time so most the time we all played cards and told old war stories to entertain one another. I was really surprised with Big Mama Red she was getting good going through the optical course with all kinds of machine guns. And as a unit we got tighter and with one another as well. Lieutenant Cob is a man of his word he did pay us all for all the coke we stole from the Jamaicans, but it was nothing we can do with the money while we were in the farm. Mister Price didn't let, us gamble while we were there or get high to me that was the hardest part to me.

The month when fast now were all going back to the warehouse and wait for word from lieutenant Cob.

When we got back to the warehouse, we all were so happy it was like we had a party and Mister Price join us drinking snorting coke and drinking getting fucked up. While we were all having a good time, Vita thought because I was nice and high, he could slide back up on me and get some pussy. And as much as I wanted to fuck, I was not giving him no more pussy. I shut that shit down and when up on the third floor and played with myself in the shower and I came three times. And I when to bed and I slept like a baby high as a fucking kite.

I GOT A RUSH JOB

The next morning Big Mama Red was back in the kitchen throwing down the smell of that bumping ass flavor of the food woke me up. I quickly went and got washed up and dressed. I laid out four lines of coke on top of my nightstand. I snort up the four lines of coke right quick. I go downstairs as Big Mama Red is serving Fat Poncho and Vita their plates of fish and grits. Soon as she set them down on the table she jumps up and hugged me telling me with a big smile, "I'm so glad to be home, girl you just don't know come sit your ass down and get some this grub looks like you need it."

Then she points at my nose uttering, clean that up girl and sit your ass down and eat. I will make your plate."

I go sit down at the table with Moon, Jitta and Stump. I bump fist with each one of them while they were eating. Big Mama Red came with my food setting it in front of me with a big bottle of hot sauce. So, I am eating and talking shit with the boys when it is a big knock at the door.

Fat Poncho yelled, "could one of y'all see who at the door, please."

Stump and Moon both whip out their guns walking up towards the door. They both peek out the door and opening it its lieutenant Cob with one of his men Black Cobra holding a suitcase he walks up to the kitchen area where we eat at talking loud wow that smells good, he walks over towards me speaking with a smile on his fat grill, "good morning, Lex."

"Good morning to you, sir. Hey, I want you to meet one of my men this is Black Cobra." I shake hands with him, "nice to meet you, Lex. I heard a lot about you."

"So, what brings you here early in the morning lieutenant

Cob?"

"Well, I have a rush job. I need you and some people from your team to do something for me."

"Okay, you say a rush job."

I uttered, "it's a fucking test."

"Yeah, but it is paying 250,000 dollars for two days work you in."

"Sure, I'm in is that for each man?"

"Yes, that is for each man who sign on."

"What about the money you gave us with the Turkish dope boys job?"

"I need you to do this for me right now this is another client of mine. Who wants this done and that is a whole different separate thing over here, okay?"

He thinks I don't know it's a fucking test to see how we move and do things so he can evaluate are performance he's not slick I got this motherfuckers number from the door.

Stump shouted, "I'm down with that!"

Moon answered, "I'm in as well."

Jitta yelled, "me three I'm in!"

I looked up at lieutenant Cob asking him, "how many men you need?"

"Five or six should do it." I waved over Big Mama Red to the table I said, "the man here has a rush job 250,000 dollars for two days work."

"I'm in fuck that, Ma."

I replied, "okay, what's the job?"

"It is a guy with two methamphetamine labs one is in Camden New Jersey the other one is in Potts Town. I want y'all to put them out of commission. He hands me a piece of paper, 'this is the two locations."

With the smoke from his cigar flying in my face. I take it looking at it is putting it in my pocket fast and I light up a cigarette with him looking me in my face again. Fat Poncho walks over still chewing his food mumbling, "what is going on?" "We have a rush job 250,000 a man. Are you in?"

"Oh, hell yes, I'm in when the fucking job is?"

"Tonight." Lieutenant Cob points for Black Cobra to clear the table top off he do it swiftly he set the suitcase on top of the table, and he opens it and it's filled with fat envelopes of money. Lieutenant Cob talking loudly but he is looking for me in my face. He gave each one of them one it is 150,000.

"You will get the other half of it when the job is done that is how I work."

After Black Cobra hands each one of us the fat envelopes filled with loot, he hands me a phone verbalizing call me when it's done don't lose that phone okay. *And he wickedly winks his eye at me I know just what that means no fucking up.*

Black Cobra close the suitcase and he smile at me and he walks with lieutenant Cob right by his side I walked behind them towards the front door as they walked out quickly. I close the door still holding on to my envelope. When I walked back in the kitchen area everybody looked happy ready to go to work but Fat Poncho.

I can see it in his face, but I did not say shit about it. *I know that look on his face he is feeling some type of way because Big Mama Red is part of the job, and I am running shit too. Some men don't want their women to rise or be beside them and plus he knows he's not in charge of this outfit anymore, so he'll do something crazy to derail what's going on.*

I just must keep my eye on his ass and when he crosses the line, I'll blow his fucking head off his fucking fat shoulders from the door. Now we all talked shit and played around but I got down to busi-

ness I send Moon and Stump out to get us two new trucks and I had Vita and Fat Poncho to go toon up the green monster. That is what I call the green bullet proof van me and Big Mama Red took care of all the guns machine guns and ammo making sure we had all the clips and all the bullets we need for this job.

The first place I want to hit is the joint in New Jersey after everybody did what they had to do I gather everybody one bye, one in the front room lounge area. Fat Poncho came last and really slow I tell them where it at and how were going to do it everybody was cool with it, but I can see in Fat Poncho eyes he could care fucking less.

Just as long as he does his fucking job, he can pout like a baby all the fuck he wants too he better know I'm running shit now or I'll have to show him what time it is. I make sure everybody doesn't get to high on this job because I know this is are debut working for Lieutenant Cob so we have to show out tonight like a motherfucker.

THE METHAMPHETAMINE LAB HIT

Mister Price hung around with us at the crib getting high and bull shitting with us, so I ask him if he was going to do the hit with us now that I need a wheel man. *We bumped fist smiling now I really know he wants to be down with the Jungle crew me and him don't like the name, but I'll roll with it until I rename our crew after I kick a whole lot of asses in the process.* He looked at me and replied quickly sure I'll help y'all out with this it just might be fucking fun. We could have done it without him but now that I know he is really cool now I said to myself. Why not plus he really got close to all of us for real?

He started out being a real prick, but we knew what that was all about trying to show lieutenant Cob he was doing his job we all broke his ass down after being around us having fun. Now it is night fall I gathered everybody up so we all get on the same page with our headsets and earpieces so we all be on the same channel so we can talk to one another that way we have a clear communication and no fuck up's. We load up the green van I call the green monster made the quick trip over the bridge in the dark of the night to Camden New Jersey.

It's me riding shotgun in the green monster with Mister Price behind the wheel with Vita and Big Mama Red in the cargo area ready to get to it and super confident glowing in their eyes. Fat Poncho is driving the black explorer one of the trucks Moon and Stump jacked earlier.

Mister Price had the location on the GPS soon as we got close to the area it's near an industrial park surrounded by nothing, but abandon burned out buildings. I knew this was a good spot for them to set up but it's also very good to trap somebody inside trying to hit them. But I'm quarterbacking this shit from the door, so I got just the trick for their ass if they try something slick. We arrived but I tell Mister Price not to get to close while we wait on Fat Poncho and the second crew to meet us up the block from the industrial park. We already peeped they had cameras posted all around it I did a quick surveillance of the place front and back. When he drove around it one time. It has a large steel gate all around it with thick weeds and brush that all in our favor in our point of attack and wipe their ass off the map. I started talking to Fat Poncho through the headset and I told him to drive up the front and while you're doing that, we will hit their ass from the back door I'll tell you when to go.

He yelled back, "fast you got it Lex!"

I say to Mister Price, "all right, I'm need you to drive up near that brush over there and let Big Mama Red out." I looked at her and announced," you know what to do baby girl make me proud."

It's her first mission of this kind but I can tell she was not shook, in this moment of truth. Mister Price drives slowly letting her out with two rocket launcher stingers and a machine gun. I told Vita in the cargo area get ready okay Mister Price started creeping up on these motherfuckers! He started driving up towards the back gate with all the weeds and trash every fucking where soon as he got close.

I spoke to Big Mama Red, "okay, Big Mama light there ass up!"

She quickly turns towards the rotting tore down houses close by on the left she took aim *Wasssuuuuhhhhh!* **Kaboom!** She quickly dropped the rocket launcher picking up the second one and she took aim towards the back gate on the right, and she hit it with position and accuracy **Kadoom!**

I yelled out to Fat Poncho and his crew, "all right niggas do your thing!"

As they speed toward the large steel gate spitting hot shit as a group of rag tag gun men is running out firing back to engage their attack. Now where flying through the back gate Big Mama Red just took out for us with the flames still shooting up in the air and were riding up into hell ready to take some heads out. Mister Price speeds up closer to the back entrance me and Vita jumped out with our machine guns I am in front of him covering him because he has the payload bomb were going to shove up their ass to take out the whole fucking joint. It's only a few men jumped out on us because we really surprised their ass with my counterattack on the ran down houses behind them. I knew they had people back there for back up from the door when I peeped it.

I been at this shit for a while now niggas don't fool me not one bit. Most of them was really running for their fucking life's then fight us back when they did jump out on us. But that don't stop me and Vita mopping up shit smoking the low life flunky's that did come out shooting the first five that were brave soul's me and Vita ripped through their ass like a chain saw in a fucking pillow factory. Blood was squirting all over that industrial park lot. After those the other four men is running their ass off shooting back just to cover their ass in the fucking wind.

Me and Vita reach the backdoor and nobody was there to stop us from rolling inside to do what we came to do. We get a little deeper inside of the brick dwelling all we see is test tubes piles of chemical products and boxes stacked up on long rolls of shelves all around. Vita quickly runs up in the middle of this place putting the bomb on top of this long steel table hitting the buttons setting it yelling to me let's go! While we are running out towards the door.

We ran in Mister Price when around picking Big Mama Red up and Fat Poncho and them, done killed about 15 men at the front and the rest of them bug out fucking fast like the bitch made motherfuckers they are. Mister Price drive up on us haft way outside of the lot we jump in huffing and puffing jumping in the green monster.

I yelled to Fat Poncho, "Y'all can take off the shit is about to blow!" They take off heading back towards the highway as were doing the same thing speeding right behind them hauling ass up the dark road towards the highway burning rubber. Soon as we got about 100 feet away, we heard the place blowing up me and Mister Price is looking out the rearview mirror seeing the bright glow of fire and fury going up in the air. We can see the smoke fire and debris flying in the air me and Mister Price did a quick high five while laughing. Then I turned to Vita bumping fist with him in the cargo area he reaches up and kiss me mumbling you can't stay mad at me forever Ma.

Big Mama Red is sitting back laughing, "I knew y'all get back together." I just smiled at her giggling. I kissed him back he was right I could not stay mad at him, but I was horny now.

So, I'll give him some and shut his ass down later after I cum about ten times on the late-night tip and torture his ass the rest of the week. We make a clean get away from this job and we took out the whole fucking place, but we have another one to do so we can get the rest of are loot. It took us about hour to make it back to the crib and me and Vita did even stay with the others getting high in the lounge area like we always do we when right upstairs and got right to it like two lovesick teenagers hot in the ass with are flesh on fire.

Soon as we got upstairs, I close the door to are room and I started taking off my black gear swiftly Vita is doing the same but he damn near falls on the floor taking his pants off. We laughed about that as I walked over helping him up off the floor. I knew why he fell over because he could not take his eyes off me, I can feel his eyes lusting for my body he reaching to feel me up.

I pushed him off me playfully giggling but I help him take the rest of his clothes off am stripped down with nothing on and I'm really sweaty hot and super wet ready to fuck his brains out for real. I quickly grabbed him by his big black Dick pulling on it and leading his ass towards the bathroom turning on the shower, but I don't let go of his thick dark meat playing with it gently watching it grew in my hand like magic. While still Jacking Vita off with my left hand I test the water running with my right hand seeing if the water is ready to get inside. The water is nice and warm but I'm about to burst at the fucking seams super-hot dripping I quickly step inside grabbing the soap off the rack rubbing myself soaping up he's enjoying the view holding his huge manhood.

I'm looking at Vita standing outside of the shower gazing at me with his Dick getting harder. I'm under the water with the water rushing all over my body with the soap bubbles and I turned to Vita pointing at him seductively coaxing him to come in with me. He steps in slowly taking the soap out of my hand and he started rubbing me up on my shoulders nice and firm along with my titties kissing me I'm ready to fucking melt right on the shower floor right about now with chill bumps running up my ass. Vita started gripping my ass slowly soaping it up. I take the soap out his hand and I started washing his lovely, black tattoo sexy body of his soon as I washed his hard-on off.

I rinsed it off with the water pointing the shower head. I started sucking on his neck then his hard-beautiful dark chest and I quickly when down and started sucking on his erection popping up in the air. With the water falling on both of us but I had his ass moaning loud with me sucking him off like. I was possessed out my fucking mind I'm thinking he was going to bust right in my mouth right then and there. *When I looked at his dripping wet hard-on, I knew he was ready to get at this pussy with a fucking vengeance.*

I quickly stopped and I leaned up on the shower wall sticking my ass up in the air waiting for the impact for him to run up in my sizzling hot wet pussy. *I'm peeping back at him on the low holding his huge tool waiting for him to fucking give it to me good.* And oh, my Gawd did he deliver. As soon as I can feel the head of his sweet black meat sliding up inside of me really slow at first Owwwwwo. Then Vita turned into a sexy human jack hammer beast smacking me on my ass all at the same time rocking my spot. Now after a good hot twenty minutes I'm gushing out another

rock blocking orgasm oooh shit! My consciousness just slides into a world of ultimate cum boiling pleasure.

My body goes limp, and loss and Vita is fucking me like a rubber fuck doll with me pushing my ass back on his erection drilling deeper with each stroke. He reaches upholding me by both my arms out long Dicking the shit out of me with my hair flying from side to side with the loud echoes of us yelling in deep pleasure and slapping meat together. *The sizzling hot rhythm and the sounds alone inside of this shower turns me on even more in the middle of this good fucking he is putting on me oh, yeah nigga tear this pussy up!* The water rushing down on us feeling like tingles up my back down to my ass and into my freaky soul. Vita is pumping inside of me like crazy. I'm out of breath screaming then Boom! He shot his hot load inside of me I feel like I was going to fucking explode just like the super-hot jizism.

He just ejaculated in my hot wet cunt.

He is shaking making that face like he's retarded breathing hard he turning to me kissing me were both exhausted. Shit he is holding me in his big strong arms it is like he's really holding me up because I'm fucking done now lightheaded. Vita quickly steps out of the shower sitting on top of the toilet trying to get himself together and bend over talking in tongues or something.

I'm fucking numb out of breath and I have that I just got fucked well grin on my grill. I finish washing off and step out of the shower grabbing a towel off the rack. I uttered to him nice and sexy, "are you alright, nigga?"

He giggled loud rattling on, "hell yeah, you put it on me Ma! We both laughed as I walked over kissing him then I started fixing my hair still giggling. With the whole bathroom is filled with steam floating all around like a heavenly bliss in the air kissing one another giggling and laughing.

MISTER PRICE HAS A PROBLEM.

The next day I got up at 10 O'clock. Vita is knocked out sleep what got me up is smelling that good down-home food.

Big Mama Red got jumping off downstairs flowing through the whole crib. I quickly washed up got dressed and made that mad dash to get me a hot plate. I go downstairs and roll into the kitchen and Big Mama Red give me that big bright smile of hers speaking loudly I know you had a good night not a hood night with that look on your face girl. I laughed bumping fist with her "A very good night girl you know it."

"Where is Poncho at?"

He told me he had something to do, He said, "he'll be back to do the work don't worry."

"What you got jumping off this morning, Mama Red? It smells so fucking good!"

"Oh, just some home-made Jacks, cheese and bacon omelets.'

She quickly made my plate as I looked over uttering good morning to the others sitting down grubbing their ass off talking loud to one another. They all wave and speak back cheerfully. Moon, Stump and Jitta are all sitting together but Mister Price is sitting by himself looking sad. I take my plate and I go sit next to him.

"Are you all right Mister Price?"

"No, not really Lex and I do not want to talk about it."

"What with me you don't want to talk about it you're just fucking with me right?"

"Well, it is really personal you know what I'm saying. Look even after that shit with you and me in New York and that thing here in Philly we got pass that, so I know you and me, is fucking brown as shit, now right?"

"Yeah, you are right I found out that you are really alright once I got to know you. "

Vita came downstairs he is walking over with his plate in his hand he kissed me and was ready to sit down. I spoke what's up baby I have to holla at Mister Price about something we be right back okay. Sure, thing baby he sat down and started eating fast. I tapped Mister Price and said come back here so we can talk Mister Price get your plate come on.

He picked up his plate slow and sad and he followed me back to the gym area where I set up two chairs and a table for the two of us and started talking look eat something before you tell me about this, please. He smiled but he did start eating the food in front of him and I was eating too.

He looked up answering this is good. I know that is why I wanted you to eat some of this before you told me your little problem over here. "

"Well, it is more of a big problem and it nothing I can do about it."

"Well tell me any way what happen? I didn't tell you this before, but my daughter Peggy works for the CIA too."

"Oh yeah, she followed into the family footsteps you did tell me your father was an agent see I remember that shit my father was a no-good crack head thief. We both started laughing loud. See you can still smile yeah but finish telling me the story."

"Yeah well, she is married to the son of the head of the bureau his name is William Cassidy. His father Theodore Cassidy he was the former director of the bureau.

But this ass hole William he is one big piece of shit. He beats my daughter Peggy all the time."

"Why don't she just leave his fucking ass!"

"It is not just that simple Lex it makes him, and the bureau looks bad plus he will track her back down. It's hard to hide from people like this with power and access to everything at their fingertips. My daughter wants to get away from this man and start a new life, but she is trapped into this fucked up situation." "Wow, that shit is deep Mister Price. What is that your daughter do is she in the field like you are?"

"No, she just a secretary in one of the departments and might I add I am retired from the bureau. I did more than thirty years in the field I am done."

"Check this out you said you did thirty years in the bureau can't you get some old friends to help you out here?"

"All of them are scared as shit of Theodore Cassidy pay back and reprisals."

"Come on now you must have one crazy ass dude out there." "Yeah, I do but he when rogue and he is selling drugs in Hong Kong somewhere."

"Okay do you love your daughter Peggy?"

"Yes, with all my heart. I do I will do anything for her too. Good because I am going to hold you to the words you just said out your fucking mouth Mister Price."

"Why are you saying this to me I told you it is nothing I can do about this shit, Lex. Theodore and his peoples are old school evil."

"I don't care about that motherfucker just track down your rogue drug dealing friend of yours. I'll get my peoples together and you give me some of the share of the money you're getting to do these jobs. And I'll get your daughter out of all that bull shit, okay."

"You sure about this Lex it is not going to be a walk in the park here. I know that shit I got this shit just do what I ask you to do.

I'll take it from their Mister Price trust me."

We bumped fist as he started smiling.

Later, that same night we were all ready to take down the other meth lab in Potts Town we all load up in the green monster Mister Price behind the wheel. Along with me Big Mama Red and Vita. In the other truck is Stump, Jitta but Moon is driving this time and Fat Poncho is riding shotgun in the Explorer but when he did that. I knew he had something up his sleeve. I told everybody in the van with me that Poncho is going to try something tonight keep your eyes open. It took us an hour and haft to get there but this joint is in the middle of the fucking woods God's country.

When I looked around and see this place it is perfect for an ambush, but I already put a bug in everybody's ear about what this nigga wants to pull off. Soon as we got closer, I told everybody in the earpiece. "Okay, everybody get ready!"

The second I yelled that we see bright lights blinding us in front of us shining in are faces. From out of nowhere coming from the left and right is two vehicles riding up on us hard Vita and Big Mama Red sprang into action in the cargo area. I got my bravo company machine gun Vita has an, 50 caliber machine guns, on a mount ready to go. Big Mama Red straps on her flamethrower as she quickly opens the sliding door as Mister Price makes a 380 turn at the same time. *I don't know how the fuck he did it, but he stopped on a dime and hung his arm out the window getting busy with his pistol shooting with all of us picking off bodies one by one.*

Whauusssss! Kackacktata! Kapacka! Boom! Boom! I am spitting my machine gun blazing hot hitting the windshield of this vehicle on the right of me. I smoked the two zipper head motherfuckers with blood and glass flying in the air. Vita is working that 50 calibers like a fucking surgeon ripping the vehicle on his left to shreds with the metal flying from off the body of it. With the men inside jumping out trying to fire off shots but Big Mama Red is torching the two ass holes hopping out yelling like a bitch trying to fight and run. They both fall to the ground with the blood curling death screams echoing in the large, wooded area. I jumped out the van whipping out my flashlight my machine gun in the other hand. I'm yelling in the earpiece where the fuck you at Poncho I know your Fat ass got something to do with all this shit!

I glanced over at Big Mama, and I can see the look in her eyes that her man got something to do with something foul and she didn't know anything about the shit.

Me, Big Mama Red and Vita jump out looking around with their flashlights as well for the Explorer in the dark wooded area and it is nowhere in fucking sight. After walking a little way from the van Vita spoke you hear that.

I answered quietly, "I don't hear anything."

Big Mama Red replied, "I hear it man it sounds like somebody mumbling or something."

Vita spoke softly, "it sounds like its coming from over that tall part of the grass over there." He is pointing as we all walked a little further in the dark. We all looked down and its Stump Moon and Jitta tied up on the ground with duct tape over their risk and mouths. Everybody helps me to stand all of them up still looking around in the dark wooded area both ways. I quickly pull my knife from my side pants pocket but soon as I cut both of them lose from the duct tape, we all can hear a truck speeding off in the distance. I'm yelling in the earpiece to Fat Poncho because I know he can hear me, "you're not going to get far motherfucker! You know I'm going to find you!"

Cutting in real fast is the excited voice of Big Mama Red cried, "Poncho! Poncho! Don't do this shit Poncho! So, you just going to fucking leave me here Poncho!"

I didn't want to look up at her but when I did, she had tears in her eyes I just hugged her and said everything is going to be alright.

Mister Price came driving up yelling out the window, "I hate to break up this tearful reunion, but we have a fucking job to do over here!" As fucked up as it was, he was right doe.

I shouted, "okay by the looks of it your boyfriend done made are job easier all we have to do is blow the joint up."

Mister Price cutting in uttering with an angry tone in his voice, "yeah, you already know Poncho already killed and robbed everybody in the warehouse. He was just setting us up when we got here."

"Your right all we have to do is blow up the place and get the fuck out of here."

I looked up at everybody and spoke, "well y'all heard the man let us go the fuck to work and get this done."

We all piled in the van drive up to the warehouse and its bodies all scattered around the place like dead flies in pools of blood. Vita quickly set the bomb in the middle of the dwelling while we were all waiting in the van in an extremely far distance he came running out as Moon and Big Mama Red took aim with the rocket launchers soon as Vita was clear from the blast running up towards the van **Wassssshhhhhh! Wassssssshhhhhh! Kaboom! Kadoom!**

The warehouse goes up in a giant ball of flames as we all jump in the green monster and take off down the dark lonely highway heading home. *We all talked on the way back home about the shit going down with Poncho but when we got to the crib, we got more fucked up then we ever did before all of us got twisted with Big Mama Red crying all fucking night.*

A week blaze by and I got everybody that is going to help me with the thing with Mister Price Stump, Moon and Vita is down. It was not about money this time it's all about us being together it's about crew love. It is 7A.M. Waking me up all curled up next to Vita its lieutenant Cob and I am still fucked up high and he's talking all fast yelling with that hard voice of his.

"Yo, get your shit together, Lex you're flying out to Los Angeles to meet with Omer Kaya and his right-hand man Yusuf Oz-turk." "When?"

"Right now, so pack your shit up my secretary Miss Ward should be at your door right about now with your tickets and reservations and things."

Along with Mister Paul and his team to dress you guys up. *I was half asleep and fucked up from all the coke weed and gin from last night, but I sat up and wake up after he told me that.*

I yelled, "man I know how to fucking dress I don't need a fuck-ing stylist to make me look good, lieutenant!"

"Your right you do know how to dress but you're playing a part Lex. Your Trina Ice a high-end Midwest drug dealer that have. a direct line to the Chinese mob pipeline of Fentanyl. They need to mix with all the heroin they have do you feel me. And they dress a certain type of way and I know for fucking sure you might not need any help with your clothes, but your men sure do."

"Okay your right I am down with the masquerade over here was she a real person Trina Ice?"

"Yes, she was but she is dead now, but they don't know she's dead they worked with her before but never met one another just by phone and middlemen working shit out.

"Well, I don't have to fuck this guy, do I?" Lieutenant Cob is laughing his ass off on the other end of the phone. You might he is one horny ass motherfucker Lex but make sure you get that information out his ass before you do kill him for me, please. They don't know you speak nine different languages, so you have a very big advantage over them so make sure you make this shit count. And make sure you let Vita know about this shit before y'all go I don't want him fucking this up for us. I'll take care of it. "

"Okay, make sure because if he messes this up, he's dead make sure you tell him that too!"

"I sur,ely will lieutenant."

"Okay Miss Ward is telling me she is at y'all front door right now. Go let them in so they can go to work and good luck see you on the other side."

I jumped up and put on my house coat. I wake Vita up shaking him hard yelling, "get up I just got the call from lieutenant Cob we all have to move out!"

Vita sits on the side of the bed stretching his arms out and yawning looking up at me saying, "move out to where Lex? We going to LA to do the Turkish dope dealer job that is up right now we already got haft the money for that job so now we have to go do it now."

"Look I have to go let Miss Ward in the house with this stylus could you go wake everybody up for me please baby."

"Okay I'll do that right now while you're getting the door." I quickly ran downstairs I open the door. Miss Ward walked in smiling, "good morning, Lex this is Mister Paul and his peoples there going to help you and your peoples with their wardrobe for this mission. Here are your tickets first don't lose them please." As four well-dressed people came pulling in this long black wardrobe cart and bags of all kinds of shit man, they had everything you name it. Two men two women all of them are young I would never think they would be working for a fucking black bag operation dressing a motherfucker up.

As the others started coming downstairs checking them out. *Well soon as all of us was together Mister Paul introduce us to his high-fashion, team to everybody pointing to each one of them Jill, Pam, Steve and Ray and they when to work on us like a world wind of magic elves. The down ass white girl Pam did me and Big Mama Reds nails and she hooked up all of our girly accessories for all of our outfits. The Sharpe slick black girl Jill did both are hair. Steve and Ray two good looking fly guys hooked up Jitta, Stump, Moon and Mister Price clothes and their hair.*

I can't front lieutenant Cob was right we looked like whole differ-ent people all together man a make-over for dope Jackin crooks, killers' thieves, and fucking paid assassins I know this shit will never make it to network TV any time soon. I looked at myself in the mirror knowing we can pull this shit off in my true psycho bitch fashion. Miss Ward gave us the once over speaking loudly smiling now this will work just fine. Miss Ward shakes my hand then she bumps fist with me too winking her eye at me some real sister girl hood shit. They even gave us the high-end luggage to go with are new look first class all the fucking way. Wow I can get use to shit like this for real. The cherry on top of all this was the Bentley limo white waiting outside of the door. I saw it when Mister Paul rolled out the door with his funny ass walk and metrosexual tendencies. Miss Ward stood in front of all of us lining us up running it down to us establishing all our roles really fast on this mission.

Miss Ward pointing at each one of us talking like a hip ass, "okay you Mister Price you're her number two man with power over everybody when she's not in the room or whatever." You Jitta, Moon, Stump, Vita and Big Mama Red is the highly paid muscle of the outfit you got me? All of us at the same time say yes! *And we all burst out laughing loud.* Then she quickly pull-ing me to the side telling me in my ear. "Joe said don't forget to holla at your boy Vita about the Omer Kaya thing just in case it, do jump off.

"I told the lieutenant that I got this Miss Ward."

"Okay good one thing before y'all roll I want y'all to meet your driver."

She quickly when to the door waving her hand and this tall dark skin hunk of a man with a black suit on walked in. Miss Ward is pointing at each one of us speaking. "Lex is the boss here isMister Price the number two top Dawg and the Sharp-ley dressed thugs over here is Vita, Jitta, Moon, Stump and Big Mama Red this is Nick Lit." He waves not speaking a word.

Miss Ward said, "okay, my job is done here."

Vita came walking over picking up one of the bags Miss Ward yelled oh no that's Nick's job the whole time all of you are together everybody have their eyes on you.

Nick is the driver and valet he does all the work like this you guys are the top notch hired guns for Trina Ice remember that ladies and gentlemen.

Miss Ward blurted out, "okay, good luck to you all and I'll see you on the other side one!"

I spoke fast, "okay, let's get the fuck out of here I walked out with Vita and Miss Ward as Nick Lit is carrying all of the bags putting them into the white limo trunk."

Miss Ward walked over to her whip as her driver jumped out opening her door, she jumps in wave at all of us an takes off down the street. I waved Mister Price over to me before I got inside of the limo, I ask him what you know about this guy I seen the way you were, looking at him when Miss Ward made the introductions.

HOLLYWOOD SWINGING

He is an ex Ombre general five star's stone-cold killer from the door.

Vita uttered, "I never heard of them before."

"Mister Price barked, "oh yeah well ask Jitta. He'll tell you he just got out of prison he can give you their run down on them animals. They are no joke for real."

I quickly take Vita to the side before we got into the limo.

"Look, were on a mission here and I just might have to get some information out on this guy. So, your going have to be cool, okay."

"Oh, so you're telling me you just might have to fuck one these guys. Is that's what you're telling me? Then no, I don't like this shit, Lex."

"Well, you are going have to put up with it until this shit is over the lieutenant told me if you mess this up for him your dead."

"So, I am going to need you to put your big boy pants on and deal with this shit just like I did when I saw y'all fucking them hoes that night, okay."

"Yeah, okay I'll be cool."

I quickly grabbed him and looked him in the eyes shaking him. "Listen, don't fuck this up and get yourself killed, Vita. I signed up for this shit. I'm not a fucking rotten lousy ho. I'm a bitch that will survive at all costs! And I don't care what anybody thinks about me if I must suck and fuck a guy to kill a nigga that's what I do just know that Vita' I was like that when I met you and I'll be like that after your ass is dead." *I see that look in his eyes if this nigga doesn't get it" it's something wrong with his ass it's not like I enjoy that shit I just use the best weapon in the fucking world on men to make them weak and that's sex some time.* He looked back at me, "I get it, Lex it is all work to get the job done."

"Now, you get it let us go you don't have to be like you're defending my honor or something nigga!"

"I'm a real psycho bitch when I'm on duty I only get an orgasm when I see blood gushing out of somebody's head. Your one sick bitch Lex!" We both started laughing jumping into the limo.

When we get to the airport, we all jump on a private jet I never been on one before wow, this thing is fucking lovely. We partied all the way their and talking a whole lot of shit. I slipped to the side in the bathroom to holla at Jitta about these Ombre prison gang motherfuckers. He told me their real old school, but it is a Black gang of killers but ironclad doe. I just wanted to know what kind of nigga I have in my mist when shit jumps off from the door. Four hours later we touch down in sunny Los Angeles ready to go to work the Jungle crew is fucking Hollywood swinging and ready to wreck shit from the gate.

"I'll run down my game plan on the crew when we get to the hotel room and work out the escape plan when I check out the landscape."

Soon as we got off the jet it is a limo waiting for us to take us to the hotel on the way there. I get the call from Mister Cesar, lieutenant Cobs right hand man. That all the samples and the product is waiting for us in our hotel room. So, we pull up at Ritz Carton 900 West Olympic Boulevard this place is luxurious I had pep in my step when we rolled in, and we all were playing the role to the fucking tee. The concierge Albert was nice and made our check in smooth and pleasurable Nick Lit helped with all the bags with the bellhops soon as were all

ready to go up to all our suites we have the whole 10th floor to are self's. A young dark skin Hispanic dude came walking up to me verbalizing fast excuse me Miss Trina this is for you.

He hands me a small envelope and he walked away quickly. I opened it and it said can't wait to meet you tonight Omer come to the penthouse suite 11'O' clock. We all head towards the elevator with Albert showing us to our rooms and we all get on then this couple jumps on and their arguing in French. I overheard the tall slender woman with a tight black dress on yelling, **"Dis a ce cocho de garder sa main sur mon cul** *Tell that pig to keep his hand off my ass!"*

I wanted to laugh, but I didn't want them to know I understood what they were talking about.

The tall very hairy plump man spoke I need for you to be more understanding about this. She quickly slapped the shit out of him he just stands their pissed off all of us on the elevator is looking at them. He yelled out, **"Vous Con!** *(You Cunt)"*

She shouted back with her eyes on fire," **Va te faire foutre!** *(Fuck you)."*

My eyes widen, and they both knew I understood what they were saying the elevator stopped at the 8th floor and they got off still yelling even more up and down the hallway. I made a mental note of what floor they got off on looking over at Mister Price who dug it as well.

So, when Albert shows us to our rooms and its off the hook the view is breathtaking the whole room is done up in white and light sky blue the ultimate upscale luxury at its finest. Everybody were happy with their rooms we all next door to one another I told everybody family meeting in one hour everybody agreed and quickly going to their rooms.

I went to my room to check on the samples and the product that was under the bed where he said it was in two large steel suitcases. I quickly set them on top of this king size bed opening them up I have ten sample bags and 50 keys of Fentanyl. I still count them quickly and put them back under the bed I make myself a drink at the bar on the right-hand side and light up a cigarette plotting my next move.

One hour on the dot I have my meeting with the crew, and it went smooth only thing. I was worried about was this new guy with us. I don't know if he's here to spy on us or help us kill these mother-fuckers or not a wildcard.

I chilled until it was time to meet the big man in the pent-house, I gathered everybody together in my room before going with all the details and codes we all worked out I told Nick Lit to stay in my room to keep an eye on the drugs. So, we don't get backed doored. We arrived a little after 11 O' clock in the pent-house they had about ten goons with guns and machine guns standing around their head of security name is Berkan.

He's a tall dark skin plump man with a thick mustache and a long beard with beady dark eyes. I can tell by the look in his pitch-black eyes he done killed a man of men from the door. I know the look. He had two sidekicks that never leave his side name Alp and Abi these two are young wild thrill kill killers loving the excitement of the game and danger is what they live for every day like a drug. I got these crazy motherfuckers clocked from the door. *I know just what to do for their ass and I got something really fucking brutal planed out for them.* Berkan meets us at the front door of the penthouse with his two dark skin gorilla goon gunmen. Berkan is babbling on Miss Trina Ice, I finally get a chance meet the ice queen of the Midwest welcome my name is Berkan! He points to his two air head goons talking loudly this is Abi and Alp my best men please come this way. I bump fist with him grinning his ass off with his yellow fucking teeth checking all of us out from head to toe.

It is not that many people when we walk inside of the place just a few hoochies to keep them entertain to suck and fuck. The three stooges walked us up to this fancy ass long-wooded table where Yusuf Ozturk a slim good-looking well-dressed man he looks like a fucking bookkeeper then an international heroin dealer. He is standing in front of the table. He came walking up to all of us speaking, "hello how was your flight, Miss Trina? I'm so glad you could make it here to speak with us."

I shake his hand replying nicely, "I would have not miss, this meeting for nothing in the world, Mister Ozturk."

"Oh no none of that you call me Yusuf please."

He turns to Berkan and announced, "you can go now so we can talk to the young lady and her associates."

His eyes are getting wide wanting them to leave him quickly because he's really annoyed with their presence. *I can tell they're just the fucking help and he treat them like there not shit* and the feeling *is mutual.*

I verbalize to him, "this is my right hand in my organization this is Mister James."

"Nice to meet you Mister James (Mister Price) and my security team Jay (Jitta) Miss Green (Big Mama Red), Mister Mack (Moon) Vince (Vita) and Mister Sam (Stump). "

He shook all their hands with his best ass kissing smile he bows and started pointing speaking loudly right this way ladies and gentlemen he walks over towards their large door opening them walking us all inside.

Sitting at this big desk with a woman sitting on his lap a big cigar in his mouth and a drink in his other hand is this fat dark skin man in an expensive black suit on Omer Kaya.

He jumps up fixing himself smiling speaking loudly in his thick Turkish accent hay you made it I should kiss you after that last deal. Trina, you really know what the hell, you're doing out here?"

I'm the fucking best Omar you should know that by now."

"Yes, you are please, have a seat would you like a drink or something I got your favorite gin. I have a shit load of blow I just got fresh from Hong Kong that will blow your fucking mind for real."

"Yeah, I would love a drink right about now. Just as long as you're talking about some real money this time. That is all I know about honey, and you should know that too."

He turns to the woman that was sitting on his lap babbling on, "this is my special lady Mi- Mi could you get us some drinks please?

Mi- Mi and get that coke from out of the back safe for me please honey so I can entertain our guest here sweetheart."

Mi- Mi the big butt blonde, white girl with deep blue eyes and big Dick sucking lips quickly walks over to the large bar on the left making the drinks. As everybody sits down in the leather chairs front of this huge desk along with Yusuf.

While were in the meeting with Omer Kaya fat ass and his ass kissing partner four mask men is creeping inside of my room in the dark. They quickly making it inside of the room looking around soon as one of the men find the suitcase under the bed. Nick Lit drops down from the ceiling with an ax in his hand soon as he falls on top of the mask man, he collapses, to the floor hard. Soon as Nick Lit stood up after knocking the first men down two of the mask men attacked him with knifes and he when to work on their ass. He sides steps the first man with speed and agility swinging his ax and it landed right into the second man neck Ouuffff!

Then he quickly ripped the bloody ax out of his neck and swang it is chopping the head off flying up hitting the ceiling and bouncing around like a ping pong ball. The first man soon as the third man ran hard charging towards him with a knife like a raging bull Nick Lit swings upwards with his ax hitting him right into his chest going deep. The fourth men came at Nick but Nick still holding on to the end of the ax, but the ax is stuck in his chest he swings him into the fourth man with all this tremendous force knocking him to the floor Blam! He rips the ax out of his chest with all his might he swinging it chopping the third man head off clean off his head flu into the wall bonces to the floor like a rubber super ball.

He quickly swinging the ax like a wind milled Swisssssshhh! Decapitating the fourth mask man with his head landing in the beautiful white brick fireplace glowing with neo blue lights. Nick Lit covered in blood walked in the bathroom pulling off his blood-soaked clothes pulling out his phone calling Mister Cesar talking out of breath I need a clean -up on aisle 10! When I got the text on my phone while I was in the meeting, I smiled now I know this wild card I have on my hands is a real vicious killer by nature. We're all getting high kicking the Willie Boo- Boo on the surface I already know they tried to fuck us. I articulated to him, so you want more keys of Fentanyl that's why you had me come here right? Yes, I need a whole lot more than 2,000 keys I got the last time. So, what are you talking about one metric ton? Yes, one metric ton to start with and in two more months or so two more metric tons if shit runs right and we have no problems bringing it in.

"Well, we have to sit around and crunch numbers on this shit Omer on that kind of operation. I can hook you up on the first metric ton but I'm going to need all the money. No, half of its cash and carry."

"Come on you guys know I am good for the money you have to work with me here I'm buying a whole lot of shit here. Mister James (Mister Price) cuts in talking fast. We understand you are a very big valuable customer with us but why don't you just buy what you can than flip that and come back. Buy a little more next time why rush it when you're playing into someone else sand box. Yusuf looks up at his partner then he stands up walking next to him whispering in his ear. *We already know the Mexican's have all of the heroin locked down in LA and these ass hole's is trying cut in on some of their market on the low. They don't have to tell me who the client is we just know he is fucking Mexican.* Then his phone rings on his desk in front of him he picks it up swiftly. He's nodding and grunting his head at first than I heard him speaking in Turkish **Ne?** *What.* **Hepsioidu** *Their all dead!* **Uyusturucu almamislar** *They didn't get the* *drugs. He quickly hangs up knowing we stuck it right up his ass trying to be slick I wanted to laugh but I had to hold it in, and I got something special in mind when I kill his ass too.*

He looks up at us, "well, maybe your right-hand man over here is right we will buy what we can, but I need to speak with you alone on this other deal."

"What other deal you talking about, Omer?" The one we talked about on the phone about the French men. Okay let me holla at my peoples and you and me can go talk about this shit. Omer, he points to his partner Yusuf to take Mi- Mi dizzy ass out the room I stood up walked a little way from where they were and huddle up with my team.

I spoke softly, "if I don't come back in three hours make your move and obliterate all these motherfuckers."

All of them just nodded their heads and slowly walked out the door with Yusuf Ozturk and Mi- Mi fussing right behind them closing the door behind them. Soon as the door closed, he gets up pulling a big fat yellow envelope out the desk draw and he stands up in front of me handing it to me I stick it my pocketbook.

He's spoke, "we agreed to 180,000 ahead for the chemist Ethan and his wife Eve this is half of the $180,000. You get the other half when the job is done but you have to do that shit tonight. They both are staying here in this hotel would you like another drink?"

"Yes, I would how about if I want more money?"

While he is making my drink, he said, "Look I don't have time for this shit Trina. I already told you I must kill this guy tonight before his partner Gabriel Chapelle hook up with them other Gooks. I will lose a shit load of heroin."

I knew his fat drunk dumb ass would bite on it and man he took an excessively big fucking bite too. He hands me my drink with his eyes getting wide pointing at the cocaine on the desk for me to snort some more of it.

I sipped on the drink and spoke loudly with my hands in the air. "You know this kind of fucking tight for a hit Omer man."

I stood up snorting some more coke from off his desk. I can't front that Hong Kong blow is really fucking good too. I put my head back to feel the drip even more as the drug started working on my brain flowing.

"Look, could you take that for now and I'll make it up on the back end when we do the deal with the drug's I just need for you to take care of that shit for me, please."

"So, when do I get the other haft of my money Omer, I'm not fucking playing because I'm doing this shit dirt cheap over here?"

"You will get your money tomorrow night, and we can work everything out with the drugs."

I stood up and yelled, "If you don't have all my money Omer man, I'm going to fuck you up for real." He came up on me closer putting me into a bearhug putting both his hand on my ass gripping both cheeks and we can work out some other things too baby. I just smiled I put my arms around his fat neck, and I looked him in his eyes I don't do quickies Omer you can break that white girl off in a few minutes with that weak sloppy shit player but a bitch like me like to cum if I'm fucking so you're going to need more time more Dick and some Viagra if you want some this good hot black pussy big man. He started laughing loud, "let me go run over to the desk. I snorted three more lines of coke off the desk. He is mumbling oh I can handle it baby your one sexy ass thing! He is looking back at me with his eyes all glassy and wide filled with lust. I started walking towards the door he quickly grabbing me by my arm really fast I just hugged him as he pulls me into him.

I started talking to him in my best sex kitten voice you do want me to take care of this thing for you right big daddy. He kissed me on my neck and then down near my breast. I let him do it giggling playing the role. He is grinding on me I feel his dick is hard but he's not working with much.

He is high and slurred, "I would love for you to call me big daddy while were in the middle of fucking, baby."

I pulled back nice and slow kissing him right in the mouth and looked him in his face. I said, "slow and sexy like we must take care of business before you and me, take care of the hot monkey business okay."

"Your right, baby. I do need this done tonight."

As he is kissing me on my neck not wanting to let me go but he does it slowly giggling. I told him you are going to walk me to the door daddy. "Yes, I'll do that, but I don't want you to go how about a quickie baby."

"I told you from the door I don't do quickies sweetheart I want to cum and gush it all over your dick your mouth if you like?"

"No quickies love that is some shit I just don't do. I love the part about you squirting your hot juices in my mouth. I know you do you, freaky ass motherfucker."

We both laughing with his arm around me walking out to the front door. Soon as we get to the front door of the penthouse, I kissed him long and deep he's like putty in my arms. I stopped pushing him off gently okay player tomorrow night the real shit will jump off.

He backs up muttering loudly, "it surely will baby I see you then."

I waved goodbye and I started switching my ass good walking away down the hallway towards the elevator. I am thinking to myself. I didn't have to fuck that fat piece of shit.

I called Mister Price to find out what's going on with Nick Lit killing them men in my room trying to steal the product. I jumped on the elevator on my way down to my room getting my phone out. Mister Price picks up on the first ring talking where you at. I just came from out of the penthouse with Omer fat freaky ass.

"Well, I'm glad you made it out of there look Mister Cesar got your room all clean up as good as new."

"Where you at right now?"

"I'm in your room waiting for you with Nick Lit. I can't wait to holla at him for real."

"Well, he is here me and him is eating pizza we will save you a slice okay. I'm almost to you one."

I get to my room and it's sparkling clean like I left it. You never know four men died with their head chopped off inside of there. I walked in the two of them are in the little lounge area eating pizza I bump fist with both of them and sit down blowing out air. I have to eat something fast because I have to go kill this dude right quick. I started eating the pizza wolfing it down.

"Mister Price, so that was the side deal he was talking about. I'm thinking he wanted to be alone with you so y'all can fuck or something."

"Well, he had that in mind too with his fat horny ass, but I played his ass. I got both the names of the French men and I didn't have to suck no Dick or fuck him thank Gawd. But you're still going to kill the dude we can just kill all of them tomorrow night and our job is done."

"Man, this pizza is good as I eat another piece. With a mouth full of food, I am talking but I want to suck him all the way in."

If the French man is not dead, he will get suspicious, and he might take off or something and our whole mission is fucked. So, I have to do it."

I turned to Nick Lit I have to say I thought you were suspect nigga."

"Na, Ma, I'm as real as they come that's why I'm here."

"Well, I know that shit now nigga welcome to the team motherfucker!"

We all started laughing as I bump fist with him.

"Where you from Nick?"

"North Philly."

"I'm from Beirut."

"Shit no wonder your tough as fucking nails. So, before I go smoke this French man and his wife. What is your story?"

"How you got into this bull shit?"

"Wow to make a long story short. I took out a cell of Nazis and Mister Cesar dropped me in with y'all." I quickly jump up going to the refrigerator getting me a beer opening it guzzling it down. I must go I started taking my clothes off walking towards the bedroom moving like a blur. I quickly go to the closet with the large spy wardrobe change Mister Cesar gave us before we took off for this assignment. I pick out the waitress outfit I slip it on swiftly. I check both my guns putting them in the back of my pants with this corny ass uniform on. I also make sure I have my magnetic door card that can open anyone of the doors here in the hotel I stick that deep down in my pocket.

I quickly go to my pocketbook pulling out a nice size sack of blow I open it up and dump out some the white powder on top of my bar. I shuffle it up making four fat lines on top of the smooth surface I snort up the four lines of coke. I put my head back feeling the drug immediately making my whole face numb and a buzzing freeze on my brain now I'm ready to kill shit. I came out the bedroom I bump fist with Mister Price and then Nick and I told them I be right back.

When I go out the front door, I head towards the exit door on the left that way I'm not seen on the hotel cameras. I go down to the basement where the kitchen at.

All long the large hallway is food carts where people already ate their food, they were there to be cleared off and someone comes to wash the dishes. I quickly take one of the used food carts, pulling it with me quickly. I started fixing it up making it look good as it I was going to serve somebody; I can't front I did make it look really nice. I quickly walked to the elevators real cool and calm I press the button and its only three people waiting on the elevator the people waiting on the elevator don't pay me any mind.

It is like being invisible when you're doing a service job these white motherfuckers don't even look at you as if you're a piece of shit on the sidewalk there trying to ignore. I press the eighth floor a long with three people going up to the tenth floor. Bing! I get off real fast pushing the food cart I'm just another nigga working in the hotel. I go up to the door and I knocked not too hard after a few minutes I can hear the man on the other side of the door Ethan speaking who is it? Food service sir. He gets closer to the door yelling, "we didn't order any food!" I put the pistol with the silencer on the end of it up to the door. **Pooouufff!** Shooting him right in the head I quickly reached in my pocket pulling out my magnetic card up to the door the light turned green. I swiftly pushed the door open stepping over Ethan dead body on the floor. I walked in smooth and very slowly his wife Eve was sitting on the bed smoking a cigarette in one hand and a drink in the other. Soon as I walked up on her She is in shock with her eyes getting wide and dropping her drink out of her hand. **Pooouufff!**

I shot her in the middle of her head she fell back on top of the bed with all the blood splashing all over the white silk pillows and sheets.

I stick my pistol in the back of my corny ass uniform. I promptly creeped towards the front door. I closed the door back as I was leaving and I went towards the back, exit doors and I got ghost like a motherfucker. I 'm back in my room on the 10th floor faster than I could blink my eyes. Soon as I open the door, I can smell the weed smacking me in the face Mister Price and Nick is getting their puff on with a bottle of Jack Daniels whiskey.

I walked up to them at the table and giggled, "I'll be joining the party with y'all in a few minutes."

They both giggled blowing out big clouds of smoke while I when in the bedroom taking off that corny ass slave outfit shit putting my black jeans on along with my black killing the game t shirt on. I swiftly came out of the bedroom when over to the bar getting a glass filling it with ice and I when and sat at the table sitting my glass full of ice on top of the table with the Hoodfellas. Mister Price slide the bottle of whiskey over to me I caught it and I poured me a nice size drink for sure.

Mister Price winks his eye at me and Nick past me the fired up blunt with the smoke flying in the air I take it out of his hand. I started puffing talking to both of them all we have to do now is wait for phase two and were out of here.

Mister Price said, "I think we should smoke there ass now then get the fuck out of here I would feel a hell of a lot better." We all started laughing we got high for the next three hours talking shit and having a good time before both of them when to their own rooms we all were nice and fucked up.

The next day I sleep a little late. I was still buzzing from last night I called up for room service I got my favorite steak and eggs with some coffee and everything bagels. I got my grub on and just laid around my room smoking cigarettes getting all my rest now before I know were going have to put in some real mad work in the next two days. Soon as I dozed off sitting up in my bed the phone wake me up, I get it fast and its Mister Price.

"Yo, what's up?"

"Yeah, the cops were up in here looking into those murders on the eighth floor."

"Oh yeah. Yeah, they had some hot shot detectives checking shit out."

"I know they looked at all the hotel videos."

"Yeah, I know just what they found nothing!"

We both started laughing out loud because we both know that Mister Cesar was already tapped inside of the hotel's video system. Leaving the cops frustrated and fucked up in the head that somebody can walked up to their room and kill two people and never be seen like they were invisible.

PHASE TWO MOP UP

I called everybody from our team to be on standby until I get the call from Omer or Yusuf. So, we can make our move. I played this shit like a real pro, and I knew I'd be hearing from one of them real soon it's 10:30 P.M. I'm chillin by the bar when I hear this knock on my door. I get up going to the door and I peek out and I see that same young Hispanic dude with an envelope in his hand. I slowly open the door and this dude smile got wider speaking what's up sweetheart this is for you. I took it out his hand and I said, thanks, what is your name?"

"My name is Don Juan the lover give me an hour and I'll rock your lovely sweet chocolate world baby girl!"

Too tell you the truth I wanted to take him inside of my, room and fuck his fine Puerto Rican brains out but something told me not to do it and I always follow my first mind. I laughed uttering with a smile,

"I bet you could, Mister dark and fine. Don Juan but if you got some big mama Trina it just might blow your Puerto Rican mind."

He giggled and gave me his best Mackin a bitch stare I close the door in his face I walked back over to the bar where I was chillin at. I leaned back in my chair opening the small envelope I read it and it said, "great work love can't wait to see you tonight at midnight Omer."

This crazy motherfucker has a fucking nerve to put two little hearts and a smiley face on this note. I just giggled sipping on my drink I got your fat ass now. What's funny that this fat Turkish gangster motherfucker think he's getting some pussy tonight. I hit up the team there already to get this show on the fucking road and close this mission out.

An hour before I go meet up with the fat man, I link up with the whole team in my room checking on our earpieces I made sure that were all on Channel three. I looked up at Big Mama Red and I ask her, "how you feel? I'm, good to go, girl."

We bump fist smiling I love the look in her eyes filled with confidence and excitement to get to work. I'm checking everybody else out everybody and there already to do their thing now I can't wait until midnight come.

We all got a little high, with a little toot here and a puff their nothing crazy not like we always do but I made sure none of us got to fucked up to take care of our business. We just joke around and talk a lot of shit. I love this because this is how we all got tight. I think that happen when we were all got fucking stuck on that farm when we were training not knowing if we were going to live or die.

It is midnight and were all on are way up to the penthouse I let everybody know that soon as I smoke Omer fat ass the shit is on to the break of dawn. We get up to the large doors. I'm knocking on the door after a few minutes. Abi one of the ass hole twins opens the door and I can tell he was higher than a motherfucker. He is talking, all loud Trina Ice and her crew come on in here girl and make yourself at home. Mister Price looks at me looking around seeing their much more loser.

Mister Price talking under his breath speaking low, "damn their all fucked up high."

"Yeah, and real sloppy to is all of y'all digging this shit."

As were all walking inside Moon mumbling, " just because you see a dog laying down don't mean he's easy to kill just know that shit y'all."

I uttered low your right about that shit we all must stay focus on the job at hand no matter how easy it might seem to be. My team is ready to go scoping the whole room. I walked toward the back of the large space to the big doors. I open the door

I slowly stroll towards Omer's desk. He's sitting on top of his desk with his arms wide open to hug me. Omer shouting, "you did a good job for me, thank you."

"Well, you know me I'm the fucking best you know that so where is my fucking money at big man."

"Let me get it for you, sweetheart. I have it right here."

He sits down at his desk he quickly opens the draw just at that moment I whip out my pistol from behind my back pointing it right in his face. Drop the gun and give me the envelope with my fucking money! Omer giggling, "I was not going to pull a gun on you Trina."

I quickly walked around the desk with my pistol in his face yelling, "if you move one fucking muscle and I'll put a hot slug in your fat ass quicker than you can blink motherfucker!" *But in the background, I can hear all this shooting and yelling in the other room now I must work fast.* When I got closer, I mashed the gun up to his head. I reach down to open the desk draw and I was right he has his hand on the gun ready to whip it out on me. See you lying ass fat fucker drop the gun now! From out of nowhere two goon gun men came popping up on the left and right of me both have machine guns. Without hesitation I shot Omer in his head **Pooouuufff!**

The two goons open fire on me **Kackapkata!** I ducked down low behind the desk as they came towards me fast shooting and the bullets just missing my ass. Just as I peek up to fire back at these two asses holes the door flu open and its Big Mama Red spitting hot shit at the two goon gun men ripping both to fucking shreds. I can see their flesh flying from their bodies with the blood splashing all over the desk and some of it got in my face as well. I stood up, "Gawd damn, girl I'm glad to see you!"

"Look, we have to move the party done got started early in the other room girl let's go!" I quickly picked up the machine gun from the dead man's hand. We both ran towards the back-exit door on the other end of the penthouse on the right-hand side.

Soon as I pushed the door opened, we started running down the steps we get halfway down and its four men running up the steps yelling and shooting at us. I quickly pushed Big Mama Red to get on the side of the wall with me. I can hear them stomping up the steps even faster towards us soon as they got a little closer. I stepped out letting them have it. **Kapackata Ratta tat tat tat Kapackacka!**

I hit the first two men up front we quickly ducked inside the exit door on my left on one of the floors soon as the door closed. I put the machine gun strap on my shoulder I pull out my pistol with the silencer shooting the light fixture out and I laid down flat on the floor and Big Mama Red did the same with me. We can hear them huffing and puffing the first man slowly open the door looking inside in the darkness Pooouufff!

I shot him in the middle of his head the second man started running away. I jumped up and ran after him soon as he made the turn to go down the steps Pooouuuff! I shot him right in the side of his neck as the mist of blood flying in the air hitting the walls and his bloody body fell down the stairs as we can hear his last death scream.

Big Mama Red came running behind me muttering, "I hope it is not any more of them so we can get the fuck out of here."

We quickly started running down the steps and we make it to the ground floor. Before I open the door and walk out of there, I pulled out my phone calling Mister Price. He quickly answers yelling, "where the fuck is y'all at we all had to get the hell out of there the shit when sideways."

Me and Mama Red is at the exit doors on the ground floor near the dock area. Hole on I'll be right there to pick y'all up! I peeked out the door slowly I don't see anybody there I heard the car pull up I quickly turned to Big Mama Red, "let's go! You don't have to tell me twice, honey!"

I pushed the door open fast soon as we started running to-wards the truck from out of nowhere is a fucking barrage of bullets.

We both ducking down near these dumpsters shooting back. I'm thinking this is it for both of us. When I looked up shooting at these motherfuckers it is the ass hole twins Abi and Alp along with their fat ass boss Berkan with some other goon zipper head dark skin foreigner shooting at us. As me and Big Mama Red is pinned near the dumpsters and sparks is flying every fucking where with us blasting back at their ass. Mister Price rolling up shooting at them from the truck. Popping up from out on the left of us is Stump with a flamethrower strapped to his back.

He's so low to the ground the shooters never seen him running up on them until he lets them have it with the flamethrower. Wooooooffffffffff! He set all four of their monkey asses on fire there all jumping screaming as me and Big Mama Red started running for our life towards the truck, we made it and jumped in the truck out of breath as Mister Price floored it.

I yelled out, "what about Stump? Mister Price just smile your boy Vita got him don't worry Trina Ice."

We all started laughing while he is driving off towards the highway. I shouted out, "what about are shit at the hotel, Mister Price?"

"What happen they were already shooting before I could smoke that fat motherfucker?"

"Well, your boy Omer was going to kill all of us after his partner made another deal with somebody else. With that metric ton of Fentanyl cutting him out of the deal, he was asking for and all of our shit is packed up waiting for us at the next location. Do you know who he made the deal with?"

"Yeah, Mister Cesar told me it is a guy name Sabokey ,this crazy ass African drug lord!"

Omer Kaya partner Yusuf Ozturk double crossed him made a deal with Sabokey some of the men got wind of it and all hell broke loose soon as you were going to kill Omer. Don't tell me that's our next job right Mister Price? We have to talk to lieutenant Cob about that shit. Now if the client wants us to get the metric ton of fentanyl and kill Gabriel Chapelle the other chemist that's cooking it up for them, he'll have to pay out more loot for us to do that shit do you follow me now.

"Yeah, I know it all about the Benjamins is the name of the game."

Mister Price started laughing puffing on his cigarette.

"So, what about are thing with your daughter Peggy?"

"Do not worry I got a foolproof plan where we can still get that done and do this job to trust me."

"Well, if you're crazy enough to think we can pull it off I'm with you."

 "Well, I did what you ask me to do, and I called my boy in Hong Kong."

He told me he's down to help me. He's going to meet us at the next location we got two weeks to get ready for this next mission. While we're all getting ready for that we're going to go get my daughter come back and do that job I got it all figured out Lex. "Hey, you are the man with the fucking plan. Let's us do this shit."

We all started laughing as he is flying up the highway. I looked in the rearview mirror seeing this truck coming up behind us. I tap Mister Price," yo, it is a truck hot on our ass! That is just the others following us we all good Lex trust me."

He pulls out his phone he hits the button yelling, "just keep following me up their Vita."

"Oh, don't you worry. I don't know where the fuck I'm at."

"I'm right behind you man."

I felt so much better hearing his voice Big Mama Red was falling asleep. It took us another two hours to get there we arrived at this huge grape Orcherie. Over two hundred acres of beautiful farm-land and fresh air were all surrounded by God's country and fuck-ing blue skies wow. I turned to Big Mama Red shaking her to wake up we are here getting her up. Pulling up right behind us is Vita and the others.

Walking up to the truck is a familiar face it is Miss Janet from the training farm in Pennsylvania. Mister Price rolled down the window. Miss Janet stuck her head inside of the truck with a big smile speaking.

"Hi, y'all doing I know y'all got to be hungry after that long trip up here."

I quickly replied, "you damn right we are."

We all started laughing as we all got out of the truck the same time the others started getting out. I quickly walked over to Vita hugging him he, is whisper into my ear, "I am so glad you are aright, Lex."

"Me too, what the fuck happen?"

"Man, the shit jumps off faster than we could get ready for good thing. We know what the fuck were doing, or we would all be dead out this bitch."

Stump Moon and Jitta came up hugging me and Big Mama Red one by one telling us with deep concern that they are glad to see us alive. *We were all laughing and bull shiting with one an-other but now I know are crew is super tight now.* Miss Janet led, the way to this large beautiful Spanish style Villa I only seen shit like this on TV and in magazines at the doctor's office. We all went inside sitting at this long wooden table eating to-gether like family, I was really loving them.

I KNEW IT WAS SOME SHIT WITH THIS DUDE

We all ate like wild Vikings having a good time too. After we were finish eating. We see the same people from the Pennsylvania training farm Frank, Billy and Andy showed us to are rooms. Soon as I flop down on that bed, I toss my backpack on the floor I was done. I was horny, but I needed to rest up before I get my shit off. I took my clothes off and I quickly jumped in the shower soon as I came out the shower drying myself off. I rolled me up a Dutch with a fat ass blunt. I didn't even finish it all leaving it in the ash tray haft smoked. I was rocked out on the bed.

I'm sleep and in the middle of the fucking night I can feel this rock-hard tool rubbing on my ass pumping. I started giggling and I turn over and it's Vita smiling wide.

I moaned, "that really feels good, but I got something for your ass nigga."

He started laughing, "I got me some rest too so bring that shit on baby."

I turn over kissing him then I quickly took off my panties. I climbed on top of this sexy ass dark skin man kissing and sucking on his nipples. *That nigga was making more noises moaning as if I was sucking on his Dick or something.* He's feeling me up on my ass while I'm going to work on his sexy black ass. Then I stood up over him and I squad over him as I reached down grabbing his thick black tube steak. I aimed it towards my awaiting wet box anticipating his steel soldier to rock my moist muffin and make me blast of into the cum filled stratosphere. I sat down on his rock-hard rod slowly making fit my dripping wet pussy.... Sqush! Ooooohhhhhhh! I started bouncing up and down on him like a hobby horse not to fast at first, I placed both my hands-on top of his chisel hard tattoo chest rocking back and forth. The more I dug my nails into his chest the more he started stroking me upward with his large strong black hands on my round brown ass. With me pumping my hips hard and I can feel that tingling sensation bubbling that I'm about to cum. And Boom! This nigga beat me to it I can feel his hot jizzim filling me it felt so fucking good I let mind go. But I exploded like a geyser it shot out all over the fucking place it shocked Vita, I seen it in his eyes. He played it off later, but this nigga jumped like a bitch because I never came like that before. We had to both get up because I made a large wet spot in the middle of the bed.

I think he was a little upset that we had to change the sheets. But I didn't give a fuck I got my shit off I quickly pulled the sheet of the bed and I tossed it in the corner. And grabbed my pack of smokes from off the nightstand lit up a cigarette and sat in the chair on the side of the bed puffing my ass off floating on a fucking cloud. He got a cigarette off me, and I lit it up for him we puffed and talked a little while he kissed me. Then he climbed back up on the bed laying down avoiding the wet spot breathing hard trying to get his shit together. I fell asleep in the chair. The next morning, I hear a big knock on the door I was still laying in the chair from last night. I'm still in a fucking deep sleepy haze.

I hear this excited voice on the other side of the door yelling, "Lex get up he's here he wants to talk to you!"

I'm trying to get myself together, so I yelled back as I'm jumping up.

"I don't have any clothes on, Mister Price. Hold on motherfucker!"

I'm scrambling, to find my panties on the floor I put them on in a dash up on my ass. I quickly slipped on my jeans and a top I pulled out my suitcase right quick. I looked over on the bed and Vita is knocked the fuck out sleep with the covers pulled up over his head balled up. I lit up a cigarette and quickly walked to the door I peek out and see the two of them. I open the door and I step out and I looked up and this so-called Hong Kong Harry character is this well build good looking nigga I'll fuck him in a heartbeat. I was expecting this dumpy ass white man with a fucking bad haircut this motherfucker was a gorgeous Black thing.

Mister Price in his heavy voice, "Lex, this is Jelly" Jelly this is Lex.'

'Nice to meet you Lex I heard so much about you from Mister Price here."

"Well, he didn't tell me shit about you and you don't look like you're in the CIA to me, nigga!"

"You look more like a drug dealing hustler from the streets. I know the type."

They both started laughing loud Jelly barked out with a smirk on his good- looking grill, "that's why I am so fucking good."

"Yeah, we will see about that shit, homey. Look, I have to Jet right now I will link up with you later so we can rap about what we are going to do with this operation."

"Cool, I'm with it. I holler at you then sweetheart. Mister Price just bump fist with me and I when back into my room to get washed and dressed.

An hour blaze past we all bust a grub talking a whole lot of shit with the crew then we all when and took a walk near the horse staples. It is me Big Mama Red, Stump, Jitta, Nick Lit, Moon and Mister Price Vita came running up at the last minute. Soon as he looked up, he locked eyes with the dude Jelly. I looked Vita in the face. "

Do you know this dude" He whispered," he looks like some dude from Brooklyn we had a beef with not too long ago."

Me and Mister Price did most the talking on how we were going to do this shit and we made a date for when we are going to move out two days from now, we all agreed while we wait on lieutenant Cob give us the green light on are next move. I'm thinking it this black ghetto macho thing with the dude Jelly and Vita not knowing it was going to be some real sparks flying between them. We all walked back towards the farmhouse with Vita putting his arm around my neck as were walking. Running up behind us is the dude Jelly pointing his finger in Vita's face yelling. Now I know you're getting some big-time loot now you can pay me for those ten bricks you and your crew took off me! Stump steps up pulling out his gun pointing at Jelly face shouting back up from my homey nigga! Moon and Jitta whip out their guns as well ready to smoke this guy.

I'm wondering what the fuck is going on with them I knew it was shit between this dude and Vita. They both squared off putting up their fists every stepped back to let them go at it. Vita, sucker punched him right in his jaw Blam! The guy Jelly fell back but he came right back with a left upper-cut punch hitting Vita up under his chin **Kook!** *Vita fell back right on the back of his ass Doom! Vita jumps back up charging Jelly swinging a haymaker and it landed right on the side of Jelly's head knocking him sideways.*

There ready to get back into it again to tango when. Mister Price gets in the middle of them all yelling with his face turning red what the fuck is going on here! Jelly started talking loudly this nigga robbed me and my homey's a couple years ago in Brooklyn and I had to replace them motherfuckers or I would have got smoked. Mister Price looking over at Vita and the others asking is this true? All of them not saying shit rolling their eyes looking up in the air and sucking their teeth.

Mister Price talking with his hands up in the air, "yeah, I can see it in all in your eyes!"

"Look, were all on the same team here now you guys are going have to put all that street shit to the side for right now!"

Jelly steps up shouting, "no, fuck that shit. I want to be fucking compensated today or were going have a big fucking problem!"

Mister Price is blowing out air before he started speaking, "okay, Vita gives him half of it today and the other half after we get paid from our next job or your going have to leave the team today."

All of us is looking at one another as Mister Price walks up in Vita's face talking that's the only way, I see it this is my farm and my decision to keep the peace over here.

Vita eyes are on fucking fire yelling, "yeah, but Lex is in charge of the whole crew not you motherfucker!"

Mister Price yelling back. "Lex has nothing to do with this shit from the past just give him the money or just pack your shit up and go! You didn't say nothing but a fucking word you white motherfucker. I'm gone!"

I quickly grabbed him by his arm, "look just give him the money to squash this shit right quick and we can keep it moving and get this money baby."

He pulls his arm from me fast with deep anger pulling out his gun sticking it in my face. I whip out my pistol with the silencer on the tip at the same time getting in my gun stance.

Vita is yelling at me, "you of all people should know it's not the money it is the principal of the fucking matter!"

"Put the fucking gun down so we can talk Vita don't let this shit get you killed nigga!"

"Oh, you're going to kill me over these no-good cracker motherfuckers!" He spit right in my face a big gob of it too. Soon as it hit my face I snaped out Pooouuufff! Pooouuufff! Pooouuufff! I shot him in the head once and twice in the chest. His lifeless body hit the ground as if it was in slow motion or something Doom! Big Mama Red bend over to check on him while all the others just stood there not saying a word in shock.

Big Mama Red muttered, "he's dead."

Nick Lit checked him too putting his hand across his neck

speaking with his heavy voice, "it's a done deal."

Moon looked at me shouting. "that's fucked up, Lex man."

I'm pissed off wiping the spit from my face still holding my gun looking at everyone's expression on their face seeing who I'm going to have a fucking problem with after killing this nigga.

Jitta looked me deep in my eyes, and he spoke up loud shit,

"I would have shot that nigga too if he spit in my fucking face!"

Nick Lit shouting, "me too, fuck that shit Lex he had it coming to him!"

"Don't worry about that shit Lex.I got your back!"

Mister Price speaking with a sad face, "I tried to end that shit peacefully. Now this is going to cause big riff within the crew here. I'll get somebody to clean this shit up."

Mister Price wave at Nick Lit to come with him and the guy Jelly walked away. *But I keep seeing that nigga Jelly looking at me and Big Mama Red. I'm thinking he's checking me out.* Moon looks down at Vita's bloody body and he walks away. I called out to him, "yo Moon hold up man let me holler at you right quick."

He just waves me off and he kept walking towards the house. Stump walks up to me speaking, "I'm still with you, Lex."

Big Mama Red cuts in, "yeah me too I'm still down with you bumping fist with me."

Jitta walks up in front of me uttering, "look, I'm going to go talk to him aright and I'm still down with you as well. I'm old school if a nigga did that to me. I would have done the same thing, sis. So don't feel guilty about that shit, okay."

I put my gun in the back of my jeans and me and Big Mama Red walks towards the house *the sun is in my eye's, but I really don't feel bad about the shit.*

An hour later me and Big Mama Red was in my room sitting on the bed snorting coke and talking shit drinking beer when it is a knock at the door.

I yelled out, "who is it? It is me Mister Price!"

"Yeah, come on in. He just looks at the two of us speaking I took care of everything, and your boy Moon is packing his shit up to leave us."

"Well, that's cool if he's rolling out nobody is going to stop him, he's a grown ass man." Big Mama Red blowing out a big cloud of smoke from her cigarette cutting her eyes at me speaking, up "why don't you go and talk to him. Lex he just might stay if you go holler at him."

"No if he wants to go, I have to let him go because later on he just might want to do something fucked up to me down the line" Mister Price looking at both of us, "your right but to tell y'all the truth he can't leave he knows too much about me and lieutenant Cob with his eyes getting wide."

I know just what that means without him saying shit. I stood up from off the bed I'll go talk to him I'll be back. I quickly walks to his room, and I bang on the door.

He yells on the other side of the door, "who the fuck is it?"

"It's me Lex!"

"Go away I don't want to talk to you!'

The door opens really fast its Jitta jumping up and down yelling. 'I'm trying to talk to this hard-headed motherfucker. I'm telling him if he leaves here, they are going to fucking kill his Black ass!"

"You know your father is right you know too much for you to jump up like a little bitch and roll!"

"So, what are you here to do the fucking deed for them Lex?"

"No, I won't have to that nigga Jelly is going to be the one to put a hot slug in your dome for y'all talking his shit from two years ago."

He stops cold from packing up his shit in the suitcase looking up at me talking nice and calmly, "now, you want to know what you're right."

He looks at me then his father with his eyes getting wide.

"So, you want me to tell Mister Price you're not leaving right?" "Yeah, but I did not like what you did to Vita that shit was cold Lex!"

Moon you see it one way and I see it another. People in a crew don't always see things eye to eye he pushed one of my buttons, but I don't want to see you get killed over that shit."

I walked over to him hugging him uttering, "were still family."

He laughed talking loudly, "yeah, were all still family you crazy ass bitch!"

"Good now can I go back and get my groove on in my room now nigga."

"Yeah, I holler at you later and thanks."

Jitta walks over to me hugging me thanks I been in his ear for the last hour or so trying to tell him what time it is. He continues jabbering on with me just giggling. Jitta walks me to the door smiling his ass off knowing that I stop his son from getting killed. I'm walking back to my room when I run into Miss Janet telling me that its dinner time.

Soon as I walked back to my room, I'm looking down the hallway and leaning on the door smiling and laughing. Is this nigga Jelly talking to Big Mama Red leaning on the door. Damn I'm thinking this motherfucker was digging on me. I said to myself I'm not going to hate on my girl she needs some Dick too shit wish I could jump in and fuck him as well. But I know my girl don't get down with no freaky shit like that. I walked up on them, and I speak What's up? Big Mama Red spoke in her sex kitten voice, "This handsome ass man asks me would I sit with him at dinner."

"Oh, hell yes and after dinner for dessert. You have to sit on his face and ask him how sweet it is."

We all started laughing. Still laughing I said, "y'all go and have some fun and don't pay me any mind girl you know I'm crazy!"

I looked Big Mama Red in the face whispering to her, " get some for me girl that nigga is fucking fine."

She quickly gave me a pound (Bumping fist together) I walked and open the door while they went down the hallway. I can hear both of them giggling echoing down the hallway. I was happy for her to get some shit. I just smoke the nigga fucking my lights out. I walked into the large dining area with that thick aroma of some down-home food that make your mouth water. I see everybody sitting at the table talking shit I went over and got my food. I walked over to where Moon Jitta and Stump is sitting at. Big Mama Red is not too far all Booed- Up and I'm just loving it for real. Nick Lit comes and sit with us speaking to everybody with his plate in his hand. Mister Price didn't eat with us I know something is about to fucking go down I just get that feeling. But on the surface, everything is all good in the hood. After we bust, a good grub Mister Price came up to me waving towards me to come see him. I get up from talking a whole lot of shit with the boys. I Surry over to him fast he walks me down the hall talking my man Jelly is hot. What the fuck you mean he's hot Mister Price. We both strolling out the door on the side of the dining area Look I just found out from my man on the inside this guy just Jacked the client list from lieutenant Cob. "Oh, shit then he is going to come here and kill his ass, right?"

"Yeah, but this is a fucking opportunity of a lifetime. If you and I get that client list, you and me, can split it and run are own shop." "I'm down only if I can trust you Mister Price."

"Oh, shit you do not trust me bye now Lex?"

"Do not take it personal, Mister Price. I don't trust a living soul on this fucking planet earth for real."

He looks me deep in my eyes pronouncing with that fucking boy scouts of America tone in his voice, "you can trust me Lex I will not fuck you okay! I want my own just like you do."

I looked back at him replying fast don't you make good money with Fat Joe? "I would make more if I had my own shit!

"Or I would not tell you about this shit while your girl is fucking his brains out you and me can go in his room and get it off his computer."

"It sounds like a plan but suppose he go to his room?"

"I know your girl better then you do if she going to have sex with that dude it is going to be in her room where she feels more comfortable at."

I looked at him and he bumps fist with me smiling barking," you got to give it to me you want to bet on it then Lex? No but how is we going to break into his computer? "

"I will do that I'm an expert at that shit trust me and I'll have Miss Janet will watch are back."

"What?"

"Yeah, she works for me, and she done this shit before you can trust her too, I took good care of her."

"Okay I'm in but if anyone of ya'll move kind of fucking funny on me I will kill both of y'all and keep getting up you do know that shit right. "

"You already tried to kill me twice already Lex just do this with me, and you can write your own ticket. We both laughed as I bump fist with him.

And just like he said they went to Big Mama Reds room later that night me and Mister Price make are move while everybody is doing their thing. Getting high watching TV playing cards while the three of us creep up to Jelly's room at the end of the dark hall. The shit when off smooth we go into the room with Miss Janet standing outside of the door with her big gray cart with towels soap and rags like a hotel.

We rolled up in the room Mister Price sits down at the desk he had the computer up on. He opens his laptop computer sticking in a flash-drive typing super-fast then I can see popping up on the screen it is copying the files. But I'm on edge hoping no body come walking by. It took a little time for them to copy but he got it all done we walked out nice and smooth. What fucked me up is that Miss Janet was so cool and calm. Me and Mister Price walked off but when I looked back, I could see Stump walking up to her putting his hand on her ass taking her by the hand down to his room.

Me and Mister Price when to his room to look at the files on his computer and he did what he said he was going to do. *What he didn't know was I had my hand on my pistol with the silencer on the tip the whole time. If one thing looked funny or shady, I would have blown, his head off and took the whole list for my fucking self.* He split the list with me, and he put it on a flash drive for me soon as I rolled out I when and checked it to make sure it was not a fucking trick, but I was good to go when I checked it out on my laptop computer. Now I wish I had somebody to celebrate this moment with I just when to my black backpack. *I still had a lot of that shit left in the big suitcase.*

And I pulled out some the coke I had in there. I got my mirror I dumped some the coke on top of it and had me a little party by myself. I made some fat ass lines and snorted them up until I got twisted and so fucked up, I laid across my bed and passed out. I'm sleeping like a fucking baby when I hear this loud sounds of machine gun fire and some yelling outside my window **Kapackatakacka!** *And the loud roar of a lot of motorcycles everywhere.* I jumped up getting my pistols and my machine gun cocking it back when it a loud banging on my door.

I looked out the window real fast I ran to the door yelling, "who is it?"

"It's me Mister Price let me in hurry up!"

I opened the door he rushed in gum flapping on and on from his lips with a machine gun in hand and a backpack on his back. We got a bunch of fucking Nazis running around shooting everything that moves!

"I thought this place was fucking secret Mister Price. It was someone sold us out for some loot!"

"So, who the fuck are they after?"

"Your new crew member Nick he took out a whole cell of Nazis motherfuckers some time back!"

"Look, can we get the fuck out of here I know you got a back way out this place?"

He smiles, "just get your shit and let's go!"

"What about the others?"

"I got them too you just come on so we can go, Lex!"

I quickly grabbed my suitcase with the handles and put my backpack on to my shoulder along with my machine gun. I ran out into the hallway Mister Price pointing his finger talking low to me just go to the end of the hallway and wait for me and the others okay. I did what he said I started walking towards the end of the hallway. But I kept looking back and I and I did not stop until I got to the end of the hallway. I can see Mister Price banging on each one of their doors telling each one of them to be quiet about it putting his finger over his mouth. I waited in the dark with my hand on my pistol the first person I seen is Big Mama Red and Jelly running up this narrow dim hallway. I hugged her real fast she uttering what the fuck is going on? I started talking low its some Nazis after Nick.

Soon as I said that we can hear a loud crashing sound **Kaboom!** It shook the whole house knocking us to the floor all I see is dust and smoke flying in the air. I can hear machine gun fire getting louder and closer Mister Price came running up with Miss Janet, Billy, Frank, Andy, Stump Moon Jitta and Nick Lit. They are running and shooting back at these men dressed in black coming up behind them. Frank, Andy, Billy is up front. Stump, Moon, Miss Janet, and Nick Lit is locked in a gun battle in the narrow hallway back and forth. It sounded like thunder from the sky but right next to you fucking ears with bullet humming past your, head.

Bullets is flying all over the place filled with smoke and loud noise of machine gun fire along with wood chips flying in the air from the hallway from the impact of the bullets hitting them. I can hear men screaming falling to the floor I did not know at the time that Andy and Frank got cut down fast. *We could not start shooting with them because we would have hit Moon, Billy, Stump, Miss Janet and Nick Lit because we were in front of them in this narrow wooden hallway.*

Mister Price after shooting at the men coming up the hallway in front of the three of them pushing me and Big Mama Red and Jelly yelling, "come on!"

They got Andy and Frank! All of us is running behind him in this dark hallway with the lights flashing on and off smoking and motherfuckers shooting at us I'm thinking were in death trap to tell you the truth my heart is pumping fast filled with anxiety. Mister Price started running towards this room on the left with him yelling, "move your ass, let's go!"

Soon as all of us is in the room he quickly shut the door I am thinking were all trapped still hearing men yelling with machine guns spitting bullets in the background getting closer. Mister Price hit the light switch and the whole floor started moving going down as if it was a big giant elevator going down. I don't know how far we when down, but it was far, and it was making a loud hydraulic sound. When we looked up, we were all in a warehouse well-lit filled with cars and trucks with that deep smell of gasoline and oil. Mister Price started yelling come on everybody step off the platform hurry the fuck up I have some Nazis to blow up. We all got off the platform quickly and with a big smirk on his face Mister Price ran towards the wall on the right-hand side of this warehouse. Mister Price started pressing these big red buttons then we can hear these loud explosions. We are all looking at each other wondering what the fuck is going on. Miss Janet looked at me smiling uttering, "no more motorcycle riding Nazis."

'What just happen Miss Janet?"

Mister Price had the whole place rigged to blow just in case something like this happened. *I just wish I could have seen them racist motherfuckers getting blown up. I would have been jumping up and down with some cheerleading pom-pom like a zit face teenager enjoying every fucking moment of it.* I am sitting on the ground trying to get my shit together then I notice Mister Price take his computer from out of his backpack leaning on this truck going through his computer a little way from all of us. All of us is catching are breath when Big Mama Red came over to where I was sitting asked, "where the fuck are we and what the hell is next girl?"

"I do not know I'm just glad we got the hell out of there in time. I know and what's up with Mister Price?"

Jelly came walking up over hearing what we were talking about replying with a smile on his face he is looking at all the phone calls from the farm and find out who sold us out that is what he's doing. After ten minutes Mister Price puts his computer back in his bag sitting it back on top of the hood of the truck.

He walks over to where the three of us is at talking low, "Lex lend me your pistol for a minute, please."

I looked up at him not saying a word I whipped it out handing it to him. Standing not too far from us is Billy Miss Janet and Stump all talking with one another Mister Price walks up on them nice and smooth with the pistol with the silencer behind his back. In a blink of an eye, he took aim Pooouuufff! shooting Billy right in the middle of his head Billy fell backwards with the mist to blood flying in the air and his body hit the ground

Doom!

Stump jumped back reacting to what just happen, but Miss Janet was so calm with her hands on her hips as Mister Price winks his eye at her. Moon , Jitta and Nick Lit walks over to us with Moon talking low, "with his really deep voice well now we know who told the Nazis where we were at."

Jitta looking over at me asking are we still going to go get Mister Price daughter? I don't know ask him he is walking back over here now. I stood up and Mister Price hands me my gun back telling me thanks. Jitta looks him in the face and asked, "Are we still doing this thing with your daughter or what?"

"Yes, it is still a go were moving out in the morning and don't worry it safe here nobody know about this shit for sure. Big Mama Red cuts in barking, "where the hell are we?"

To answer your question, "honey, we are about 200 feet under-ground from my farm this is an old bomb shelter from World War two."

"I have one more question Mister Price where is your daughter at?"

"She is in Seattle Jelly got some people in Canada where were taking her get some rest you're going to need it. I have all the keys of the trucks and cars on the wall over there as he points towards his right so you can get some sleep."

He taps me on the arm so I can walk with him, so I walked with him towards the truck he had his bag on top of. Mister Price talking low everything is all set, right? Yeah, I took care of that thing for you. Good I am going to get some sleep but before I do that, I have a gift for you. Mister Price hands me an DVD just go take a look at it when you get a chance okay. I looked up at him holding it in my hand what is it? Go look at it I'll talk to you in the A.M. I quickly stuck it in my pocket and walked back to where everybody is at. Then I walked over towards the wall on the right where the keys were hanging. I got the keys to this

Chevy truck.

I walked back picking up my backpack and my machine gun and dragging my suitcase trying the remote to see which on it was when it started beeping, I turn to everyone uttering I'm going get some shut eye. I dragged all my shit with me to the truck tossing it inside I climbed in and shut the door and laid across the seats I was beat down tired. While I was trying to get some sleep, I can still hear the others talking until I drifted off into La- La land.

The next day I got up and I pulled out my computer from out of my backpack I put the DVD that Mister Price gave me last night. Soon as I peeped it, I started smiling it's Bloody Mary Gomez meeting with Mark Pain and their both talking about how they set me up making AK and others think that I killed Angel and Binky. Oh" shit that just made my fucking morning I was really excited this was like a weight lifted off my ass. I put my computer back in my bag and I step out the truck and Mister Price came walking over to me bumping fist with me.

He is telling me you can go over there towards your left I have some where for you to get washed and get yourself together before we roll out. "Where at?"

"Way over there as he is pointing, I said to myself shit I never thought this place was that fucking big. Before I when back inside of the truck to get my shit. I looked up at him uttering, "where did you get that DVD from thank you."

"I hacked it off Miss Ward's computer that's my gift to you for helping me out with my daughter Peggy."

"Thanks again, I'm going to go get my shit together. You, Better and he laughs bumping fist with me. So, I went and got my suitcase got my things out and I put it inside of a big plastic bag soap, deodorant wash rag, towels and all that shit but I had my pistol in the other hand."

I took that long walk but then I hear a voice calling me telling me to wait up. I looked back and its Big Mama Red she jogs up to me. "Gawd damn girl you walk to fucking fast for me!"

I just laughed she uttered with her eyes getting wide, "why you got the gun?"

"Just in case if we run into some bull shit while. I'm trying to wash my ass you know me girl. I don't trust a motherfucker living or breathing on this planet girl."

We both fell out laughing with her yelling and laughing loud, "your one crazy ass bitch! And when we got there, it was a large clean area closed off for us to wash with showers with roes of sinks mirrors and toilets nothing fancy kind of military like."

But very clean and old school like back in the fucking 1950's or something but clean smelling doe I have to say that.

Soon as we were going to get started to get washed, I heard somebody coming inside I took aim and I see it was Miss Janet she was yelling, "don't shoot me, Lex it's me!"

When I looked down, I seen she had a big wet spot in her pants. Me and Big Mama Red is laughing are ass off she was really pissed off. But after we were fucking with her, she came around laughing and joking with us soon enough.

On the way back to the truck I seen all this fucking hardware lined up on the floor everywhere all over the fucking place but neat in order he had enough shit here to start World War three for real. Shit when I got dressed real fast I when back and got me some hand grenades and some extra clips for my, machine gun and boxes of shells for my, pistol in my backpack just in case I needed them. So, no matter what goes down if I get into a jam. I know I am going to fucking get out of that shit with a motherfucking bang for sure. And Gawd help any dumb ass hole that is in my way because Lex makes a way out of no way you better believe that

GETTING THE JOB DONE.

An hour later we all packed up and gassed up all our vehicles and put on are bullet proof vest we were on the road going to Seattle. Big Mama Red and Jelly drove with me in the dark blue Chevy Silverado truck. Mister Price took the lead in a black Pathfinder Miss Janet riding shotgun and Stump in the back seat. Moon is behind the wheel of a black Benz with Jitta Nick Lit following behind Mister Price and I'm in the rear. It took us about six hours to get their and that's speeding the whole fucking way. But the plan is for me and Mister Price is to go and get her, but he would wait for her in the car while I go and get her out of there. Now were in this all-white suburban neighborhood but nobody paid me any mind maybe somebody think I'm the fucking maid or something. When I walked up to her and rang the doorbell. Soon as she opens the door she smiled and blurted out, "so your Lex."

"Yes, that's me honey are you ready to go?"

"Yes, give me a hand with these bags please."

I grabbed her suitcase she quickly walked out locking the door up getting her other bags talking low where is my father at? He is around the corner waiting for you don't rush just be cool we have to be as normal as possible Peggy. "I'm just so excited to see him that's all."

"Yeah, I know that, but I do not want people to think I'm kidnapping you okay."

"So, we walked around the corner and Mister Price came driving up she jumps in fast, and I pointed to him telling him to pop the trunk."

I tossed it inside and closed it fast and they drove off smooth then Jelly came driving up picking me up. I jumped in. He waited for Moon to drive behind Mister Price, and he started following Moon. What fucked me up nobody seen us leave. We all drive to this motel before we get to the Canadian border so we can all rest and Mister Caesar was going to meet us there because he heard about what happen at the farm. *I know the job is ready, but we all don't know what the fuck it is doe. Plus, this fat white motherfucker what he really doesn't know this is my last fucking job for his fat ass too. We arrived at this old motel it looks like it's been frozen in time from the 1970's or something. Then it started pouring down raining really hard we all park in front of the roes, of beige and brown motel rooms it's pitched dark outside. Man, it looks like a scene from one of them twisted horror movies or something. I see Mister Price walking towards me holding an umbrella signaling for me to roll down my, window. I rolled down the window feeling the rain hitting my face.* Look I'm going in here and get us some rooms keep your eyes open I be right back. He quickly walks inside of the motel office I have the radio on playing it is on some old school rock station because *Walk on the wild side by Lou Reed is on.*

I never notice that it had that color girl line in that shit. I looked up and Mister Price came back, and I rolled the window down again. I turn down the radio Mister Price hand me the keys. Soon as he did that from out of nowhere springing out of the darkness a tall man mashed a gun to Mister Price head **Pooouuufff!** I quickly whipped out my pistol taking aim and I hear a voice yelling, "don't shoot it's me,Mister Caesar Lex!"

I looked really good, with the rain coming down even harder in the dark and it was him.

I yelled, "why the fuck did you shoot, Mister Price for?"

"I was told to do it for an old very important client and I'm taking over for Mister Price. Now listen up good the job is ready to go I need to talk to all of you guys."

Let's all meet in your room go talk to the others and I'll meet you there in a few minutes or so. I just nodded my head yes quickly but when he walked away, I hear him speaking Russian to the four men behind him in the dark I, know right then and there something was not right.

But I am still holding my pistol upward am really stun for real. *I'm thinking to myself the only one who told him to do that shit is Peggy's husband William Cassidy and his father-in- law Theodore Cassidy.*

Jelly quickly muttered, "what are we going to do, Lex?"

"We going to grab Peggy and were getting the fuck out of here."

Big Mama Red cuts in, "your right Lex this whole shit going down here is fucking shady!"

I looked at Big Mama Red cover me okay Jelly get behind the wheel were getting the fuck up out of here. Soon as I seen Mister Caesar running over to this big black GMC truck to getting out of the rain. I jumped out and I looked down at Mister Price on the ground in the rain, but the blood is still gushing from his head even doe the rain is coming down hard. I step over him talking to his dead wet corpse sorry my friend, but I will get your people out of here like we planned. Me and Big Mama Red ran over to the Black Pathfinder with Miss Janet Stump and Peggy I banged on the window Stump open the door yelling what the fuck is going on with all these men all around us? Look I know you guys could not see but Mister Caesar just killed Mister Price. I looked up at Peggy she started crying I quickly uttered to her I'm not telling you not to cry but don't make a whole lot of noise because we're, getting the fuck out of here. Nick Lit and Jitta came running over in the rain up to me speaking what's going on Lex? It's really dark out here and I know y'all did not see Mister Caesar just killed Mister Price. Jitta looked me right in my grill saying so what are we going to do here? We going to make a run for it that what the fuck were going to do! Nick Lit cuts in fast yeah then they are going to kill us!

What your Black ass don't know there here to kill us any way they're going to grab Peggy and take her back to her husband! Plus, he has a bunch of fucking Russian mercenaries with him I heard him talking to them! Jitta looks up at me talking low so what are we going to do then? What you think we're going to do we are going bang it out with these ass holes is what the fuck were going to do nigga! My phone started ringing I pull it out quickly and answer it yeah! Mister Caesar with his booming voice ripping out of the speaker tell everybody to go to your room right now I be right there! I'm talking to them now hole the fuck on okay. Just do it bitch I do not have all fucking night. He hangs up I started thinking fast I quickly text Moon telling him to get out the car I need to holler at him right quick. I look at everyone standing there talking low me and Big Mama Red is going to kick it off Peggy you're coming with us so go get into the truck right now. She quickly walked and got into the truck still crying. I continued talking to the others with the rain coming down on all of us, but we really didn't care this shit is life and death right and it's no time to fuck up. *The Black psycho bitch just showed up for duty!*

Stump I'm going to really need you on this one my nigga you down? I'm ready to kill anything in our path with anyone fucking with us and you know that shit. Good *we bumped fist I swiftly whispering what I wanted him to do he smile showing me all of those yellow teeth but I'm loving it right about now I know what this little motherfucker is capable of. He's our secret weapon out this bitch and were going to fuck them up really good too!* Yo" were going to get ghost out this motherfucker everybody got it. Moon came over and huddled up with us I pointed at him. Telling him were going to make a run for it we don't have that much time just jump in your shit and take off if we get separated, we all meet at the cabins in Buffalo. I quickly lean on the truck looking up at Jelly stand your ground I'll let you know when we roll out okay. He just nods his head yes slapping a clip into his AK-47. Soon as I gave my Football coach style death march speech with confidence of a four-star general. We when to work Stump ran around to get in back of them real stealth like in the dark. Out the corner of my eye I can see that Frankenstein looking like ass hole is making his move two groups of four and some of them in the middle. Moon jumped in the Benz shooting back at them with Jitta and Nick Lit hauling ass. **Skkkirrrrrrrrr!** The came at us fast and hard **Brrrraaaatttttt!** Sparks is flying bouncing off the trucks me and Big Mama Red got low firing back moving to the left and right like old pros of fucking war getting behind the two trucks as they started charging us spitting hell fire and fury.

I laid down flat am already soaked down to my panties pointing low spitting bullets chopping up and shedding the shit out of their kneecaps and legs. *I know that shit hurts because I'm fucking their ass up turning their legs and kneecaps into Hamburger meat.* Big Mama Red is holding her own leaning on the truck giving them motherfuckers the business without a suit. Miss Janet is on one knee spitting hot shit at the men coming towards us in the darkness. What fucked me up is Jelly rolling down the window with his AK-47 joining in on the party hitting about three them Russian ass holes dressed in black. Some of them backed up off our ass a little seeing that we were not a fucking push over thinking they were going crush us like a cock roach running across the floor on the run. Then from out of nowhere the sounds of sweet music to my two ears ripping from out of the darkness. As were going back and forth shooting at one another in the middle of this fire fight in the rain. All we can see is muzzle flashes from the machine guns and smoke like real dogs of war cold, sore, wet, miserable and tired. But were fighting with every fiber of our being.

Stump came behind them shooting his MP5 machine gun those motherfuckers that were left didn't know what fucking hit them falling like rag dolls killing the last five men shooting at us. From what I could see in the dark is blood gushing into the puddles of water in the parking lot. Soon as I see one of the trucks backing up super-fast spedding off in the other direction. I know its big bad bitch made CIA agent bugging out he knows I out played his ugly ass. *These ass holes must have forgot they trained us for situations like this.* I'm yelling to Big Mama Red let's get the fuck out of here right now! I pointed to the Black Pathfinder Big Mama Red ran over jumping inside of the back seat of the Black Pathfinder. I can see a fucking blur running towards their direction its Miss Janet with a machine gun going after them shooting like she is going crazy. I yelled at her, "let them go! Come on let's get the fuck out of here!"

She is still trying to run after them screaming, "no they killed Mister Price they have to die. "

Stump came running up smiling. "Man, go get your, girl those motherfuckers are gone after we done kicked their ass!"

Stump quickly jogged over to Miss Janet just standing in the darkness with her machine gun still smoking from the tip. He walks her back with his hand on her ass pushing her along. I jump inside of the truck looking Jelly in his face floor this motherfucker! I know there coming back after us this shit is not over. Jelly takes off with Miss Janet is right behind us taking off pissed off I quickly call Moon to see where he's at.

He picks up on the first ring. "Yo, where you at Bro?"'

"My GPS is telling me were somewhere outside of Mill Creek."

"Okay pull over and wait for us there we will link up with you there."

"Okay, I'll see you when you get here one! Jelly looking in his rearview mirror talking loud check this shit out we see red and blue flashing lights behind us coming up really fast.

THE MUD DUCKS TAKE OUT THE DRAGONS.

My Phone started ringing I answer it swiftly, "Yeah, It's me Janet someone must had called the sheriff while we were at that motel don't worry about it, I'll take care of them it only two of them."

'Y'all just pull over when I do and I'll take them out. Jelly slow down and pulled over at the same time Miss Janet did with the red and blue lights flashing bright. I'm trying to look out of the mirror on the left I couldn't even see that good. Miss Janet jumps out the Black Pathfinder she tossed two fucking hand grenades Jelly took off like a fucking space rocket to the moon after a few minutes **Kaboom! Kadoom!** I looked in the rear-view mirror seeing two big fucking fire balls with black smoke floating up in the air. Jelly yelling Gawd damn she took care of it aright. She sure did looks like some shit I would have done. Peggy mutter from the back of the truck cab I think all of y'all is fucking crazy if you ask me! We all started laughing. A few minutes later we see a set of headlights behind us Jelly is laughing it her I quickly call her she picks the phone up giggling I put it on speaker. Yo good job Miss Janet. *With my little giggling.* Those fucking Hill Billy is eating corn on the cob in fucking hell bye now and she hung up laughing.

We all busted out laughing riding down the dark road and it finally stop fucking raining. The from out of nowhere we can hear this loud whipping sounds the closer it got the first thing that popped in my head is choppers. Jelly yelled out oh shit it two fucking choppers coming down on us! The first one flu bye us the one behind that one is started shooting at us while we are driving up the road, I rolled down the window and leaned out the window shooting upward missing. Soon as I did that, they shot back making me duck back inside of the truck. Then the second chopper came lower shooting at the Black Path-finder it sounded so loud I was thinking that it hit us too. I told Jelly slow down and stop so I can get out. What are you fuck-ing crazy or something Lex? Look if I get on the pay load, I can take out one of them fucking Helicopters if we keep running like this, they will cut us down after a while. He looked at me while he is still driving fast with more bullets raining down on us **Kapackpatacka!** Jelly uttering you want to know what you're right, I wish we had a fucking rocket launcher or some-thing. Let me call Miss Janet and let her know what we're going to do. She picks up on the first ring these motherfuckers came from out of nowhere ya'll. Look we going to stop, and I'm get-ting on top of the pay load and take these fucking helicopters out. You want to know what that is a fucking good ideal! Jelly started slowing down I put my backpack on my back soon as he stopped. *My heart is racing but I have to do this shit.*

I jumped out with my machine gun pointing it upward as the two helicopters made another past hurling by shooting like a sonic death machine out for vengeance. I got low on the side of the truck soon as the barrage of bullets hit the ground the mud slashed up in my face getting into my eyes from the im-pact hitting the ground. I did not panic I just stayed low until I could wipe my eyes right quick with my wet shirt the shit sting but fuck it! It's better to put up a good fight then giving up hope and lay down dead and take it up the ass all night. Soon as I could see Stump came out getting in front of the Black Pathfinder staying low and Miss Janet came running over next to me as the helicopters started coming back but I notice now they are staying high in the sky now that we both stopped. I looked up and their coming back side bye side I climbed up on the back of the truck laying down getting a good aim on these motherfuckers. And I just started squeezing off shots, but I took my time knowing that they are coming at us with a lot of fucking heat. They came shooting at me I quickly jumped up off the payload when they got closer, and I got up under the truck getting all muddy on the shoulder of the road. But when they were going after me on the payload Jelly jumped out with his AK-47 helping Stump and Miss Janet shooting upward hit the bottom of one the other helicopters **Brrrraaaattttt!**

I heard it when I rolled back out from under the truck, I know this was going to be it. This time when they came back shooting one helicopter is low, and one helicopter is high. The one that's low came from the right I stayed behind the truck and I lit that motherfucker up I started seeing it smoking turning black it flu off towards the left. When the helicopter that was smoking tried to turn around it was going up and down sputtering, but it could not go higher like the other helicopter, but it still came after us spitting hot led letting us know it still had teeth to bit into our ass really good the muzzle flash was red and orange with thick white smoke. All four of us knew we were going to take that bitch down I can see it in all of our eyes pure determination glowing in all of our eyes in the darkness. Plus, that gangster shit that sticks in your gut most motherfuckers will never know about unless you been in the middle of some real shit when it's life and death dancing at your doorstep. The four of us started shooting that motherfucker all at the same time we can hear all the bullets ripping into the metal then as it, fly's by still shooting back at us I heard **Busssshhhhh!** It when up in fucking flames the dark sky turned orange. The helicopter on fire the black smoke getting thicker it, fly's off towards the left and just exploded in the sky **Kadoom!**

As the second helicopter came in for the kill shooting another barrage of hot led on our ass, I took out four hand grenades throwing them with all my might **Boom! Boom!** Miss Janet did the same thing tossing hand grenades at it **Boom! Boom!** Jelly and Stump stayed rock study shooting their machine guns but all four of are assault started working. My first two miss just exploding but the concussion from the hand grenades it rocked the helicopter making it go from side to side making look like a toy on a fucking string or something. Then my third one hit that motherfucker while it was hovering shooting at us **Kaboom!** Ripping a hole in the side on the right and it started smoking it quickly started flying towards the left, but it turned around swiftly coming in low not too far from the road. The helicopter came back firing more bullets we all got low all of us jumping up under the truck getting all muddy. Soon as it when by we all jumped back to are feet ready to do battle gripping our machine guns even tighter. I yelled out this is it y'all the helicopter when up, but it looked like it lost control right before it started coming towards us going from side to side, we all can see that it was struggling like a fucking beast that's wounded still out for blood. Smoking like a broke stove we all started shooting we can all see all the sparks flying inside of the frame of the helicopter **Kadoom!**

The helicopter blew up and crashed on the road up a head of us about a good 100 feet from us. With metal debris flying everywhere flames and smoke gushing from its large green frame. We all ducked hitting the deck when I looked up, I was praying that none of the fucking scraps of burning metal did not hit any of us. *I can't front this is one of them shit in your pants type of moments, but you know me I just played it off like it was another fucking day at the office.* We all came to are feet slowly looking down the road of this big ball of fire slapped each other five cheering loud like we just hit the fucking power ball lottery. But were all covered in fucking mud breathing hard and glad to be alive. *Shit I done did a lot of fucked up shit in my life, but I never took down a fucking helicopter before! Knowing them motherfuckers is dead inside of it makes me want to cum on myself for real even with all this mud on my ass.* Miss Janet quickly ran to the Black Pathfinder and I jumped into the dark blue Chevy Silverado truck smiling my ass off yelling let's go we got that son of a bitch! Jelly bumping fist with me laughing wow we got both of them ass holes the mud ducks took down the fucking dragons. And he floored it riding up the dark road. Jelly pulls out his phone and started dialing his phone. I glance over barking who the fuck are you calling? I'm calling somebody from my crew to get us the fuck out of here.

I quickly whipped out my gun sticking it in his face yelling why you didn't call them motherfuckers when Scarface and his fucking Russian goon hit squad was going to fucking waste us at motel hell? I have some peoples in Everett to get us to the East coast I already had this shit planned Lex. I don't trust you, nigga! Your, supposed to be helping Mister Price and the rest of us with Peggy over here to get her to, somewhere safe. I'm going to keep my word and do just that, but I have to get away from anybody connected to Lieutenant Cob or I'm dead!

Oh Yeah keep talking motherfucker! Look I took something very important from lieutenant Cob and I have to get the fuck out of dodge okay that's all I'm going to fucking tell you Lex! *He does not know I already know what he stole from lieutenant Cob I am going to keep it to myself. And now I know he's not going to try anything fucking crazy. But If he acts just a little bit funny, I'll smoke his ass on the spot.* Okay what about the others is this way out of here for all of us? Yes, it is open to everybody who want to get the fuck out of here. *He's one lucky motherfucker because if he said no, I would have shot him the minute we got out of the truck faster than he would had blinked his fucking eyes.*

I hit my GPS on my phone seeing how close we are from Mill Creek. Were only one mile from where there at. Peggy leans over talking to me my father picked the right people to help me get away, but my husband will stop at nothing to get me back. Look your husband and your up-tight father -in- law will never find you where I'm taking you okay. Jelly pulls up behind the Black Benz Moon is standing outside leaning on the car on the side of this dark road. I jumped out walking up to him he's mad with his face is all twisted up yelling you know we got a price on all of our heads now with your little break away from the fat man's henchman shoot out! There were there to kill us all Moon I got a plan and the golden ticket my nigga trust, me. I think it some bull shit I say we all split the fuck up now you go take Mister Price Daughter to wherever you're going to take her. So, what are you telling me your out now? Yes, that just what I'm saying you talked me into staying at the farm now everything done turned to shit! How about if I told you that Jelly is going to get us all to the East coast, he got some peoples in Everett. Okay let me go to this guy and hear him out but I don't trust this motherfucker all that much neither.

He quickly walked over to his window yo Lex said your, going to get all of us out of here to the East coast. Yeah, they're going to call me back at any minute now. Check this shit out please don't be Capping are heads up with this shit or I'll- Jelly's phone started ringing loud he looks at Moon uttering see I'll put it on speaker for you scene you don't trust me like your girl Lex. That's when I walked up to hear this fucking call too. I hear the voice talking loud yo Jelly were coming up near you right now we got three cargo vans. Good Mook you'll see us you can't miss us it's 9 of us counting me. That's cool we got room for every-body to get you the fuck out of there. Okay I see you when you get here. Just like he said pulling up is three gray cargo vans Jelly is shaking hands with the dude, name Mook driving the lead van along with his two other guys with him Big Eric and Shank.

We grabbed all of our shit from out of the truck with the quick-ness and we got into the first van me Jelly and Big Mama Red. Jelly sat next to Big Mama and Peggy sat in the back by herself still looking sad. In the second van is Moon Jitta and Nick Lit and in the third van is Stump and Miss Janet. We left both the shot-up vehicles on the side of the road. I notice that Jelly paid all three of them on the spot it looked like he paid them three stacks each and he did not ask us for a fucking dime. They had food and water inside of the vans I still really don't fully trust this guy, but I did get some sleep while we jumped on the road. We made a few stops along the way to go to the bathroom at rest stops in Wyoming the countryside was so beautiful. I they even gave us time to change our clothes and wash all that mud off our ass as well. A day later when we got to Denver Colorado, we when to the airport and got on a private jet Jelly had hooked up.

Soon as we got on the jet, I ask Jelly where is this motherfucker going to land at? He looks at me smiling we will be in New York in five hours' time so relax I told you I was going to make sure you get to where you're going but once we get there, you're on your own. *When we get to New York I know just what I'm going to do I'm going to link up with Uzi-Boy from the old gang in Philly so I can clear my name. The first time in a long time I got to relax, and we started partying like a motherfucker having fun snorting coke drinking champagne the whole way there. Shit even Peggy got down with us she smoked some weed, but she would not touch any of the coke I just don't know why but she did get her smoke and drink on with us doe.* When we landed in New York I was sleep Big Mama Red started pushing me to wake me up were here talking really nice. Look Lex I'm rolling out with Jelly you're not mad, are you?

LINKING UP WITH
THE OLD GANG

No, you're a grown ass woman why would I be mad do your thing girl. When I looked out the window, I notice these trucks coming over unloading the jet extremely quick with his two goons Shank and Big Eric and some other men. I stood up and hugged her replying with a big smile good luck to you baby girl. And the same to you Lex it's been fun. They quickly got off the jet I looked over to Moon and Jitta carrying their bags ready to get off is y'all rolling out on me too? No were going with you to drop of Peggy. Jitta bumps fist with me smiling. Stump came walking up talking loud and me too don't forget about that shit. Good! I looked at Miss Janet she smiles I'm going anywhere Stump is going. I pat him on his back see that what you needed a ride or die bitch and you got one! All of us started laughing. We all got off the jet and Jelly came up to me talking, you can take one of the trucks I hooked up for y'all the keys is under the mat on the driver's side. He pointed at it in the far distant airport parking lot and good luck to you Lex if you ever need some work look me up okay handing me one of his cards. Thanks for everything and take care of my girl or your going have to see me motherfucker! He smiled I will. Jelly walks off with Big Mama Red waving goodbye. We started walking to where the truck was at with Peggy right by my side as were walking it didn't take us no time to reach the truck. Moon open the door of the Black GMC truck I'm driving now where are we going first? Stump and Jitta helped us with are bags inside of the back of the truck. We going to a five-star hotel and check in and then were going drop Peggy off in the morning.

Your good with that Peggy? Yes, I'm good with that why can't I stay with y'all? Moon Stump Miss Janet and Jitta started laughing loud. I don't think you know this Peggy but were a bunch of fucking criminal's baby girl I don't think your father would have like that you are staying with us. Well, he is dead now and just like you told Big Mama Red I'm a grown ass woman and I don't have any little kids to hold me back. I don't think so Peggy we are taking you to the cabin in Buffalo and you will be safer there okay. Please get inside of the truck she gets into the truck uttering I need to talk to you alone when we get to the hotel. Cool I got into the truck sitting next to her Jitta sat next to his son and Stump and Miss Janet sat in the back of the truck. I said

loud please take me to the Baccarat hotel on 28 west 53rd street Moon am Jone-ing some fucking luxury! You got it Lex! The laughter filling the truck as he took off down the street. One hour later we all checked into this five-star hotel I brought out the whole six floor I'm in fucking heaven now thank you Jesus!

The first thing I did was order two bottles of champagne to my room ice cold they brought it up fast too and I tipped the guy 50 dollars. Then I just jumped across the large soft bed. I started working the horn I called up that fine ass butter pecan nigga with a big Dick Chi- Chi. The phone rings about five time before he picks up speaking who is this. It's me nigga Lex. Oh, shit where the fuck you been at girl! I been thinking about your sexy ass for a long time now! Well, I'm back in town and I need some blow can you hook me up? Yeah, how much do you need you know I got it. I need a haft a brick can you get it for me some good shit now. I sure can baby! Look Chi-Chi please don't tell anybody I'm back in town sweetheart. Oh, I would never do no shit like that when you told me you were going to Boston, I was thinking somebody smoked your ass or something. Why you say that shit? Because Fat Poncho was running around here talking shit that he burned you and your crew for a lot of keys of drugs. He did burn me and my crew for a big shipment of methamphetamine.

Wow that's fucked up Ma the last time I hollered at you" you, told me you wanted me to work for you. I was holding then well fuck all that right now how soon can you get here? I'm on my way right now I'll be there in a haft hour tops. Good I see you when you get here. I hang up I called Uzi- Boy the phone rings three time before somebody picked up hello the voice on the other end is Alice Black yo who the fuck is this? It's me nigga Lex. Lex so why are you calling this phone your one dead bitch you do know that right! Yo" hold on Alice I need to tell you that was not me who did that shit for real doe. Yeah, right Lex you would say anything slick out your mouth when you were the one who shot and killed your own friends. *Uzi-Boy came into the room barking who are you talking to?* Look you don't have to believe me, but I have proof that I did not do it Alice you have to believe me let me talk to Uzi- Boy! Alice talk-ing loudly.

It's your lying ass girl Lex on the phone and she quickly hand him the phone. Yo what the fuck is you calling me here on the phone bitch! Yo Uzi-Boy you got to believe me it was not me and I have proof I didn't do it man Mark Pain and Bloody Mary set me up to take the fall from the door I have a DVD that will prove that it was not me. Well, I have to see that shit. Do you have a computer I can download it to you for you to see it! You know damn well I would not do shit like that to Binky, and Angel I loved both of them! Well download that shit to me and let me see what the fuck is you talking about my email is Uzi-boy.@ yahoo.com. I quickly when got my lab top at a breakneck pace.

YOU HAVE A NEW SECRETARY
IF YOU LIKE IT OR NOT.

I already had the DVD inside of my computer I turned it on talking to him give me a few minutes I'm hooking it up now laying my computer on my bed. My computer came up I quickly when to my yahoo.com account and I downloaded the clip to him Bing! He waited on the other end I can hear him say I got it now, I'm going to peep it right now Lex. He calls Alice over to him so she can see it at the same time he's looking at it. *I can hear both of them mumbling and signifying under their breath loudly.*

I just waited really nervous looking down at the phone then I can hear his voice uttering man that really fucked up Lex I didn't know Ma! All this time I'm thinking you did that shit. I told you man! Alice cuts in yelling I'm sorry Lex I was thinking you did it like everybody else did my bad! Yo AK need to see this shit where you get this DVD from? I Jacked it off of one AK's CIA shadowy friend. Well, you might not know this shit scene you were gone I'm running shit in Philly now I'm at the head of the cipher table. Oh, shit wow congratulations nigga you been a number two cat for a long time it about fucking time! Yeah, you got that one right look, I'm going to take the green light off your head with the gang and I'm going to get with AK myself and let him know about this shit! And plus am going to show him this DVD with them two snake ass motherfuckers that set you up.

Thank you Uzi I been wanting to hear that shit for a long time coming now. Well now we got all of that horse shit out the way if you ever need to put in some work, you know who to fucking call Ma. I can always use someone with your skills to help a nigga out you know what I'm saying. I'm glad you said that Uzi-Boy I need to holler at you about some serious business I got going on now I'll be back in Philly in a few days so we can sit down and rap about this shit okay. Okay I'll text you my new address where am at now baby girl. *In, the background I can hear someone knocking on the door I hope that's Chi- Chi with his fine ass.* Sounds good look I have to go don't forget to send it to me after I hang up with you Uzi and thanks again Moja! Moja! *I flu to the door thinking its Chi- Chi to come fuck my brains out I get wet just thinking about the shit. I looked through the peek hole and its Peggy white ass! I opened the door as she came storming in with a super pissed off look on her pail grill.* I closed the door yelling what is it you want Peggy! Look I already know what you're up too my father told me about you and him stealing the client list from off Jelly's computer with her eyes getting wide.

So, what you know what we did what is it to fucking you! Yeah, did you tell the others what you're up to? No but I will it's my crew bitch so don't worry about it okay! Now tell me how are you going to approach any of those people on that list did you think about that shit? I know how to talk to people I'll get it done don't you worry about that suburban white girl! Peggy started laughing uttering the minute you call one of them people they will let lieutenant Cob know and nobody will fuck with you! Okay I'm listening Peggy tell me how am I going to hook all this shit up?

Your, going to let me talk to them first most of them know me because of my father I'll set it up tell them the prices and I talk to you to see if you can do the job. Are you sure you want to do some shit like this Peggy it really fucking dangerous work here! You can just set back, and you will have it made with the money your father set up for you to have. Yeah, I know about that to but that is not what I want to do. I want to be a part of something like you guys I see how all of you fight together live and eat with one another I need that kind of shit in my life right now. As you know all that shit is not so easy as it looks now and its' not what you think it is neither Peggy! Look just go find a nice guy this time and have some babies or something not this shit we're doing. No because I bring a lot to the fucking table now, I'm going to be your new secretary if you like it or not Lex! Do you really think you can do this shit Peggy for real? I was born to do this shit I worked for the CIA for 12 years Lex I know a whole lot of shit you would never know about in a million years. Plus, I'm going to prove it to you! Now how in the fuck are you going to do that Peggy? I'm going to hook you up with General Ed Kowalski he's a rogue army general who runs his own Black bag operations and he's ten time more powerful than Joe and he hates Joe Cob guts.

Why are you hooking us up with another white man to tell us what to do I don't get it? He's not going to have you doing shit for him just as long as he knows that you double crossed lieutenant Joe Cob, he's going to love you and your crew trust me. *It's a knock at the front door.* Look Peggy don't be getting us into more shit than we can handle over here girl! Do you trust me? I just look at her look Peggy I don't trust a living soul on this planet but if it get you go while I'm trying to get my shit off yes now could you leave me please. She kissed me on the cheek giggling I'm going to go make the call okay! Okay! Okay now get the fuck out of here already! I quickly walked this crazy ass white bitch to the door I opened it and its Chi- Chi with that big sexy ass smile of his.

Chi- Chi looks at me talking loudly who the fuck was that Ma? That's my new secretary just bring your fine ass in here and shut the door I got something to show your hot fucking haft Black Puerto Rican ass! Yeah, well I got something to show your fine chocolate self too Ma- Ma! He came in strolling over to me with that macho ghetto strut of his kissing me soft and tender feeling on my ass with both hands rubbing it too. Oh, did you miss me motherfucker! I sure did here you go a haft a brick baby. Okay you know what to do go get that cart over there and start dumping it out and making some lines while I get us something to drink, I started walking over to the bar on the right taking off my clothes.

I started doing it slow and sexy I know that nigga could not take his eyes off of me I can feel his eyes burning inside of my skin bubbling for some action. And just like I knew it when I glanced over to him giving him that I'm going to fuck the shit out of you smile on my face. Chi- Chi is chopping up the coke making lines on top of the cart and looking at me like he is going to have me for fucking breakfast lunch and dinner. I'm in my bra and panties grabbing two champagne glasses in one hand and the bottle of champagne in the other. I sit next to him on the bed, and I popped the champagne bottle Poooooo! It gushed out from the top of the bottle and I sucked some of the fizzling foam in my mouth some of it is dripping from my mouth and chin falling to the floor. He is watching me uttering that kind of shit keep a motherfuckers Dick hard baby girl. I know that's the whole ideal handsome! Then I pour both of us a glass and I handed him his glass as are eyes is locked into, I can't wait to fuck you stair on both of are grills we both touched glasses together Clink!

We both down the glass of champagne giggling at one another just looking at this fine ass motherfucker is getting me wet. Chi- Chi scooped up some of the coke with a 100-dollar bill he had holding it up to my nose so I can taste it. I snorted the white powder super-fast soon as it when up my nostrils my face started getting numb. Wow that some really good shit baby. Nothing but the best for you sweetheart. Kissing me and we both had lust glowing in are eyes. I quickly took off my bra and I tossed it in the chair nearby. He looks at my, titties licking his lips he takes his left hand and started feeling on them. I reached over taking the 100-dollar bill out of his hand I scooped up a big pile of coke and I sprinkled the coke on both my titties uttering it's time you taste it too baby! He jumps licking my titties feeling them up with two hands while I took off my panties when I lean back letting him suck them for about five minutes or so. But I'm ready for this motherfucker to do some real freaky shit to me.

I sit up pushing him gently with a smile grabbing the bottle of champagne in my right hand and I reach over scooping up another big pile of coke I lay back a little sprinkling the coke on to my stomach down to my pussy. He did not disappoint me he started slobbering down on my stomach and he started working his way down to my wet box glazing like honey.

I sat up with the bottle of champagne pouring it down on my twat watching him lap it up like a true-blue freak. I thought I was going to hit the roof jumping up and down it was feeling so good. Shit Chi- Chi eats pussy as good as he fucks while I'm rocking my hips pumping in his face groaning loud. I am getting thrill bumps rushing up my back and that overwhelming feeling of my first orgasm spewing out my pussy lips. **Oooohhhhhh!** The sucking and slurping sounds was freaking me out just like his thick lizard tongue wiggling around inside of my sugar walls. I'm rocking on the end of the bed with my left hand on top of his head pouring more champagne down on my cunt then I came again, and he sucked it all out with the champagne. *Oh, my Gawd my legs are shaking like a small tree in the middle of a fucking hurricane.* Then he just stops standing up and when I glanced up, I see his butter pecan one eyed snake hard as a brick in the wintertime.

He grabs at both my ankles with them big hands of his lifting both my legs up in the air pointing his large man hood at my super wet muffin ready for a real good fucking. Chi-Chi slides in it into me nice and smooth ooh shit! I locked my legs around his hips, and he started pounding faster and harder with each stroke. We both moaning loud, and I am in a sizzling hot zone floating into that world of ecstasy after I came for about the third time now and that coke kicking in as well. *He just doesn't know while he's rocking my pussy like it's the last one on earth I'm floating into space in the middle of Andromeda.* Chi- Chi is grunting loud and I'm screaming until I'm just out of breath lightheaded with my head bopping up and down and my hair flying from side to side with him fucking me like a rubber fuck doll. And out of nowhere **Boom!** Chi- Chi is yelling as his whole body is going into convulsions with his face all twisted up and I can feel that hot jizzim filling me hot sticky and warm. Chi-Chi leans down kissing me with his sweat from his head dripping down on me I am out of fucking breath kissing him back and my whole body is tingling and sweaty. Chi- Chi got up off of me slowly lying next to me giggling and me and him did some deep down catching up. We snorted some more coke and he told me about everything that's going on in New York.

After him telling me all the extra gossip and bull shit on who is fucking who he got down to the good part about Fat Poncho. Chi-Chi uttering yeah that fat motherfucker made a come up after selling all that methamphetamine to them bikers and Dominican gangsters he is selling coke for Coo- Coo this big time Dominican Cat my boss wants his ass dead he is taking most of our customers. Oh yeah you know where they hang at. I sure do but if you do it, I want to come with you. Why should I take you with me if I'm putting in work? Because it would bump up my street cred to the fucking third power that's why. How you know I'm going to kill them? Because I heard stories about you that's why. What kind of stories you heard about me Chi- Chi?

I heard you were a top lieutenant in the 24th street cartel in Philly they said you killed more than 100 men. And you done killed haft of Big Sammy crew and you robbed his money drop spot and plus you took down his fentanyl stash spot in New Jersey. And took more than 200 bricks of shit with your titties out killing everybody in sight and you got away with it without a fucking scratch! They say they have a green light out on you, but I think there fucking scared of you Lex to tell you the truth! We started laughing Is that all I did more than that Chi-Chi you just don't know the fucking haft of it nigga.

Oh Yeah like what? You ever heard of the MMC here in New York. Yeah, most of them guys got smoked. Yeah, I'm one the people who smoked them. Somebody told me that the 24th street cartel took them out, but I did not believe them. Okay enough about ancient history do you know where Big Sammy hang out? No. Okay I'll take you with me only if you fuck me really good in the shower for round two. His eyes got wide with that sexy ass smile of his giggling. I jumped up to my feet in front of the bed slapping him on his leg yelling come on nigga you ready!

Round two was super-hot and off the hook just like round one we both fell asleep after we were done drained. I got up around 10A.M. I got washed and dressed and I order room service for both of us steak and eggs. With coffee and orange juice I snorted some more coke he brought to me I paid him for the coke and told him he has to roll so I can get some shit done. Because if he stayed any longer all I will do is fuck him until I pass out. Chi- Chi didn't want to go but I told him I would call him when I make my move on Fat Poncho and his boss Coo- Coo. He didn't believe me walking away with sad puppy dog eyes. Soon as he was gone, I called up Peggy and told her to come to my room a few minutes later she came. I pointed towards one the bar stools for her to sit down and she did it with that goofy ass expression on her pail face.

How good are you tracking people down? I'm one of the best Lex why? I need for you to find this guy he's a drug dealer name Big Sammy his real name is Saul Williamson and he's 34 years old and he's from here in New York city. Give me one hour and I'll have everything you need. Good soon as she walked out the room, I text everybody saying family meeting in one hour. The Hour blazed past quickly Peggy came to my room first with all of these papers in her hand and a cigarette cocked in the side of her lips. I pointed at the bar again as she sat next to me giving me the run down on Saul Williamson joker. Check this out Lex, he is working for this guy name Pedro Morales in Columbia. But know what's so funny about this case here? What's that Peggy a dude name Juna Garcia wants him dead because your boy Big Sammy killed his sister Tina in a wild shoot out in the

Bronx. Juna can't kill him because all of the family in Columbia would come down on him but if we do it that's two million dollars, we can go get for you smoking this shit bag.

That is to low Peggy he must give us five or better and we can do it. Okay I'll talk to him this way you can get your pay back on this guy and get paid for it as well. Okay set it up and call your General friend too were going to need somebody to have are back with all this shit were about to do. I already did that he said he almost pissed in his pants laughing when I told him what happen. I looked at Peggy smiling as she just smirked back at me as if to tell me I told you so type of shit. Then she continued talking he's going sit down with us tomorrow at 7A.M. at the airport at hanger 18. *I looked up at her because I'm really impressed.* Well, Gawd damn Peggy your one bad bitch! You better fucking know it! Lex! Soon as I said that the crew started coming one by one. Stump and Miss Janet walking all hugged up. *They do make a cute couple I have to omit.* They came first than Nick Lit followed by Jitta and Moon came last singing he must got some pussy last night he always do that shit after he gets laid. Me and Peggy just sat there at the bar patiently while everybody is full of chitter chatter. I looked up at everybody talking loud it's time we when back to work! Moon how are we going to get back to work when we are marked for death. I got that covered were meeting with general Ed Kowalski early in the morning at the airport he hates lieutenant Cob, and he will have our backs. Nick Lit are y'all sure about this shit and what the fuck is Peggy still doing here don't tell me she's going be down with the click now? Yes, she is she just saved are ass by hooking us up with the general okay! Let me explain something to you all me and Mister Price stole a copy of the client list from Jelly he Jacked from Miss Wards computer. Just like he told me it was an opportunity of a lifetime, so I took it.

We are all moving forward if you want to continue to move forward with us good if not speak now or just step the fuck off. Moon steps up talking loudly I'm with you 100% Lex, but I think that guy Jelly when and took that metric ton of Fentanyl from Gabriel Chapelle along with that client list. That is why I think Mister Caesar came to kill us all thinking we were down with all that shit in the mix. I think your right Moon and plus William Cassidy Peggy's husband and father-in-law came to kill Mister Price on top of all that. Look we all been in a world wind of shit for months now this move we are about to make is going to be the light at the end of the tunnel. I came to tell you all Peggy is going to be our new secretary from here on out and she is an excessively big asset to are crew. Miss Janet cuts in yelling so what about me and what is the name of this fucking outfit. We all started laughing. Well to answer you Miss Janet I didn't like the name at first but Moon, Stump Jitta and who is left like me called it the Jungle crew now I love it. Now if you want Peggy to be down with us raise your hand if not yell out no. Moon, Jitta, Stump Miss Janet raise they hands way up in the air now everybody is looking over at Nick Lit. Than he slowly raises his hand we all started cheering loud the Jungle crew. I bump fist with her now you're fucking in officially bitch! Now come over here and show her some love before we start talking about some more fucking business at hand. All of them walked over to Peggy hugging her and shaking her hand.

Okay! Okay let get back to it now Peggy you just fucked up you just when and joint the gang! Everybody started giggling now we about to get the phone call from Juna Garcia to do this hit on Big Sammy one of my enemies what is great about this shit were going to get paid for killing his ass. Jitta yelled out shit that a fucking win-win if you ask me Lex. Its sure fucking is brother! Now I know were putting all this shit together fast but it's just like all the shit that has been thrown at us and we faced it and made it to the other side of the bull shit. So, I know were going to be highly successful if we all put are heads together and get this shit done. Peggy's phone started ringing she looks at me barking I got to take this it's Juna's middleman Ju-Ju. I point to her go in the bedroom over there. Peggy quickly walks towards the bedroom on the left I put my hand up talking quickly to the others look that's him I be right back let me go handle this. I quickly walked behind Peggy, I tell her to put it on speaker she hit the button and we both hear this heavy voice with a thick Hispanic accent.

Yeah, is this the party that can take care of what we need done. I speak up fast yeah but five million is just to week for us to do it doe. Is this the girl everybody been talking about in the streets name Lex? Yeah, that's me player so what's up? He started laughing I heard a lot about you Mommy the pleasure is all mine baby. Well, I don't know if you heard this about me poppy, but I don't fuck around so bring your weight up a little more and we can get this shit done as soon as possible. I like that Mommy ten is all my people will go to get this shit done. Sound good haft before and the other haft when it done and if you cross me not only your dead but you whole family as well you got me. Don't even sweat that shit Ma meet me in one hour at Starbucks 111 Worth street in Chinatown I'll be there with one of my men I'll have the dark blue suit on. Good I will find you see you there one. Peggy looked up at me now, I see why you told me you know how to talk to people. Shit when you're talking to people like that you have to know what the fuck to say. Shit I like that feeling the way you handle him. Yeah, you will get use to it and did you tell him who I was Peggy? No, he must did some digging around it sure was not me Mommy. We both started giggling. I quickly walked back in the room telling the others its on I'm meeting up with the Juna dude in one hour I am going to need you Moon and Nick Lit to watch my back. Moon bumping fist with me uttering let us do this shit Ma. I look Nick Lit in his eyes to get him pumped up you ready for this bro. I was born ready baby girl. Okay I'm going to go change my clothes meet me back here in a few minutes you two go tool up by the time you get back here I'll be ready. I turned to Stump, and Miss Janet I'll talk to y'all when I get back okay. Sure, thing Lex me and my baby will be in our room when you need us, and I have to say things are really looking up after all the crazy shit we been through. He came over to me hugging me and so did Miss Janet smiling and they both when out the door.

I quickly slipped on my black power suit and checked both of my guns and made sure both my silencer is on tight I looked at myself in the mirror fixing my hair and I was ready to roll. Right before I was about to go I bumped fist with Peggy mumbling good luck. Soon ad I walked out the door Moon and Nick Lit were waiting for me with their black suits on. I looked at both of them bumping fist with both of them looking good let's roll. It only took us twenty minutes to get there and like he said he was sitting near the window with this Big bodyguard standing up. Moon and Nick Lit stayed in the background while I walked over to the table and I sat down in front of him he smiles talking smooth nobody told me you were sexy as well as deadly Mommy.

With that he wants some pussy cute smirk on his dark handsome Latina grill on his ass. He reaches out his hand I shook his hand replying I would say nice to meet you but I'm all fucking business poppy so who told you who I was? Some crazy ass powerful general you suppose to meet in the morning he gave me your long bloody resume I'm really impressed. Okay than I got the job then where is the money at poppy? Its on its way as we speak that give me some time to talk to a living legend in the game my name is Ju- Ju. Why thank you poppy but I'm really busy you know what I'm saying not to be rude your cute and all, but I don't know you. I understand you don't know me, but you will really get to know me after you take care of this thing for us maybe we can sit down and have a drink next time? Sure, I would like that once I get to know you. He looks out the window talking low the money is here a white Bentley is coming in the drive throw. Go get in that car right there my driver will take you where you have to go haft the money is in the trunk five million dollars meet me back here after its done and we will do the same thing so I get you the rest of your money and you will see that I know how to take care of business sweetheart. Okay I stood up shaking his hand nice to meet you Ju- Ju see you when it all done poppy. I walked out the door with Nick Lit and Moon right behind me all in step cool and calmly. We all jumped inside of this white Bentley I sat next to the driver this dark skin man with a dark blue suit on in his 30's he speaks hi

you doing where you want to go? Drop us off at West 27th street and we will be all good. He just nodded his head like a down ass soldier that been around for a minute in the game. He takes off nice and smoothly he took us there swiftly like an old pro he popped the trunk Nick Lit and Moon quickly grabbed the two suitcases, and we walked a block up to the hotel everything jumped off super smooth. We when to my room to check the money and it was all in order wrapped in yellow bands. *Gawd knows I love the smell of new money.*

Me Moon and Nick Lit sat at my bar in my room we had some drinks they had gin while I had Vodka with a lot of ice, we all were snorting the coke I got off of Chi-Chi. I dumped on top of the bar laughing and talking shit. Moon talking loud now that was super smooth so when do we hit this motherfucker Lex. Friday night in New Jersey when he go see his baby mama. Nick Lit y'all got all that information that fast on this dude. No not me Peggy did here I was trying to get rid of this bitch the whole time and she's the fucking golden ticket to this fucking business for real. Man, I was thinking she was a fucking square snitch white bitch.

Yeah, you got to remember she worked for the CIA for 12 years and she know a whole lot of shit plus all the shit her father showed her. And I'm sorry about this my niggas were going have to cut all this shit short so we can get up and meet the general it was fun while it lasted but we got to go get this money. They both started laughing uttering oh yes, it's all about getting that bag baby! Bumping fist with me with that hood killer grin on their faces. Moon stood up mumbling your right Lex I holler at you in the A.M. and came over and hugged me and Nick Lit did the same as I walked them to the door giggling and bull shitting the whole way there. I had another drink and when to bed taking my clothes off going to bed with sweet dreams of running my own Black bag shop Mister Price would be proud of us.

The next day I got up early at six know we had to be at the airport at 7 on the dot and I did not want to be late. Soon as I got out the shower Peggy was already knocking on my door, I rushed to let her in I open the door this bitch is already dressed. She quickly came in my room shutting the door fast yelling I need a gun. What the fuck you need a gun for Peggy. Look all of y'all have guns shit you carry two of them with a fucking silencer on them. Look Peggy just be yourself you don't need a gun okay. Yeah, but I want one. Okay I'll give you a gun if you know how to fucking use it. I gust your right will you show me how to use one? Sure, I'll show you soon as we get back from this meeting. I got finished getting dressed me and Peggy dash out the door when she told me she rented a new truck for this meeting the keys are at the desk as we run into the others in the hallway. Jitta, Moon, Stump, Miss Janet and Nick Lit we all bumped fist and hugged one another then she just stopped right before we were going to the elevator talking low in my ear where you got all the money at? It is all in the room do not worry if anybody take it, they will not get far I rigged the room with hand grenades and the money so don't worry about it okay. Wow I didn't know you can do that. See we both can educate one another about a whole lot of shit in this crazy ass world. We both laughed we got the key from the front desk while Moon still singing when and got the truck he brings it out front so we can get to the airport to meet the big man. *I'm a little nervous but I'm playing it off with my South Philly Swag.* We arrived on time at hanger 18 soon as we pulled up it about ten men with machine guns in army green outside of the hanger. When I glance up from the passenger side every one of them men look like they were not playing any fucking games. A tall young black soldier steps up to the driver side window as Moon rolls down the window with a cigarette cocked in the side of his lips. I leaned over and spoke up loudly its Lex to see general Kowalski.

The tall young soldier he carefully looks inside of are truck front and back super-fast like he lifted his hand and the gate opened from the left and right. Moon pulls inside this well-lit large space as he drives up towards this big green Jet in the middle of the hanger. I'm like damn it a Lear jet when we got closer it looked like the motherfucker was tricked out to me. Walking up on the passenger side is this tall white dude in his green army get up with a cigar hanging from his mouth. He is puffing big clouds of smoke and a big smile with soldiers on each side of him one black one white and that kill anything that moves glair in their eyes. General Kowalski sticks his hand out towards me with his deep smoke voice speaking let me shake the hands of the people who killed Mister Caesar and his Russian death squad. He shakes my hand smiling from ear to ear then he quickly hugs me then he when down the line shaking everyone's hand and he kissed Peggy on the cheek. Your dad would be proud of you sweetheart he points to the chairs on the right-hand side of the big army green color jet. We all sat down, and he sat in front of his in his chair and his men standing on each side of him. He smiles at me and he waves his hand yelling bring them in right now. Coming towards us is a large group of men pushing Jelly and his goons Big Eric Shank and Big Mama Red all in handcuffs all dirty and beat up in front of us while he is laughing looking at are reaction. The general looks me right in my eyes barking you know these people. It's a fucking shame you girl fell in love with the wrong guy again. *I looked at him.* And he started laughing uttering yeah, I know the whole story about Fat Poncho.

Don't worry I'm going to spare your friend she had nothing to do with them ripping me the fuck off! I was about to say something when he stood up pulling out his green 45 automatic. He is yelling this ass hole not only he took three thousand keys of heroin and two metric tons of cocaine from me working with your boy lieutenant Cob in Hong Kong. The general steps up putting the gun to his head looking at all of us uttering any last words motherfucker! Jelly started yelling that was not me who did that shit I took it from lieutenant Cob and his peoples I never took shit from you! He cocks the pistol back he quickly points it at Big Eric at the last minute Kapacka! Blowing his brains out the blood splashed on Big Mama Red Jelly and Shank his body fell like a big red wood tree in the fucking woods Doom! As one of the generals' men cuts the duct tape from their risk. He looks Jelly in his face loudly talking your one lucky ass motherfucker! My people told me that it was not you who took are heroin it was your boy here and he put the word out you were behind it.

Now I am going to make one demand with this rag tag group of good soldiers' you guys have here that you all work together! If you want me to have your back from here on out. And if all of you keep fucking over all of my enemies, we will have a very good understanding from this day forward! *Every last one of us is nodding are head yes.* Jelly Looks over at us rubbing his risk nodding his head yes as well. *I just let out some air of relief soon as he started nodding his head in agreement. Shit I knew Jelly was not as dumb as he looks if he would have said no, they all would have been dead, and they would never find their bodies like Jimmy Hoffa.* He stood in front of all of us with that wicket ass grin of his still talking I would go and party with you guys, but I have some where to be in a few hours he hands me Jelly, and Peggy his card this is your get out of jail free card do not fucking lose it! He taps me and pulls me to the side swiftly good luck to you and we will talk next month on my private island okay! He bumps fist with me yelling fire up the jet were the fuck out of here! Some of his men jump on the jet with him and the others just lined up on the left and right-hand side of the hanger. The giant bay doors to the hanger opened as we all got out of the way. As the jet rolled out on the runway speeding as we stood there watching it take off and flying off into the wild blue yonder. Big Mama Red came over hugging me and Jelly shaking my hand smiling. *I would never tell him about the client list we took from him and if he dose find out I'll blame it on Mister Price isn't that what everybody do blame on someone dead some real classic shit.*

I quickly blurted out welcome to the firm everybody started giggling loud Peggy came walking up speaking see it all worked out like I told you it would. We all just looked at her like she was crazy I turned to her uttering yes you told us Peggy let's just get back to the hotel and get high and celebrate the birth of are new company okay. Moon stepped up talking we do not have enough room for everyone to get into the truck. I just said we just make two trips that all take them first then come back for us. Peggy, you go with them and check them in for me please. Sure, thing Lex. Moon standing next to Peggy waves Shank Jelly and Big Mama Red over to the truck they jumped in and took off from the hanger.

An hour Moon came back to get us, and we partied hard until Friday came like a fucking blur, I gave everybody their game plan. *We named our firm the Price Firm after Mister Price Peggy cried when we got the business card printed up and next week, we move into brand new office building space me and Peggy hooked up after we sobered up and I showed her how to shoot at a gun rage and in the woods.*

This was the best time to hit Big Sammy, he only took six men with him when to see his peoples. So, it me Moon Nick Lit Stump and Miss Janet in the Black GMC truck Jelly gave us when we first split up when we got to New York. Jelly Big Mama Red and Shank is in the other truck Peggy rented. Peggy is at the hotel watching from the two monitors on the drone camera following Big Sammy's whip with his thuged out escort. Big Sammy is driving on the expressway in his 500-S Benz with three of his goons inside the car with him. and another car trailing him with three more ass holes. We all have on earpieces and bullet proof vest. Am talking to the whole team as we get closer behind them. Okay Jungle crew were going hit them fast hard and get the fuck out of dodge y'all got it! Moon speed up ahead getting right beside this big white 500-S Benz so we are waiting on the second car to get in position. Now I'm coaxing Jelly along so we can get this shit clean come on Jelly! Come on Jelly! With Peggy in my ear yelling tell him to fucking hurry up! Then she screams that's it smoke that shit bag! **Pooouuuff!** I shot the driver inside of his left eye falling on top of the wheel with the car swaying to the left. Big Sammy panicking leaning over to grab the wheel of the car. **Pooouuufff!** My second shot I hit Big Sammy on the top of his right eye when the blood shoots up on the window I just about came on myself. Simultaneously squeezing off a shot is Shake hitting the driver in the middle of his forehead the car swayed off making a hard right hitting another car **Kablam!** The car flipped over crashing into truck and a pile of cars exploding on fire. Both of are cars speed off smooth and stealth flowing into traffic like it was easy as Sunday Morning and gone in fucking 60 seconds. As we all are bopping are head to DMX's *Where my dogs at.*

The next day I made the call to get the rest of our loot we meet back up at the same joint Starbucks soon as I got there with Nick Lit and Moon Ju-Ju is smiling his ass off yapping about that drink. I told him to meet me later on I made a fast rendezvous to his canary yellow Rose Royce and fucked him in the front seat we never made it up to the room. I came three times we drove all the way to Philly just to get some cheese steaks and came back snorting coke all the way up there and all the way back having a fucking blasé. And Oh yes, I plan to see his ass again because that shit was good. After that everything was a drug induce burly fucking haze and the week blazed past and I never knew it, but I felt my power rocking in my ass. We moved into the front at the fancy ass officer building in

New York, but out real fall back is back to warehouse palace back in Philly and we hooked the green monster the beast back up too with some new gizmo's.

A month when bye before we when back to work I met up with Uzi-Boy in Philly and told him what I wanted to do and him and his whole crew is down. but in the back of my mind is how lieutenant Cob is going to come back at us. When I woke up that morning, I got a phone call I I'm haft sleep I reached for the phone on my night-stand and put it up to my ear. Who the fuck is this calling me so early in the morning! It's the man you wish you never double crossed that who the fuck it is bitch! I sat up on my bed, but I did not panic lieutenant Joe Cob who nice of it you to fucking call. Let cut out all the fucking small talk I have your Uncle Big Hank! And if you and Jelly don't turn over the metric ton of fentanyl and the three thousand keys of heroin along with the client list, or he's fucking dead! You want to know what I when for all you bull shit about working for you, but I soon found out you were setting us up for a suicide mission! Well, if you say so Lex you have 48 hours to produce all of my product, I'll call you where to meet up at! He hangs up. I sat back and started laughing because if they have my Uncle Big Hank, they just don't know what the fuck there in for real.

I jumped up and got myself together and called a family meeting in the lounge area near the bar letting everyone know what the fuck was going on. Jelly was the only one that looked like he was going to shit on himself. Then he asks me why are you so cavalier about this shit Lex? I smiled looking out at everyone talking loudly if they think they got my Uncle Hank he wanted them to take him where they are laying their head at and he's going to fuck all of them up. My Uncle was one of them hard core gang war cats from back in the day and by tomorrow they will wish they never even picked his ass up! Jelly stands up talking in a panic I know you looked up to your uncle from back in the days, but his skills just might have diminished over the years Lex! And we worked so hard to get to where were at now with new client lined up all this month. Peggy looked up at me talking do we need to be worried Lex tell us the truth please. No! Plus, we already sold the metric ton of fentanyl to BoJack and them in Chicago and the heroin to my friend Uzi-Boy from the 24th street cartel. Moon stands up from the bar talking if you say we got nothing to worry about then that's just about it then. As he's looking over at Jelly. Miss Janet sitting next to Stump stands up and announced, "we still strap up just in case shit goes sideways Lex. Look, we always have to be ready no matter what we're doing in this fucking game."

"Yeah, strap up, but when I'm right again don't come to me talking that I believed you from the door bullshit, okay."

Then it is a big knock at the door everybody jumped up scrambling grabbing their guns and machine guns aiming towards the door. I just looked at all of them I'll get it smiling my ass off. I peeked in the peephole, and I could not believe my fucking eyes. I opened the door and its AK and Jackie standing right in front of me.

With AK in his deep voice, "Miss, are you interested in reading the watchtower bitch!'

I fell out laughing hugging him then Jackie blurted out, "I thought I never be saying this after all this time, but I miss your crazy ass bitch!"

Then from out of nowhere Big Boogie came picking me up from my feet giving me this giant fucking bear hug yelling, "family!"

He puts me down than Bizzer bumps fist with me and he came over kissing me on the cheek.

"My family, please come on in."

AK looking around uttering, "damn, they kept this motherfucker up I see!"

"Yeah, Rock did I just brought it back off of him for my crew to lay low."

As the four of them walked in I started introducing them to my new crew one by one. After I was done AK taps me on the arm whispering, "why don't you get one your peoples to make my wife and Bizzer a drink while we go over here in the gym so I can rap to you right quick. Don't worry about lieutenant pale face showing up here I got men posted up all around here, okay."

I pointed to Big Mama Red, "could you please make everybody a drink while me and AK step off to talk."

"Sure, thing Lex."

Big Mama Red quickly went behind the bar fixing everybody a drink. Me, AK and Big Boogie walked into the gym in the back. Soon as we went to the back sitting down. I looked up at AK and he began to speak, "this like is a fucking dream. I never thought this day would ever come after all the shit I been through."

AK looked at me right into my eyes, "look, I'm really sorry about putting that green light out on you, but I really thought you did it, Lex."

Big Boogie cuts in, "yeah, and after you took all that coke off us, we really thought you did it."

"Well, I did take the coke, but did y'all get my gift I replaced it and then some."

AK laughing, "I don't want to ask you where you got it from but thank you, we got more pills than we can handle."

"Well, I had help from my new secretary finding that monster shipment of Oxycodone going to the Midwest."

AK raised his eyebrow, "so, the white girl is good then."

"Oh, hell yes, she worked for the CIA for 12 years she knows a lot of shit."

"Well speaking of the CIA your old employer sends me here to kill you."

"So is that why you're here instead of the apology."

"To tell you the truth, yes that was before I got the call from Uzi-Boy letting me see the video and him telling me that you outsmarted lieutenant Cob by Jacking the fucking client list. But after he told me to kill you, he never said nothing about that client list."

"After all this time working for him, I found out he was just using me like everybody else."

"So, what are you asking me over here, AK? I know you, nigga you never beat around the fucking bushes."

"Okay, I came to cut a deal with you. I'll keep lieutenant Cob off your back, and you share some of the client list with us."

"Well, not to be funny I already got that shit from general Ed Kowalski. You can't trust that crazy white motherfucker."

"Your right, I can't but this is what I propose I got an open line from Ju-Ju the Columbia middleman working for Juna Garcia."

"You hook me up with Death Struck in Los Angeles and King Darius down South and we all can be one big happy family again."

AK looks over at Big Boogie he's smiling nodding his head yes. "I already talked to Uzi- Boy and BoJack about this ideal they told me to ask you to work it out."

"Yeah, I'm with it that's a fucking deal. Now you word is good as gold I know that, but I don't trust Kim."

"Don't worry about Kim my son will deal with that bitch soon."

I stood up and we both hugged then I hugged Big Boogie.

AK yelled, "okay let go get fucked up and celebrate this shit!"

"I down for that shit, but what are we going to do about lieutenant Cob white ass?"

AK and Big Boogie started laughing. Big Boogie still laughing, "we send Neno to his ass before we came here so don't worry about it if he escapes from that shit, he's one lucky ass."

 Like he said we went and the other room and started getting twisted.

And don't worry about it because Neno is one of the deadliest hit men in the game and he's down with the 24th street cartel for life. While we celebrated our new reunion for bigger and better things to come. By night fall on the other side of the bridge lieutenant Cob with 12 of his best men and his new attack dog Black Cobra. They have my Uncle Big Hank tied up in an abandon factory in New Jersey waiting on word from AK for my death. My Uncle been working on the duct tape and ropes most of the day wiggling around and making them lose sitting in the dark.

Two men are on post outside of the dusty ass storage room they have him in. Lieutenant Cob is pacing the floor not too far from where they have him at yelling. "What taking that motherfucker so long to take them the fuck out!"

Black Cobra quickly spoke, "well lieutenant Cob Sir you did tell me you trained them sir?"

"So, what the fuck that got to do with anything?"

"I hate to say it sir, but that means they will be harder to kill give him another hour or so if we do not hear back, then we know something when wrong."

Bursting out of the storge room door is Big Hank tackling one of the men on post.

Making him drop his machine gun the second guard is pointing his machine gun toward the two men tussling on the floor. Lieutenant Cob is running over yelled, "shoot his ass!"

The second men yelled back, "I'll hit our own man!"

"Shoot him! Fuck that, shoot him!"

Soon as he when to take to pull the trigger **Pooouuuffff!** The man holding the machine gun is shot right in the middle of his head blood shooting up in the air as he falls to the floor boom!

Lieutenant Cob and Black Cobra pulling out their guns ducking down looking both ways. All the lights go out and all they both see is sparks from up top on the left **Pooouufff! Pooouuuff! Pooouuuff!** Killing three more of his men.

Big Hank finally snaps the neck of the man on post **Karacka!** He is feeling on the ground in the dark finding the machine gun he stays low soon as he seen some shadows moving around, he lets them have it!

Barrrrraaaaaa! He gets down on the ground Big Hank is crawling on the ground towards some little bit of light he sees near a doorway. Then from the right four more shots. **Pooouuufff! Pooouuufff! Pooouuuff! Pooouuufff!**

Killing four more of lieutenant Cob's men. Lieutenant Cob is whispering to Black Cobra where is this son of a bitch! Big Hank makes it to the door on the left he pushed the door wide open, but he stays low crawling outside. With that little bit of light lieutenant Cob can see him and he started shooting at him just missing him. Black Cobra quickly grabbing lieutenant Cob up and started running towards the right. The four men that remain jumps up from lying flat on the ground. **Pooouuufff! Pooouuufff!**

Two more of his men are hit in the back of their head falling to the floor really hard they all can hear their death cries. But Black Cobra pulls running and pulling lieutenant Cob out the warehouse and two of his men they are all running towards there Black GMC truck soon as they got close **Kaboom!** The impact from the blast knocked all four of the men to the ground. The truck is engulfed in flames with black smoke gushing out of it. With all their ears ringing loud all of them rolling around on the ground. **Pooouuufff! Pooouuufff!**

Hitting the last two men of lieutenant Cob's men. Black Cobra jumps up grabbing lieutenant Cob up from off the ground making him run with him running towards the highway. Two more shots just missing them as Black Cobra pulls lieutenant Cob near the hill of the freeway and they both fell at the bottom of the hill right near the black top of the road. As cars and trucks are speeding by Black Cobra yelled to him you stay down if we don't get out of here were dead this ass hole with that high power rifle is good.

Black Cobra runs out on the freeway with his machine gun standing in the middle of the road as a truck is speeding towards him while he points upward with the machine gun **Eee-eeerrrrrrrr!** The red pick-up truck stops right in front of him he quickly ran over snatching the truck driver from out under the wheel of his truck. The truck driver scared to death runs off in the opposite direction yelling head off. As Black Cobra ran over pulling lieutenant Cob to push him into the truck. Black Cobra get behind the wheel of the pick-up truck taking off up the dark highway.

Meanwhile back at the warehouse were all fucked up telling old war stories with AK Jackie Big Boogie and Bizzer laughing drinking snorting and smoking having a fucking ball. What made it even more fun was that Uzi- Boy along with his wife to Alice and her brothers Ducky Black Billy Black and their cousin DeShawn. *Well, when I laid my eyes on him, I said to myself God Damn look like a bitch is going to get some tonight after all.* My phone is ringing off the fucking hook, but I don't know the number I step off to see what the fuck is going on I'm high.

So,I go in the other room to see who the fuck it is. "Yo, who is this?"

"It's me, your uncle, motherfucker!"

I almost jump twenty feet in the air when I heard his voice.

"Uncle Hank are you alright?"

"Yeah, I'm good right now I had to get the fuck out of there, but I had to say I had some help getting the fuck out there.

Somebody came there killing all of his fucking men from out of nowhere."

"Did you see who it was?"

"Hell, no but if I do find out who he is I'll buy him a fucking drink I tell you that shit!"

"You want me to come get you or something?"

"No, I'm good I'm over a friend house right now that why you did not know the number, they took my phone."

"Just as long as you're alright I feel a hell of a lot better."

"Well, I will feel a lot better when you give me some money so I can relocate sweetheart."

"I got you Uncle Hank come past the warehouse and I'll hook you up."

"Good, I'll be past there in the afternoon. I'll see you then good night."

Soon as I hung up, I made a bee line towards that fine ass Black man. This is one the best days of my life I got my company off the ground plus I'm back in with the gang as well. We all know it is going to be raining fucking money now when I walked AK and Jackie to the door when they were going back to Miami. AK turns to me uttering, "I'm so glad you back into the fold and he hugs me."

And one by one Jackie, Big Boogie and Bizzer I was so happy.

And just like I knew if I got him up to my room and got a real pleasant surprise when we got down to fucking. After everybody went home his Dick hooks to the left. I saw this shit on porn movies before, but I never got some Dick like this live and in person.

He made me cum five times. Shit, I was seeing fucking stars after he was done with me and I was sore. What really turned me on about him is he loves to talk a whole lot of nasty shit to me while he's fucking me, I love that shit. I love being back in the fold, but I found out fast was that I stayed busy and my thirst for revenge got replace by stack in up chips for my future. I never thought that this Black bag operations shit was so lucrative. I knew it was good money but not like this it was fucking crazy. I reach one of my golds by buying my first condo building in the suburbs'. And every week end I had two men I was having sex with come over De Shawn and Chi- Chi but he was starting to get on my nerves because he kept talking about killing Fat Poncho. I think he told his boss that he will get me to kill him that's why he kept pressing me to do it.

So, De Shawn started being my main nigga after time when by I use to see Ju-Ju once in a blue moon when he comes to town, but I never took him where I lay my head at. Me and Ju-Ju use to go on wild adventures after we have sex and we fucked all over the place outside and all kinds of strange places. One day he told me he was going to take me shopping one time, so I shouted why not right now motherfucker! He jumped up on Saturday morning and yelled I'm taking you shopping in downtown Rome in Italy I told him he was bull shitting me.

So, he called up his peoples an made it happen. We jump on his private jet, and we stayed for a couple days too. But before we were going to go back you would never fucking believe this shit, I seen Fat Poncho sitting in a restaurant eating but he did not see me. Ju- Ju looked at me asking me what is wrong. I did not want to tell him, but I broke down and told him the whole story. He told me that we were on vacation leave that shit alone get his ass another time. I told him no this would be fucking perfect than I ask him why he don't get one his men to find out where he is staying at. He did not want to do it, but he got one his men name Giorgio to find out where he is staying when we when back to the hotel to pack. An hour later Giorgio told me where he is staying and when he leaves.

Ju-Ju looked at me muttering why don't he let Giorgio do it. I told him it not the same I want to do it myself it more satisfaction in it for me. He looked at me and smiled okay he leaves tonight to pop his ass on the way to the airport and we get the fuck out of here! I hugged and kissed him. So, we lay low snorting coke and drinking champagne while he sends Giorgio to rent a car and got me the tools I need as well.

We are staying at the Hassler Roma Piazza Trinita Dei mont 6, Rome. Fat Poncho is with this coke selling bitch name Taffy Richardson all of her brothers are in the game and every last one of them swear for Gawd that their bad too. Fat Poncho and Taffy is staying at The ST. Regis Rome Via Vitorio Emanuele Orlando 3, Rome RM. Right before it was his check out time Giorgio drove me to this beautiful hotel. We laid in the cut waiting for them to check out when a cab came rolling up Giorgio whispered to me here, "we go make sure you get a good clean shot at him don't miss."

I laughed not saying a word this motherfucker does not know me very well. We watch both of them get in as the cab driver helps them with their bags in the trunk. What they both do not know that the cab driver is cussing them out in Italian that the bags were so heavy. I was cracking up listening they both jump in and take off down the road.

Giorgio follows them as they drive towards the airport. He stayed with them not being too suspicious the way he was driving but soon as the road got wide on both side Giorgio speeds up on the side Fat Poncho is sitting on, I line up my shot Pooouuufff! Hitting him right in the center of his head on the bridge of his nose. Soon as he fell back on to that bitch Taffy with the blood gushing out, I yelled out Bingo! Giorgio speed off laughing talking loud I did not know you were that good I would not have given you that little speech. And we were gone with the sun going down the shit looked cinematic.

We got back to the hotel with are bags already packed up as Giorgio is talking to Ju- Ju in Spanish how good I was. Ju- Ju is laughing his ass off telling Giorgio to talk in English because that woman can speak nine different languages fluently, so she knows every word you're saying. He is in shock uttering for real boss. My way of thanking him for letting me do the hit in

Rome I gave Ju-Ju a super head special sloppy ass blow job soon as we got on his private jet in the bathroom. I thought he was going to have a fucking heart attack I sucked his Dick so good.

I really drained the cum out of the head of his Dick. I was gulping it all down like a sweet sticky ass vanilla milk shake. This motherfucker was hyperventilating holding his chest after I was done with his ass. He had a big wide grin on his face all the way home when we touch back down in the states.

THE LAST THREE

After me smoking Fat Poncho in Rome I never seen Ju- Ju after that but the plug he hooked me up with this chick name Gi- Gi was still jumping off, so I really did not give a fuck. The same thing with Chi- Chi he when an fell in love with some bitch in Brooklyn having two babies with her. I'm not mad at him because life for me was getting better each day. All I did was stack shit up while the Price firm was booming with new business. After AK hooked us up with his drug contacts you would think we were born millionaires.

Two years flu by like a blur we all worked hard and played even harder. Me and DeShawn became a study thing, but I still fucked some hot guys when I wanted too but it became less and less when I didn't have the time I use to have before, so I got my shit off with him most the time. I met his whole family as shit got deeper with the two of us, I met his mother Miss Terry she is nice. His brothers Mango who works with is older brother Fat Wally who run the crew. He works for this high-profile gangster bitch name Almasi. Her name is ringing bells in the streets right about now. She used to run the BSN The Black Syndicate Nation.

Now she got her own thing flowing but when I met his cousin Zab at a dinner party, they had for DeShawn's mother Miss Terry at this small hall in North Philly.

I got a real bad vibe about this nigga I didn't know if I was tripping or not, but I know this nigga from somewhere. DeShawn kept telling me how tight he was with his cousin running off at the mouth they were like brothers not just cousins. He went on about how much work they all put in together in the streets while we were sitting at the table with him. It did not hit me until his cousin was on the dance floor dancing and he took off his shirt when I see the tattoos with his wife beater t-shirt on, *I would never forget it two machine guns crisscrossing with the thick lettering saying death before dishonor.* I knew that was one of the niggas Bony Irons send to the crib in New York to kill me. I was upset *now I'm thinking to myself only some shit like this would happen to me once I'm feeling this nigga.* I stood up telling DeShawn I had to go he quickly following me out of the door asking me what is wrong. I did not want to tell him I quickly walked to my car with him right behind me pulling at me to tell him what is going on with me. A voice in my head told me to tell him and another one was telling me to just get the fuck out of there and don't say shit about it to him and kill his ass and his cousin too. I jumped into my whip pulling my keys out of my pocketbook.

He jumps into the passenger seat yelling at me, "I'm not letting you go until you tell me what's up with you."

I acted like I calm down and I slowly reached in my bag getting my pistol inching it out slowly.

Right at the moment I'm about to pull my shit out his cousin Zab is at the front of the doors kissing on some girl laughing and giggling. A car came speeding up the street letting off a barrage of bullets all we can see is the muzzle flash and flames shooting out from the tips. DeShawn jumps out with his gun shooting at the speeding car, but it was too late the car was gone it sped off into the darkness of the Verizon. I quickly jumped out to see his cousin Zab bloody body with the Dall yellow lights shining down on the pool of blood he is laying in. People started running outside to see what happen in deep shock and horror screaming and yelling. *I looked at DeShawn with tears in my eyes he might think that I'm crying about his cousin. But I'm crying knowing about him and I don't cry for a motherfucker no time in my life.* I hugged him talking low with my voice cracking, "I have to go sorry about your cousin I holler at you later."

I jumped in my car and got the fuck out of their because I know the cops are coming, I do not want to see them motherfuckers.

What I did not know this was the beginning of a war between ONSH The Original North Side Hustlers and Kim's group of hoods she uses to be down with the 24th street cartel now she broke off from them and her click is called JFK Just for killers.

Two weeks went by, and I was really avoiding DeShawn, but he kept calling me every day I did not call him back neither. The day of his cousin's funeral after the services he came to my crib at my condo banging on the door like he was fucking crazy. I ran to the door to let him in yelling at him what the fuck is wrong with you! He rushed inside of my place I quickly closed the door and walked inside of my living room as he is yelling at me. "So, what are you dumping me for some other nigga or what?"

"No, that not it I found out about you that's why I stopped calling you, okay.

"You found out what about me? You sound like all these other crazy bitches out here. What is you talking about? Spit it out!"

"You were the fourth shooter that tried to kill me in New York!"

"That was not me I drove the car I never went inside of the house. I never knew that was you Lex I swear to Gawd."

"Your fucking lying when I saw your cousin's tattoo. I know it was y'all. It was 7 years ago, but I never forget shit like that! You two are lucky because I was going to kill him and you before that drive by went down once."

I saw that tattoo on his fucking chest death before dishonor! What's really fucked up I was falling for your fucking black ass too."

"That was not me go ask that dude Fat Poncho!"

"You can't ask him I killed him."

"Well ask Big Sammy he is the one who set it up!"

"You cannot ask him neither I could not stand his ass and he is dead too because I killed him too."

He sits down on the couch, "shit, Lex who you did not kill."

"I did not kill you yet."

I pointed my gun right at him.

"Just admit it was you. I just want you to tell me before you die motherfucker!" He is backing up with his hands up in the air still muttering, "It was not me, Lex!"

Right before I was going to squeeze the trigger.

DeShawn screams out his mouth, "I know go ask that fat bitch fat Poncho was fucking who had the speakeasy in Brooklyn!" *I'm thinking to myself how the fuck he knows her.*

I lower the gun uttering, "you mean Big Mama Red?"

"Yeah, that's her she did not know the name of the target, but she was there when we put the whole thing together."

"She knew we were from out of town to put in work it was me Lance Lucci, Mikey, Zab and this dude name Sleam he was the fourth shooter not me. I was just driving the truck."

"How much did Big Sammy pay y'all to do that shit?"

"We split 60K fast money for some niggas working from out, of town shit three large a piece."

I pulled out my phone calling Big Mama Red she pick up after three rings, "Yo, what's up girl? I need to holler at you about some shit that went down in your spot some time back."

"Sure, when you want me to come to your house?"

"Is an hour too quick for you girlfriend I really need to clear this shit up with this nigga or I'm going smoke his ass and I think he's lying to me again? "

"Okay I'm on my way can I bring Jelly with me?"

"No, I just need you because Jelly don't need to know about this shit because Fat Poncho was all up in the middle of this shit."

"Okay, see you in an hour one!"

I looked up at him you want a drink because I sure need one right about now. "Sure, I will take one Lex."

I waved for him to join me at my bar on the right-hand side. *We both walked over slowly with me rolling my eyes at this nigga he's lucky I like this motherfucker, or he would be dead already.*

With him uttering out his mouth, "how the fuck did you know this bitch?"

See it a small world after all nigga she is my home girl she was down with me when we put the crew together to Jack this Puerto Rican drug dealer in North Philly. DeShawn sits in front of me while I make his drink Jack Daniels and coke on the rocks. I made me just Vodka on the rocks. I set the gun down in front of him it's a test he doesn't know I have my other gun in the back of my jeans. He sips on his drink looking up at me muttering, "what was that about you falling for my Black ass?"

"I don't want to talk about that right now until she comes and clear this shit up about you motherfucker. Just because I did not shoot you right now don't mean I will not do it, nigga!"

"So, sit back and enjoy your drink it just might be your fucking last one. Now that is the Lex, we all know and love that cold ass gangster bitch! Well after she come here and clear my name from this shit, I need to ask you something."

"You want some coke?"

"Yeah, I can take me a snort right about now as well. I walked to the other end of the bar to get the large zip lock bag of cocaine and see if he will reach for the gun."

I am watching him from the corner of my eye he never reaches for the gun he just might be telling the truth. I walked back dumping a big pile on top of the bar. I get one of my playing cards to chop the shit up and I hand him a cut off straw. He takes it out my hand looking me in my face talking all smooth I don't know why you don't believe me Lex. I just started shuffling the white powder on top of the bar I just looked back at him not saying shit. I make my first four lines and I snort them up real fast and sipping some more Vodka. Then I hear the doorbell ringing I quickly walked to the door I looked in the peek hole and its Big Mama Red.

I opened the door and I hugged her, "please come in."

As we both walked back to the bar. She speaks to DeShawn sitting down I go behind the bar snorting some more coke than I look at her and asked, "now were you there when these niggas were talking about doing a job?"

"Yeah, it was him that guy Zab, Sleam, Mikey and Lance and they wanted DeShawn to drive the others were to get the drugs and give them back to Bony Irons Fat Poncho put all of them together to do it on the low."

DeShawn pointed at me, "I told you!"

He jumps up kissing Big Mama Red on the cheek yelling, "thank you for telling the truth, baby!"

Big Mama Red looks at me could you give and asked. "Can you please give me a drink before I ask you something, Lex?"

"Sure, I already know what you're going to ask me while am making her drink real quick Vodka on the rocks with a little bit of cherry red Kool aid."

"You don't know what I'm going to ask you before I ask you Lex."

I sat the drink in front of her now you got your drink.

"What do you want to ask me?"

"Did you kill Fat Poncho?"

I just nodded my head yes.

She lowered her eyes, "why you did not say that out your

mouth?"

"Because you could be fucking wired bitch!" Me and DeShawn started laughing loud. After that we talked for a little while and I got Big Mama Red out the door very quickly so we can be alone. Now me and DeShawn had some serious ass down home fucking making up to do. He fucked me right on the floor right near my bar.

He yelled, "your daddy's little fuck squirt cum queen and I'm going give you a really good cowboy fucking!"

Laying me on the floor pulling my panties off and tossing them up in the air and they landed on the ceiling fan. We both burst out laughing as each hot stroke sends chill bumps up my ass grunting and moaning with my legs up on his shoulders pumping like a high-performance sports car piston on a race-track sizzling hot.

He is tearing this pussy up. I just love make-up sex. I jumped up and got on top of his sexy Black ass. I wanted to ride the lightning in this storm of orgasmic pleasure and pain. He was Captain Hook, and I was Sally Star riding that Dick into the Valley of erotic bliss and cum fulfilling ecstasy. Just like an explosion from off a volcano a serendipitous moment happens electrifying both our hot sweaty bodies we both came together. "Wow!! Oooooooooooo! Oh, my Gawd!"

I was screaming at the top of my lungs falling into a cum coma with my head getting light feeling that mind blowing sensation. He is twitching and jumping up and down like he just got struck with 9000 votes of electrodes on the top of his fuck happy brain. Making that ugly wild snarl then crashing into an ocean of hot sticky love gushy juice dripping down both are legs. As both our souls melting into the Milky Way kissing one another like we been a part for two years or something thug love will fuck your whole life up for real. We both breathing hard giggling like two school kids who just heard a dirty joke. Laying down next to one another tingling with every touch every kiss every jester my leg still bopping up and down on him laughing. Then he hit me with, "Lex, I really didn't want to ask you, but I need your help."

"I do anything in the world for you DeShawn but I'm not getting in the middle of a fucking war unless it's one of my wars you feel me, Harry Handsome."

He giggles, "I know Kim for years she came up under us, so I know the bitch is real."

"Y'all don't know who you're fucking with I do."

"So, you're saying we will lose going up against her?"

"No, what I'm saying is let Faheem wild ass crew take that bitch out and you and me go get this money with my Black bag operations."

He looks at me I put my hand up in his face, "it is up to you, boss up or go get fucked up love that's on you."

His eyes told the whole story this nigga want to go get this money.

His phone ringing in his black jeans on the floor he quickly runs to get it he put it to his ear and his whole face drops filled with sadness. He is stunned lost in a fucked-up haze of some kind.

I quickly stand up, "what happen DeShawn?"

"Nas is dead!"

"Who is that baby?"

"He was the head of our gang ONSH *the original North Side Hustlers.*"

I quickly walked over to him and hugged him to console him he looks like he got hit by a fucking truck. I walked him over to the bar and made him a drink, but I never said the words out of my mouth I told you so. We got high and this nigga went to sleep for the next two weeks.

I was working with Peggy so she can track down the last three Mikey Sleam and Lance Lucci. What I love about her she got all of them clocked and she also tell me the best place to get rid of their ass next month. She told me that we have a job in New York that is when I can take care of one of them.

One month went by fast but the war with Kim's JFK and ONSH niggas raged on and I kept DeShawn out of all of that shit. I kept his ass busy working with me making sure everybody had their product counting loot running errands for me and fucking me every other night. All his boys disown him telling him he's pussy whipped. I told him it's better to be pussy whipped than being dead. He fell out laughing.

Its Monday time for me to make our move with this job the client a Chinese businessman who is not connected with the Triads (The Chinese Mob) wanted his brother-in-law dead so he can take over their import outport business. The businessman's sister is in on it as well she will collect the insurance money and get some pay back on his ass too for him stepping out on her. He told us every Monday he goes to see his mistress to have sex in a Manhattan apartment high rise. Me and Nick Lit when to take care of it I have Nick just in case shit goes sideways and we both could shoot are way out of shit. But the way we have it set up everything should go smooth. We get to the high rise early laying low on are marked to just walk right into it.

Nick Lit is in the parking garage were both on the same page with are radio earpieces. Nick took care of their video surveillance system taking out the whole 17th floor. I'm in the exit waiting on this dude I look at my watch I peek down the hallway and this motherfucker is right on time. I wait for him to get closer to the door he's walking with that silly as grin on his grill he just doesn't know. The second he got near the door I popped out from the exit taking aim **Pooouuufff!** I hit him in his right eye he falls backward to the floor I ran up **Pooouuufff!**

Pooouuufff! Putting two more slugs in his head to make sure he's dead and I quickly walked back to the exit walking down to the parking garage.

Soon as I get their Nick Lit drove up in the Black BMW I jump in, and he took off and we when straight to New Jersey to a massage parlor Mikey loves going to at this strip mall. I looked at my watch were making good time it 10:30 P.M. It took us about hour to arrive at this little strip mall we sit and wait. We park not too far from the door, but it is kind of dark that why these guys come here they don't be seen going inside. This Dickhead did not get there until 10" clock We see him jumped out of his whip by himself he quickly started walking to the door. I ran up behind him soon as he when to open the door I lift my gun to the back of his head **Pooouuufff!** I hit him in the middle of the back of his head it exploded like a cantaloupe the blood splash up on the door of the joint he fell forward face down. I give him two more **Pooouuufff! Pooouuufff!** Soon as I when to walk away some dumb ass fat guy walking out the door falling over his body and he looked up at me. I have a mask on, but I shoot him anyway in the mouth **Pooouuufff!**

With no hesitation and I ran back to the car telling Nick to take off he sped off down the dark street. I say to myself one down and two to go after we hit the expressway. I took off my mask blasting J Cole Motiv-8 and ATM repeatedly. We made it back to Philly and had a little party with me Peggy, DeShawn and Nick Lit.

Four months go by like a blur I'm sleep in the bed with DeShawn I reaches for the phone on my nightstand am half asleep. I put it to my ear mumbling, "yeah, who is this?"

"It's me AK."

"Hey what is going on did you get that thing?"

"Yeah, I got It I'm not calling about that. I'm calling to tell you I'm putting all hands-on deck because that bitch Kim shot my son up Faheem."

I sat up right quick, "what when AK?"

DeShawn lifts his head up listening.

"About an hour ago. Where you I'm on my way!"

"Were at?"

"Jefferson hospital be careful she still might have some of her people lurking out there Lex."

"I will I see you in a few one."

I quickly called my peoples at the warehouse palace hitting up Jelly he picks up on the fourth ring,

"Yo, what's up Lex?"

"Check it, I'm going to need one y'all to bring me the beast to my condo for me please."

"Sure, I'll ask Moon to bring it to you so what's going on Lex?"

"This war with Kim just when to another level Kim people just shot up AK's son Faheem."

"Yeah, but I thought it was between ONSH and Kim's JFK thugs why they shoot Faheem isn't he down with the 24th street cartel?"

"Yeah, it is an old beef after Kim split from the gang."

"Oh, Kim was down with the 24th street cartel at one point then."

"Yeah, some time back."

"Okay I'm telling him now."

"Hey, Lex Need you to drive the beast to her condo."

Moon take the phone out of Jelly's hand speaking I'll be right there Lex! Thanks Moon man one! *It took him less than a half an hour because I'm not too far from the warehouse he had his father Jitta to follow him in his whip a Lexus SUV so he can get back home.*

I strapped up with my two guns two machine guns and four hand

grenades my favorite. I made sure DeShawn had two guns as well since he wanted to come with me. After I got my shit together and me and DeShawn snorting a little blow my phone rings. I look at the caller ID its Moon.

"Yo, I'm outside Ma. I'll be right there, bro!"

I double check my guns and me and DeShawn head outside. I bump fist and hug Moon and Jitta with him uttering to me, "watch your ass out this motherfucker baby girl. these cats are not playing any games out here."

"Don't I know it!"

Me and Jitta giggling. I wave to them as me and DeShawn jump in the green van, we all call the beast I get behind the wheel and take off. It doesn't take us long to get to the hospital I park it in the parking lot right across the street from the hospital I ask the woman at the information desk.

She told us he is here I think he is still in surgery the family is in the waiting room on the emergency room side on the right. "Thank you, Miss."

Me and DeShawn walked over to the emergency room side soon as I walked in there, I see AK and Jackie. I hugged both of them asking them about Faheem condition.

AK just looked at me uttering, "we don't know yet he's still in surgery."

"Wow you two got here fast from Miami. "

Jackie just turned to me whispering, "we came into town a few days ago on the low to take care of some business with a couple of are properties."

Uzi-Boy and Alice Black came over to me hugging me and bumping fist with DeShawn. Uzi-Boy waving me to the side. I step off with him as he is talking.

"So, what up with your boy here?"

"He's my man, Uzi -Boy why?"

"I just want to know who side this nigga is on alright we got one of your niggas right now at the scrap yard."

"Who?"

"You know some nigga name Chi- Chi?"

"Yeah, I was fucking him why?"

"Well, he said he drove here, and he has a gift for you we gripped his ass up. We're holding him there. He said he was trying to call you, but you never picked up on your phone."

I was knocked out I got high and when to bed early I quickly looked at my phone and I see five miss calls. "He's right I never picked up. Well, when were done here I take you to him to get this shit straight?"

Two hours later Faheem makes it out of surgery, but he is going to be alright. *Thank Gawd but I already know all hell is about to break loose in this city for real.* AK told me we are all going to meet up later on tomorrow he going to call us telling everybody when and where. Me and DeShawn along with Uzi- Boy and Alice rolled out I followed them in their whip to the scrap yard. Soon as we pulled up in this dark scrap yard this joint it brings back a whole lot of fucking memories. We both park in front of the brick building and we both jump out. Uzi- Boy and Alice walks in first waving for us to follow them. Soon as I walked in the door, I see a few familiar faces Travis- War Horse ran up on me hugging me along with Newmoe Debra Gee and Jasul.

We all are laughing and talking and carrying on.

Uzi-Boy shouted, "I hate to break up this big fucking family reunion, but I need one of you, nigga to bring out that dude so we can get this shit over with."

Jasul and Debra Gee when to the back bringing Chi- Chi out arm and arm soon as he seen me, he started smiling.

Uzi- Boy pulling out his gun yelling, "so what is this gift you got for my sister here?"

Chi- Chi with his hands up in the air is yelling, "it's in the back of my car go see for yourself. I am not fucking with y'all."

Uzi- Boy muttering, "it might be a fucking trick let us go to your car motherfucker!"

So, Uzi-Boy along with Alice me and DeShawn walked out to the dark yard quickly. I do not care how long it's been that bad smell make you think how many people got smoked out here.

We all walked up to his car and Chi- Chi s it's in the trunk man. Uzi-Boy pointed his pistol to his head yelling, "open it, nigga!"

All of us pulling out are guns getting ready for whatever Chi-Chi open it swiftly and it is a dead body inside I took my phone using the flashlight gadget I shined the light on the dead man and its Sleam no good ass. I bumped fist with Chi- Chi. Uzi- Boy is shrugging his shoulders yelling, "who the fuck is it, Lex?"

"That's one the niggas that tried to kill me in New York. his name is Sleam I just killed one of his bosses Mikey Irons. "

Alice glances over at Chi- Chi asking him, "why you bring him here for Lex why you just did not just take a picture nigga?"

Everybody started snickering. Chi- Chi quickly uttered, "this is a better audition bringing him to Lex to see for herself."

Uzi- Boy lowing his gun still giggling, "yeah, but you almost got killed doing this shit motherfucker."

Chi- Chi began rambling, "I really need a job right about now this was the only way I could get all of your attention."

Uzi- Boy looks over me than he peeps over at Alice we both nodding are head yes not saying a word.

Uzi-Boy yelling, "okay nigga you got a job but clean this shit up first and go inside with Travis and the others we have a lot of shit to do tonight."

I hugged him fast as he is whispering my ear, "thank you."

He waves at DeShawn smiling as we started walking to the van.

Uzi- Boy said, "hold up, y'all let me go tell these niggas what's going on and we can all roll out together so wait for me." So, we wait on Uzi- Boy and we all said we were all going to his place so we can all get high and talk shit. I follow him out on to the street we are driving down the road not speeding or anything when I see red and blue flashing lights behind me."

The cracker ass cops I hate these motherfuckers. I'm ready to shoot it out with these motherfuckers but when I looked up, they came from all sides of us a swarm of cops and detectives in plane cars shit! They got Uzi- Boy pulling him out his truck along with Alice then us yelling telling us to get the fuck out the van. I get out with my hands up in the air and they slammed me up on the van yelling you are under arrest for the murder of five police officers! DeShawn is gazing over at me like were done. I laughed telling the detective putting the handcuffs on me I'll be out in an hour motherfucker! The hard nose detective looked up at me and said, "I don't know what planet you're on mommy, but you will do five life sentences for this shit miss Jorden!"

I wish they had the fucking needle in New York because that is where you are going tonight.

Then right at that moment I see the two New York cops on the side smirking and slapping each other five. So, they take me downtown first and they toss me into a cell with a bunch of fucking hookers and thieves. I know what's going to happen next, they are going to work me over before they take me to New York. I just sitting there when I hear this girl with a cell phone chatting her ass off. I spoke to her softly if you let me use your phone, I give you four stacks.

The tall dark skin woman eyeballed me like I was fucking crazy. "How the fuck are you going to get me the money?"

"Give me your phone and you can find out for yourself please."

One the women yelling over to us.

"That bitch is a cop killer her ass is done for honey you'll never see that money!"

I yelled back at her, "I'll be out in a fucking hour you want to bet on it, bitch!"

The tall dark skin woman hand me the phone mumbling this bitch sounds real. I get the phone and start dialing general Ed Kowalski number. I made sure to memorize it from the day he gave it to me.

He picks up after three rings, "yeah who is this?"

"It's Lex. I'm locked up here in Philly they had some New York cops came down with a fucking warrant."

"Okay, that's the work of your old friend lieutenant Cob."

"Do not worry my man will be there with in a half an hour and he hangs up."

I hand her the phone back smiling. A half an hour went by really fucking slowly sitting there in that funky ass cell."

Then I can hear this loud voice yelling out, "Alexis Jordan let's go!"

The dark skin tall woman uttered, "I knew it!"

She is pointing at the girl who was talking shit, "I told you that bitch was real!"

She turns to me, "you're still going to hook me up, right?"

"Yeah, and I'm going to give you five stacks. What's your name?"

"My name is Pam Turner!"

"Nice meeting you Pam. I'll make sure you get you money when my people come bail you out, okay."

"Thanks girlfriend."

I looked over at the woman that was talking shit and I winked my eye at her and walked out. When the fat Black female cop walked me out her face was twisted up mad, she didn't even want to look at me. Now I walked out towards the front desk and it this short bald head man with glasses holding a suitcase and an expensive blue suit on he sticks his hand out speaking my name is Mister Smithfield.

"Nice to meet you, Mister Smithfield. Are they going to let my peoples out as well?"

"Yes, there getting them now general Kowalski told me a lot about you he told me you do very good work. Thank you."

The cop behind the desk hand me my belonging in a clear plastic bag. We both can see they two New York cops going the fuck off because they have to let me go. You would never think this little man was so powerful and that he worked for the NSA and him and the general is tight. De Shawn Uzi- Boy and Alice came out hugging me as they give them their things in a plastic bag.

I looked at all of them putting my finger up to my lips for them not to say anything in front of none of the cops standing there. The cop who put the cuffs on me is cussing up a storm calling me all kinds of nigger criminal bitches.

I walked over to him muttering, "I told you I be out in an hour motherfucker!"

He lunged towards me as his detective partner held him back while I was laughing in his fucking face. All the others just giggled as we when out the door with Mister Smithfield. When we got outside of the station as we were yelling and jumping up and down Mister Smithfield smile as he watches us celebrate. He taps me on the arm so I can walk with him on the side as he tells me general Kowalski wanted me to tell you that Kim has join forces with lieutenant Cob so it going to be harder for you to kill her. And the person that sold Faheem out fingering him was his girlfriend's name Violet Pryor. "Thank you, Mister Smithfield for everything. Well in a few months' time I will call in this little favor I did for you."

"Sure, anything you need you can call on me to do it."

"Just remember what you said Miss Jorden both of your vehicles are over there with everything you had in them guns hand grenades and all."

Mister Smithfield shook my hand smiling he lifts his hand up and a big black limo came speeding up and he jumped in taking off up the street from the parking lot of the police station. *I quickly called up Peggy to bail out that girl Pan Turner and give her five stacks and she did it within that hours-time.*

We when back to Uzi- Boy's luxury apartment in center city and we got fucked up talking about what just happen to us. Uzi-Boy with a beer in one hand and a blunt in the other laughing, "did you see the look on that cocksucker face when Lex told him I told you I would be out in a fucking hour!"

"Man, I thought I was going to fucking die laughing right on the Gawd damn spot."

Alice is snorting off a big pile of coke on the coffee table asking me, "where did you get that dude from, Lex?"

"He is a good friend of the general I didn't know that motherfucker from Dick's hat band."

De Shawn taps me on the arm and asked, "who was that guy Chi- Chi at the scrap yard Lex?"

"He was somebody I met before I met you sweetheart why?"

"I just was asking baby it no big deal. I just wanted to know."

"DeShawn, I'm going to tell you something and I don't want you to forget this shit I'm in love with you and I never loved any man in my life like I love you. So, let the past be the past okay."

Alice cuts in, "Awwwwwww!" As me and DeShawn kissed. The party we had raged on until the next day when we got home to my spot, I got the call later on that afternoon after me and De-Shawn got some sleep.

We were just chilling all hugged up all lovely dovey on the couch when my phone rings I pick it up answering it, "yeah, who is this?"

"It's your old friend Lance Lucci bitch!"

"What the fuck is you doing calling me nigga and how did you get my number anyway?"

"Well, I called to tell you I got a few exceptionally good friends of yours from your Price firm Peggy, Jelly and Big Mama Red if you want them to live. I want 80 million dollars, or I'll kill every one of them motherfuckers and ship you their fucking body parts!"

And he hangs up I'm thinking he's bull shitting, so I called Moon to check the warehouse palace my heart is pumping hard when he goes to check it out. He calls me back telling me their gone. I jumped up yelling, "stay there I'm getting dressed."

I quickly put my clothes on super-fast DeShawn, asking me what happen?

"That son of a bitch Lance Lucci just kidnapped Peggy, Jelly and Big Mama Red from the crib."

"Who would know where they were at somebody sold you out, Ma?"

"Your aaright somebody sure fucking did!"

Me and DeShawn meet Moon at the warehouse palace we looked everywhere as I told Jitta, Nick Lit, Miss Janet and Stump what happen. They help us looking around at their apartments and everything their nowhere to be found. Now I know the shit is real! What fucks me up somebody help this nigga get the upper hand on me and I cannot figure out who did it right now. My mind is going in a thousand different directions and I'm fucking furious.

THE END.

[b1]

ABOUT THE AUTHOR

Dartanya A. Williams Sr

Dartanya Williams was born and raised on the south side of Philadelphia. Raised by his mother Catherine and his three brothers. Birthed into a family of great storytellers Dartanya inherited the gift and continued the tradition of storytelling. Dartanya from ex-gang member to a hardworking citizen.

A strange twist of fate, Dartanya suffered an accident on the job getting hit by a car not able to walk for months. He had to learn how to walk again during that period he turned tragedy into triumph completing eight novels and hundreds of short stories from dark gritty street tails that range from odyssey to wild fantasy roller coaster. Adventurous journeys in other worlds to deep introspective tender novels about relationships new love, lost love in this some time happy and unforgiving metropolis we all live work and play. Throughout it all embarking on his literary journey Dartanya is blessed with the knowledge of knowing his purpose.

BOOKS BY THIS AUTHOR

Killadelphia Soldiers

After Anthony Kilson(AK) is busted for smuggling heroin from Afghanistan into the United States working for a Black bag CIA operation while he was serving his country. Anthony Kilson formed a gang in federal prison awaiting his trial with the help of his well-paid lawyers, his wife Jackie and a well known black CNN reporter helped AK miraculously win his case. Soon after he hit the streets taking down banks to get even with the government and to fund his drug criminal network with ex-marines, navy, and army veterans and training criminals with skills and high potential to join the gang. Soon after the gang grows and become one of the most powerful drug cartels. The Mexican hire them to put in work providing transportation and muscle then chaos ensued all around the gang with jealousy from the Italian mafia and other local drug crews all jockeying for position in the bloody brutal drug trade. Once the gang expands into major cities and drug markets as the gang bulldozes their way to the top of the heap building an empire.

Almasi Aka Glock Mommy

Sharonda Miller was just another poor ghetto statistic. She had to step into the parent role at a young age because of her mother's drug addiction taking care of her little sister Robin. One night from the result of her mother Dotty dirty underhanded dealing with a group of young wild drug dealers. Who was tired of performing sexual acts with Dotty who owed them money for the drugs she been smoking most of the night? Dotty made an unscrupulous decision unlocking her daughter's door and letting the young men loose on Sharonda unknowingly while she was sleeping. The young men raped Sharonda while her mother stood by the door shamelessly. From that chain of events thrusted Sharonda the victim into self-empowerment finding out who she really is along the way and what she really wants in life.

Changing her name to Almasi that means Diamond in Swahili set out with a burning desire for revenge for the men who did her wrong. As the drug gang, she was initiated into BSN, The Black Syndicate Nation turned her into a professional female assassin her along with the gang would one day rule the black underworld and the streets of Philly. Her bloody rise to power changed her life forever and the landscape of organized crime in Philadelphia and all over the country.

After her transformation putting in mad work for the gang she was known as Almasi aka Glock Mommy and she will leave an indelible mark on your senses as she tells, her story in the first person. She will take you on her incredible journey of lost love, death, tragedy destruction and triumph in her life. And after you read it, you will never forget it as long as you live.

Almasi 2-Queen Of The Streets

Sharonda Miller aka Almasi found out everything in her life was one gigantic lie. She escapes a life sentence in prison by the skin of her teeth. Almasi finds herself trapped into the very game that pulled her up from the very hell most of her family has been stuck in for generations. Surrounded by ignorance, death and drugs Almasi is smart enough to know that living life at a crazy off the hook blistering pace that your luck can't last forever. The crown of being the queen of the black underworld has a heavy price on your soul and your mental capabilities.

Almasi can handle the pressures of the game better than most men, but she can't handle the betrayal from the very angels that saved her from a life of being trapped into a life of poverty and abuse. How easily the Kings of the game from the mansions to the prison cells can turn on you. The bullets of betrayal and deceit are gunning for Almasi's soul. On a quest to escape what made her into the Queen of the Streets. Almasi wants to get out of all the bullshit in one piece and live the life she wants to have. This story will take you on a heart pounding ride into the dark twisted and ultraviolence streets of the Philly underworld having you on the edge of your seat still wanting more.

www.ingramcontent.com/pod-product-compliance
Lightning Source LLC
Chambersburg PA
CBHW071523260626
47170CB00002B/478

* 9 7 8 1 7 3 2 6 1 2 2 5 9 *